UFUO...

THE
CHURCH
GIRL

THE CHURCH GIRL

By Ufuomaee

ISBN: 978-1720191957
Independently published

This story is an adaptation of the fictional story series written by Ufuomaee and published on **blog.ufuomaee.org.**

It is a purely fictional work. Any resemblance to real persons, organisations or events is merely coincidental.

Unless otherwise stated, all scriptures referenced are from **www.blueletterbible.org.**

Cover photo credit: www.shutterstock.com

Book cover design and book layout by
Paul Ikonne for Axenic Arts.
www.axenicarts.com.

DISCLAIMER: Please note that this story contains some sexually explicit content, violence, and offensive language. It is not appropriate for children nor an immature and sensitive audience.

REVIEWS

The Church Girl is for anybody who thinks they have made 'too many mistakes' to be forgiven by God and have a better chance at life. It is also serves as a caution to people who are fast to give up on others. The book really proves that there is indeed redemption in God.
— woman.ng

The author weaves a tale of faith, the encompassing love of God, and the frailty of human nature. It's a moving story that teaches about salvation, patience, holiness, the power of forgiveness, and the benefits that come with putting your unwavering trust in the Almighty.

Although its fiction, this book is so relatable, it is about real people, with real issues and flaws so big only the grace of God can cover. You are sure to recognize a few people you know in Mary, Ifeanyi and the other characters.
— Today's Woman

DEDICATION

This book is dedicated to everybody who still believes in true love.

TABLE OF CONTENTS

BOOK ONE

TABLE OF CONTENTS

BOOK TWO

PREFACE

T he Church Girl was a fleeting idea in my head, one day in February 2016, when I thought it would be funny to tell a story about a Christian girl and a player, who finds out that she's not such a good girl after all. It was meant to be a short story, not more than 1500 words, like all the stories on my blog were before it. I had never written a story series then, but from the first part of the series, I realised that I couldn't complete this story in one sitting.

I returned the next day to continue the story, but at that point, it was no longer *my* story! God had taken over, and I was telling the story without knowing where it was really going. It was as exciting for me as it was for my readers. But I was a bit afraid. I thought I was getting over my head and kept anticipating that the story would conclude the following day.

I wrote the original seven chapters of the story every day for seven days, as I followed the Holy Spirit's leading to go deeper. It was a beautiful happy ending for Mary and Ifeanyi after so many twists and turns. At that time, people said it should be in a book, but I thought it was much too small a story to convert to a book.

After writing a couple more story series on my blog, I felt bolder to try to extend my first story series, The Church Girl. I rewrote the story as 'The Extended Version,' adding a new twist that prolonged Mary and Ifeanyi's journey to marriage. Writing 'The Extended Version' was a real challenge for me because all my stories have the purpose of glorifying God, and I wanted this story to teach godly lessons and help singles learn how to walk with God and discover His will for their lives.

The problem was I didn't have much insight to draw upon. I had to learn. And I did a whole lot of growing up as I wrote 'The Extended Version.' I dropped a few ideas I had about love, relationships, and intimacy before marriage, and you can see that in the way my main characters developed, forsaking old ways and learning to trust in God.

Well, the story didn't end there. I revisited the story, with a new leading from God, and told the story of their lives in marriage. That is BOOK TWO. So, while BOOK ONE focused on their lives as singles, BOOK TWO told of their lives as a married couple, dealing with the various challenges couples face in marriage. The theme of BOOK ONE is '**Dying to Self**,' which is essential for us to know the will of God. The theme of BOOK TWO is '**Maturing in Love**,' learning to love one another as Christ loves us.

The Church Girl is also divided into eight volumes and fifty chapters, with a prologue and an epilogue. Each volume has a theme (a special Bible verse). Do take note of the theme as you are reading through. It will help you not to miss the main lessons being communicated through the story.

I hope this story will help many Christian singles to learn to discern God's voice and walk in His will so they will enter marriages that glorify God. It is also my hope and prayer that those who are married and are facing various challenges will be encouraged and inspired by this story and learn how to safeguard their homes from the attack of the enemy. I hope everyone reading this story will come away with a greater appreciation of the grace of God, which we all enjoy, a deeper relationship with Him, and more wisdom to walk in love.

The love story of Mary and Ifeanyi continues in 'A Small World,' a seasonal story series on my blog, which merges my first three story series into one. Do visit and follow me at **blog. ufuomaee.org**. Thank you!

THE PROLOGUE

"For I know the thoughts that I think toward you, saith the LORD, thoughts of peace, and not of evil, to give you an expected end."

JEREMIAH 29:11

M aryann had dreams, and she told beautiful stories of princes and princesses, who fell in love and lived happily ever after. She had a wonderful imagination and drew inspiration from the few Disney classics she had to watch. She loved how, no matter how lowly the girls were, with faith, hope, and love, they persevered against all odds and won the hearts of princes. She truly believed that one day, her prince would find her, and no matter what happened until then, she would never despair of hope but would always exercise faith and abide in love.

For a little girl of her under-privileged standing, all she had were her dreams and her beauty. Even though she did not know how beautiful she was. She was blessed to have naturally long hair, uncharacteristic of African women. Her features were pronounced, even at a tender age, and she always drew the attention of men.

Her father, Efe Uwanna, adored her. She was his only girl, his darling angel. And for seven years, she was his only child. The fact that she looked like him, and had his dimples, only made her more endearing to him. He loved to listen to her stories, and he told her that one day, she would be a wonderful author, who would bring hope and joy to others through her tales of love. That made her smile.

Her mother, Elizabeth, was not too pleased. She didn't like that her daughter spent so much time entertaining fantasies. It was a hard and cruel world, and she wanted her daughter to be prepared. She didn't want her high hopes to be dashed nor to see her sweet child become bitter because of broken dreams. She had learnt that the fewer expectations you had in life, the better you fared.

Elizabeth felt she had been unfortunate to marry a dreamer, a man with more hope than promise. He was always chasing after one dream or the other, and when she was younger, she had misunderstood that for passion and ambition. But they didn't put food on the table nor clothes on their backs. Still, it didn't stop him from desiring the life of a king and seeking to have as many children as he could, even though he knew he had no legacy to leave them with.

After his first few ideas crashed and burned, she had decided no longer to hold out hope for his dreams nor hers coming true. Elizabeth had always applied herself to hard work, and her labour sustained the family. She had good employment working as a cook for a rich family, and by the time Mary was seven, she had saved enough to buy their small 'room and parlour' abode in Ajegunle. Efe hadn't been keen on buying the home. He thought the money would be better invested in one of his new ideas. She fought back bitterness and regret at her folly in marrying such a man, who she felt was so out of touch with reality.

Elizabeth passed on as much training as she could to her daughter and didn't entertain her fantasies. She busied her with chores, teaching her how to sew and mend clothing, cook and bake, and many other life skills so that she would be able to do something for herself should life turn unfortunate. Mary was naturally bright and also did well at school, which eased Elizabeth's anxieties about how she would cope in life.

Elizabeth really had no reason to be so worried. But she had always been morbid. She had a feeling that she would die young. She had had that feeling since she was eighteen, when she was pregnant with Mary. She thought she would die in labour. But she had lived. And when she carried her twins, the same feeling fell upon her.

Now, she had four beautiful healthy children, and death had evaded her each time. Still, as she watched them play, she could not shake the dark cloud that loomed over her spirit. Sometimes, she wondered if it was not her despondency with life, rather than an omen, that caused the darkness and morbid thoughts.

Efe watched his daughter, Mary, as she did the laundry in the backyard. She was no longer the cute little Annie he knew. Now sixteen, she'd blossomed into a very beautiful young lady. He sighed with regret.

He had hoped that she would be discovered and used as one of those child models in baby adverts, or even movies. When she was younger, he had suggested putting her in to compete in beauty pageants, but Elizabeth had been dead set against it. He knew someone from his village, whose daughter had been scouted, and now, they lived in a mansion in Ikoyi. The girl had gone on from modelling to acting movies, and she was even now pursuing a career in music. He didn't know why he had listened to Elizabeth. She was always shooting down his dreams.

Actually, she had believed in him at the beginning. When they met, he was a young comedian. He had spotted her at an open mic event, and she'd laughed so hard at his jokes, he had noticed her from the stage. He told her that he was going to blow up Nigeria with his jokes. There were not many MCs and comedians doing well at that time, but the few successful ones were big time celebrities. She had told him he had what it took, and he had proposed immediately.

But eighteen years later, he was still not doing well as a professional comedian nor MC. He had few paying gigs and still did open mic, hoping to be spotted. He tried his hands at other things, but he was not the kind of man to hold a nine to five. He managed to get a freelance job drawing funny comics for the local newspaper, but they didn't always publish his pieces, and even when they did, the pay wasn't much. But he still believed that one day, he would blow. He just needed to be at the right place at the right time. Just once!

"What? You mean it? They asked for me?" Efe spoke into the phone. Elizabeth lifted her head briefly from her knitting. She saw that look in her husband's eyes again, but she dared not raise her hopes. "Oh, thank you so much! God bless you."

"Praise God!" he screamed when he got off the phone. He pulled his wife unto her feet and started dancing.

Mary spied her parents and smiled. She wondered what the jubilation was all about. Elizabeth smiled, despite herself. What could it be?

"I just got the biggest gig ever! You know Prince Eddy Udo is turning 60 in December, right?"

"I heard... They are doing a big party for him. Don't tell me you're performing?" Elizabeth said excitedly.

"Okay, I won't," Efe giggled. "But you know I am! I'm going to be among the line-up for entertainment on that day! Do you know the calibre of people that will be there?"

"Oh, wow! How did you manage that, Dad?" Mary asked.

"I don't even know. It seems one of the organisers spotted me at another event. Anyway… Nothing is confirmed yet. They said I should come this weekend for rehearsals or auditions. You'll come with me, right?" Efe asked his wife.

"Of course, I will, darling," Elizabeth said genuinely. If Efe got the opportunity to perform at such a major event, she just knew their fortunes would change. She was beginning to feel hope again.

"Mum, maybe you can take some of your food? They will need caterers too. You never know," Mary said.

"Yeah, that's a great idea. Good thinking, Annie," Efe said, grinning at his daughter.

"I'm sure they already have the catering sorted out, dear," Elizabeth said, not wanting to raise her hopes. She was doing fine catering for the children's parties in their small community in Ajegunle.

"Yeah, but these days, they have several caterers, not just one. You can take some of your sweet desserts. There's always room for desserts!" Mary insisted. "Come on, Mum… Believe a little!"

Elizabeth grinned. What did she have to lose? She would take some deserts, and if they liked them, she would tell them about the other delicacies she could make. She was getting excited already, just imagining their faces when they tasted her treats. She looked up at her husband and felt a pang of guilt for not believing in him. It seemed they were finally going to break into the light.

Mary helped her mother to prepare some scrumptious desserts to take for their journey to Benin City, where the party would be held. This was just the break her parents needed. She wished she could go with them, but she needed to look after her younger brothers.

As Mary waved her parents off, the storm clouds gathered. The showers came down immediately, and she ran back into the shelter. It was strange how the weather had suddenly turned.

Heavy rain was uncommon in October. She hoped and prayed for a safe and blessed journey.

But it was not to be. Efe and Elizabeth never made it to their destination.

"Whosoever shall seek to save his life shall lose it; and whosoever shall lose his life shall preserve it."

LUKE 17:33

DYING TO SELF

BOOK ONE

VOLUME
ONE

01

"...weeping may endure for a night,
but joy cometh in the morning."

PSALM 30:5

Mary was rounding up her Sunday School class with the Youth Club. It was a good session, and she had enjoyed teaching them about Joseph. He was her favourite Bible character, after Jesus. She drew so many lessons from his life of struggle turned triumph, as someone who had had her fair share of traumas.

She sighed deeply as she remembered the scripture, "*weeping may endure for a night, but joy comes in the morning*" (Psalm 30:5). She had been waiting long for that morning, but if there was a lesson to learn from Joseph's story, it was that God is in control of our times and seasons, and He is faithful to work things out for the good of His children.

Her Faith was all she had to help her through. It was her life line, and she relished it. She smiled and hummed to herself as she packed up to prepare to go home. She was startled when someone's voice broke into her thoughts.

"You have such a beautiful voice," he said.

Mary looked up at him wearily, wondering what he wanted. She'd seen him around at church, but they had never met. She'd caught him staring at her a few times, and she'd always managed to dodge his attempts to talk to her. Now it seemed he had pinned her down.

When she didn't reply, he introduced himself at last. "Hi, I'm David. I've been wanting to talk to you for a while."

Mary took his hand politely and gave him a curt smile. "Mary. Thanks, but I'm in a hurry."

She scurried past him, out of the room. She heard his steps following her. *Oh, my goodness*, she thought. *What does he want?*

"Mary," he called, and she stopped briefly and turned to him. "I would really like to take you out. Please."

It was not the first time. There were always guys trying to pick her up, and she'd learnt the quickest way to shut them down. You just have to be as cold as possible.

She looked him up and down slowly, and twisted her mouth in a frown, before saying mockingly, "No, thanks! You're not my type."

Mary turned around and walked away, feeling bad for the guy. It wasn't his fault. And she had lied that he wasn't her type. But, what was the point when nothing could ever happen between them?

Ifeanyi Chukwueke was a player, with no plans to settle down; that was until he met 'the church girl.' He never really fancied the religious kind. They were always too frigid and self-righteous for his liking. But there was something about Mary...

The first time he laid eyes on her beauty was during registration for Nigerian Youth Service Corps (NYSC). He hadn't said anything to her at the time, but he took note of the fact that they would be going to the same camp at Iseyin, in Oyo State. He had smiled to himself that he would make his move then.

But to his surprise, Mary did not take notice of him nor fall for his charms. That was the first! He could always get the ladies to swoon with just a flash of his pearly white teeth. And if that didn't do the trick, his perfected British accent, from his few years in London, usually sealed the deal.

His friend, Chuka, saw him one day passing repeated glances at Mary. "O boy, virgin Mary no be it, oh," he mocked.

Ifeanyi shrugged. "I don't care," he responded. "She's not it, but the chase is sweeter with a fast prey."

Chuka laughed. "You're too bad!"

As Ifeanyi observed Mary with her friends, conducting an outdoor Bible Study, he wondered how far into her Faith he would have to go to win the game.

Mary went to fellowship at the Risen Christ Church (RCC) Parish at the camp, every Sunday morning for the three weeks that she was there. On their first Sunday, she noticed the tall, light-skinned man that had approached her after their registration. Damilola, her room-mate, had informed her that he was a player. He had a bad reputation in London for breaking hearts. She was duly warned.

After the service, Ifeanyi approached Mary again, with a Bible in his hand.

"Hi, Mary. How did you find the service?" Ifeanyi asked.

"It was good," Mary replied.

"I really enjoyed the praise. That's always my favourite part," Ifeanyi continued.

Mary just smiled. "Okay, well, have a good day," she said, as she hurried along to catch up with her friend, who had silently dismissed herself.

Dami laughed when Mary swung her hand through her arm and got in step with her. "Why did you diss him now?"

"I didn't diss him," Mary said. "I just don't have his time."

As they walked along, Mary wondered if it would ever be possible for a man to break through the bars she had put up around her heart. Certainly, if there was such a man in existence, Ifeanyi didn't fit the bill.

Ifeanyi couldn't believe it. Why couldn't he stop thinking about Mary? *She wasn't that pretty*, he told himself. And she was darn right rude too! Yet, she had succeeded in spoiling his appetite for other women.

Sure, he still had the odd girl in his bed now and then, but he didn't enjoy it like before. All he thought about was Mary, and he feared that it was more than a game now. Whenever he saw her, he lost his cool. He would sweat and stutter, and well, he was not himself. This had to be fixed, and the only way was by sleeping with her and getting it over with.

So, as he thought about the situation more, he realised that he'd missed a step in his play-book. He was paying her far too much attention. He would have to pull out the old trick of ignoring and insulting her. That should get her riled up.

Ifeanyi applied himself to his new strategy, and Chuka was happy to have his mate back. Their table was alive with activity and always flanked by many beautiful girls. Ifeanyi even got himself a steady girlfriend, Ijeoma, who was oblivious to her role as a stand-in girl, to make Mary jealous.

Ifeanyi succeeded in dulling his feelings for Mary, but he never forgot about her. And it hurt him to realise that she seemed unmoved by his disdain for her. If she was jealous, she certainly hid it well.

Ifeanyi was the last thing on Mary's mind. She was more con-cerned about her eventual placement, as she hoped to go as far away from Lagos as possible. She needed a new start, freedom from a haunting past that suffocated her dreams for the future.

She had been such a silly girl to have made the mistake of working for Bolaji and thinking that she could bear the toll it would have on her soul - the real price of accepting his support. And now she was in too deep, and she knew he wasn't about to let her go. Even now, she knew he was working behind the scenes to ensure that she worked right under his nose. The thought was horrifying.

"Are you all packed?" Dami asked, as she entered the small dorm they shared with ten other girls. "I can't believe it's been three weeks already!"

"Yeah..." Mary muttered, as she came back to reality. *It had been three weeks of bliss*, she thought. She hadn't even been bothered about the highly inadequate toilet and shower facil-ities, the cramped, smelly, and hot sleeping arrangements, nor even the less than satisfying meals. "It's been fun, *sha*," she said honestly.

"We should hook up in Lagos," Dami said.

"Before *nkor*?" Mary smiled, going over to Dami. "I'm going to miss you, *sha*," she said as they hugged.

"Yeah, me too!"

Dami helped Mary carry her things outside, where she was to catch a taxi to the coach station. Dami wouldn't be leaving for another two days and had offered Mary a ride. However, she had turned it down, in favour of leaving earlier.

As she got into the taxi, Mary noticed Ifeanyi looking at her with a strange expression on his face. His face was devoid of his usual grimace. A little sad, actually. She offered him a smile and a wave goodbye, which seemed to shock him. He lifted his hand in a half-wave before promptly turning around and walk-ing away.

When he got back to Lagos, Ifeanyi swiftly dumped Ijeoma. She was hysterical, as she hadn't expected it at all. She really thought she would be the one to win his heart, that she would be his 'ride-or-die' chick. She hounded him for days to tell her what she had done wrong, but Ifeanyi didn't know what to say. The truth was far too cliché. Because it really wasn't her; it was him.

Ifeanyi thought often of the last time he saw Mary and the sweet smile she had given him. It was so unexpected that it had thrown him off-balance. He didn't even realise that he had been staring at her. He knew now that he really liked her, for reasons unknown to him, and he had really messed that one up. He hoped for an opportunity, a fresh start, but he had no idea how to get in touch with her. She wasn't in his NYSC Community Development Group (CDG), and he wasn't even sure if she was serving in Lagos.

However, one day, he had some good fortune. It was a Saturday morning, and he and the guys were playing football at the City of David court, which they usually did once a month. He had invited Chuka to join his team as they had become inseparable after meeting at the NYSC camp.

During half-time, they rested at the stands and refreshed themselves with cool water. Breathing heavily, Chuka asked, "Do you still think of that SU from camp?"

Ifeanyi frowned at the derogatory reference to Mary as a religious zealot. Unsure how to answer the question, as he had not yet confessed his feelings to Chuka, he shrugged. "What's there to think about?"

"Okay. No problem," Chuka muttered. "I just thought you might be interested to know where she's serving."

Ifeanyi patted his face with a towel, to hide his excitement, and looked straight-faced at Chuka when he had composed himself. "Oh, really. Where?"

"I thought you didn't care," Chuka shot at him, running back to the field.

"Where, *joor*?" Ifeanyi shot back, a little annoyed.

"She works for my sister, dude!" Chuka said, with a smile. "I saw her the other day at the office."

Ifeanyi couldn't hide his smile.

Chuka laughed. "I knew it! Game on?" he asked, ambiguously.

No games, Ifeanyi thought to himself. This time, he would come correct!

"Oh, these are beautiful!" Aisha, a co-worker at the Browne Law Firm where Mary served, marvelled. "Who got you these?" she asked, admiring the bouquet of a dozen red roses on Mary's desk.

Mary shoved the card in her face, uninterested. It read: "*Let's start over. Dine with me. Luv, Ifeanyi*".

"Who's *Ifeanyi*?" Aisha asked, saying his name as though he was a mysterious prince.

"Just an arrogant guy from camp," Mary replied.

"Doesn't sound arrogant to me," Aisha said. "Whatever he did, this says 'sorry'! Can't you give him another chance?"

"I don't have time for guys, *abeg*!" Mary snapped. "Don't you have work to do?"

"Okay!" Aisha said, dropping the card on the table. "You know, you can do with a little lightening up. Life's too short." And with that, she went to her desk and busied herself on her computer.

Mary couldn't help but think about Aisha's words. Maybe she was being too hard on him. *But he is not a Christian*, she told herself. *Well, he did make the effort to go to church*, she reasoned. Maybe he's trainable. And it was only dinner. If there's no spark, then there's nothing lost. Maybe he'll get off her case when he realises that she's not his kind after all.

She picked up the card and looked at the flowers. *He is kinda sweet*, she smiled. Ifeanyi had scribbled his number at the bottom. She decided she would send him a text. "*Got your flowers. Thanks*" was all she wrote.

"*What about our date?*" came his instant response.

When she didn't respond after ten minutes, he dialled her number instead. Her voice, as she picked the call, was so sweet, he smiled. "When can I take you to dinner?" he asked.

"I'm free Saturday," she responded casually and added, "I don't do late nights."

"I'll pick you up at 7 pm. I'll be your perfect gentleman," he replied, beaming.

"Good. I'll text my address. Bye." And with that, she cut the call.

Ifeanyi smiled to himself when he heard her click off. He breathed a sigh of relief, as he put down his phone.

It instantly pinged with several BBM messages from neglected babes, who were still pining for his attention. But he wasn't interested in any of them now. He was planning the most romantic dinner of the century!

02

"...weeping may endure for a night,
but joy cometh in the morning."

PSALM 30:5

P astor Bolaji Akinwunmi was the Pastor in Charge at his branch of the Vessels of Honour Fellowship, a mega church with branches all over the world. The church was headed by Dr. Bishop Taiwo Adetiba, who founded it and sat as the General Overseer. As such, Pastor Bolaji, as he was often called, was a very influential man, not only in Christendom, but in the political sphere too. Many well-known personalities and celebrities were members of his fellowship, and their tithes alone ensured his kingly lifestyle was maintained.

As Mary stood in his spacious office, she remembered the very first time she had gone to meet him. At that time, she had been filled with such hope and expectation, after being directed by another sister in church to approach him. *"Pastor Bolaji is very kind. He will help you,"* the lady had said, with a reassuring smile.

At sixteen years old, Mary was an unfortunate girl to be burdened with the responsibility of taking care of her three younger siblings, after the sudden demise of her parents during a road traffic accident. They were not rich to begin with, and the little they had was used to cover burial costs and maintain them for a month or two, before she had to start desperately looking for a means to sustain them. Fortunately, they owned their room and parlour accommodation at Ajegunle. However, this small blessing was all they would enjoy, as relatives complained of their own impoverished situations, such that none considered the children worthy of support.

That fateful afternoon, she had come to Pastor Bolaji to ask him to lend her money, through the church's Community Support Programme, as her youngest brother, five-year-old Daniel, was ill with malaria. As she told her story, she broke into tears and sobs. She felt the pastor as he brushed past her to the door. He locked it and drew the curtains.

"There, there," he muttered to her, as he approached her from the back and enveloped her with his strong arms. "Don't cry. There is always a solution to be found in God's House. Just calm down and tell me everything."

Mary was startled by his inappropriate level of intimacy and turned around to face him. He smiled at her and wiped her tears with his hands. "Thank you," she murmured.

Pastor Bolaji went over to his executive chair and sat down, looking at her up and down. She was a very beautiful young lady, he thought. Her hair was braided and packed in a bun, to display a well-contoured flawless face, complete with dimples and long thick lashes. Her knee-length skirt, though loose, revealed her wide hips and firm behind, which were held up by long, slim, shapely legs. Even without make-up, and a face full of tears, she was breath-taking.

Mary had nervously continued her account, feeling like a goldfish under his stare. "My father was the only child of his parents and was an orphan when he died. Our only family is from my mother's side, but no one wants to help us."

Pastor Bolaji gestured for Mary to come to him. "Come and sit here. I can't hear you from over there," he said, patting his lap.

Swallowing hard and hiding her shock, Mary walked slowly to him and awkwardly sat on his thighs. She didn't know what to do with her hands, so she held them on her lap in front of her.

"Continue," the Pastor prompted.

As she continued to tell her story, she noticed his hand sliding up her skirt. She couldn't believe what was going on and wondered if she should stay or run out of the room. But she remembered her sick brother, who was downstairs with her other two brothers. They hadn't eaten all day, and the way things were going, she didn't know if she would have to resort to stealing to provide for them. If the Pastor was willing to listen and help, then she would suffer this humiliation - just once!

By the time Mary had concluded her story, she was topless on his laps, as he fondled her breasts. She saw that, on his table, there was a family picture of him and his wife and two kids, smiling like the perfect family. Tears rolled down her eyes as she realised what a lie the picture told. Even though it had not been her intention nor desire, she felt that she had personally hurt them.

Pastor Bolaji assisted Mary to her feet and handed her her bra and blouse to put back on. She hastily put her clothes back on and straightened her skirt. Was he going to help her? She wondered, afraid that he had only abused her without any intention to help.

Knowing the question she didn't dare to ask, the pastor answered, "I will help you."

She breathed a sigh of relief, only just realising she had been holding her breath. "Thank you, Pastor. Thank you." She couldn't add "*God will bless you,*" as was usually said by the grateful to their benefactors in Nigeria.

Later that afternoon, Mary left his office with N20,000 and a commitment never to return. She would make that money last, find a job, and send her siblings to school.

However, getting a job was much harder than she had realised. It seemed there were many more predators out there expecting her to demean herself to get any support from them. When the money had run out, in desperation, she had gone back to ask of the pastor, her head bowed down in shame.

❤ ❤ ❤

Pastor Bolaji was happy to see Mary when she came back to his office. He hadn't seen her in church since the last time she came. He asked her about it.

She complained about being busy looking for work and also not having enough for transportation to the church, which was at Apapa. The truth was that she did not want to see him nor hear him preach to her about God. She was even struggling with her faith in God after what had happened to her.

"Church is important in the life of every Christian. I want to see you at church every Sunday," the Pastor said. "You don't have to worry about work, or your brothers, because I will take care of you."

Mary was wide-eyed with unbelief. "*Really?*"

Pastor Bolaji nodded. "But you have to earn it. The Bible says, '*if you don't work, you can't eat.*' So, you can work for me, and I'll see to it that you and your brothers complete your education."

"Oh, thank you, sir," Mary said, not fully understanding. "What work can I do for you, Pastor?"

"Anything I ask," he responded, looking her straight in her eyes, so she understood exactly what he meant. "You know you are a very beautiful girl. If no one is there to protect you, anything can happen to you. If you work for me, I will protect you and make sure that you have whatever you need."

Mary looked down at her shaking hands on her thighs. "I understand," she said. Her mind was racing as she thought of how to get out of her situation. It didn't have to come to this. There had to be some other way. "Can I think about it?" she asked.

"As long as you want," said the pastor, as he rose up to show her out of his office.

Mary stumbled to the door. So, he wasn't going to give her anything? Desperately, she stopped him. "Please, we really need help. Please give us anything you can spare now, and I'll come back tomorrow with my answer."

"If you don't work, you don't eat," he responded coldly.

When they got to the door, Mary took a big gulp and gave up the fight. "Okay. I will work for you."

Pastor Bolaji smiled and locked the door. After drawing the curtains, he took her to the sofa, where she lost another precious part of herself. She cried silent tears as he forced himself into her and broke her hymen.

It had been six years since she started 'working' for Pastor Bolaji. Privately, he told her to call him 'Bolaji,' but in public, she was to refer to him as 'Pastor Akinwunmi.' Nobody knew of their relationship. She was the perfect Christian girl, and he was the revered Pastor. If she was to tell anyone of their arrangement, she was certain she would be branded a liar and a slut. And of course, there was also the financial control he had over her. She had her brothers' education to think about, even though she was now a graduate.

Eleven-year-old Daniel was in JSS1 and the twins, fifteen-year-old Samson and Samuel were in SS2. They were oblivious as to the cause of their good fortune and were happy to be going to private schools in Lagos. To keep up appearances, Mary and her siblings stayed in their family accommodation, which was well-furnished and renovated to include private shower and toilet facilities. She had only enough spending money to keep them comfortable, though she still tried to save, with the hope that one day she would have enough to break free from Bolaji's hold.

As she worked for him, she also worked in the church, which justified their relationship and frequent meetings. She was not permitted to work anywhere else, until her year of service as a youth corper and placement at Browne Law Firm. Her stipend from that was supposed to be N20,000 monthly, but when others were being paid, her madam had said that she had a different arrangement with the pastor, who had influenced her placement there. She had decided she would go to his office to ask him about it.

"Am I not paying you enough?" Pastor Bolaji asked. "Don't be so ungrateful!"

"I am really thankful for everything you have done for me and my brothers. I am, *really*," Mary said. "It's just that, now that I am graduated and have a good job, I think we will be fine."

Pastor Bolaji laughed scornfully. "Really? You have a job? Did she say she is going to keep you after your service year runs out? How much is she paying you? Do you even know how much school fees are? You're just unbelievable!"

Mary was quiet. She thought about Ifeanyi. Their first date, last Saturday, had been a dream. She had agreed to see him again, and she wanted to close, once and for all, this awful chapter of her life. Ifeanyi's family were well off. She was sure that with her earnings from the law firm, and his support as a boyfriend, she wouldn't need the pastor's support anymore.

As the pastor studied her, he realised that there could be more to it. "Is there somebody else?" he asked her.

She didn't respond.

"You slut! Does he know the nasty things you do? If he knew the type of girl you were, he would *run*!" the pastor spat at her with his words. "Or do you want to go back to the streets? *Begging*? Doing *ashawo* all over Lagos?"

Mary started to cry. "I didn't want this. I just wanted help! I'm not a slut!"

"You are a *filthy* slut!" Pastor Bolaji hissed. "Let me show you how much of a slut you are. Come here!"

Mary fell to her knees and begged. But the pastor wasn't softened. "Come over here now," he demanded and watched as she stood up and walked towards where he was sitting on his executive chair.

An awful dread fell over Mary as she walked over to him. From the evil glint in his eyes, she knew that he was going to be rough. She spied his pen knife on his desk, and for one crazy moment, she thought to pick it up and use it as a weapon.

Bolaji caught a hold of her hand, as if he was reading her mind, and twisted it, delighting in the scream that escaped her mouth. He was going to enjoy punishing her.

03

"...weeping may endure for a night,
but joy cometh in the morning."

PSALM 30:5

Ifeanyi was singing and dancing in front of the mirror to the tune of one of his favourite RnB singers, who sang about changing his ways. He smiled, thinking his player days were officially behind him now. He was still on high from his date with Mary last Saturday. It was absolutely perfect. He had outdone himself in creating the most romantic night of their lives.

Mary and Ifeanyi had enjoyed a roof-top meal at the Four Points Hotel by Sheraton, in Victoria Island. Though there were other diners present, they were secluded in a private corner, with an amazing view of the city of Lagos, and it felt like they were the only ones in the restaurant. Their section was specially decorated with lights, scented candles and flowers, and they had a dedicated waiter, who brought them their special order, fresh from the grill.

"This is too much," Mary had half-heartedly protested. She wondered how much it had cost Ifeanyi to put it all together. Was this how he treated all his ladies?

"Nothing is too much for you, babe," Ifeanyi had responded, as he slid his hand across the table to hold hers. "I think you are really something special."

Mary had blushed, despite herself. She was supposed to keep it cool. She couldn't forget his reputation. But she could already feel her heart warming towards him. He was unbelievably cute. And not at all what she had expected.

They had laughed and reminisced about their encounter in Iseyin and talked about their new placements. Ifeanyi was working at an accounting firm, and he had dreams of owning his own bank one day. Mary didn't know what her dream was. "I just want to be happy," she had told him, with a strange sadness.

She didn't reveal a lot about her past, but he knew she worked at the church and was very passionate about her Faith. He had confessed that he had never given much thought to religion. He found it a bit restricting. It was "the status quo," and he had always been a bit of a rebel. But he was open to learning about her Faith, and this made her happy.

Ifeanyi smiled as he remembered when he had dropped her off at home. It had taken everything in him not to lean in for a kiss. Instead he had given her hand a squeeze after they shared an affectionate hug. He was now thinking of their next date. He couldn't wait a whole week, so he had invited her to watch a movie with him this Thursday. It was now Tuesday, and he had only called her once. He didn't want to come off too strong. He would call her again tonight.

As he got himself ready for work, he caught a glimpse of himself in the mirror and smiled. He wondered, *is this what it feels like to be in love*?

Suddenly, his phone rang.

It was Keisha, his ex-girlfriend from London. He debated whether to answer her call, but knowing her, she wouldn't relent. With resignation, he picked up on the fourth ring.

"Hey, Keisha, long time," he said jovially.

"Hey, boo," she replied.

Keisha and Ifeanyi had dated for three years while they were in university together. He knew she had expected a proposal when he took her to dinner before he left for Lagos. However, she was stunned when he had suggested that they have an open relationship, because he didn't want to hold her back from meeting her true love! Even though he had cheated on her repeatedly, Keisha had always forgiven him because he always came back to her, and she thought that meant he loved her. For this hold she had on him, she wasn't giving up easy.

"Hey..." Ifeanyi said, cautiously. "What's up?"

"I thought you might want to know that I'll be coming around in the summer," Keisha answered, in a practised sexy voice. "My friend's getting married. Maybe we can hook up?"

"Hmmm..." Ifeanyi paused. He didn't know whether to mention Mary. "I'm not sure I'll be around," he said instead.

"Why, where you going? It's not every day you get to see me. Don't you miss me?" she pushed.

"Well... I'm kinda seeing someone," he finally volunteered.

"*So?* When has that ever stopped you?" she hissed, sarcastically.

"Things are different now, Keisha. I'm sorry I hurt you."

His confession and apology struck a nerve with her. She was not appeased. Because apparently, *whateverhernameis* had succeeded in changing him in just a few months when she had laboured tirelessly for three good years of her life! "What, do you love *her*?" she asked in contempt, holding back the tears.

"I don't know. We just started dating," Ifeanyi responded.

"What's her name?" Keisha asked. She would find that tramp and make sure she regrets the day she was born!

"Don't worry about that, Keisha. Look, I gotta go. I have to get to work," he said, impatiently.

"No probs. I'll be seeing *you* in the summer. If I know you at all, this chick will be crying tomorrow," Keisha said and cut the call.

Ifeanyi looked at his phone, shaking his head. He certainly hoped she wasn't right. He didn't want to hurt Mary, but he was beginning to realise that he didn't know himself all that well.

It was the eve of their second date. Mary sat in her room, contemplating whether to call it off. She couldn't handle the emotions seeing him again would stir up in her. She didn't have anything to offer him and was certain that he would dump her in a heartbeat if he found out her secret. Better to stop it now, she thought as tears rolled down her cheeks.

"Why are you crying?" Daniel asked, startling his sister. Mary hadn't noticed him at the door.

"Go away, Daniel. Go and eat your food," she said to him.

"Samson, Sister Mary is crying again," Daniel grumbled, as he left her doorway.

Before long, Samson was at the door. Mary quickly wiped her tears and stood up from the bed. "Are you okay, Sister?" Samson asked, concerned.

The children had noticed that their sister was unhappy, but lately, she had been crying more, and they didn't know how to help her. They knew she was trying her best to provide for them and often wondered if they were the reason for her unhappiness.

"I'm fine. It's just work. Have you eaten?" she asked him, to turn the light off her emotional state.

"Yes. We left some for you in the pot," Samson replied.

"Don't worry about me. I'm going out," Mary said, surprising herself with her decision. She would be going out after all. "You and Samuel should look after your brother for me. Don't go outside, oh!"

"Okay, Sister," Samson said, as he sat down to continue watching TV with Samuel in their small living area.

Mary looked at the time, it was 5 O'clock. Today had been her Community Development Day, and she always made it home by 4 O'clock. Ifeanyi would soon arrive to pick her up to catch the 6 O'clock movie at Ikeja City Mall, and she was a mess. She hurried up to shower and put on her most comfortable jeans and one of her nicer blouses. Bolaji always bought her clothes from his frequent travels overseas, so that she would always look good for him when she attended church. The girls in the neighbourhood liked her because she was regularly giving away her old clothes.

Just as she concluded on her make-up, which she always applied modestly, Ifeanyi called to inform her that he was outside. She came out to find him leaning on his white Toyota Camry with flowers.

The sight made her smile. She soon forgot all the reasons she shouldn't let herself fall in love with him.

"Thank you," she said, as she took them.

"Let's put them in water," he said, implying that she should let him into her home. He had not been inside her home the last time. She hadn't even told him which of the rooms in the run-down complex was hers.

"We'll be late for the movie," she said, hoping he would accept that excuse.

"We have time. Plus, I have gifts for your brothers."

"You do?" Mary replied, shocked. Then she wondered if they were pity gifts. "What did you get them?"

"I'll show you inside," he insisted, with a grin.

Reluctantly, she showed him her humble abode. He didn't show any sign of shock or disgust. Her room and parlour was actually in a much better state than the other properties in the "face-me-I-face-you" living complex.

The boys slowly stood up to recognise the presence of their guest. They greeted in unison, "Good evening, sir."

"Good evening, Daniel, Samson, and Samuel," he said, intentionally recollecting their names, as told to him by Mary during their first date. Mary was impressed he remembered, though he mixed up Samson and Samuel. "I thought you might like these," Ifeanyi said, as he presented his gifts of football jerseys.

The boys were elated! They ran to collect the Arsenal jerseys from his hands, jumping and screaming with excitement. "Thank you, thank you, thank you!" they sang in chorus.

Mary laughed as she watched her brothers, who were the happiest she had ever seen them. Even happier than when she had told them they would be going to private schools! "So, that's why you were asking which team they supported?" Mary said to Ifeanyi, recalling their conversation on WhatsApp earlier in the week.

Ifeanyi giggled. "Alright, boys, we'll see you later," he said, as he stole their sister away.

Mary hardly paid attention to the movie. She kept thinking about what Ifeanyi had done for her brothers. She passed repeated glances at him and knew that she didn't stand a chance anymore. She was in love!

Three months flew by in a haze. Mary and Ifeanyi met as often as their jobs would permit and grew ever closer together. Mary still had her commitment to her church, and Ifeanyi never questioned her about the amount of time she devoted to church activities. He actually started attending his neighbourhood fellowship, Grace and Truth Assembly at Parkview Estate, in Ikoyi. He used to drive by the church but never entered, until he started dating Mary. However, he found the church to be warm and welcoming, and he even started attending their Bible Study classes on Sunday mornings.

At times, on Saturdays, when he visited Mary at her home, they would discuss some of the things that Ifeanyi was learning at his church. Mary was quite insightful and very knowledgeable of the scriptures, and to his surprise, Ifeanyi always enjoyed their discussions. However, he still hadn't made the decision to give his life to Christ. Mary was sure that he would and prayed for him every day. Sometimes, they prayed together.

Ifeanyi remained a perfect gentleman with Mary and never once pressured her to do anything she didn't want to do. Their connection was on a level neither of them understood, and they always wanted to be together. They both knew that they had fallen in love...months before they said the words "I love you" to each other. Every time Ifeanyi told Mary he loved her, her heart hurt as she thought of the secret she was hiding from him.

Mary was nervous. Today, she would be meeting Ifeanyi's parents for the first time. The times she had visited him at home, his parents were not around. She had already met his elder sister and younger brother, and they both liked her.

"Don't worry, they will love you," Ifeanyi whispered in Mary's ear before opening the car door for her to enter. When he got to the driver's side, he looked her over and said, "You are stunning!"

Mary returned his smile and straightened her dress. It was a new one from Bolaji. It was the only one that fit her well, as her other dresses were clinging too tightly to her body.

Ifeanyi's parents were happy to meet his new girlfriend. Anybody who was able to straighten him out, and stop him gallivanting all over Lagos, was a keeper in their books! After exchanging greetings, Mary quickly excused herself to the bathroom, as she felt nauseated by Ifeanyi's mother's perfume. She apologised for her abruptness when she returned.

"It's okay, dear," Mrs Chukwueke said, looking at her oddly.

They sat at the table and engaged in chit chat until the food came. It was prawn fried rice, Mary's favourite. However, Mary covered her mouth and excused herself again. The smell was offensive. Chief and Mrs Chukwueke looked at each other and then at their son. "Is there something the matter? I thought you said she was a Christian girl?"

"What are you talking about, Mummy?" Ifeanyi asked, oblivious.

Mary walked back into the room, as Mrs Chukwueke blurted out, "She's clearly pregnant, dear!"

Ifeanyi laughed. "It's impossible, Mum. We haven't slept together."

Mary stood in the middle of the room frozen. Ifeanyi turned and looked at her. She looked as if she had seen a ghost. "Are you okay, babe?" he asked, more concerned for her health than about his mother's accusation.

Before their eyes, Mary slumped to the ground and fainted.

04

"...weeping may endure for a night, but joy cometh in the morning."

PSALM 30:5

"**N**a lie!" Chuka exclaimed. He couldn't believe what Ifeanyi had just told him. "*Omo*, she played you, oh! *Pele.*"

Ifeanyi sat with his head in his hands. He still couldn't believe what had happened yesterday. He thought he knew her. He had really believed she loved him. Was this payback? Some kind of karma?

"Payback's a bitch, *sha*," Chuka said, as if in response to Ifeanyi's thoughts.

Ifeanyi let the tears roll freely from his eyes. The sobs came after. How did he miss it? He knew her every move. Whenever she wasn't with him or at work, she was in church. Was it some-one from the church?

"These church girls, *sef*. They are such great pretenders," Chuka continued, thinking that his philosophy would console his friend. "Don't ever trust a woman, oh. That's my motto. You know it could even be someone in church."

Ifeanyi lifted his head for a minute. "Do you really think so? That she had a church boyfriend?"

"I won't put it past her, oh. All those fine clothes that she wears... You never wondered who was buying her those things? My sister doesn't pay her that much!" Chuka speculated.

"*Chai!*" Ifeanyi exclaimed. "I am a fool!"

"God is good, *sha*. At least, you didn't marry her before she got pregnant for another man!" Chuka sighed. "Then she will tell you that it is *your* baby."

"*Chineke!*" Ifeanyi called on God's name in the Igbo language of Nigeria. "What if I had slept with her? I would never have known."

"You dodged a bullet, my friend!" Chuka said, feeling happier. "Just forget about her and move on. Come out with me tonight. Let's celebrate your freedom."

Moving on was much more easily said than done. Despite himself, he still loved and ached for her. He wished he would wake up and it would all have been a bad dream.

Mary called him every day, several times a day, but he always diverted her calls. He also deleted all her messages without reading them. He didn't want her explanations. He didn't want to understand why she betrayed him in such an awful way. And most of all, he didn't want her to talk her way back into his heart. He wasn't going to be that fool!

Mary rehearsed the break-up over and over again in her mind, tormenting herself with the memory. She remembered the look in Ifeanyi's eyes when she had confessed that she had been with another man. He would not let her continue. His

THE CHURCH GIRL | BOOK ONE

words, "*how could you?*", kept ringing in her ears. "I changed for you. I trusted you. I *loved* you. *And you do this to me?*" he had shouted accusingly.

The drive to her home was tense and excruciatingly painful. She tried repeatedly to explain, but he would cut her off with, "Don't lie to me!" At one point, he pulled up and said coldly, "If you say another word, I swear to God, I will throw you out of this car!"

As she thought more about her horrible predicament, Mary drew herself ever closer to the edge of life. She had not been to the church since she found out about her pregnancy, and Bolaji had been calling and sending her messages. She didn't know how to face him. She felt powerless to do anything to change her situation.

She had no one to turn to, no one to talk to. Because of her secret, she had kept her distance from friends. Even Dami had tried to get close to her, but she had pushed her away. Now, all that kept her from killing herself was the thought of her brothers, alone, without anyone to look after them.

She could not continue like this. She had to talk to somebody. But who, she did not know. Who would understand her plight? Who would help someone like her?

"God help me!" she cried aloud. "I want to die. I want to die. Oh, God, help me, please."

Every night, she would curl up in a ball and cry herself to sleep.

Mrs Kelechi Nwachukwu had noticed a sudden change in Mary, who had been a bright and cheerful staff member over the past three months. However, of recent, her work had been poor and her presentation at the office was getting others down. She wondered what could be the matter with her. She decided to call her into her office.

"Are you okay, Mary?" Kelechi asked with genuine concern.

Mary was nervous and shaking. She didn't know how to respond to the question. Usually, she would say she was fine. But she wasn't, and she couldn't hide it anymore. She broke down in sobs.

Kelechi waited for her to calm down and stood up to offer her tissues. "Sit down and talk to me."

When Mary opened her mouth to talk, she wailed instead.

"Is this about a man?" Kelechi prompted. Mary gently nodded. "Did he cheat on you?"

Mary shook her head, pulling herself together. "It was me!" she cried.

"Oh, dear," Kelechi sympathised. "Why did you do that? You know the truth will always come out."

"It's not what you think. If I told you, you wouldn't believe me," Mary said, giving Kelechi a side glance.

"Try me," Kelechi said, looking at her with sincerity in her eyes.

Hesitantly, Mary started to recount her story. She didn't know how she was able to open up so much to her boss, but she felt she had nothing left to lose. She told her everything, right up to the day she had fainted in her boyfriend's house. As she concluded her account, and told about her suicidal thoughts, she looked at Kelechi to see if she believed her.

A tear rolled from Kelechi's right eye, and she wiped it off. "You've been so unfortunate," she said, shaking her head. "You should have told him the truth. You should have told somebody before it got this far!"

"I know. I wanted to break it off with him before, but...I wanted someone to love me," she admitted to herself.

"Look, let's get practical here," Kelechi said, as the lawyer in her came out. "Your pregnancy is actually a good thing."

"*What?*" Mary didn't understand. "But I hate the baby already."

"Don't say that! The baby needs you to love him or her," Kelechi rebuked. "A paternity test, when one can be done, will prove that Pastor Bolaji is the father of your child. We can make a case against him and also see how much you can get for compensation and child support."

"But they will say I seduced him. No one will believe me," Mary despaired.

"You will be surprised," Kelechi responded. "If he was doing this to you, he is probably doing it to other girls too. If you are bold enough to speak out, you might encourage them to speak also. And with his character questioned by the paternity of your child, he will not be able to deny the charges. He might want to settle out of court. Will you accept that?"

Mary thought for a moment. If she agreed to that, then he might continue to abuse other young girls and women and think he can buy his way out of his crimes. She didn't want that. She also wanted people to see him for the evil monster that he really was. "No, I can't accept that," she responded.

"Then you better brace up for a fight," Kelechi said. "In the meantime, you need to keep yourself, your baby, and your brothers safe. You will also need some financing. I can only do so much."

"I don't have anybody," Mary said downcast.

"What about your boyfriend?"

"He won't even talk to me. He won't help me," she despaired.

You can't give up. You need his help if you are going to get through this. He loves you, right?" Kelechi asked.

"I think so."

"Then go to him, and tell him everything, like you told me. Who knows, maybe that is the reason God brought you two together..."

"Okay, I will go to him," Mary said. "Thank you so much! I am so grateful."

"It's okay, dear. God is in control of this. Just keep praying," Kelechi said, giving Mary a hug. "Here, take this card and call her. She's a Christian counsellor. She will help you deal with your grief and trauma. Her service is free too."

Mary thanked Kelechi again before taking the card and putting it in her bag. As she walked out of her boss' office, Mary felt like a load had been lifted off her shoulders. She had hope again. After work today, she would go to Ifeanyi's house and beg his forgiveness.

Ifeanyi was in one of those moods again. He lay in his bed going through the pictures on his phone of him and Mary. Pictures that he refused to delete because they were all he had left of what was his first love.

They had been so happy. Why did she do it? Why? It didn't make sense.

He had tried to move on with his life, but things had changed for him. He wasn't that guy anymore. Every girl he saw at the club was not good enough, because they were not Mary. And the thought of having a one-night stand, as was his habit before, was now filled with an awful dread of pregnancy. He had left the club early the night he had gone out with Chuka.

He continued to go to church. For some reason, he felt like being there made him close to Mary. He was mourning her as if she was dead, while refusing to talk to her. He also hoped to get answers and started to pray to a God that he thought was punishing him.

As he lay there, lost in his thoughts, there came a knock on the door. At the same time, his phone rang. He looked at it and saw that it was Ijeoma, his ex-fling. He ignored the call. *Some people really don't know when to give up!*

"Who is it?" Ifeanyi asked.

The steward opened the door. "Oga, there's one woman here for you," he said.

"Eh, what's her name?" Ifeanyi asked.

"She didn't tell me, oh," the steward replied.

"She didn't tell you or you didn't ask?" Ifeanyi replied, annoyed. "Tell her to wait for me, I'm coming."

Ifeanyi got out of bed and slid on his slippers. He glanced at the clock and saw that it was 7:30 pm. Who would be visiting him at this time?

He strolled down the hall and began down the stairs. He almost stumbled when he saw who it was.

"Hey, boo! *Sur-prisssse*!" Keisha said with a wide smile, as she stood up to receive him in an embrace.

"Uh, what are you doing here, Keisha?" he asked, refusing to hug her.

"I told you I was coming for the summer... Why you gotta be like that?" Keisha replied, hurt by his reaction.

"Well, usually people call to confirm visits. I wasn't expecting you," Ifeanyi answered roughly.

"It's okay. I'm here now," Keisha shrugged and sauntered up the stairs, heading in the direction of his bedroom.

Ifeanyi watched her, stunned by her boldness, as she strolled up to his room without invitation. He rubbed his hand on his forehead, not knowing how to handle the situation.

There was another knock on the door. The steward promptly answered it.

Mary walked in to see Ifeanyi standing there looking dazed. Before he could say anything, she began, "Please, hear me out, baby. I'm so sorry I hurt you. If you loved me at all, you would let me explain."

Ifeanyi opened his mouth to speak, but his words were interrupted by the reappearance of his ex-girlfriend in sexy lingerie. "Who is she? Is this the *tramp* you told me about?" Keisha sneered, with venom.

Mary couldn't believe what she had just walked into. "Oh my God!" she exclaimed. *He has moved on already!* In a panic, she turned around and ran out of the house.

05

"...weeping may endure for a night,
but joy cometh in the morning."

PSALM 30:5

Ifeanyi dashed after Mary and caught up with her at the end of
the driveway. He pulled her to himself passionately. "Where
are you going?" he asked, looking intently into her eyes.

"It's okay, Ifeanyi. I'm not mad at you," Mary said, looking
away, to hide the tears that were clouding her vision.

"What do you have to be mad about? You cheated on me!"

"Yes, and you've had your own back. Let's just move on," Mary
replied, struggling to be free of his grip.

"No, Mary. That's not what you think it is. I haven't been with
anyone since we've been together," Ifeanyi said, softly. "Look,
just come inside, and we can talk."

Mary looked at him with hope. She didn't know whether to believe him, but then she remembered that things are not always as they seem. She stopped struggling, and he released his grip. She followed him as he paced back into the house, shouting, "Security!"

A security guard came quickly to his side, and he gestured for him to wait. "Keisha, please get out of my house now!" he barked up the stairs.

"You don't mean that," Keisha replied. "Come upstairs; let's talk about it."

"There's nothing to talk about. If you don't get out of my house now, my security guards will drag you out!"

Keisha laughed. "Yeah, right. How can you treat me like this? You wouldn't dare!" she glared at him and stubbornly held her position, with her hands crossed on her chest.

"Little girl, if you do not leave this house, right this minute, I *WILL* throw you out myself!" The voice came from the upstairs hallway. Chief Chukwueke stood fuming, looking at the scantily dressed woman in his house.

Keisha was mortified. She covered herself as best she could with her hands and ran to the room to change. Moments later, she walked out and gave a slight bow of respect and mumbled, "Sorry, sir," as she climbed down the stairs, brushing past Ifeanyi on her way out.

"What kind of crazy women are you bringing to this house, Ifeanyi?" Chief Chukwueke chastised his son. "And you are here, shouting all over the place like a lunatic. Children of nowadays! Watch yourself, oh!" With that final rebuke, he returned to his room, where he and his wife were watching a show on Africa Magic.

"Sorry about that," Ifeanyi said, looking at Mary, who now felt very uncomfortable. "I think it's best we go for a drive."

Mary nodded her approval of the idea.

Ifeanyi drove to the waterfront, in Ikoyi, where lovers usually went for boat rides in the lagoon. He had taken Mary on the boat on a couple of occasions, and she had loved it. Today, they would just wind down the windows, pull back the sunroof, and enjoy the evening breeze at the dock.

Their drive was much more relaxed than the last time Mary was in Ifeanyi's car. She sensed that his anger had dissipated and hoped that he would be understanding of all she was about to tell him.

For a while, both of them were silent. Ifeanyi didn't know why he had suggested this outing, or even considered her request to talk. He was working through his emotions, and they were seriously clouding his judgement. Mary did that to him. He sighed deeply, breaking the silence.

"So, you wanted to talk..."

"Yes," Mary found her voice. "Thanks for giving me an opportunity to explain myself."

"I just want to know why," Ifeanyi said, studying her as she fiddled with her hands. "I thought we were happy."

"Oh, I was ecstatic! I'm so in love with you, Ifeanyi," Mary said, looking up at him.

Ifeanyi swallowed and closed his eyes for a second. "So, what happened? Who is he?"

"Pastor Bolaji," Mary answered.

Ifeanyi sat up straight. "Say what? You're having an affair with the *pastor* of your *church*?" he asked, disgusted. "That's just sick!"

"It wasn't an affair," Mary corrected him. "It was a very, very, *very* stupid arrangement that I accepted when I was 16 years old. I've been stuck in his grip ever since."

"What type of arrangement?"

"He said he would look after me and my brothers, and send us to school, if I would do anything he asked," she said. "Sexually."

Ifeanyi was silent.

"I wanted to break it off many times, but I was afraid. He was cruel, demeaning, and controlling. He didn't let me work anywhere else."

"Those are just excuses, Mary," Ifeanyi interrupted. "That was like six *years* ago? You stayed his whore for his money. I don't understand why you would let it go on for so long if you genuinely wanted out."

Mary covered her mouth in shame. Had he just called her Bolaji's *whore*? "What choices did I have?" she asked, offended.

"I am not trying to judge you. Especially at sixteen, you wouldn't know the impact of your choices. But though the right choice may be hard, it is still a choice. You chose to have it easy."

"How dare you?!" Mary was emotional. "I hated every single time he touched me! If it was only for my education and well-being, I would have NEVER agreed to such a despicable arrangement. But I wanted a better life for my brothers. You don't know anything about hard choices! EVERYTHING has been easy for you."

"Maybe you're right, that I've had it easy all my life," Ifeanyi responded. "Yes, it has been easy for me to sleep with so many women, I stopped counting when I was 19! But I made a hard choice for you. I was celibate with you for three months and counting. That's no picnic for a guy like me!"

"That's hardly the same," Mary replied defensively.

"It's not about comparison, Mary. It's just about right and wrong. You have to accept some responsibility in all of this. Even if he was and is an awful, child-molesting bastard!"

Mary was silenced. She had never thought about it like that. "You are right," she finally said, too ashamed to look at him. "I'm sorry..."

Ifeanyi reached out and held her hand. "I forgive you," he replied. "But I hope you have stopped seeing that man," he said, with piercing eyes.

"I haven't gone to see him since I found out I was pregnant. Almost two weeks now," Mary said. "I don't know how to face him. I'm still afraid."

"How far along are you?" Ifeanyi asked.

"Three months."

"I thought you guys usually noticed these things. Didn't your periods stop?"

"I didn't notice anything because I was too happy. My clothes fit tighter, but that was about it," Mary replied.

"So, we're keeping the baby?" Ifeanyi inquired.

"There's a *we*?" Mary smiled.

"I don't know, Mary. It's a lot to take in. I don't want to be your new Bolaji," Ifeanyi said.

Mary flinched. *So, he thinks I'm only after his money*, she thought. "It's okay. I don't want another Bolaji. I understand that I come with a lot of baggage. The last thing I want is to spend my life with someone who pities me, or thinks that I only care about their money," she said, folding her arms. She was ready to go home.

"Mary, you know I love you. I also don't want to hurt you. I don't know if I'm ready to get married, let alone have a family and in-laws to look after," he said honestly. "You make me want to do things I have never done before. But before we rush into anything, I just want to be your boyfriend…for now."

Mary swallowed the lump in her throat, feeling relief wash over her. She had thought he was trying to brush her off. "I'm happy just to have you in my life, Ifeanyi," she said, letting the tears flow.

Ifeanyi pulled Mary to himself and kissed her. All was right with the world again. Except for Bolaji, who didn't know what was about to hit him.

Ifeanyi and Mary attended church together for the first time that Sunday. Ifeanyi invited Mary to join him at Grace and Truth Assembly, and she made it there by 10 am when the service started. It was a convicting sermon by Pastor William Adekunle, the General Overseer, and Mary thought she saw Ifeanyi wipe away a tear from his cheek.

When the call for those who wanted to give their lives over to Christ came, Ifeanyi was among the first to go down to the front. Mary cried and thanked God for answering her prayer. She also went down to re-dedicate her life to Christ; to trust

Him to meet all her needs and protect her from every contrary power. She had been living in fear for far too long. She needed His strength to be courageous and to stand for the truth in every area of her life.

As a first-time guest and as a new Believer, Mary and Ifeanyi were invited after service for tea and biscuits, to get to know the ministers in the church and consider making the church their home. They both enrolled for the discipleship class, a decision that bound their hearts ever closer together.

After that, their fellowship deepened, and they prayed often together. Ifeanyi hungered and thirsted for more of God and studied the Bible daily to grow in his Faith. Mary believed that, in time, Ifeanyi would rise to the occasion and show his godly potential as the spiritual leader in their relationship.

Mary called the Christian Counsellor, Ms Seto Abiola, as directed by Kelechi, her boss. They arranged an appointment for Tuesday, and Kelechi had agreed to let her leave early to make it there by 4 pm.

The first session was slow paced, as Ms Abiola sought to establish the reason for her referral. They talked about her childhood and family life, and they explored patterns in her behaviour that she was still stuck in today. Mary had found the experience to be surprisingly enlightening. Ms Abiola explained that the aim of their time together would be to help her to be more conscious about the choices she makes and to break bad habits that result in harmful choices.

Mary was pleased with the first session and scheduled two appointments a week with Ms Abiola. She made sure she thanked Kelechi when she got to the office on Wednesday, for pointing her in the right direction. She was now well on her way to recovery. The next step would be confronting Bolaji.

Mary invited Ifeanyi to join her to meet with Kelechi to discuss the case she would be bringing against Bolaji. They met that Wednesday afternoon in Kelechi's office. Mary confirmed that Bolaji was still in the dark about her pregnancy, because she had refused to communicate with him since she found out about it three weeks ago.

They then addressed the issue of financial dependency. Mary reported that Bolaji had already sent several hateful messages, threatening that he would not be paying for her brothers' new term in school. Kelechi advised her to save them for additional evidence of control.

Fortunately, the boys had already closed for the summer, and Daniel had sat his Junior West African Examination Council (WAEC) exams without a hitch. Mary would be enrolling him in a public school for his Senior Secondary Education. The twins were to commence their final year in September, but she would be transferring them to a more affordable private school in Ajegunle. Kelechi said she would pay Mary her monthly stipend and promised to backdate it, which would help significantly in managing her new situation.

Kelechi also thought it would be important to secure a restraining order that would restrict Bolaji from coming within a certain distance of Mary. This was because it was likely that he would seek to harm Mary or her baby in order to bury the evidence and sabotage their case. Mary and Ifeanyi were very much in favour of that, but Ifeanyi was still concerned that it might not be enough of a restraint. The laws pertaining to this were quite limited in Nigeria, and with the scourge of corruption in the country, he had reason to be concerned.

06

"...weeping may endure for a night,
but joy cometh in the morning."

PSALM 30:5

The story first leaked in one 'Oluwatoyin's Blog' with the headline: "**Another Pastor Caught In Sex Scandal!**" By the end of the day, it was the most popular post on Nigerian blogs, and the hashtag #BolajiSexScandal went viral across the Internet.

By the next day, the print media had picked up on the story and were reporting with various headlines. "**Pastor Bolaji Akinwunmi To Face Trial On Sex Assault Charges.**" "**Pregnant Corper Claims Pastor Bolaji Assaulted Her For Six Years!**" "**Vessels Of Honour Fellowship Refuses To Comment On Pastor Akinwunmi's Sex Scandal.**"

Within a matter of days, three more allegations were made by two former members and one current member of the Vessels of Honour Fellowship of child sexual abuse, rape, and indecent assault by Pastor Bolaji. According to one of the two ex-members of the Fellowship, now in her mid-twenties, she was only 14 years old when the abuse began. The other, who claimed to have worked for him as his house-help, accused him of raping her. She had left the job, and the church, and had been afraid to say anything because she thought she would not be believed. 16-year-old, Shade Olubunmi alleged that he sexually assaulted her over a year ago, but they continued to have relations because, in her words, *"he buys me nice things."* There was a public outcry as the church was pressed to make a statement.

Mary was surprised with how quickly the story spread. She was however not surprised to read the headlines that were less favourable towards her. "**The New Ashawo: Sex for Education**" was the title of one such blog post. "**GOLD DIGGER WATCH: Mary Uwanna Seeks Child Support From Pastor Alleged of Sexual Assault**" was another. Some of her old friends were calling her up to confirm the story, but Mary refused to give a statement, knowing how easily her words would be turned against her.

Ifeanyi did not escape getting mentioned in all of the scandal. One featured article, with the title, "**Whose Baby Is It?**", revealed: *"Mary Uwanna's ex-boyfriend is none other than notorious womaniser, Ifeanyi Chukwueke, first son of Chief and Mrs Chinedu Chukwueke. Of course, he dumped her the moment he learnt of her pregnancy!"* As he read the post, Ifeanyi wondered who was feeding them all this information, which only had traces of truth to them. Fortunately for Mary and Ifeanyi, they had each other and the truth to help them get through the ordeal.

Pastor Bolaji had no such comfort, however. His wife had kicked him out of their bed, and he was to face an inquiry at the church, where they were sure to find out that he had been stealing from the church treasury to support his many extra-marital relations. The truth, rather than convicting him, tormented him day and night.

"Aaaaaarrrrrhhh!"

Mrs Akinwunmi's screech was heard out on the streets by some paparazzi that had camped outside her family home, one fateful Saturday in August.

The children ran to their mother's side to see what was the matter and began to wail when they saw the corpse of their father, hanging from the ceiling, with a noose around his neck. The eldest of the three children, 16-year-old Femi, tried to console his mother, who had become hysterical.

When the police made it to the late pastor's house, they searched for a note, but none was found. However, in the study where he hung, on his office table, his Bible was opened to Luke 17, and verses 1 and 2 had been highlighted in yellow. The words "I'm sorry" were scribbled on the page with the same highlighter. The passage read:

> "Then said He unto the disciples; it is impossible but
> that offences will come: but woe unto him, through
> whom they come! It were better for him that a
> millstone were hanged about his neck, and he cast
> into the sea, than that he should offend one of these
> little ones."

The Bible was taken in as evidence, and the case of the sexual assault of Mary Uwanna by Pastor Bolaji Akinwunmi was solved. The pastor had hung himself by reason of guilt.

Pictures of the late pastor hanging were soon to spread through the media, and even appeared on the evening news of NTA. When Mary watched and saw that her abuser was dead, she felt the first kick of her baby as her stomach churned. Instantly, she threw up.

When asked to give a statement about the death of her abuser, Mary made this press release:

> *"What I have learnt from this horrible ordeal that resulted in the suicide of my former pastor, is that my oppressor was a coward, unable to face the consequences of his actions. All these years, I lived in fear of him and believed his lies, but I see now that I was a contributor to my own bondage.*
>
> *"When I think about the fact that I could have come out with the truth long ago and saved myself a whole lot of trauma and heartbreak, instead of now being pregnant for a man I despised, I feel like a complete fool. I am also troubled and saddened as I consider the many other young girls and women who might have been spared his assault, if I had said something. If only I had been bold enough to stand for the truth, rather than live in fear and in compromise. I sincerely apologise to his family for the anguish I have caused them, through the part I played in this scandal.*
>
> *"I want to implore every victim of abuse to speak up! Your voice is a gift you can give the world. The truth is what will set you free, so do not ever believe your oppressor when he or she says that no one will believe you or that no one else will help you. With every last ounce of your strength, speak up, before it is too late!"*

When Mary finished speaking, she was filled with an overwhelming surge of joy and passion for a new cause. Her experience had given her a gift she could give to a world plagued by injustice. She realised her new calling and became committed to speaking against all forms of abuse against humanity. She started her own blog, "Speak Now For Freedom," which quickly grew in following. She anticipated that it would soon grow in influence and become an additional source of revenue for her. She hoped to become a highly acclaimed human rights activist, working under the banner of Browne Law Firm, helping victims speak out and bringing perpetrators of abuse to justice.

The investigation into the late Pastor Bolaji's abuse of power and of church funds revealed that the late pastor was indebted by many millions of Naira to Vessels of Honour Fellowship. Some of the funds were retrieved from off-shore accounts, and the others were retrieved by sale of his properties. As a mercy to his widowed wife and three children, the church permitted the family to retain their home. However, neither inheritance nor support was available for the late Pastor Bolaji's unborn child.

In the wake of the scandal, Chief and Mrs Chukwueke called Ifeanyi into their quarters. They were sitting out on the balcony, enjoying the ocean breeze, when Ifeanyi joined them. Ifeanyi pulled up a seat across from them.

Mrs Chukwueke spoke first. "Ife, are you still seeing that Mary girl?" she asked.

"Yes, Mum. Why?" Ifeanyi asked.

Mrs Chukwueke shook her head. "So, after everything she has put you through, you are determined to ruin your life for this girl?"

Ifeanyi was shocked. What was this about? "Mum, I know what she did was wrong and foolish, but she's not a bad person. I know she loves me, and I love her."

"Shut-up-your-mouth! What do you know about love? You have never settled down long enough to love somebody, and it is *this* one that you want to marry?"

"No one has said anything about marriage, Mum."

Mrs Chukwueke laughed. "*Na wa oh*! So, you think she is just playing? You think you can have your fun and move on? Tell me, if you don't plan on marrying this girl, why are you wasting your time?"

"Well, marriage is not out of the question; it's just not on the cards right now. I don't want to complicate things."

"See me see trouble, oh!" Mrs Chukwueke said, spreading her arms dramatically to an imaginary audience. "You don't want to complicate things? How much more complicated can it get? And now she has dragged our family name into her *dirty sex scandal!*"

Ifeanyi looked at his father for support, but he was simply petting his wife to calm her down. "I don't know what to say, Mum. This is between me and Mary. If we decide to get married–"

"God forbid bad thing!" Mrs Chukwueke interrupted, getting more emotional by the minute. "What can that girl offer you, except somebody else's baby and three other children to look after? No, I will not accept. In fact, I forbid it!"

"You will do no such thing," Chief Chukwueke interjected. "There's no need to be so dramatic. You know, you were no angel yourself when we were dating."

"Ah, at least I was not a whore!" Mrs Chukwueke shot back.

"That is debatable," Chief Chukwueke replied. "But I loved you then, and I love you now."

Mrs Chukwueke sat back in her chair, dumbfounded, and sulked.

"Look, son, what your mother and I are trying to tell you is that you should not continue this relationship with this girl, unless you plan to marry her. It will not be fair to you or her, or the baby, if you decide to walk away later. We just want you to think about what you are getting yourself into because you are a bright, young, handsome, well to do man, with a lot of prospects, and we believe you deserve better. But if you really love her, you can make it work."

"Thank you, Dad...and Mum," Ifeanyi said, offering his mother a smile. "I will think about what you have said. And I hope, if and when I decide to choose a wife, you will support my decision."

"It is well," Chief Chukwueke said. "May God help you to make the right decision."

Ifeanyi stood up and thanked his parents again before leaving them. He had some thinking to do. As someone who had never been good at living up to other people's demands and expectations of him, he had to really consider what *he* wanted for himself. He didn't want to live to regret his decision nor resent his wife. He would take it to God in prayer.

❤ ❤ ❤

Mary noticed that Ifeanyi had been a little distant of late. She wondered what might be troubling him. They were supposed to see a movie tonight, but he had cancelled it for a dinner date instead. He had said those dreaded words: "*We need to talk*," which filled her body with a chill.

She was now five months pregnant and her stomach had blown up in the space of just two months. She couldn't find anything attractive to wear, so she went for comfort instead. She wore a long floral gown that showed off her bump and a pair of simple slippers.

Ifeanyi smiled when he saw her, which calmed down her nerves. "Beautiful, as always," he said.

They dined at a new Chinese restaurant in Surulere. At six O'clock, they were the only ones there. Mary looked at Ifeanyi, as he shifted on his seat. "Are you okay?" she finally asked.

He nodded. "I want to ask you something, but I don't know how."

"Just ask me," she said, nervously.

"This is a scenario... Let's say my parents forbade us to marry. Sshhh," Ifeanyi said, putting his finger to his lips upon seeing Mary's reaction. "It's just a scenario. And if I married you, I would be disinherited. Would you elope with me?"

"This is *just* a scenario?" Mary confirmed. Ifeanyi nodded. "I guess I would want to, but I wouldn't marry you without your parents' blessing. It wouldn't be right. So, I guess my answer would be 'no.'"

"So I understand, why wouldn't it be right? It's our lives after all, and we love each other... Isn't that enough?"

"If you do not honour your parents, how can you honour me as your wife? If I marry you, I marry your family. I can never come between you and your family. A marriage built on such a rebellion doesn't have much chance for success. I'd rather pray and wait on their blessing," Mary said, looking at him intently.

Ifeanyi sighed deeply and smiled. "You are right." Mary nodded, and looked down at her hands. "That's why I want to marry you," Ifeanyi said to her, as he got on one knee and revealed a 4-carat diamond ring with a white gold band.

Mary looked up and saw the ring and gasped. "No way!"

"Is that your answer?" Ifeanyi asked, amused by her reaction.

"Of course not. Yes! Yes! I want nothing more," Mary said, accepting his ring and his proposal.

He stood up and pulled her into his arms. They shared a passionate kiss to the applause of the waiters.

VOLUME
TWO

07

"Many are the plans in a person's heart, but it is the LORD's purpose that prevails."

PROVERBS 19:21

Ifeanyi was glowing, smiling like a freed man after a long sentence. He was even more attractive now that he was renewed in his mind and committed to the woman he loved, that all the ladies at Ifeanyi and Mary's engagement party could not help but be jealous of the bride-to-be. Many of those who came to wish him and his fiancée well never thought they would see the day that Ifeanyi would devote himself to one woman, nor the day that he would declare, "It's all God's doing."

Even his parents were amazed at how mature their son had become in such a short time. Though they knew his life would not be easy, they knew that Mary was a blessing to him and their family; he had made the right choice. They smiled and hugged each other. They had not done so badly in bringing him up after all.

Chuka came up beside Ifeanyi to congratulate him. "Congrats, my friend! I'm really happy for you."

Ifeanyi smiled. "Thanks! You helped to make it happen."

"Me? What did I do?" Chuka asked, perplexed but glad to be credited with bringing the happy couple together.

"You told me where she was serving. If you hadn't, who knows what I might be doing now," Ifeanyi said, his eyes alight with joy.

"Wow, I've never seen you like this!" Chuka marvelled. "You're a completely different man from the one I met in camp."

"If I tell you the truth, will you believe me?" Ifeanyi looked at him seriously.

Chuka was intrigued. Was he going to confess it was all an act? "Sure, tell me, man," he said with a lowered voice.

"Jesus is real!" Ifeanyi smiled. "I just don't want what I wanted before. He has completely changed my heart. And now, I just feel like there's so much more to life. I've been blind, and now I see."

"Hmmm," Chuka muttered, a little disappointed that it wasn't a juicy secret. "So, no more clubbing for you?"

"That's not what it's about. My time here is limited, and I don't want to waste it being where I don't need to be or doing what will not give me peace," Ifeanyi responded. "You know, I actually love spending time with Mary and the boys. They're just great. It's better than clubbing!"

"Damn! You're so sprung," Chuka said, shaking his head but also feeling a little envious of Ifeanyi's new life.

"It's all God's doing," Ifeanyi said, with a smile, before excusing himself to go to his fiancée.

Chuka watched him with envy. He had missed his friend, but now he realised that the man he knew was truly gone. But there was something to be admired and respected in this new Ifeanyi. Maybe he was on to something. Maybe Jesus is real, Chuka pondered.

From the corner of his eye, he spotted a familiar face and turned his gaze to the new guest at the engagement party. His mouth dropped open when he realised who it was. He stood, stunned, as his eyes followed the lady, who made her way across the room to make her presence known to the celebrants. There is a God after all, he thought as he sought a good seat to watch the drama that would soon unfold.

Mary was dressed in a lovely pink gown, looking like she belonged on the cover of "The Bump" magazine. She stood radiant and without a care as she chatted with her soon to be sister-in-law, Chidinma. They had gotten quite close over the past couple of months, and she had been the event coordinator for the little engagement party.

A surge of warmth coursed through her body when she felt the warm body of her fiancé from behind her as he came in for an embrace. Ifeanyi dropped his head and kissed his fiancée on her neck before resting it on her shoulder. Mary beamed brilliantly, enjoying the sensations his touch sparked.

"I'd say get a room, but..." Chidinma teased, giggling.

"Don't be a hater!" Ifeanyi retorted, jokingly. He stood up straight and came beside his fiancée, his arm around her rounded waist. "What are you guys talking about?"

Chidinma stopped short as she opened her mouth to respond. Her eyes were fixated on something behind the couple, and they both turned around, following her gaze. Neither of them could believe their eyes as they stood face to face with Ijeoma Njokwu, Ifeanyi's ex-fling from camp. She was wearing the same pink dress as the bride to be.

Mary looked her up and down before glancing at her fiancé, who had suddenly grown cold. They were both wishing the same thing as their eyes settled on Ijeoma's bump. *God, please, don't let it be Ifeanyi's baby!*

Ifeanyi stood looking at Ijeoma as if she was a ghost. He couldn't take his eyes away from her. He knew he was supposed to say something, but he didn't want the moment to pass. He didn't want to face his new reality because he knew, as did Mary and Chuka, that the baby was his. In an instant, the plans he had for his amazing life with Mary came tumbling to the ground, and he was powerless to stop them.

Ijeoma smiled to herself as she observed the reaction from the formerly happy couple. She knew that her news would be hard to take, but she hadn't even said anything yet! If only Ifeanyi would have picked her calls, maybe she wouldn't have had to break it to him like this.

As it seemed no one wanted to break the silence that had suddenly fallen over them, Ijeoma decided to speak first. "Hi, Ifeanyi. Long time! Seven months to be precise," she said, patting her pregnancy bump.

Ifeanyi swallowed hard and cleared his throat. He wanted to say 'hi' back but was surprised with his tone when he asked instead, "What are you doing here?"

Ijeoma smiled. "I heard you were getting married...and to "*virgin* Mary" for that matter. I had to come and see for myself." She gave Mary a slow once over, with a smirk as she considered the irony of the nickname. "Not much of a virgin I see..."

Mary tried to slip away from Ifeanyi's hold, but he pulled her to him all the more. He needed her now. He couldn't lose her now. She had to stand by him, and she had to know that he would choose her over anyone. Ijeoma had to know that Ifeanyi had no room in his life nor heart for her. So, Mary had to stay. He didn't know how he would stand if she walked away from him now.

"What do you want?" Ifeanyi asked coldly.

Ijeoma suddenly felt uncomfortable. Maybe he had the wrong idea. "I want to wish you well in your life together. And I thought you needed to know that you're a father. I only want my child to be considered in your plans."

"How can you be sure that I'm the father?"

"Wow!" Ijeoma was hurt. "Well, you may not believe me, but you're the only man I've slept with this year. So, that sort of rules out everyone else."

Ifeanyi looked at his fiancée, who stood uncomfortably beside him. She had managed to keep an expressionless face, and he couldn't decipher what she was thinking. They needed to talk. He needed to know what was going through her mind, and they needed to process this information together.

"Excuse us," Ifeanyi said to Ijeoma as he turned his fiancée around and left the room, to the stares and mumblings of everyone.

Chidinma stood glaring at Ijeoma. She felt so sad for her brother and his fiancée. This news would break their hearts, but she hoped their marriage would be saved. They deserved to be happy.

When they were alone in Ifeanyi's room, he finally let his grip loose on Mary, and she plumped herself on the sofa, silently processing what had just transpired downstairs. Ifeanyi sat on the bed trying to organise the many thoughts that were running through his mind. There were so many variables, so many complications to their love, and he feared that this new information would change everything.

Maybe if Mary wasn't already pregnant, they could handle one child out of wedlock. But now they had TWO! And they hadn't even made love. They hadn't even dated long. Would Mary accept his baggage, as he had accepted hers?

"Talk to me, Mary," Ifeanyi said, at last.

"What can I possibly say?" Mary looked up at Ifeanyi, glistening tears in her eyes. They had to be the most unfortunate couple to be in their predicament! She knew he had loved her despite her humongous baggage, but how could they start a life together with two small babies and Baby Mama drama to boot? It seemed such an insurmountable obstacle. Maybe they were never meant to be...

"Anything... What are you thinking?"

"It seems luck is not on our side. We're both faced with the consequences of our sinful actions, and it's just...too much."

"Too much, how? Too much that you can't handle it?" Ifeanyi looked at Mary worriedly, his heart in his throat.

"Can we really handle this? Is this really how you want to start a life together? Another baby, I can deal with, but Baby Mama Drama? I think we need to pray about us again."

"What are you saying? You don't want me anymore?"

"Of course, I want you. But it's not just you anymore. That child is a part of you and will always be in our lives. We have to be realistic."

"If you weren't pregnant, and we have only this child to think about, would you not accept me...and my baggage?"

"Let's not do the 'what if's. I can't think about that, only *what is*."

"I still want you, Mary. I can't imagine my life without you." Ifeanyi came to kneel at Mary's feet and placed his hand on her tummy. "I'm already in love with *our* child! I need to know you still love me, even with my baggage. That's the only way we can make it work."

Mary kissed Ifeanyi's head, which was bowed before her, and let the tears flow. He was being too romantic, thinking with his heart and not his head. Of course, she still loved him, but she was no longer certain that she should marry him. No matter how much she wished Ijeoma's baby wouldn't change things, it already had. Their life had been thrown into uncertainty, and she needed stability. She'd had enough traumas for one lifetime.

"I love you, Ifeanyi. But I don't know if I can do this. I need some time to work through my feelings and pray about it."

"What are you praying about, Mary? Is it because we are not married yet? If we were, wouldn't you fight for us and make it work?" Ifeanyi cried. "Who's going to love you like I love you? And accept your baby and brothers as their own? If you leave me now, then I can't believe you ever loved me... Please don't leave me!"

The intensity of Ifeanyi's love broke Mary's heart all the more. If only he didn't love her so much, then she would just walk away, pick up her heart, and hope for another love to come her way. How ever painful their break-up would be, she could handle it.

But she couldn't ignore the dread that had gripped her heart the moment she had laid eyes on Ijeoma's bump.

The dread that she and her baby would always interrupt their lives. The dread of struggling to look after two babies and her three brothers too, as they begin a new life together! The dread of always wondering if and when Ijeoma would try to seduce her husband from right under her nose.

And what about the sibling rivalry that was sure to ensue? What about Ifeanyi's parents? Would they still be in support of their marriage, knowing that Ifeanyi has his own biological child and could just as easily marry the child's mother?

She wondered if they would not even be happier to marry him off to Ijeoma Njokwu. She came from a good and wealthy Igbo family, and they probably even hailed from the same tribe. She had no sordid past nor dependents, unlike Mary. And the child in her tummy was related by blood!

No, the bright future Mary had foreseen for herself with Ifeanyi had been clouded over. The forecast was for a horrific storm, and her body, mind, and heart were too worn out to handle any more stress. She just wanted to run away, as fast as she could. She wanted to run before Ifeanyi realised that marrying her would be the biggest mistake of his life!

08

"Many are the plans in a person's heart, but it is the LORD's purpose that prevails."

PROVERBS 19:21

"Let's call it off."

Ifeanyi couldn't believe how quickly his world was crashing before his eyes. Just a few days ago, he thought he couldn't possibly be happier. That he'd finally found the one he had been waiting for his whole life. The one who made him want to be a better man. How could he not have seen this coming?

He had given Mary the time she said she needed to pray and was sure she would finally see that they belonged together. But now she was breaking up with him. Over the phone.

"Why are you doing this?" he asked, with the last of his fight, his voice hoarse with emotion. He'd begged her enough and spent time on his knees praying for God to see them through this ordeal and help him come to terms with whatever decision Mary made. But he still couldn't understand why she would throw their love away. Had she loved him at all?

"Please don't make this harder than it is. Nothing I say or you say will change what has happened. I just don't think I have what it takes. Please, let's just move on. Maybe we can still be friends..." Even as the words left her mouth, Mary knew it wasn't likely that they would remain friends. Their lives were worlds apart, and she'd had a brief moment of belonging in his world, but now, she had to face reality.

Ifeanyi kept the phone to his ear, not wanting to end the call, not wanting to move forward. He listened to her breathing on the line, knowing that it was the last time he would ever speak to her on the phone. If he had known the last time he saw her would be the last time, he might never have let her out of his arms.

The tears fell down his cheeks as he heard her click off the line. No one had spoken for over a minute, and she had just proved that he loved her more.

It was the hardest thing she had ever done. She felt like she had really let him down, that she had betrayed him. She felt wicked and selfish for leaving him because he had a child with another woman, even though he had stood by her when she'd gotten pregnant for a man she'd slept with behind his back. But Mary knew it was the right thing to do.

They really hadn't known each other under the right circumstances. And if she hadn't gotten pregnant, he may not have felt a need to assure her of his commitment by proposing marriage. They were rushing things, and Ijeoma's baby was the wake-up call they needed.

Mary resumed work on Wednesday, after taking a couple of days off. When she had called in sick on Monday, Kelechi had understood. She had been at the engagement party, and the pregnant woman with the matching dress as the celebrant was hard to miss.

Now that she had made her mind up, and they were truly over, Mary finally felt ready to move forward with her life. She really wanted someone to talk to, though, because she just lost her best friend, and her whole world seemed to have stopped.

Even her baby, who she had become fond of talking to, had been quiet of late. She hadn't been kicking as much. Maybe she knew her mother was depressed.

She couldn't call Chidinma, and even though she had re-acquainted with old friends, she wasn't close to anyone enough to confide in them about her feelings. The only person she could turn to was Kelechi. Mary hoped she would be reassuring.

"Hey, you okay?" Kelechi's voice broke into her thoughts. She had been staring blankly at her computer screen, in the middle of typing a letter. "Are you sure you're ready for work? If you want to take the rest of the week off, I'll understand."

Mary looked up from her desk and forced a smile. "Thanks, but I really need to get on with life."

"Do you want to talk about it?"

How was it that she knew just what to say? Mary wondered at her boss, now turned confidant. She simply nodded in response, as she felt her emotions welling up again.

When they were in Kelechi's office, Kelechi brought out her pack of tissues and waited for Mary to settle in her seat. "So, how are you?"

Mary tried on a smile. "Stronger than I thought," she finally responded, with a sigh. She was not in the frame of mind she had been in the last time when Ifeanyi had broken up with her. Today, she was feeling resolute. Maybe because the case of Bolaji had been finally settled, and she no longer had that trauma hanging over her head.

"Hmmm…" Kelechi returned her half-smile. "What about Ifeanyi? I hope you guys worked it out."

Mary's eyes met Kelechi's. *So, she thought they could have worked it out?* "We broke up." For the first time, as Mary heard those words, she wondered if they could have worked it out after all; if she had been hasty in making her decision. She really hadn't believed she was strong enough for any other outcome.

Kelechi frowned. "Are you sure that's what you want? I'm guessing you were the one who broke up with him...?"

The sobs came then, out of nowhere. Maybe she wasn't ready to talk about it yet. She'd avoided consulting other people for advice because she had wanted to make up her own mind, and she also needed to be sure that she was led by God and not by popular opinion. But it was evident that she was still unsure about the decision she had made.

She hadn't received anything clearly from God. She thought her circumstance was His doing and His will, and so evidently, He had expressed His mind by making her relationship with Ifeanyi hard. Surely, if they were meant to be, it wouldn't have been this hard!

Kelechi hesitated and then reached out to embrace Mary. She really wanted to keep their relationship professional, but Mary had gotten under her skin. Since the first time she had opened up to her, Kelechi felt a certain burden for her, and they had become closer over the past few months.

"Have you prayed about it?" she asked when Mary had released herself from the hug and was wiping her eyes with tissues.

"I have. I honestly can't say I've heard anything from God, though. I just feel so afraid when I think of what awaits us..."

"Maybe that's the problem. Maybe your fear is louder than your faith," Kelechi said. "I'm not saying that you shouldn't have broken up with him. I honestly don't know what I would have done if I was in your shoes. But worse things have happened, and God has been, and will always be, faithful. I just really thought you guys belonged together."

"What have I done? He's going to think I don't love him," Mary cried, the weight of her decision sinking in. She thought she had closed the door, but it had turned out to be a revolving door.

Will she ever really know what to do? Her indecision has been the hallmark of her life, and she had a bad habit of making decisions out of fear. "Do you think if I called him back, we could work it out?"

Kelechi thought for a moment. Mary was clearly emotional and indecisive. She didn't want to make it worse by contradicting her decision. "If you want my advice, I'd say give it time. You've already ended it, and perhaps it is for good reason. Let your mind settle. Rest in God, and wait on Him. I believe He will make His will clear to you in time. If you called Ifeanyi back now, he may think you're unstable, and who knows if you will not still regret your decision."

Mary nodded her agreement. She didn't trust herself to stick to any decision she would make. Maybe time was really what they needed. Maybe things would be clearer when the babies were born. Maybe...

"How about the baby?" Kelechi asked, offering a kind smile, hoping that the shift in focus will make Mary feel better.

"Okay...I think," Mary said, unsure.

"Why do you say that?" Kelechi lifted a brow in concern.

"I haven't felt a kick in about two days. Is that normal?"

"No, that's not normal. But maybe you just haven't noticed. Or maybe, she knows you're feeling down," Kelechi said optimistically. "But you know what, go to the hospital and have a scan, just to be sure everything is okay."

"Thanks, I will."

"Take the rest of the week off, Mary. Go to the hospital, and then go home. I think the stress is much for you. You have to think of your baby." Kelechi gave Mary another hug when she stood up to leave. She couldn't help her big heart, as she added, "Call me if you need to talk."

Mary hugged Kelechi tighter. She was so grateful to have her in her life. It was amazing the ways God provided for her. "God bless you. Thank you."

The nurse had just concluded the scan and had excused herself to call the doctor. She said she wanted his perspective. Mary lay on the hospital bed, looking out of the window. She turned her head when the door opened again, and the nurse walked in with the doctor.

"*Mary?*" Doctor Oziegbe, as his tag revealed, said in surprise.

Mary looked at him, trying to recollect his face. Nothing. Maybe he knew her from TV, she wondered, starting to feel embarrassed.

"It's me, David. From Vessels of Honour?" Still nothing, but Mary offered a smile all the same. "I guess you don't remember me. Maybe that's a good thing," David said, returning her smile and resuming his professionalism.

Doctor Oziegbe frowned as he looked at the results of the scan. He asked Mary a few questions about her pregnancy then said, "I hate to be the bearer of bad news, but you lost the baby, Mary."

Mary looked at him as if he had just spoken French. "What?"

"Yes, unfortunately, though uncommon, this happens from time to time. Particularly when there has been a lot of stress in the pregnancy. Your baby has been dead for some days now. We need to get her out, quite urgently actually."

Mary couldn't believe her ears. She had lost the baby? She didn't know how to feel about it. After losing Ifeanyi, nothing seemed so important anymore. Silent tears began to drop from her eyes, for the life that would have been. It seemed her baby was as weak of heart as she was and had given up on an uncertain future.

Mary didn't think about the cost of the procedure until after it was completed and she lay in bed, devoid of her baby. She wondered why they had not brought a bill to her. She thought to ask the nurse who was attending to her.

"Your account is paid up," the nurse said after verifying with the accounts department. "Isn't your husband coming?"

"I'm not married," Mary said, just as Doctor Oziegbe returned to the delivery room.

"But your boyfriend knows you're here, right?" the nurse continued in her presumption.

Mary lay her head back on the pillow and looked up at the ceiling in dismay. "I don't have a boyfriend. The father is dead."

"Oh, I'm sorry," muttered the nurse. She received a look from the doctor, indicating that she should leave. She quickly concluded her task and left the room.

"How are you feeling, Mary?" Doctor Oziegbe asked, looking kindly at Mary.

"I feel fine. Can I go home now?"

"I just have some final checks to make, and then I'll give you the all clear."

"Okay," Mary turned towards the window again.

"I know this is not the best of times, but I don't know if, or when, I will see you again, Mary." His voice had changed. It was husky with emotion. Mary turned to him again, and finally, she remembered the man she had met in early January after church, one Sunday. He was fiddling with his hands like he was a teenager. "I heard what happened between you and Pastor Bolaji. I'm sorry I didn't know and wasn't able to help you. But if you need a friend..."

"Thank you. I'm sorry about how I responded to you last time. I'm not really in the right place to consider a new relationship, but I wouldn't mind a friend," Mary responded, with a kind smile.

David smiled with relief. "That's good. So, can I call you?" Mary nodded her approval, and his smile widened. "Well, I guess, there's nothing else to confirm. You're free to go."

Mary looked at him with both shock and amusement. Was that the final check he needed to do to release her?

David gave her a lingering parting look as he left her room to give her a chance to change and leave. He looked so cute with his sheepish grin, Mary thought. She had to be careful of this one, though. Her heart was not ready.

09

"Many are the plans in a person's heart, but it is the LORD's purpose that prevails."

PROVERBS 19:21

There was a knock on the door, and Mary put on the last of her clothing. She wondered if the doctor had something more to say. She quickly pulled up the maternity pants she had worn to work that day and called out, "Come in."

It was not the doctor. It was someone more unexpected. Ifeanyi stood at the door hesitantly, then walked determinedly over to Mary and wrapped her in an embrace. She melted in his arms, and for a long minute, neither of them said anything. It was as though they hadn't seen each other in years.

"I'm sorry," Ifeanyi said, at last. "I'm so sorry."

"It wasn't your fault," Mary said, as she pulled out of his embrace. "How did you know?"

"They called to approve payment of the procedure. I came as soon as I could."

"It was so kind of you to approve. I promise I'll pay you back as soon as I can."

Ifeanyi raised an eyebrow at her. Was she serious? "Don't be silly, Mary. You don't owe me anything."

There was an awkward silence, and both were aware that things had changed between them. Would the loss of the baby make everything okay again? They didn't know.

"Are you cleared to go home?" Ifeanyi broke the silence. Mary nodded. "Can I give you a lift?"

"Thank you. I'd appreciate that," Mary smiled, shyly.

They drove in silence all the way to Mary's home. Mary kept wanting to speak and then deciding against it. She rehearsed speeches in her mind and discarded them. He wouldn't be able to concentrate in a deep discussion, she finally concluded. They would be able to talk properly when she got home.

Ifeanyi struggled with his thoughts and feelings as he drove. He had decided he wouldn't fight nor push any more. The ball was in her court. He had already shown, beyond a shadow of a doubt, how much she meant to him, and well, he couldn't handle her rejection again. He was fulfilling his duty by taking her home.

When he had parked the car, he half-expected her to open the door, say goodbye, and leave, but she just sat there, so he wound down the windows and switched off his engine. More silence.

Mary finally found her voice. She turned to him and swallowed hard. "You know I love you right?"

Ifeanyi's gaze was steady as he nodded. He had doubted, but he knew.

"I loved the baby too, but I feel...*relieved. You know?*"

"I know. Like you've been given a blank slate?"

"Yeah... It changed my life, and now I feel like my life is my own again, and I have more choices now."

"Hm hmm. Did you feel you had to marry me?"

"No, I wanted... I want to... It just kinda made it seem as though that was what we had to do. I'm sure you felt like you had to propose?" Mary said, looking into his eyes, looking for the truth.

Ifeanyi looked away and sighed. Was she right? Was it the baby that made him propose? "I guess, in a way... I may not have proposed for several months if you were not pregnant," he answered at last, feeling a bit uncomfortable.

He remembered how his parents had urged him to make a decision. But they had only caused him to do what was right, and he wouldn't have done it differently, given the same situation. He had proposed because he loved her.

"I guess what I'm saying is that...this is a chance to take it slow, to really get to know ourselves. Without pressure. I needed you. I said "yes" because I *love* you, but I needed you... I guess I feel our circumstances pushed us together, and I want a chance to choose you, without the feeling of desperation. I want...no, I *need* my love to be proven."

"So, what are you saying?" Ifeanyi asked. He didn't want to lead her on. She'd never felt in control of her life, and he knew that she was fighting for some sort of control over her destiny. And he was beginning to see that fate might have something else in store for both of them.

"I want to be friends. And maybe there will be more for us in time, but I really want to be friends with you. I want to know you from a different perspective. I want to know me... I don't even think I know who I am, so I really don't want to be in a committed relationship right now. Do you understand?"

Ifeanyi nodded. He did. He really did. And she was brave.

He also wanted to be friends and hoped that he could put away his feelings for her - and dreams for them - and let her find herself and, hopefully, find her way back to him. But she needed this time. He knew that now. It wasn't about him. It was about her realising what she had to give in a relationship, and he would be a good friend and let her do that.

Mary took in a deep breath of relief. The God of second chances, she marvelled. Just when she thought He had dealt her a fatal blow, He had given her a new lease on life. The first thing she wanted to do, more than discovering herself, was to know Him more.

❤ ❤ ❤

After their talk, Mary felt like a weight had been lifted from her shoulders. She had returned the ring to Ifeanyi. She no longer felt guilty for her decision to end her engagement to him. She strangely felt like she was breathing the free, clean air for the first time in a long time. But she knew that she had to be careful. She would use this free time and independence wisely and not let herself get caught up in something she shouldn't.

She used the time to draw closer to God by praying, studying her Bible, meditating on scripture, and trying to apply the lessons to her life. She began in search of a new congregation to call home, as she didn't want to continue going to the Island to attend Ifeanyi's church. She wanted to be an active part of the Body of Christ and grow by serving in a capacity, as she had done at Vessels of Honour. She missed teaching the Youth Club.

David called her on Friday evening, two days after their meeting at the hospital. He invited her to his church in Surulere that Sunday. It was an Anglican Church, like the one Mary's parents had belonged to before their passing. Mary said she would be happy to attend.

They talked briefly on the phone. She learnt that he had left Vessels of Honour about a month before the scandal broke out. He didn't ask her much about the ordeal, and she took it as him showing sensitivity.

Mary called Ifeanyi on Saturday. He was pleased to hear from her. They chatted briefly about their week, and she asked about Ijeoma and the baby. He didn't have much to say about that. There was some awkward silence, and she excused herself, saying she just wanted to see how he was doing. Ifeanyi thanked her for the call and promised to keep in touch.

Mary also got in touch with some of her old and new acquaintances via social media. She decided to call Dami, her room-mate from NYSC camp. She'd invited her to the engage-ment party, but Dami had said she couldn't attend because of a conflicting family engagement.

Dami was cheerful when she picked up the call. They talked for a long while, as Mary opened up about her new status, being no longer a mother and no longer engaged. Dami encouraged her to trust God to lead her, believing that there was something better on the horizon.

After concluding her calls, Mary joined her brothers in their small living area to watch a programme on Africa Magic. Soon, the twins would complete their Secondary Education and would hopefully continue into Tertiary, funds permitting. They were both brilliant boys, and she was already looking out for scholarship opportunities for them.

Daniel turned to look at his sister. He felt so protective of her and was happy to see her smiling again. He went over to sit close to her, between her legs, on the floor. She patted him on his head and eyed the twins, who were about to tease him. They smiled and resisted the temptation.

The boys had asked about Brother Ifeanyi and had been sad to hear about the break-up. But they wanted their sister to be happy, above all else. And if she was happy, they were hap-py. Contentedly, Mary sat back and enjoyed the show on their small flat-screen TV.

Ifeanyi threw himself into his work as a way to pass the time and busy his mind with something other than Mary. And time did what it does best; it healed the wound caused by her aban-donment, and eventually, Ifeanyi could get through a day with-out thinking of Mary and feeling regret and sadness.

However, he still lived with the consequences of his actions from earlier in the year, when he had chosen to have a fling with Ijeoma to make Mary jealous. How ironic, he thought. He had hoped to build a life with Mary, and now, his distraction had be-come a very real focus of his life.

Even though he didn't love Ijeoma, Ifeanyi was happy to be a father. He had already been expecting to father Mary's child, but now he had his own, and in the cocktail of his emotions, there was a trace of joy. He was excited at the changes fatherhood would bring in him and felt challenged to rise to the occasion and become more responsible.

Whatever her faults, Ijeoma was also a nice person, who Ifeanyi genuinely liked. They got on well, and as they resumed communication, because of the child they shared, Ifeanyi grew to respect her as the mother of his child. Eventually, Chidinma and the rest of his family accepted Ijeoma as well and were friendly towards her because of Ifeanyi's child. But Ijeoma was not Mary.

In the first week of December, with the smell of Christmas in the air, Ijeoma went into labour and was delivered of a bouncy baby boy! A picture of Chief Chinedu Chukwueke's first grandson in the arms of his adoring father was published in the tabloids, along with a half-baked story about Ifeanyi's romance with Ijeoma, his "NYSC sweetheart." Ifeanyi marvelled again as he wondered who would be feeding the press such trash.

Ifeanyi had kept in touch with Mary as promised, but it was harder than he'd thought. At first, he had to resist the urge to call her when he was really missing her. But then when he finally did call her, he had enjoyed their brief conversation so much that he was convinced that their continued correspondence was not a good idea if he was going to get over her, so he withdrew instead. He found other ways to cope by talking to his male friends and, on occasion, Ijeoma. Soon, he had to prompt himself to return Mary's calls because he really did want to stay friends with her, but it was hard to keep the balance.

However, Mary and Chidinma had remained close. She was among the first to learn about the birth of Ifeanyi's child. Chidinma had called her while they were at the hospital, and she had handed the phone to Ifeanyi. He thought she sounded genuinely happy for him, and she had even asked to speak with Ijeoma and express her best wishes.

Ifeanyi looked down at the cute bundle in his arms. The little boy looked just like him, and his heart was filled with love for him. He caught Ijeoma looking at him with admiration and what looked like desire. He was well aware of her feelings for him, and her hope that they would become a happy family. But he didn't want to fuel her dreams nor raise her expectations in any way. As much as he was happy to be a father, he wasn't about to marry anyone out of obligation.

But he had also learnt never to say never.

10

"Many are the plans in a person's heart, but it is the LORD's purpose that prevails."

PROVERBS 19:21

David woke up in a cold sweat and sat up in bed, breathing heavily. He had had the dream again, and this was the third time. He was sure of the meaning, and he felt that, this time, it was a warning not to let her pass him by again, but to let her know that she was meant for him.

In his dreams, there was a beautiful woman in a white dress who was walking towards him. A veil covered her face, so he couldn't see her well. At the altar, when she met with him, he kissed her. And in the next moment, they were rolling on the bed, making love.

Usually, he never saw her face, but he knew in his heart who it was. Tonight, as he had lifted the veil to kiss his bride, her face was clear. It was Mary. She was the one!

David lay back in bed, his heart beating fast. She had to know how he felt about her. He couldn't go on living his fantasies in his head. He had finally broken through to her, and they were now friends. But that was a dangerous place to be. He didn't want to be stuck in the 'friend zone'. It had been over four months since they met in the hospital, and though he didn't want to rush her, knowing that she was getting over someone else, he believed it was now time to make his intentions known.

After thinking of his plan of action, and praying for God to open Mary's eyes to see him as her husband, David snuggled back under the sheets and slept off with a smile on his face. He was sure about his future. He was finally going to make his dream come true.

Mary woke up on Sunday morning feeling a little strange. Over the last few months, she had been attending the Anglican Church she used to attend as a child. Initially, she had been excited about the prospect of becoming part of that traditional church and having that Faith connection with her parents. But it wasn't long before that wore off, and she slowly came to the realisation that she was not an Anglican.

Even though she appreciated that they were very communal and liturgical, she didn't connect with them in worship, and she didn't feel nourished by the sermons. She had been giving more time to personal Bible study and worship and found that really exciting and uplifting. She'd been journaling what she'd been learning from God and was feeling strongly in her spirit that her time at that church had come to an end. She needed to move on.

So, on this bright Sunday morning in February, Mary did not feel like going to church. She had a burden to stay home, pray, and fellowship with her siblings. When she told them that she wanted to stay home today, she was not surprised at their jubilation. They'd murmured that they found the church boring, but she hadn't paid much attention to them, knowing that if given the choice, more children would probably choose to stay home than sit in a church for two to three hours.

Then she got a text message from David. She'd forgotten about him. She wondered how he would take the news that she wouldn't be returning to his church. She clicked through to open his message. It read: "*Hi, Mary, how are you this beautiful Sunday? Please stay a while after church. I want to talk to you about something :)*"

Mary raised a brow at the message and took a deep breath. *Ummm*, she pondered. Was this God's way of telling her she should go to church today? She thought to reply that she wouldn't be coming in but then decided to make this her last visit and tell him face to face that she would be seeking another place to fellowship.

"Sorry, boys, change of plans! We're going to church," Mary said to a chorus of grumbles. "Hurry up and have your bath, we're already late!"

Mary smiled to herself, listening to the murmurings of her brothers as they scurried to take their baths. She looked for something nice to wear and wondered what David might want to talk about. She had an inkling that he was going to ask her out, and she didn't know how she felt about it. He was a very nice gentleman, and they got on well. But he wasn't Ifeanyi.

She'd never given him much time, though he often tried to get her to do things with him. She didn't want to lead him on. Only once had she accepted his invitation to attend a party with him, and that was during Christmas, and at his family home. Since she didn't have a family of her own, he'd offered that she could share his family for a day. They were also really nice people.

She sighed, thinking of Ifeanyi and his family, who she had grown to love as her own. She and Ifeanyi hadn't spoken in a long while. Maybe he had moved on and was adjusting to his new life as a father. Maybe it was time for her to let him out of her heart and move on too. Her thoughts were interrupted by the shout from Samson that the bathroom was now free.

♥ ♥ ♥

Mary waited after service, as David had requested. She'd seen him when she came into church, just a few pews from the front. Being late, she'd sat close to the back. A few times, she saw him turning around to seek out her face. When he eventually did, they exchanged friendly smiles.

"Hi, Mary," David greeted when he had finally passed through the crowd, greeting as many as he knew personally, before greeting Mary with a hug.

"Hi, David," she replied. "Is everything okay?"

He looked at her intently and smiled. "Yes, let's take a stroll outside. Where are your brothers?"

"They went to get ice-cream."

"Oh, I would have taken you all to KFC," David said, a little disappointed.

"You still can," she giggled. "Let me call them."

"No, let's talk first," he said, pointing to a bench in the small garden area outside the church building.

Mary sat down, feeling a little nervous now. He sat beside her and started fiddling with his hands again, the way he did when he was nervous.

"You know how I feel about you, right?" he said, at last. Mary blinked and gave a small smile. "I don't want to be just friends anymore. I'm looking to settle down, and I have it from a good source that you're the one."

Mary giggled at his last remark. "Are you proposing marriage? Who's the person who told you I am the one?"

"Not yet, just to begin a courtship. And don't worry about my source."

"Why shouldn't I worry about it? What if he's a quack? Why say it if it's not important, anyway?"

"Trust me, He's not!"

"So, who is it? Was it the bishop? The priest?"

"God."

Mary laughed. "Are you joking?"

"Don't laugh, Mary. I'm serious," David said, a little curt. Why would she doubt him and laugh? "God has given me three dreams about you, and I know He will make His will known to you too. But I just want you to know I'm serious about you."

Mary was quiet for a moment, thinking of what this revelation would mean for her and Ifeanyi, if it were true. She didn't want to believe it. David was a good catch, and she knew any woman would be lucky to have him, but she felt some resistance in her spirit...or was it her heart? She decided that rather than regard his dreams as anything, she would be better off considering him as an option and praying over it before committing herself to a serious relationship.

"I'm not ready for a serious relationship, David." His face fell. "But maybe we can start with a few dates...?" He brightened up. "Then we can see how we go and take it from there."

David took her hand and squeezed it. "Okay. So, we're dating?"

"Hm hmm," Mary nodded with a soft smile, thinking again of the man that she still held in her heart.

David drew Mary into his arms and breathed in her scent. He closed his eyes as he told her, "I'm going to make you fall so madly in love with me. You're my treasure." He felt Mary relax in his arms and hug him back.

"Can we go now?" Daniel's voice interrupted their moment, and they broke free from their embrace to look at Mary's brothers, who had just appeared out of nowhere.

"Yes. Who's up for KFC?" David asked with a huge grin.

"Yeah!" the boys chorused, and Mary giggled.

Ijeoma was at her family home in Lekki. Being an unwed mother, she lived with the continual nagging of her parents to find a man who would look after her and her baby; preferably the father of her child. She'd been feeding her mother the story that she and Ifeanyi were falling in love, and she knew he would soon propose, to ease the pressure. But two months after Baby

Chukwuemeka was born, and there was still no proposal, Mrs Ngozi Njokwu was concerned.

"Ijeoma," Mrs Njokwu called her daughter's name on entering her bedroom. "What is happening with Ifeanyi?"

"Mummy, we're fine. There's no problem."

"Are you sure he's serious about you? Because you don't have time to be wasting on someone who is not serious! Your baby needs a father, and it is better you find someone now, when he is still cute, than when he has become a loud mouth!"

"Mummy, stop worrying, eh? He's just got a lot on his plate with work. You know he's helping to look after Emeka. He's just waiting for the right time, I'm sure."

"Look, listen to me. Let me tell you how we can speed up this waiting period," Mrs Njokwu conspired. "You need to get pregnant again."

Ijeoma looked at her mother alarmed. Her look revealed too much.

"So, you're not even sleeping with him? I thought you said you were in love?"

"He's celibate, Mother."

"Celibate, *ke*? Is he not the famous skirt chaser? *Abeg*, leave that thing!" Mrs Njokwu said. "Every man has his weakness, and his own is women. Don't wait until another woman comes to *carry belle* for him! Hmmm!"

"What do you want me to do, Mum? He's really not the same person I knew back in camp. I haven't been totally honest. He puts up with me because of Emeka, but I think he still loves that Mary girl," Ijeoma lamented.

"Okay, this is what you will do. Your birthday is next month, right? We will throw a big party, and he will come. When he does, you will be ready."

"What do you have in mind?" Ijeoma asked, curiously.

"Just do what I tell you to do. Trust your mother," Mrs Njokwu said, with a kiss on Ijeoma's forehead. She was up to her old tricks again.

Ijeoma watched as her mother left her room with a new spring in her step. She looked at herself in the mirror and wondered if they could really pull it off. And if indeed Ifeanyi would end up falling in love with her. Whatever the possibility, it was worth the risk. Emeka needed his father. And he deserved to grow up in a loving family. She just hoped Ifeanyi would forgive her deceit.

Baby Emeka stirred in his crib, where he was napping, and Ijeoma soothed him back gently to sleep. She couldn't afford to wake him up now. She was exhausted and needed to catch some shut-eye herself. Motherhood was tiring, not at all like she had imagined. Her parents had refused her requests for a nanny, lest she gets too comfortable staying in her family home. Her mother helped when she could, but in all respects, she was a single mother.

But with any luck, that would soon change.

11

"Many are the plans in a person's heart, but it is the LORD's purpose that prevails."

PROVERBS 19:21

David and Mary had their first official date set for Valentine's Day, which fell on the Friday after their meeting at church and trip to KFC. Though he used that to observe how Mary was with her brothers, David said the KFC outing didn't count. Mary also observed David's interaction with her siblings. She could tell he was trying hard to please.

Now that they were officially dating, David called Mary every night to talk and sent sweet messages to her throughout the day. Even though he was a busy doctor, he made out time to talk to her for at least 30 minutes each day. He was very inquisitive and wanted to know everything about her day. She would run out of things to say, but he wasn't short of stories. Working in a hospital gave him many events to draw upon.

By the time Valentine's Day came around, Mary was both excited and nervous. She wondered if they would have much to say to each other, seeing as they had covered quite a lot from their daily conversations and frequent text exchanges. She noticed, however, that he still hadn't asked about her past, and she wondered why that might be. For a brief moment, she wondered, sceptically, if he had a secret as bad or even worse than hers, but she shook off the thought.

Moments after she arrived at work that morning, Mary took delivery of a dozen cupcakes David had bought for her to mark Valentine's Day. There was also a card with a lovely message:

> *"Roses are red, Violets are blue, All day long, I'll be thinking of you. Happy Valentine's Day, Mary. Love, David."*

"*Love?*" Aisha snatched the card from Mary's hand. "You've already hooked another one?!"

"He doesn't love me. It's just what people say on Valentine's Day. We're actually going on our first date tonight," Mary said.

"Ummm. *Abegi*, this one is a keeper! I want to hear all the gist on Monday," Aisha said. She floated her hand above the cupcakes, hoping for permission to take one.

"Go ahead," Mary said with a chuckle. She went around and shared her cakes with the two other staff and Kelechi.

"So, who's this David guy?" Kelechi asked, when she collected hers.

"He's just a guy from church."

"Well, just be careful. You don't want to rush into anything. But I'm happy you're moving on," Kelechi said.

Mary smiled and returned to her desk. The cupcakes were lovely. She called David to tell him, and he was pleased. And like a charm, his sweet card made her think of him all day long too.

For their first date, David took Mary to a new Chinese restaurant in Ikeja that he had been wanting to try. It was actually close to his home, which was located inside the Government Reserved Area of Ikeja (GRA), and he drove past it each day on his way to and from the Hospital.

He picked her up at 7 pm, after closing his shift, wearing a smart, black shirt and jacket, on top of dark blue jeans. Mary thought he looked very dashing. He was definitely an attractive man.

Mary wore a fitted black and white, knee-length dress that could have been worn to work at a fashion magazine and was even suitable for church. The dress did well for her figure, which she had regained since the termination of her pregnancy, almost five months ago. Her braided hair was wrapped in a new style that showed off the natural beauty of her angelic face, which she had enhanced with some make-up.

As they walked into the restaurant together, they looked like a perfect fit. The doorman opened the door for them, and they were shown to their reserved table by a waiter. The place was packed because it was Valentine's Day. Each table had a tall vase with a single long-stemmed red rose, in honour of the occasion, and the soothing sound of Kenny G's saxophone could be heard through the speakers.

"Wow... This is a nice place," Mary said, taking in the ambiance, as she settled in her seat.

"I'm glad you like it. I've been wanting to come here with someone special," David said.

Mary blushed.

"You look very nice, by the way," he said, for the first time.

She smiled and muttered, "Thanks. So do you."

Mary turned her attention to the menu, as did he. There were so many options, she didn't know what she should go for. She considered settling for her usual; the Special Fried Rice.

David soon signalled for the waiter to come over and placed an order for one of the house special dishes for two, and then he asked Mary if she was happy with his selection or if she would like to add something to it. Mary said she quite liked the grilled prawns, so it was added to their order. They also placed their order for drinks. David thought she might like to try a certain fruit drink, and he mused about its health benefits. Mary approved with a nod.

Mary's phone beeped, and she brought it out of her purse to look at it. She saw notification of two messages from two chats on WhatsApp. She thought to open it to read but decided it might be rude, so she put her phone aside.

"Who is it?" David asked curiously, his eyes intent on her.

Mary looked up at him. "I don't know, I didn't open it."

"Probably one of your many admirers sending you Valentine messages," David replied, trying to disguise his jealousy with jest. The phone pinged again.

Mary decided to check it. No new admirers. Just Ifeanyi. She hadn't heard from him in a long time. His messages read, *"Hi, Mary," and "How are you doing?"*

The other message was a random Valentine's broadcast from one of her contacts. "No new admirers, just an old friend," she said.

"Is that your ex? Ifeanyi is his name, right?"

"Yes," Mary muttered and took a sip of her glass of water, which the waiter had just poured from a big bottle they had ordered. She hadn't spoken much to David about Ifeanyi, however, she could sense that he didn't like him.

Her phone pinged again, and this time, she decided she would respond. Ifeanyi's message read, *"Are you busy?"*

She replied, *"Yes, sort of. Let me buzz you back later."*

"It seems he wants to talk to you. Maybe he misses you," David swallowed, his jealousy less concealed, as he studied Mary.

"Maybe," Mary replied, putting away her phone. "What about you? No exes?"

David observed her desire to change the focus and sighed. "None that I still care about."

Mary didn't miss the accusation behind his words. What did he expect her to do with her residual feelings for a man she had wanted to marry? "Have you never been in love?" she asked instead.

"I have. Once," he sighed deeply. "She cheated on me."

Oh, that explains a bit, Mary thought, thinking about his apparent insecurity. "Oh, I'm sorry to hear that."

The first course of their meal arrived. Chicken and sweet-corn soup.

After their waiter left, Mary asked, "Were you serious about her?"

"Well, we weren't planning marriage or anything. We were just two people who were crazy about each other, at least that was what I thought." He leaned in closer. "We broke our rule not to sleep with each other before marriage, and I wanted to continue to abstain afterwards. It seems she was not satisfied with that."

"Awww... Her loss," Mary said, with an encouraging smile.

"Did you and Ifeanyi ever...ummm?"

"No, we didn't. I know his reputation precedes him, but he was a good guy. He *is* a good guy."

"Hmmm..." David muttered, not at all convinced. He sipped his soup. "But he got another woman pregnant?"

Mary was shocked at the direction of their conversation. "That was before us," she said in Ifeanyi's defence.

"Look, I don't want to taint your image about him or anything," David began. "But guys like him don't ever change. I wouldn't be surprised if he was good with you but was still up to his old ways."

Mary swallowed hard. She didn't believe him. And she didn't like what he was suggesting; that Ifeanyi was sleeping around while they were together. Why was he trying to ruin the good memories she had of him?

Why wouldn't he? You still love him, and he's jealous!

"I know what you're thinking; I'm just jealous. And you're right! Why wouldn't I be jealous? I just think you deserve someone better. And the sooner you realise it and get over him, the better," David said, reaching across the table to hold her hand. "I want to show you what real love feels like, and I just need a fair chance. I hope you will give me that."

Mary tried a smile and nodded, not able to look him in his eyes. At least he was honest that he was jealous. And who knows? Maybe he was right, and maybe he had a good point about her hanging on to the past.

No, don't believe him. Ifeanyi was faithful and true to you.

Mary wasn't sure where that came from, but she tucked the thought away in a secret compartment, to revisit later.

They appreciated a few moments of silence as they ate their second course. David tried to lighten the mood by telling a funny story from work that day. Mary gave a low giggle in appreciation for his efforts, but her mood remained deep and retrospective.

"What are you thinking about?" David eventually asked.

There was quite a lot going through her mind, and she didn't know where to begin, so she started with her deepest insecurities. "I... I am just trying to figure out what a guy like you would want with a girl like me. You know, I'm not squeaky clean."

"Uh... You mean your relationship with Pastor Akinwunmi?"

"Uh huh."

"Yeah... That's true. You know, I used to look at you as some angel. I had you up on a pedestal for years..."

"*Years?*"

"Yup. When the news broke out, it was a major blow and a major relief. Because you were human again, and attainable. And the fact that he abused you, and victimised you in that way, made it easy to sympathise with your situation, and want to be there to protect you. I was both shocked and pained for you, and I think I loved you more."

"You *love* me?"

"Yes, I do. You're real, Mary. Genuine. And you're beautiful. I just want to be there for you." David stroked her hand lightly.

A sole tear escaped Mary's eye, as she considered the man in front of her. Could he truly be the one God had in mind for her? Was Ifeanyi the distraction? Could she really grow to love him as passionately as she had loved Ifeanyi? Her heart was torn between letting go of Ifeanyi and facing what looked like a promising future with David, a man who apparently loved her deeply.

"Thank you," Mary said finally.

David took her hand and kissed it, feeling her warming up to him. Soon, soon, she would be his woman. And he could hardly wait for that day to come.

Mary got home at 10:30 pm, which was rather late for her. But she had enjoyed her evening out. David had planted a soft kiss on her cheek before driving off.

Mary sneaked in quietly past her brothers, who were asleep in the living room, where they shared a double mattress. She got onto her bed and checked her phone. Ifeanyi was last seen on WhatsApp at 9:30 pm. She wondered if he had already gone to bed but decided to send him a message as promised.

Mary: *"Hey, how are you? Sorry I didn't get back to you earlier."*

Five minutes passed…

Ifeanyi: *"Hey, Mary. How was your evening?"*

Mary: *"It was fine, thanks. And yours?"*

Ifeanyi: *"~~I missed you~~. It was okay. Were you on a date?"*

Mary: *"Yeah. How did you know?"*

Ifeanyi: *"Well, I'm sure I'm not the only guy with good sense in Lagos. LOL!"*

Mary: *"Lol! Thanks ☺"*

Ifeanyi: *"So, who's the lucky guy?"*

Mary: *"Just a friend from church."*

Ifeanyi: *"What's his name?"*

Mary: *"David."*

Ifeanyi: *"Haven't you mentioned a David to me before?"*

Mary: *"Yeah. He is the doctor that attended to me."*

Ifeanyi: *"Oh. Okay. So, you guys are dating?"*

Mary: *"It was our first date."*

Ifeanyi: *"Okay. Cool. ~~How was it?~~ Well, I actually just wanted to see how you were doing. I'm glad you're happy."*

Mary: *"Thanks for getting in touch. How's Fatherhood?"*

Ifeanyi: *"It's no piece of cake, but I'm happy. Emeka's amazing ☺"*

Mary: *"That's great. I'm happy for you too. When are you doing the churching?"*

Ifeanyi: *"In about two weeks. He will be three months in the first week of March."*

Mary: *"Oh, cool. How time flies..."*

Ifeanyi: *"Yeah... I know it might be strange for you, but ~~it would mean a lot to me~~ I would appreciate it if you come. We're doing it at my church."*

Mary: *"Oh, ok. Yeah, no problem. I'd like to come."*

Ifeanyi: *"Good. Thanks. Well, Happy Valentine's Day, Mary."*

Mary: *"Happy Valentine's Day, Ifeanyi. Did you do anything special, btw?"*

Ifeanyi: *"~~I took Ijeoma and Emeka out for lunch~~. I spent some time with Emeka :)"*

Mary: *"That's nice :) ~~I miss you~~. Well, I'll see you later."*

Ifeanyi: *"Yeah, see you. I'll send a text reminder about the thanksgiving."*

Mary: *"Please do. Bye."*

Ifeanyi: *"Bye."*

Mary read their correspondence again and wondered what Ifeanyi must be thinking about her dating David. She hadn't intended for him to find out until she was sure that she was serious about David. But now he knew, and she wondered if he would begin dating himself. Or maybe he would get back with Ijeoma. If she was honest, she was quite surprised that he hadn't started dating yet. Maybe there was already something brewing between him and Ijeoma, she wondered.

She wanted him to be happy. He had a family now, and if they could work things out, it would be for the best. So why did her heart ache so much at the thought? Why did she feel like they were running out of chances to make things work between them? Did she want Ifeanyi back, even with Ijeoma and Emeka in the picture? Even with David's profession of love and a chance at a fresh start?

"Oh God, please help me to make the right decision, not from fear or jealousy, but from love and wisdom," she prayed. "Please make Your will clear to me, and let me have peace about my decision; even if neither are meant for me. Lead me Lord and guide my heart, in Jesus' name. Amen."

12

"Many are the plans in a person's heart, but it is the LORD's purpose that prevails."

PROVERBS 19:21

"I can't believe you're insisting on going, even when I've told you how I feel about it!" David shouted into the phone.

"And I can't believe you're insisting that I dishonour my friend's invitation to church just because you don't like him!" Mary retorted.

"Problem is, he's not just a friend, is he? Why else will you consider his feelings before mine?"

"Oh, I'm seriously fed up with tiptoeing around your feelings. I can't even imagine what you think will happen between us, with all his family around, and at *church* for that matter."

"So, why can't I come?" David asked

"Because...because we're not official, yet. I don't want to give the wrong impression. This is a man I was engaged to, and I don't want to go and act as if I'm flaunting you in front of him and his family."

"Mary, you know I'm serious about you. If after all this time, you don't know how you feel about me, then what are we even doing? I love you, and I want to be with you, and yes, I want the whole world to know it - especially Ifeanyi!" David said.

"You're asking too much of me, and I told you I'm not ready to commit. This is all I can give right now. If it's not enough, then I'm sorry. I can't do more."

There was a brief silence. "What if I just come, not as your guest, just another churchgoer?"

Mary laughed. "To spy on me? Because you don't trust me? Please, I don't even know why we are arguing about this. I'm going, and you're not invited!"

"Mary... Mary?" David called her name in what she perceived as a condescending tone, with the implication that she should fall in line.

"David, I have to go. See you later." With that, she hung up the phone.

That was their second fight in as many weeks, since their first date. The first one was when she had finally told him that she was looking for another church, and he had insisted that she stay in his church because they needed to have spiritual unity and fellowship. She'd told him until she is married, she is free to fellowship anywhere and wouldn't be told where to attend church. He'd replied that during dating and courtship is the best time to begin to learn to submit to your husband. She'd told him not to 'count his chickens' just yet.

He later came around and apologised for being so 'full on,' explaining that it was only because knowing that he can lead 'his woman' was important to him. He didn't want to tell her what to do, but he did want her to appreciate his opinion and make some compromises for their relationship. Mary said she understood, and she apologised for insisting that she shouldn't be told what to do. She knew his perspective had merits, but it also was very important for her, while she was still single, to develop a strong *personal* relationship with God.

However, today's argument had been exasperating. She was beginning to see him as controlling and possessive. His desire to lead and protect insisted on being able to dictate what she should or shouldn't do, and it was robbing her of the joy and liberty to choose. She felt like she was being caged again, when she had just been delivered from a prison of sorts. She found herself reacting to even the most innocent suggestions with strong emotion and disagreement, simply to show him that he couldn't control her. They were locked in a bad pattern, and she didn't like how she was responding to him.

Mary took some time to pray for her spirit, and for God to prune her of anything that was hindering her spiritual growth. She asked for more humility and the strength of character to stand for what is true. She committed David and her relationship with him into His hands, and she prayed that God would make His will for them more evident and grant her the wisdom to choose wisely. After her brief prayer time, she got herself ready and left for Ifeanyi's church in Ikoyi.

It was a good service at Grace and Truth Assembly, and Mary realised what she had been missing at David's church. She found the praise and worship really uplifting to her spirit. She knew the songs and sang along without inhibition. She also found the message to be quite challenging and nourishing. It felt like she had returned home.

When Ifeanyi's and Ijeoma's friends and family were invited to come forward to join them in thanksgiving, she also made her way to the front. Prayers were said for the sleeping baby and for his parents, who were entrusted as guardians to raise him in the fear of God, with the support of the Church and community. Afterwards, those who came bearing offerings dropped them in the baskets and proceeded to greet Ifeanyi, Ijeoma, and their parents.

Mary received a warm hug from both Chief and Mrs Chukwueke. She greeted Ijeoma and her parents, but they didn't seem to acknowledge her presence. Finally, she got to Ifeanyi, whose gaze seemed fixated on her, even as she had greeted others. They shared a smile and a brief hug.

"Congratulations again," Mary said, trying not to notice the way his stare was turning her body to mush. She had forgotten how dashingly handsome he was.

"Thanks for coming," he replied. But before they could say more, others pushed their way to get his attention and extend their wishes. She waved goodbye and returned to her seat.

After the service, Mary lingered, hoping for a chance to speak with Ifeanyi before going home. She chatted with Chidinma for a while until she saw Ifeanyi approaching them. Chidinma excused herself to catch up with a friend.

"Hey, Mary," Ifeanyi said.

"Hey," she smiled.

"Where's David? He didn't come?" Ifeanyi raised an eyebrow.

Mary wasn't sure if he was joking. Had he expected her to invite him? "I didn't think it was appropriate for me to come accompanied. Besides, we're not that serious yet."

"Hmmm... Really?" Ifeanyi replied. "Well, I was kind of hoping to see my competition."

"*Competition*?" It was Mary's turn to raise an eyebrow.

"Well, I think I still stand a chance... Or am I eliminated?"

His stare was disarming. What was he doing pulling out all his charm on her now...and here...in church - during his baby's thanksgiving? Mary realised that she had a wide grin plastered on her face. She tried to straighten her expression but ended up covering her smile with her hand instead. "This is hardly the place to be hitting on me," she chastised.

Ifeanyi smiled mischievously. "I was just checking something."

What? She wondered. What was he checking?

Whether you still have feelings for him, dummy!

And her expression had given her away. Maybe David had been right all along about wanting to come with her.

"Ijeoma's having a birthday party next weekend. You should come," Ifeanyi said.

"Should I bring David?" Mary asked, teasingly.

"Only if you don't want me to hit on you," Ifeanyi replied coolly. He leaned across and kissed her on the cheek before whispering in her ear, "You look amazing as always!" Then he was gone.

Mary swallowed hard, looking down at the black and white dress that she had worn for her first date with David. What was he doing to her? She'd forgotten what a charmer he was. Now, she couldn't remember why she ever thought they should break up. She watched him as he walked away towards his parents, her heart beating fast.

While still watching Ifeanyi with amazement, and a hint of desire, Mary was shocked back to reality by the glare of a woman scorned. Ijeoma was not a happy woman, having observed the father of her child flirting with his ex-fiancée in front of their friends and family! Mary gave her a half-smile before turning around and heading for the door.

Maybe Ifeanyi hadn't had enough drama in his life, but she most certainly had no plans of going to Ijeoma's home to stir up trouble. Even though Ijeoma had crashed her engagement party, she would be the bigger person. Besides, she now realised that Ijeoma was not her competition. She had never been.

By the time her birthday party came around, Ijeoma was ready. She'd prepared an irresistible trap for Ifeanyi, with the help of her conniving mother. Her excitement built up as all the guests arrived. But there was only one she was interested in, the one for whom the party was thrown, and she couldn't wait to see him walk through the door.

The party was well underway before Ifeanyi showed up. For a while, Ijeoma had been scared that he would humiliate her by not making an appearance. When she spotted him by the door, she strategically made her way over to him, making some polite conversation with other guests and enjoying the way he was looking at her expectantly. Finally, she reached his side.

"Happy Birthday, Ijay!" he greeted and presented his gift and card, with a kiss on the cheek.

"Thank you, Baby Daddy," she flirted, fluttering her lashes at him.

"Have you seen Mary?"

The question shocked Ijeoma to the core, and she couldn't help the scowl that crossed her face. "No. I hope you didn't invite her!"

"Why not? She's my friend," Ifeanyi replied. "Since I'm family and all, I thought I could at least invite a couple of my friends."

"Not your *ex-fiancée*, Ifeanyi. Try to be a little sensitive!"

"Sorry, my bad. So, how's it going?"

Ijeoma's smile returned. She took his hand and led him to the mini bar, where she proceeded to talk his ear off. Because it was her birthday, Ifeanyi indulged her. However, he refused the second alcoholic drink she offered in preference for a non-alcoholic cocktail, knowing that she could not be trusted.

"So, I stumbled on this store in VI that has these cool baby things. I couldn't help myself! I practically bought the whole store!" She giggled, touching his hand fondly. "Do you want to see?"

"See what?" Ifeanyi asked, hardly paying attention anymore. He kept scouting the room, hoping to spot Mary.

"The things I got for Emeka. Come with me, you have to see them. I can't bring them down, otherwise I would."

Ifeanyi stood up from his stool and followed Ijeoma, who led him by the hand. He took one more look around, disappointed that Mary hadn't shown up, before he climbed the first step leading to the private quarters of the Njokwu residence.

As Ifeanyi followed Ijeoma up to her room, leaving the noise of the party behind, he felt some resistance in his spirit about what he was doing. However, he was sure he could handle himself, so he ignored it. Even though he was aware of the possibility of seduction, he actually hoped that Ijeoma would prove him wrong and that, indeed, she was only going to show him the things she had gotten for their baby, which she couldn't bring downstairs.

When they finally got to her room, amid the stares of some gossips, Ijeoma closed the door behind her, and Ifeanyi observed the room, hoping to see some cute baby things. Instead, he saw a room lit with scented candles, a bed arrayed with rose petals, and he inhaled a strong fragrance in the air. He bit his bottom lip as he turned to face Ijeoma, who now had her back against the door.

Ijeoma slowly zipped her dress open, revealing the sexy, one-piece lingerie hugging her petite frame underneath. Even after just having a baby, she still had a very sexy figure, and her breasts were full and inviting. She stepped out of the dress, and for a moment, she just stood there, afraid of his rejection.

Ifeanyi was of two minds. To stay and play a little or to run. It had been a very long time since he had been with a woman, and the last six months without Mary had been torturous. While they had been together, at least he had been able to appease himself with the knowledge that she would soon be his, and his waiting period would be over. But now that he was single again, with no prospects for marriage, his longing for sexual satisfaction had peaked, and he'd been struggling to keep the thoughts out of his mind.

"Ijeoma, what are you doing?" he asked.

Don't ask questions, just run!

"Get out of the way!"

Ifeanyi reached the door, where Ijeoma had stretched herself and writhed sensually against, blocking his exit. She looked into his eyes and stroked his chest. "I'm just lonely like you. Can't we make each other feel good - just once? No one needs to know."

But I will know. You were bought at a price.

His spirit man was not at peace, as he knew the biblical thing to do was to flee from temptation. But his body was already responding to the visual sight of Ijeoma and her sensual touch.

Surely, God would allow for *one* sin... He was still a man, after all, and he just needed to get it out of his system, his flesh soothed his conscience.

Giving in to temptation, Ifeanyi reached for Ijeoma, pulled her in his arms, and kissed her. He pulled away briefly, breathing heavily, to say, "This doesn't mean anything, okay?" She nodded, trying not to be offended, thinking only of the victory of having her way with him. "It's just sex. We're not together," he continued, before resuming his kiss and running his hands through her body.

Ijeoma locked the door behind her and led the way to the bed, as they continued kissing and caressing heavily. Ifeanyi frantically took off his trousers, revealing to Ijeoma how excited he truly was. She smiled in anticipation. Then he paused.

"I don't have protection."

"Don't worry, I got that covered," she said, pulling him onto the bed, on top of her.

Ifeanyi closed his eyes, as his head nestled in her cleavage, delighting in what was about to transpire. He was shocked by the image that played in his mind instead. He saw a blood-stained Jesus on the cross. He quickly opened his eyes and lifted his head from between her breasts.

"What's wrong?" Ijeoma asked, sensing a change in him. She slid her hand down and touched him where he was hottest. He went wild and quickly peeled off her lingerie. It was as if he wanted to get it over with, before he could think any more about what he was doing or what he had just seen. He would deal with the guilt later.

Ifeanyi closed his eyes once more, and he heard the mockers at the foot of the cross. In the same instant, he saw Jesus' eyes open, and it was as though they were fixated on him. Ifeanyi jerked and jumped from the bed. "I can't do this!"

Ijeoma sat up quickly, looking at him dazed. What was happening? "Is this *still* about Mary?" she asked, her voice filled with pain.

All Ifeanyi could do was shake his head. His whole body shook as he quickly put on his clothes, the image of the crucified Christ stuck in his mind. "I'm sorry," he said when he reached the door. He unlocked and opened it, then dashed out.

When he got in his car, he lay his head on his hands, resting on the steering wheel, and began to cry bitterly. The tears were uncontrollable. And this time, they were not for Mary.

VOLUME
THREE

13

"Trust in the LORD with all thine heart;
and lean not unto thine own understanding. In all thy ways acknowledge
him, and he shall direct thy paths."

PROVERBS 3:5

"How was church today?" David asked Mary, settling down on his sofa for their daily chat on the phone. Mary had finally found a new fellowship to call home. She had been pretty excited about the small Pentecostal church she had visited just the week before, and this would be her second week in attendance.

"It was great, thanks," Mary replied cheerfully. "How about you?"

"It was good as usual. So, what was the sermon about?" David asked.

"The Body of Christ," Mary answered. "Pastor John talked about how we all make up the Body of Christ, and about how we are becoming Christ as each member finds and fulfils their place in the Body. It was quite inspiring."

"Hmmm…" David muttered. "We are *becoming* Christ? I thought we *are* the Body of Christ?"

"Yes, *becoming*. Like Paul said in Ephesians four thirteen, '*until we all reach unity in the faith and in the knowledge of the Son of God, as we mature to the full measure of the stature of Christ*,'" Mary replied. "We are in a process of transformation, being built up to unity."

"So, what are we while we are waiting for the other members to 'find' and 'fulfil' their place in the Body?"

"We are still the Body, just not complete and not unified yet," Mary replied, sensing another religious disagreement on the climb.

"Well, that would suggest that Christ is divided. But Jesus Himself said that '*a house divided against itself cannot stand*,'" David said.

"Okay," Mary replied, not wanting to argue. "So, what was the message at your service?"

"Why are you changing the topic? I'm trying to show you something," David said, a little annoyed by her attempt to side-step.

Mary sighed.

"The Spirit of Christ is whole, whether it is fully abiding in God the Father or in God the Son or in the Body of Christ. The Body of Christ is already united in Spirit, it is the visible manifestation that is pending. Like it is written in Romans eight nineteen, '*the creation waits in eager expectation for the revelation of the sons of God*.'"

"I think we are saying the same thing, David."

"No, I think there is a distinct difference. Your doctrine is dependent on the individuals finding and fulfilling their purpose, while mine is dependent on the Spirit, and on the realisation that it is already *fulfilled* and *finished*," David said.

"It's not my doctrine, David," Mary said, now annoyed at his insinuation. Why did he always feel the need to argue and to teach? They were running out of topic areas where he wasn't a know-it-all.

"Okay, your church or whatever. The point is–"

"Look, David. I don't think this is going to work," Mary interrupted him.

"What's not going to work?" David sat up straight, wondering what he had said wrong.

"*Us*. I don't think we're connecting. I think we are trying to force something here."

"No, we're just exchanging ideas. I love to talk about spiritual things, and you are a spiritual person, and I thought you would love to talk about God too. You used to teach Sunday School, so you should understand the importance of such discussions. Iron sharpens iron, remember?"

"Except for the fact that in our relationship, you think *you're* the teacher. And you keep trying to get me to bend to your understanding without appreciating mine," Mary replied.

"That's not true, and it's not fair. The other day, we discussed women's roles in Church, and I agreed with you about women being able to teach."

"You *conceded* that women can teach women and children, not that women can teach men. Look, I don't want to argue. You're a great guy, but..."

"Don't do it, Mary. Come on... Why are you always running? Relationships take work, and everyone has issues. At least we know that we are both Christians...and love God. We can work out the rest."

Mary was silent. This was the third time in a week that she had felt that she should end things with David. It wasn't getting better, no matter how much she prayed to understand him more and follow his lead. He made it so hard to follow him. Her heart was heavy a lot of the times they discussed because there always seemed something to argue about.

It was never that way with Ifeanyi. Maybe because Ifeanyi wasn't a believer when they met, and she had been in the teaching role. Could it be that she was hard to teach?

David swallowed hard. Why did Mary seem so elusive to him? Why did she resist his leadership so much? He knew what he had expected in a wife, but she was so defiant. However, he was still sure she was the one. Maybe he just needed to soften his approach. "Baby, I'm sorry. Let's talk about something else."

Now, what was with all the "I'm sorry"s, Mary wondered? He seemed to say sorry to sweep the issue aside, only for it to rear its head another day. And there was really nothing for him to be sorry about, except for the fact that they were incompatible.

"I don't want to, David. I know you think I'm running, but I don't think it's supposed to be this hard. It seems every day we are arguing about something, and I'm…I'm just tired. Let's just be friends."

"No, Mary, I don't accept that," David spoke softly into the phone. "I know you've never had someone fight for you before, but I will fight for you. I'm not going anywhere."

"Okay. Well… *I'm* going. Bye." Mary hung up the phone and was instantly irritated when it rang again. It was David. She ignored it.

She'd really missed the crazy, clingy, and controlling signals that he must have been emitting before. How was she going to get him off her case? Her phone kept ringing until she decided to take out the battery for some peace of mind.

Mary woke up from her Sunday nap and remembered that she had switched off her phone. Everywhere was quiet. Her brothers must have been playing football outside, like they loved to do on Sundays. She put her phone back together and switched it on. It rang immediately. *Dear Lord*, she thought to herself in exasperation.

She looked down at the phone, and it was Ifeanyi. Relief flooded her as she clicked the button to answer the call. "Hey!" she answered with a big smile on her face.

"Hey, been trying to call you," Ifeanyi said. "Were you busy?"

"Was napping. Had my phone off. What's up?"

"Nothing much. I was calling to check on you. Is everything okay?" Ifeanyi asked.

"Yes, everything is fine. The boys are out playing, so I am enjoying a peaceful Sunday," Mary smiled as she spoke with Ifeanyi.

"Good. I'm glad. I was a bit concerned. I had a dream about you last night," Ifeanyi said.

"You did? What about?"

"I can't really remember the details, but I could sense you were in trouble, like you were trapped or bound by something," Ifeanyi said. "Just be careful, okay?"

"Hmmm... That's funny," Mary said, pondering on his warning. "I have been feeling kind of trapped actually. Well, suffocated, more like. But everything is okay now."

"Suffocated by who or what?"

"My relationship with David. I ended things with him today."

"Oh... Well, I'm sure you did the right thing. You shouldn't be feeling trapped or suffocated in your relationship," Ifeanyi replied, a part of him, relieved, and another part, excited at the realisation that Mary was single again.

At that moment, another call was coming in on Mary's phone. It was David. "In fact, he's still calling me. He doesn't want to get the message."

"Hmmm... So, he's one of those guys that are hard to shake," Ifeanyi said, feeling a little concerned that maybe his dream would still come to pass. "Do you want me to talk to him for you?"

"No, no need, thanks. I'm just going to ignore him. He'll give up eventually," Mary said.

"Let's hope. So...you're single again..." Ifeanyi couldn't help saying that with joy. Mary giggled, and it filled his heart with hope.

"Yeah, I am," Mary said, playing with a braid. Her tummy was filling with butterflies again, the way it usually did whenever she spoke with Ifeanyi.

"You didn't come to Ijeoma's party last week," Ifeanyi said, sadly.

"I know. I didn't think it was right," Mary said. "How did it go?"

"Let's just say, I would have loved for you to have been there. But I understand."

"Didn't you have fun?" Mary asked. She added playfully, "Gist me *nau*."

Ifeanyi shifted uncomfortably. He wasn't ready to talk about what happened between him and Ijeoma. He also knew that he wasn't ready to entertain a relationship with Mary either. He was learning to listen to God's guidance and to grow his relationship with Him. Right now, the Spirit was prompting him to get off the phone and pray so that he wouldn't give in to his desire to be with Mary. "I'm sorry, Mary. I have to go."

"Is there something wrong?" Mary was concerned. He was behaving strangely.

"No, everything is fine now. Be careful of David, okay? I'll talk to you later. Bye." Ifeanyi waited for Mary to say "Bye," before he hung up the phone. His heart was heavy. He really wanted to take the opportunity presented by Mary's break up and get things started between them again. But he knew that he would be acting contrary to the Spirit.

He had learnt to be sensitive to Its leading over the past few days. He had realised that he had been going about in his own wisdom and strength, and so he had fallen into Ijeoma's trap and could have really sabotaged his future. He still loved Mary, but right now the Spirit was saying "no," and he had to obey and trust God. He got on his knees and prayed for more grace and strength to wait on God's direction and timing.

Mary was startled by how Ifeanyi had hurriedly ended their conversation. Didn't he want her anymore? Had she said something wrong? Maybe something had happened at the party that he didn't want to talk to her about. Maybe something was going on with him and Ijeoma. Oh, her heart was aching again. Was she going to lose him after all?

She sat with her legs folded on her bed and watched as her phone rang again. David was unrelenting. She picked up and put the phone to her ear.

"Mary, Mary... Please talk to me. I want to see you," David said, emotionally.

"David, please stop calling me. I don't like what you're doing. We're over. I'm not the one for you." Mary hung up the phone again and then put it on silent. She had about 30 messages from him on WhatsApp, but she didn't care to read them. She ended and deleted the chat. She was tempted to block him but decided against it. Hopefully, he would get the message and stop bothering her.

She got on her knees again and began to pray. She thanked God for helping her see that she had made the right choice in letting David go and asked that He protect her from anything he may try to do to entrap her again. She prayed for Ifeanyi, Ijeoma, and Emeka; that God's will would be done in their lives. She also prayed that God would change her heart and deliver it from its apparent bondage to Ifeanyi if he was not for her. She prayed to be able to love, completely, the right man that God would send her way and not miss him by being stuck in the past.

When she was done dealing with the matters of her heart, she raised up the issues of life before God, committing her brothers and their academic needs into His hands. She remembered Kelechi, Chidinma, and Dami too, praying for them and all that concerned them. She prayed fervently and in the spirit. Mary was nourished in her soul as she laid every weight at the feet of Jesus.

Her prayers were interrupted when she heard the boys come in, grumbling about being hungry. It was time to work on dinner. She thanked God and rose up, renewed in peace, hope, and joy.

14

"Trust in the LORD with all thine heart; and lean not unto thine own understanding. In all thy ways acknowledge him, and he shall direct thy paths."

PROVERBS 3:5

M ary arrived at work to find a massive bouquet of flowers on her desk, with a big red envelope. She was already sure who they were from, but for curiosity sake, she opened the envelope. On the outside of the card was written in big bold lettering: PLEASE FORGIVE ME, and inside: "I make mistakes, but loving you is the one thing I do right!"

Mary rolled her eyes, chucked the card into the bouquet, and placed them on the floor by the bin. She had become bored of his romantic gestures. He seemed to be playing a character in a one-way romantic movie, and she was tired of being his co-star.

"Love on the rocks, heh? What did he do now?" Aisha couldn't help herself as she observed Mary from her desk.

Mary simply shrugged her shoulders. She didn't even have any strength to talk about him. "It's not that serious, abeg!" she replied, at last, dismissing the discussion. She began to sort out her desk. *How did all these pile up*, she wondered?

Since completing her National Youth Service in January, Mary had been retained at Browne Law Firm as a Clerk, and she also worked part-time as a Counsellor, taking on cases of abuse, which had begun to flood in since the Bolaji scandal broke out last July. People wanted to talk with her specifically, and she had to manage that alongside her normal administrative duties for the company, since these clients were not bringing in money for them.

That day, she had arranged to see two new clients, who had reached out to her from her blog. She wanted to be done with her other official duties before they came in at three O'clock, so she could give them an hour each. Monday was the only day she scheduled such appointments, as they usually got busier as the week went on.

The cases were always so heartbreaking. Most of the time, the women and girls she counselled spoke about past sexual assault and childhood molestation. Some were by family members, others were friends and neighbours, and on the rare occasion, absolute strangers. Many years later, these women and girls finally found the courage to speak about what they went through, but even still, many were afraid to come out publicly with a case against their abuser. It was so much more heartbreaking when Mary heard about abuses committed by close family members, who the victims still related with.

Her first appointment was with a 19-year-old girl, called Debra, who had been recently assaulted by her boyfriend. She didn't want to press charges because she thought she had led him on and it had been half her fault. She came to enquire about how to break up with him because she was now afraid of him.

Mary encouraged her to see that it wasn't her fault; that no one had a right to her body if she had not given them permission.

She encouraged the girl to open an official case because abusers continue to hurt their victims and others by capitalising on their shame and silence. The girl wasn't convinced because she was afraid of her parents. They had warned her to stay away from the young man, but she hadn't listened to them.

Mary helped her see that she was sentencing herself to suffer in silence, when the very people that could help her were waiting for her to speak up. She drew on her experience with Pastor Bolaji and the many years she lost living in fear. Eventually the girl said she would talk to her mother, who she felt would be more understanding and able to mediate the discussion with her father. Mary was pleased and encouraged Debra to keep her in the loop, in case she needed legal representation.

Her four O'clock appointment was with a 29-year-old woman called Tejumola, who had been sexually abused for many years as a child. Her case was particularly sad because she was now married, and her past was complicating her present. She came, not for restitution, but for counsel on how to save her young marriage, because she was no longer able to control her sexual urges.

Mary told her about Jesus, that only He could restore her brokenness. However, the lady was too embittered by her past to entertain much discussion about God and Faith. Mary could sense that she was disengaging from their session and left her with some choice wisdom to ponder on. When the woman left, Mary felt strongly in her spirit to pray for her and her husband. She hoped that the seed she had sown would bear fruit in their marriage.

"Ijeoma!" Mrs Njokwu called her daughter from her bedroom.

"Yes, Mum," Ijeoma called back and lazily climbed the stairs to her mother's room. She was getting tired of their scheming, and she just wished her mother would drop her expectations once and for all. "What is it, Mum?" Ijeoma asked when she was at the door.

"Sit down," Mrs Njokwu said. "Eh heh, are you still taking those fertility pills I gave you?"

"No, I'm not. I don't need them, because nothing is going to happen between me and Ifeanyi."

"Don't say that! Patience, my dear. You have to keep taking them. I have another plan."

"Mother, please. It's enough. I don't want to do any more *juju*! It was probably the *juju* that scared him off in the first place. I've never seen him so terrified!"

"Ijeoma, Ijeoma. I don't like the way you are going, oh. Is it because you are comfortable in this house that you think life is so easy? Don't be so naive! Don't you know that even the Bible says that the Kingdom of Heaven suffers violence, and it is the violent that take it by force? Have you not read where Jesus said that we should learn from the shrewd servant, who connived to secure his future? If you like, stay there and be doing good girl!"

Ijeoma was quiet, and her mother continued talking. "You are our only child, Ijeoma, and we want to make sure you marry well. You know business hasn't been going well for your father, and this relationship with the Chukwuekes has really turned things around for us. You have to think of your family, oh. You have to think of your baby too!"

"Okay, Mum. What's your plan?"

Mrs Njokwu beamed. This one was a sure-fire. She edged closer to her daughter and revealed her ingenious plan.

David left the Hospital promptly at the end of his shift on Friday evening. All week long, Mary had refused to pick his calls or respond to his messages. She hadn't even said anything about the flowers he had delivered to her office on Monday, nor the chocolates he sent on Tuesday, nor the cupcakes he sent on Wednesday. She must be really upset with him, he thought.

Well, this would make up for it. He had the most romantic evening planned for them. He would go to her house and serenade her, and she would see how much he loved her and was willing to lay down his pride for her. He had also bought her a gift of jewellery, and he couldn't wait to place the gold necklace on her neck and share their first kiss over a romantic dinner. He smiled to himself through the side mirror of his Peugeot 508 and drove off to his destiny.

Mary lifted her head from the novel she was reading as she heard a strange sound in her neighbourhood. Someone was playing a guitar and singing. She wondered briefly if one of the street preachers had gotten some new inspiration. Shrugging, she returned to her reading. When she realised that the sound wasn't fading, she got out of bed and left her small accommodation to see what was happening.

A crowd had gathered, and some people were laughing at the man causing the disturbance. She was dumbstruck to see that it was David! He was the strangest sight, dressed in his smart suit, strumming a guitar, and bastardising classic love songs. When David saw that he had gotten her attention, he began from the top, singing off key.

Mary couldn't believe her eyes nor her ears. This guy had serious issues! What would it take to get him to leave her alone, she wondered? She had some ideas, but they seemed either too cruel or too lame. Finally, she decided to call the only one she knew would be on hand to help.

"Hi, Ifeanyi... No, I kinda need your help. Are you busy?"

Ifeanyi was settling down to watch a series with his brother, who had just returned home from the States, where he was doing his undergraduate course in Civil Engineering. The two brothers had planned to catch up and bond over their favourite

TV series. They were just at the first commercial break when Mary's call came in.

"Hey... You okay?" Ifeanyi asked, happy to hear from her. They hadn't spoken since he called her on Sunday. "No, I'm not. What's up? Oh, really? Don't worry, I'll be right there!"

"You're leaving?" Nomnso asked, a little disappointed.

"It's Mary," Ifeanyi said as an explanation.

"Oh, okay. Good luck!" Nomnso teased.

Ifeanyi ignored him and dashed out of the house. His palms were damp, and his heart was beating with excitement. Why was his body acting as if she had asked him on a date? He had to tell himself he was only going to help out a friend.

Ifeanyi got to Mary's place and observed the scene. David was still playing his songs and was in the middle of Daniel Bedingfield's "If You're Not The One" song. He sat in the car and pressed his horn twice.

Moments later, Mary ran out of the building and entered his car. "Oh, please, let's get out of here!"

Mary threw her head back and laughed from the pit of her stomach as Ifeanyi pulled out of his parking space and sped off down the street. She turned around to see a dumbfounded David staring after them in disbelief. She looked over at Ifeanyi, who was trying hard to stifle his giggles.

"Oh, that was too cruel, Mary!" he said, watching her as she giggled happily beside him.

"I just hope he finally gets the message. I tried to be nice!" she sighed deeply and smiled at Ifeanyi. "Thanks for coming to my rescue."

"Don't mention it." He returned her smile and then composed himself. He had no idea what they were going to do or where they were going. He just kept on driving on autopilot.

Mary settled into her seat and enjoyed the breeze that blew her hair and cooled her face as they drove fast on the highway, with the windows and sunroof down. She didn't know where Ifeanyi was going, but she was happy just to be with him. Her heart was light with joy, and she sat smiling to herself as if she was having a pleasant dream.

Before long, they were in Ikoyi, and Ifeanyi realised where he was going. He was driving to their favourite spot by the lagoon. They had many memories there, and that was where he wanted to spend the evening with Mary. Mary looked up at him when she realised where he had driven them to. They hadn't spoken on the ride, being both lost in thought. It was almost 8 O'clock at night, and it was getting dark.

Ifeanyi parked the car and reclined his seat. "I hope you don't mind that I brought you here."

"No, I'm glad you did. Thank you." She breathed in a sigh and closed her eyes, enjoying the ocean breeze and the relaxing sound of crickets and nature.

For a while, neither of them spoke, and they just enjoyed each other's company and the ambiance. Eventually, Mary turned to Ifeanyi. He turned his head in her direction, and they just looked at each other.

"So, what were you doing when I called?" she asked.

"Nothing much. I was just hanging with my brother," Ifeanyi replied.

"Oh, so Nomnso is back?"

"Yeah, just for the Easter Break."

"Cool. How is he?"

"He's doing great. He asked after you, actually," Ifeanyi said.

"Hmmm, what did you tell him?" Mary smiled.

"I told him I don't know. You know, we don't talk like we used to. I was pleased when you called."

"Hmmm..."

"So, how are you?" Ifeanyi asked seriously. "Are you happy?"

"I am. Are you happy?"

"Hmmm," Ifeanyi giggled. "Sometimes. Ahh, this is a bad idea..." He breathed out a deep sigh.

"What? What's a bad idea?" Mary lifted herself from her reclined position and looked down at Ifeanyi, studying him.

Ifeanyi sat up too. "I should take you home."

"What are you not telling me? What are you afraid of?" Mary asked, concerned.

"Being with you like this, takes me back to where we were. But so much has changed. I don't want to hurt you."

"My feelings for you haven't changed," Mary said, swallowing the lump that had been growing in her throat. Being without him made no more sense to her, and she just knew she was ready for whatever that meant.

Ifeanyi leaned against the car door, afraid of what he might do at the revelation that Mary was still in love with him. He ached for her so badly. Maybe he shouldn't have gone to her after all. How was he going to resist her looking so beautiful and saying that she still loved him?

God, how he still loved her... But was it right? Could they really work it out? And was God in support of their love? He was reminded of the Scripture in First Corinthians chapter seven, which said that *"it is better to marry than to burn..."*

His silence broke her heart. *He doesn't love me anymore*, she thought. She looked away from him and brought her seat upright. "It's okay if you don't feel the same," she said, fighting back tears.

That about did it. Before he could think it through, he said the words that hung at the tip of his tongue. "Marry me, Mary."

Mary's hand flew to her mouth as she turned to him in shock. She let out a small whimper, as the tears rolled down her cheeks. She wasn't expecting that. But she already knew what her answer would be. "Yes, yes, I will," she said, as she reached out for him passionately.

Ifeanyi caught her in his arms and held her in a passionate embrace. He kissed the top of her head, her forehead, her nose and cheeks...every part of her face except her lips, where he longed to kiss but had promised himself and God that he would honour Him by waiting until marriage to kiss the woman he loved. "I love you so much," he said between kisses.

Mary looked up at him, expecting his kiss, but he placed a finger to her lips instead, saying, "Let's save it, darling. I want to do it right this time." Mary hugged him tighter. She didn't know she could love him more...

It was going to be hard, but she knew that there was nowhere else she would rather be. Ifeanyi was the one man she was ready to follow and submit to, and she felt comforted and protected knowing that he too was submitted to God. Whatever the days ahead had in store for them, she was ready to face them with him and stand by him.

15

"Trust in the LORD with all thine heart; and lean not unto thine own under- standing. In all thy ways acknowledge him, and he shall direct thy paths."

PROVERBS 3:5

Chuka was surprised to receive a call from Ifeanyi early on Saturday morning. They had lost touch over the months, with Ifeanyi being tied up with family, work, religion, and all. However, he was pleased to see that he was missed. He picked up on the fifth ring.

"Hey, man, long time! To what do I owe the honour?"

"Haha... Sorry, man. It's life, you know? How are you?" Ifeanyi replied cheerfully.

"I'm good. We can't complain. And you?" Chuka asked.

"I'm great! I'm getting married..."

"For real? You and Ijeoma?"

"No... Mary. I asked her last night, and she said yes!" Ifeanyi grinned.

"What about Ijeoma?" Chuka asked, feeling annoyed.

"She's okay. Nobody knows yet. We're actually going to tell the family over dinner tonight, and I just wanted to give you a heads up. I'll be needing a Best Man..."

"I can't believe you are just going to leave Ijeoma alone with your baby! You're so *selfish*!"

"Hey! What brought this on? Why do I have to marry her and be miserable the rest of my life because we made a stupid mistake? It's not like I'm not taking care of my child!"

"Oh, give me a break! Have you even thought about how hard it will be for her to find someone else with that baggage you dumped on her? Or are you the only one who deserves to be happy?"

Ifeanyi was speechless. Why was Chuka being so emotional about this? It's not like he loved Ijeoma... Oh, *wow*! Ifeanyi finally pieced it together. Chuka still had feelings for Ijeoma. He now remembered that Chuka was the first to spot her during registration at the NYSC camp, but Ijeoma had flirted with Ifeanyi instead. He hadn't thought twice about taking advantage of her.

"Oh, man... You still have feelings for her?"

"What do you care? I don't even know why I thought you were my friend! You never think of anyone but yourself! Happy married life! I hope your whore of a wife gets pregnant for someone else!" And with that final word, Chuka hung the line.

Ifeanyi stood shocked looking at his phone. He knew he had been selfish back then, but was he still being selfish now? Was it wrong for him to want to be with the woman he loved, who loved him back? Did he have to marry the mother of his child, simply because she was the mother of his child, even though they were not good for each other?

He couldn't believe how cruel Chuka had been, calling Mary a whore and wishing such evil on his marriage. Had Chuka always been so bitter and envious towards him, and he had just never noticed? Ifeanyi wondered if Chuka would tell Ijeoma about his engagement. He decided he had better be the one to break the news to her.

He tried her number, but the line was busy. When she didn't call him back within 10 minutes, like she usually did, he thought the worst. The news was out, and not in a good way!

Ijeoma got off the phone with Chuka. He had just asked to see her. He said he had something important to discuss with her. She wondered what it might be. They had agreed to meet at an eatery on Admiralty Way in Lekki at 1 pm.

She saw the missed call from Ifeanyi and was about to return the call when another call came in. It was one of her aunties calling to ask her about Emeka and Ifeanyi. She stayed long on the phone answering her many questions and thanking her for her advice. Before dropping the line, her aunty prayed and prophesied over her life. By the time the call was concluded, Ijeoma had forgotten about Ifeanyi's call that she hadn't returned.

Ijeoma met with Chuka at their scheduled time. She had taken Emeka to a family friend's place for a play date. Her parents had travelled for a wedding that weekend, and she didn't want to leave him at home with the house help.

"You look good, Ijay," Chuka said, when he got up to hug her.

She smiled at him. "Thanks! You do too." She sat nervously, wondering why he had asked to meet with her so urgently.

"How's Emeka?" Chuka asked, collecting the menus from the waitress and passing one to Ijeoma.

"He's fine, thanks," Ijeoma said. "So, what's this about?"

"I thought maybe we could eat first," Chuka said. "Or at least talk seriously over the meal."

"Is this a date?" Ijeoma raised an eyebrow.

"Would that be wrong? Are you not single?"

"Ifeanyi is your friend, and I'm his Baby Mama."

"Ifeanyi is nobody's friend," Chuka muttered under his breath, then collected himself. "I'm sorry. Can we not talk about Ifeanyi for now?"

"What happened between you guys?" Ijeoma asked, concerned.

Chuka looked down at his menu, wondering if he should come clean about his feelings. Would she understand? What if she laughed at him? "Look, I just think you should start seeing other people and stop waiting around for the likes of Ifeanyi. You deserve to be happy too."

"Awww... That's so sweet," Ijeoma beamed at him. "It is hard to meet new people with Baby in tow. It was hard enough meeting a good guy when I didn't have Emeka."

"Hmmm," Chuka muttered, enjoying the way she was being free with him. "Don't worry. You're a beautiful, kind-hearted lady. I'm sure you will meet someone. You just have to be open."

Ijeoma could already tell that Chuka was trying to communicate his interest in her, and she was flattered. She thought it was odd that he would do so behind Ifeanyi's back, and then she wondered if Ifeanyi knew. What if Ifeanyi had put him up to this? Was Ifeanyi passing her off on his friend? She suddenly felt sick.

The waiter came back to take their order and didn't linger long. Ijeoma couldn't keep her suspicions to herself. "Does Ifeanyi know you are here?"

"No, he doesn't. In fact, I didn't want to tell you now, but... Ifeanyi is getting married."

"What do you mean Ifeanyi is getting married? To *whom*?" Ijeoma asked incredulously.

"Mary."

Ijeoma was frozen in shock. She hadn't known what to expect, but she would have been happy to hear any other name but that! What was it about this Mary anyway? What kind of *juju* hold did she have on Ifeanyi? She put her head down on her hands and started to sob into it.

Chuka came up beside her and comforted her. "I'm so sorry. I didn't want to tell you like that. I wanted you to have fun and realise that you deserve so much better than him." But Ijeoma's silent sobs were increasing in volume. "Are you going to be okay? Should I take you home?" Ijeoma nodded and grabbed her handbag.

Chuka dropped some change on their table and apologised to the waiter who had taken their order as he departed with an emotional Ijeoma.

Chuka collected Ijeoma's keys, insisting that he would drive her home, as she was in no condition to drive. When they got to her house, it was quiet, as no one was there. Chuka followed Ijeoma in, and she comported herself and offered him something to drink. He said he would help himself to something at the bar so that Ijeoma wouldn't stress herself.

He came back and offered her a glass of wine. Ijeoma nodded her approval. "Do you still love him?" Chuka asked.

Ijeoma took a sip of the wine and thought for a minute. "Honestly, I don't think I ever did. I just loved the idea of us, you know? And when Emeka came into the picture, I just wanted a perfect family. I mean, I'm not a bad person."

Chuka was relieved to hear that. "No, you're not a bad person. You were just unfortunate. You know, I had a crush on you back in camp."

Ijeoma looked at him, surprised. "You did?"

He nodded and gave a shy smile. "I kinda still do. But I don't want to rush you or anything."

Ijeoma put down her glass and went to him. Someone loved her. Despite her situation, someone loved her. It was music to her ears. She leaned in to him, and he claimed her lips with a kiss.

After some passionate kisses on the sofa, Ijeoma led Chuka up to her bedroom, where they continued making out. Chuka pulled himself together and stopped Ijeoma. "I want to make sure that this is what you want, Ijay. If not, we can just cuddle."

Ijeoma wasn't having it. She had been starved of love and sex for more than a year. She was ready to be taken, and she continued kissing and touching him until he threw reason and caution out of the window. When they were done, they lay in bed and cuddled.

Chuka kissed Ijeoma's shoulder and watched her fall asleep in his arms, unable to believe his luck. If he had only known, he would have made his move sooner.

Mary was still ecstatic from her rendezvous with Ifeanyi last night. She stood in front of the mirror, smiling from ear to ear as she put on her make-up and jewellery and checked out her appearance for the dinner party Ifeanyi had organised at his home. She was the guest of honour. It would be the first time since their engagement party that she had been inside their home.

The boys were over the moon too! They had liked David, but they loved Ifeanyi. They were just as excited about Ifeanyi coming over as his fiancée. When Ifeanyi had arrived and was parking, Daniel ran to alert Mary that her prince had come.

Ifeanyi entered Mary's small abode and waited in the living area with her brothers. Mary was surprised to see him without his usual bouquet of flowers when she departed her room. "No flowers for me today?" she teased.

He rather fell on one knee and presented her with a small velvet box. She screamed with glee. He had purchased a new ring for her, which was even more glorious than the first. She leaned in to him instinctively for a kiss, but he pulled her in for an embrace instead. He kissed her cheek and returned her cheeky smile. It would take some getting used to.

They said goodbye to the boys and went on their way.

Chief and Mrs Chukwueke received Mary warmly, not sure why a special meal had been called. They looked at Mary's hand for a clue but found none, and then at their son, whose smile gave nothing away. Chidinma hugged Mary fondly, and Nomnso gave her a side hug. They all made their way to the dining table, which was already set for the occasion.

"So, what's the reason for this special occasion?" Mrs Chukwueke couldn't contain her curiosity any longer.

"Mummy, you can't wait until we finish the first course?" Ifeanyi asked, looking sweetly at Mary.

"No, *abeg*! Stop killing us with suspense. What is it?" she retorted.

"Well, you will all be pleased to know that Mary and I are back together."

"I think we all figured that one out..." Chidinma teased.

"And we have decided to get married," Ifeanyi concluded. "I proposed to Mary last night, and she said "yes"!"

Everyone was quiet. Chief Chukwueke broke the silence. "Is she pregnant again?"

Mary and Ifeanyi looked at each other in shock. "No, I'm not, sir," Mary answered.

"So, why the hurry to marry? I thought you guys would like to take it slow this time?" Mrs Chukwueke made her contribution.

"Because we love each other. We are sure we want to be to- gether. I thought you would all be happy for me. For *us*?" Ifeanyi replied, surprised at their questions.

"You know things are not the way they were before. You're a father now. Does Mary understand your responsibilities and relationship with Ijeoma?"

Mary nodded. "Yes, I do, ma. I love Ifeanyi very much, and I know we can make it work."

"So, what date are you looking at?" Mrs Chukwueke enquired.

"Four months' time. We want to marry on the anniversary of the date I initially proposed last August."

"That doesn't leave much time to plan a wedding. Are you sure you wouldn't rather marry at Christmas? It will also give you more time to get reacquainted and decide if you are ready for marriage," Mrs Chukwueke said.

"No, we don't need a big wedding. We will be happy to keep it small. And we will have enough time for three months of pre-marital counselling at my church," Ifeanyi said, feeling disappointed that no one seemed as excited for them as they were.

"Son, I take it you have prayed about this?" Chief Chukwueke asked.

"Yes, Dad, I have."

"Okay, and I hope you will let your mother and I pray about it too, so we can give our blessing."

Ifeanyi looked at Mary worriedly. Were they going to withhold their blessing when they already gave it? Mary squeezed his hand to calm his nerves and offered him a smile. "Okay, Dad. When can we expect your feedback?"

"Give us a week or so. We can't rush these things," Chief Chukwueke said, and then served up his meal.

Ifeanyi looked at his sister and brother, who gave him hopeful looks. Was he missing something? Why was everyone acting as though they were wrong to want to marry? Ifeanyi ate his food quietly.

Mary was surprised at the response from the Chukwuekes. She was sure they would have been dancing and talking about wedding dresses by now. She looked into her heart, in search of a clue and a word from God. There was nothing. She was not relieved. She would have one week of wondering...and she longed for the peace of assurance.

16

"Trust in the LORD with all thine heart; and lean not unto thine own under-standing. In all thy ways acknowledge him, and he shall direct thy paths."

PROVERBS 3:5

Anxiety kept Ifeanyi up all night. He couldn't understand why his family had not been as excited as he had been about his proposal to Mary and her decision to marry him. He was afraid that they would try to use reason against his passion. Would they really prefer for him to marry Ijeoma, even against his wishes? What was he missing?

At 1 pm, he gave up on trying to sleep and got out of bed to pray. But he was also afraid to pray. He was afraid that God would oppose him too. He knew that he had acted in passion when he had asked Mary to marry him. He had intended to wait until he had a clear leading from God to proceed with their relationship. However, he felt that he was only being honest with himself about his desire. After all, the Bible did say that *"it is better to marry than to burn."*

"Oh, Lord, please... Make a way for us. Please, Lord, I pray that they will grant their blessing, and that Mary and I will be married and be together at last. Oh, Lord, please..."

Am I to serve you or are you My servant?

"I am Your servant, Lord. But please, I need Your blessing on my marriage."

Why have you not asked what I want?

"I am afraid. I am afraid that you will ask me to do what is impossible for me. I love Mary so much..."

More than Me?

Yes. "No, Lord. I don't know... God, I just want to be happy!"

You are carnal. If any man loves his wife more than Me, he is not worthy of Me.

"Please, Lord! What should I do?" *Please don't tell me to let go...*

Silence.

"But I've already proposed, Lord. For the second time. Will she ever forgive me if I withdraw my proposal now? Lord, I can wait. We can have a long engagement."

The answer he desired did not come. He wrestled with his spirit all night, knowing what he should do but too afraid to confess it and too unwilling to do it. He would wait on his father's decision. Hopefully, his parents will give their blessing, and they will have the go ahead to proceed. Maybe God will come around after he is married...

Three days later...

"Ifeanyi, Daddy is calling you."

Ifeanyi was in bed, staring blankly at the TV and lost in thought. He looked up at his brother, Nomnso, who had just entered his room to deliver the news. He wondered if his parents had arrived at a decision already and wished that it would be in his favour. "I'm coming," he said as he dragged himself out of bed.

"Ifeanyi, why am I hearing about your engagement to Mary from others? I thought you were waiting on our blessing to go public?" Chief Chukwueke asked, looking sternly at his son.

"What? I didn't tell anyone. Well, except Chuka... Oh no! Who did you hear it from?"

"So, you have told people that you are getting married, even after I told you to give us time to pray about it?"

"No, I didn't, Dad. I told Chuka before our dinner that night. I didn't think he would go and blab. He was supposed to be my Best Man."

"I'm so disappointed in you. You have totally lost all reason over this girl!" Chief Chukwueke said.

"Hey, that's not fair, Dad. I didn't mean for it to get out. I'm sorry," Ifeanyi swallowed hard, hoping to appease his father.

"Well, I've made my decision." Ifeanyi held his breath. "You will be married in four months, but not to Mary. To Ijeoma."

"*WHAT*?!" Ifeanyi raised his voice.

"And I forbid you to see that Mary girl again!" Chief Chukwueke met his challenge.

"*W-WHAAT*? You can't be serious, Daddy! You can't make me marry someone I don't want or keep me from the woman I love!"

"As long as you bear my name, and live under my roof, you will honour my authority in this house! Ijeoma will make a good wife for you. And you will grow to love her, as you do your child."

Ifeanyi was shaking his head, fighting against the sobs bubbling in his throat. This was too unfair! "Daddy, please! You can't do this. I didn't go behind your back. You know me. You are just angry."

"I've said all I want to say," Chief Chukwueke said, turning his gaze back to the show on his widescreen television.

Ifeanyi fell at his feet. "Daddy, please... I can't marry Ijeoma. I love Mary."

His father didn't answer him. He turned to his mother instead. "Mummy, talk to him. This is not fair. *This is not done!*"

"Sorry, son. But I'm with your father on this one. You need to be wise, and you are not being wise here. You will thank us later."

Ifeanyi stood up again and wiped his nose with the back of his hand. "No. I won't. Because I won't *ever* marry Ijeoma! I am old enough to choose my wife, and I will marry Mary, even without your blessing."

"Don't be stupid, Ifeanyi," Mrs Chukwueke arose from her seat to calm her son down. "How do you suppose you will look after her and her siblings with what you earn? Your father is serious. You just have to calm down and see reason."

Ifeanyi withdrew from his mother, shaking his head frantically. "No, Mum. I can't accept this. This is the rest of my life we are talking about. NO! If you like, disown me. But you can't make me marry Ijeoma!"

With that, he ran from their chambers and out of the house. He got into his car and drove off. There was only one place he wanted to be right then, and it was in Mary's arms.

Mary was surprised to see Ifeanyi at her place at 8:30 pm at night. They didn't have a date planned. She saw quickly that he was emotional. His puffy, bloodshot eyes revealed he had been crying.

"Hey, babe, are you okay?" she asked, as she welcomed him into her private space. The boys were watching TV in the living area where they also slept.

Ifeanyi held Mary in his arms, comforted by her embrace. He withdrew briefly and looked into her angelic face. "They said 'no,'" he said soberly, and swallowed the lump in his throat.

Sadness fell over Mary upon realising the cause of his pain. They were not going to get his parents' blessing to marry. "It's okay... Let's keep praying and give them time to change their minds."

Ifeanyi shook his head. "They won't. They want me to marry Ijeoma."

Mary tucked in her lips to hold back her emotions. "It is well. God is in control," was all she could say, as pain began to grip her heart again. She had been so sure they would give their blessing.

"Let's elope," Ifeanyi muttered quietly, his head bowed.

Shocked, Mary turned to him and lifted his head with her hand to look him in his eyes. "We can't do that, Ifeanyi. You're not thinking straight. Trust God. If it is His will for us to be together, we will marry with your parents' blessing."

Ifeanyi looked in her eyes and knew that she would soon be lost to him forever. Unless... Unless... He kissed her with all his passion, and she returned his kiss. They sat on her bed, kissing. He let his hands stray to cup her breasts, and she shrank away from his touch.

"What are you doing, Ifeanyi?" Mary asked, seriously concerned for him now.

"Let's go somewhere private," Ifeanyi whispered quietly. He kissed her lips again.

"Let's stop, before we do something stupid, Ifeanyi," Mary resisted him, wriggling out of his embrace.

"Mary, I love you. Maybe if you had my baby...maybe they will let us be together." A tear rolled down his cheek.

"No, Ifeanyi. What's happened to you? Baby, please stop," Mary said, as she felt him slide one hand under her blouse to fiddle with her bra hooks.

"Don't you want to be with me?" Ifeanyi asked, as he kissed her neck softly.

"Of course, I do. But not like this," Mary said resolutely and stood up from the bed, moving away from Ifeanyi. "If we go against God, we have no hope of ever being happy together. I want you, but I want God's blessing too. I think you should leave now."

"I'm sorry, Mary. I will stop. Just come and sit with me. I promise I won't do anything," Ifeanyi said, soberly. He swallowed. "I just can't bear the thought of living without you. I don't want to live without you."

Mary returned to sit beside him, keeping her distance on the bed. "I know. I don't want to live without you either. But God knows best. We have to remember that. Maybe there is something we are not seeing. We just have to trust and obey."

"My dad forbade me from seeing you again. Can you believe that?!"

Mary just looked on, sad and heartbroken. Their love didn't stand a chance against all this opposition. The tears found their way out of her eyes as she looked with despair at her beloved.

Ifeanyi held his head in his hands and sobbed. Mary went to him and held him in her arms, sobbing quietly over him. It was to be her last cry, before she closed the emotional chapter that was Ifeanyi.

Ifeanyi lifted his head again to kiss Mary, and she let him, tears streaming down her cheeks. He leaned into her until she was lying on her back on the bed, and they continued to kiss passionately.

"You need to go home," Mary said, after a while.

"I'm going to miss you so much," Ifeanyi said, nestled by her bosom, as they both looked up at the ceiling. "I'm going to miss the boys too."

"They will miss you. I will miss you more. But I know you will be fine. We will all be fine."

They lay quietly in each other's arms for a long while, both lost in their thoughts and grief. It was well and truly over. Mary wondered how she would get over him.

Ifeanyi wondered if he would end up marrying Ijeoma and if he could ever love her the way he loved Mary. He seriously considered moving out of his parents' home and living by himself for a while...until he decided what he would do with his life. It seemed better than agreeing to marry Ijeoma so that he could stay in his father's good graces.

"It's getting late," Mary said, when she heard her brothers snoring. She sat up in bed and tidied her hair and clothes.

"Why are you rushing me out of here? If this is our last time together, shouldn't I savour it? Let me spend the night," Ifeanyi pleaded.

"No, Ifeanyi. It's enough. Let's not make this a long goodbye," Mary said, pulling Ifeanyi up from the bed. "Go home and pray. You need God to help you through. I think you are losing sight of Him."

"You see why I love you so...? You always lead me aright. You're just the kind of woman I need in my life. If only I had known then what I know now. I was so stupid to mess around with those girls. I was playing with my destiny, and I didn't even know it. Pray for me, Mary."

They stood and held both their hands together. "Lord, I thank You for who You are, and I worship You for who You are. You are the God who knows all things, who is all wise and all loving. All Your ways are good and just. Lord, we pray to You, being comforted in this truth.

"Lord, I thank You for Ifeanyi. I thank You that I met him, and that I knew him, and that I loved him. I thank You for all that You did in our lives together, and all that You will do in our lives as we go our separate ways. Lord, we know that all things work together for the good of those who love You and are called according to Your purpose.

"Lord, I thank You for the calling on Ifeanyi's life. I thank You that he is not the man I knew in camp, and he has matured, and he has given his life over to You, to live it to please You. I pray, Lord, that he will come to know You more. I pray that this time of trial and testing of his faith will result in him drawing nearer to You and being placed right where You want him to be. Lord, please grant us both greater grace to abide in You, dependent only on You, our ever-present Help and Salvation.

"Lord, please forgive us for every way we have strayed from Your love tonight. Please have mercy on us in our time of weakness, and make us strong by Your word. Let Your wisdom direct our paths now, and lead us not into temptation. Let our lives honour You, Lord, so that others will be blessed by our witness, and not hindered from coming to You. Please cleanse us of all unrighteousness and renew in us a right spirit.

"As Ifeanyi returns home, Lord, please minister to him. Please grant him safe journey across the bridge and all the way home.

Please watch over him and all his family. Lord, I pray that Your perfect will will be done in his life. And if Your will is for him to marry Ijeoma, I pray that You will put that love in his heart for her and grant her the grace to be the woman he needs. May his marriage and home be fruitful and blessed. I pray that his relationship with his parents will be restored, and that Your peace will abide in his home again.

"All this, and many more things, we commit into Your hands and pray in Jesus' mighty name. Amen."

"Amen," Ifeanyi replied soberly. "You've refreshed my soul. God bless you, Mary."

Mary smiled at him and then looked down at her hand. She had forgotten about the ring. She pulled it off her finger and offered it back to Ifeanyi.

"It's yours, Mary," he said sweetly and folded her hand with the ring inside. "I would have given you the world, but this is all I can give you. Please keep it and remember me."

Mary shook her head and sniffled. "I can't. I have to let go."

"Then sell it and move out of this place. Start a better life for yourself. I don't want it. I bought it for you, and I want you to have it," Ifeanyi insisted.

Mary began to sob again and thanked him through her tears. Her lips trembled to kiss him again, but she resisted the temptation, knowing that if she gave in now, she would not be able to withhold him from taking all of her. Ifeanyi held Mary's hand as they walked to his car to say their final goodbyes. The two lovers hugged and parted, without hope of ever being reunited.

Mary lamented as she watched him drive away, a new song of forsaken love playing in her soul. *They were never meant to be...* She returned to her room and wept bitterly. She cried into the early hours of the next day, mourning a life that would have been...

17

"Trust in the LORD with all thine heart; and lean not unto thine own under- standing. In all thy ways acknowledge him, and he shall direct thy paths."

PROVERBS 3:5

There was a knock on the door. Before she opened it, Mary knew who it was. She knew she was too weak to see him now, but she couldn't bear to shut him out. She opened the door and looked up at Ifeanyi.

His face came down and their lips touched in a sweet kiss. Mary whimpered. Ifeanyi carried her the short distance to her bedroom and lay her on the bed. She couldn't think of anything except for how much she loved him and wanted him in that mo- ment. He straddled over her slender frame and kissed her lips again.

Like a starved baby, she returned his passionate kisses and cooperated with him as he removed her nightgown eagerly. He took off his shirt with slow determination and undressed completely before her eyes. He returned to plant kisses all over her body, caressing her curvaceous figure.

There was no stopping now. Reason had no say in their passion. She was surrendered to him, and he claimed her body as he slid easily into her. Mary cried as Ifeanyi made love to her. It was all she ever thought it would be.

In the morning, her body still tingled with the sensations of their love making the night before. She turned around, hoping to find him lying beside her, but he was gone. He had left a note.

"Last night was incredible, baby. I'm sorry, I had to slip away for work, but I can't wait to see you again. Let's have dinner! I'll call you. Love, Ifeanyi."

She smiled as she read it. It wasn't a dream... She had been fantasising about their first time together for many nights now. But last night had been real.

With that realisation came the flood of guilt. They'd given in to temptation and had no intention of stopping themselves. How could she reconcile what had happened between them and her faith in God?

Thoughts of the night before played in her mind again, and she soon forgot her guilt. She couldn't wait to see Ifeanyi again. She couldn't wait for tonight.

Ifeanyi and Mary had dinner at the Sheraton Hotel in Ikeja. She had always wanted to go there, and she marvelled at the richness of the resort. They had their meal by the poolside, under a blanket of stars. They couldn't keep their eyes off each other.

"So, I booked us a suite for the night. I thought we could do with some privacy and a little luxury tonight," Ifeanyi said.

Mary smiled at him shyly. She knew of his intention, and it was also her desire to spend the night with him. She just wished they didn't need to sneak around. She suddenly didn't know what to say to him, because she knew what they were doing was wrong, but she was afraid to say something. She didn't really want to stop.

After their meal, Mary followed Ifeanyi to the suite he had booked for them. It was indeed luxurious. She had a quick look around before settling down on the bed.

Ifeanyi poured himself a glass of wine and offered her a glass too. She took it from him and drank, almost rushing it down her throat. She was so nervous.

Ifeanyi knelt before her and put her hand to his chest so that she could feel his excited heartbeat. "This is what you do to me, Mary. I love you to Heaven and back. I promise I won't hurt you as long as I live..."

Mary drew his face towards hers and kissed him passionately. Then she began to undress, her eyes locked with his. All thought of right and wrong was expelled from her mind. They were just two people in love, doing what lovers do...

The days became weeks, the weeks became months. Mary and Ifeanyi continued their secret love affair, all the while plans were being made for his wedding to Ijeoma. But Mary had crossed the point of no return. She had broken out of her shell sexually and had become much freer with Ifeanyi. She lived for the brief moments they shared together, making love at hotels and occasionally at her home, when her brothers were not around.

It pained her deeply that Ifeanyi was going ahead with the wedding. But she had rejected his proposal to elope, and she still refused to marry him without his parents' blessing. She felt stuck, unable to leave him for her love and desire, and unwilling to be joined with him legally for the opposition they would face.

One Saturday afternoon, they lay in bed together after making love. Mary realised that she didn't have much to say to Ifeanyi apart from asking about Emeka and complaining about his pending marriage. They had stopped talking about God long ago, as neither were willing to acknowledge nor forsake their sin. They were drifting apart, even though they were more physically intimate.

Ifeanyi rolled to his side and began to dress up. "I have to go and pick up my suit from the tailors," he said.

She sat up and swallowed as she watched him. "I still don't understand why you are going through with this sham of a marriage."

Ifeanyi breathed in deeply. "What do you think I can do about it? You know I would rather marry you. So, if I can't, I might as well marry the mother of my child."

"You don't have to marry her or anyone, you know? Can't we just tell them we're still together, even if we are not getting married?"

"You are forgetting that my dad forbade me from seeing you! If I announce that we're still together, then I will be forfeiting my inheritance. And I know *you* don't want that..." Ifeanyi said.

"What's that supposed to mean? I want you, I don't care about your money!"

"Believe me, you do. My life would be completely different if I was broke. I wouldn't be the same guy you love right now," Ifeanyi said. "Look, this way works out best for everyone, including Emeka."

"What about Ijeoma? She's going to expect you to make love to her too..."

"So?"

"What do you mean by '*so*'?" Mary asked, wide-eyed.

Ifeanyi sat back on the bed and held her hand. "It will just be sex. You're the only one I make love to."

Mary withdrew her hand and shook her head. "You can't seriously expect me to be okay with that..."

"Mary, you can't expect me to deny her that. I promise I won't enjoy it," Ifeanyi joked. He stroked her face with a finger.

Mary slapped his hand away. "This is not funny! God, what are we doing? So, I'm going to be *the other woman*? An *adulteress*?"

Ifeanyi was quiet.

"You're going to have to choose, Ifeanyi. Me or her?"

He stood up and robbed his hand against his head. "I think you mean you or my family? I thought you said you would never come between us!"

"So Ijeoma is your *family* now?"

"That's not what I meant... But yes. Yes, she is my family. We have a child together."

"What if I'm pregnant?"

Ifeanyi froze and then turned towards her, looking at her excitedly. "Are you?"

"No. But I could be. What if I got pregnant for you and you are already married? What about our child? What about us?"

"You're overthinking this, Mary. We will cross that bridge, *if* and when we get to it. But for now, I have to do what I have to do, for us... Please try to understand," Ifeanyi said. Then rifling through his wallet, he brought out N20,000 and handed it to her. "Get yourself something nice, bae. I have to go now. I'll see you tomorrow."

Mary didn't take the money, and he placed it on the bedside table. This was wrong on too many levels. She watched him leave and then broke down in tears.

Ifeanyi and Ijeoma's wedding day finally came. Mary was not invited. It was a big spectacle that even got live coverage on Channels Television. Mary couldn't bear to watch it. She was in torment.

The worst part was that she couldn't pray. She didn't want to be one of those people who apologised for a sin they still intended to commit. And she knew that when Ifeanyi returned to her arms, she would be holding nothing back from him.

But she needed God. She needed Him desperately, but she had chosen to follow her heart...and the two could not be reconciled.

After his two-week honeymoon with Ijeoma, Ifeanyi paid Mary a visit. She fought and wrestled with him with all her might, shouting insults at him, which he took without resisting, before he finally arrested her and claimed her body again. She was helpless in his arms. She had missed him so much, but being with him, knowing he was married to someone else, was far more painful.

"I can't do this anymore. I can't be your secret lover," Mary said in agony when they lay in bed together after making love. This was not what she had had in mind. She needed to be celebrated...to be his *one and only*.

Ifeanyi didn't pay any attention to her protest. He rather began to kiss and caress her body again. Mary squirmed in his arms, hanging on to him like her life depended on it. They both knew she couldn't and wouldn't leave him. She would just have to get used to the new arrangement.

Months passed, and Mary grew more miserable. Ifeanyi did not appear so conflicted. He was enjoying the best of both worlds.

The news soon broke that Ijeoma was expecting her second baby. Mary found out with the rest of the world, as Ifeanyi had kept it hidden from her. She wanted to die!

She hadn't heard from Ifeanyi for a few days actually, which was unusual. Today of all days, she expected to hear from him, or even that he would pay her a visit. He didn't. Several more days passed in silence, and Mary assumed that he had finally let her go, but she was angry with him for not being man enough to tell her to her face that they were over.

Then one day, there was a knock on the door. Mary opened it slightly, blocking his entrance into her home. "What do you want?" she asked, coldly.

"I came to see you. Are you okay?" Ifeanyi replied.

She wanted to throw a tantrum. Was he really asking if she was okay? "Go away! I never want to see you again!" She shut the door in his face.

He continued knocking. "Come on, Mary. You don't really want me to leave. Let me in, let's talk about it."

"Go away!" she shouted. "Leave me the hell alone!"

"I'm not going anywhere, Mary. Open up. Please. I love you."

Enraged, she flung the door open. "You don't love me! You don't love anybody! You are a selfish *bastard*, and I never *ever* want to see you again! Get out of my life! Get out of my life!"

"Get out of my life! Get out of my life!" Mary was tossing and turning, crying and sweating, and shouting in her sleep.

"Sister Mary! Sister, wake up!" Samson nudged his sister awake from her nightmare.

Mary woke up, heaving and looking tormented. It had been a dream... All of it! She looked at Samson, who looked at her a little frightened, and pulled him into her arms and cried. *It had all been a dream.* She hadn't slept with Ifeanyi, and he hadn't married Ijeoma. But what a dream it was... It had felt so real.

"Are you okay?" Samson asked his sister.

"I will be. Thank God," she replied, the memory of the dream still very real. It was clear that God was warning her of falling into temptation and going against His wisdom. It was sure to end in misery.

Samuel and Daniel came in to see their sister, and she embraced them too, glad to be in touch with reality again. "We're off to school," Daniel said. He added with a smile, "Don't worry, we made breakfast."

Mary smiled at him and kissed all her brothers before they left for school. She needed to get ready for work too, but before she did, she got on her knees and glorified God. She thanked Him for the dream, which left lessons that she wouldn't easily forget, and for saving her from her fleshly desires. She prayed for more grace to flee from temptation and live a life holy and pleasing to Him. She prayed also for Ifeanyi, that God would also grant Him grace and wisdom to walk according to His will.

When she had finished her prayer, she got ready for work. She was about leaving her home when her phone rang. It was Ifeanyi. Her instinct was to pick up his call, but she chose to heed the warning in the dream. She had to forsake him. And she couldn't risk having him as a friend she secretly loved.

It was over, and she was moving on.

18

"Trust in the LORD with all thine heart; and lean not unto thine own under-standing. In all thy ways acknowledge him, and he shall direct thy paths."

PROVERBS 3:5

A couple of days before...

"Hey, it's time you left. My parents will be home soon," Ijeoma said, throwing Chuka's shirt at him, before picking up her bra to put back on.

Chuka shoved the shirt aside and pulled her to him again. "I thought you said they are not coming 'til the evening. Are you tired of me already?"

Ijeoma kissed him. "I just don't want to chance it. Come on, get up!"

Chuka kissed her back, caressing her body. "I can't get enough of you. You're so not what I expected at all."

Ijeoma giggled. "Neither are you!" She picked up his shirt and threw it at him again. "Get up! Emeka will soon wake up, and he's already due for his feed."

Chuka slid the shirt on and got out of the bed. He found his trousers and slid into them. "So, when can I see you again?"

"You have my number. Use it," Ijeoma replied, with a cheeky smile.

"Okay, ma'am. I'll call you later," Chuka said, pulling her back in his arms for another round of kisses.

Ijeoma escorted him to her driveway and watched him enter his car and drive through their tall black gate. Moments after he drove out, her parent's car drove into the compound. Emeka began to cry. Relieved at the excuse he had presented, she hurried back into the house to attend to him.

"Who was that that just left the compound?" Mrs Njokwu was at Ijeoma's bedroom door with a frown on her face.

"Welcome back, Mum. You're back early." Ijeoma turned to look at her mother briefly, as she made herself busy attending to Emeka.

"Are you not going to answer me?"

"He's a friend. Ifeanyi's friend actually. He just came to see Emeka."

"Oh..." Mrs Njokwu's eyes narrowed. Ijeoma had a certain glow about her. She could tell she wasn't telling the whole truth. "And what about Ifeanyi? Did he come over this weekend like we planned?"

Ijeoma took a deep breath. "No, Mummy, he didn't. Don't you want to know how Emeka is doing?"

"What's that supposed to mean?"

"I don't know, Mum. It seems you're not interested in him at all. All you care about is Ifeanyi," Ijeoma replied, rocking Emeka in her arms while she fed him with a bottle.

"I don't know how many times we need to have this discussion before you understand. Is it not because of Emeka that I worry so much about you and Ifeanyi? Your baby needs a stable home, and you are acting like you don't care," Mrs Njokwu replied, marvelling at her daughter, wondering how she got the nerve to be so rude.

Ijeoma didn't say anything. She continued to feed Emeka and hummed to herself.

Mrs Njokwu sat on the bed next to her daughter, feeling guilty. "How's he?"

"Who? Emeka? He's fine, thanks."

"And you? I hope you weren't too lonely while we were gone."

Ijeoma smiled to herself and looked at her mother. "I'm fine, Mum. It wasn't too lonely. Emeka kept me company."

She remembered how she had spent the evening with Chuka. They'd gone together to pick up Emeka from his play date in the late afternoon yesterday, and he had also picked up his car from the restaurant where he had left it. He had decided to stay over and keep her company. They'd ordered take out, looked after Emeka together, and talked well into the night.

"There's something different about you..." Mrs Njokwu said. She cleared her throat. "So, what about Ifeanyi? Why didn't he come around?"

"Because he doesn't love me, Mum. He loves Mary, and they are getting married," Ijeoma said, looking blankly at her mother, whose jaw had dropped. "And you know what, I'm happy for them! I don't love him either."

"Married, *ke*? He told you he is going to marry that girl?"

"No, Mum. He wasn't even man enough to tell me himself. His friend, Chuka, did! It's over, and Emeka and I are going to be just fine."

Mrs Njokwu got up and put her hands on her head dramatically. She couldn't believe the turn of events and how Ijeoma was just letting someone else take her husband. It was time she took matters into her own hands. "It is well... It is well," was all she said as she left Ijeoma's room.

Mr Njokwu picked up his phone to call Chief Chukwueke. His wife hadn't stopped nagging him since she discovered that Ifeanyi was engaged to marry another woman apart from their beloved daughter.

"I thought you said you guys had an arrangement? How can we be hearing about his engagement from the street?! This is dishonourable! You have to talk to him, oh. You have to talk to him. The way I am feeling now, I can just go there and give them a piece of my mind! As if my daughter is not better than that tramp! What a disgrace..." Mrs Njokwu had ranted in his ears.

"Chinedu, how *nau*...? We *dey*, oh. What is this I am hearing about Ifeanyi getting married? Eh, Ngozi told me. We were very sad to hear it, oh. I thought you said you were going to talk to him? Yes, Ijeoma is very upset too. *Abeg*, make you talk to him. It is better. Thank you. Thank you, sir."

"Congratulations!" Kelechi sang to Mary when she resumed work on Monday morning. "Let me see the ring!"

"You're engaged?!" Aisha piped in, enthusiastically.

"What?" Mary looked at them surprised. How did Kelechi know about the engagement? "How did you know?"

"Are you forgetting that Chuka is my brother? He told me of course. I was actually disappointed that you didn't tell me your-self. But I forgive you. Come on, let me see it!"

"I'm not wearing it. We are not supposed to tell anyone yet," Mary said, but she smiled. "We're waiting on his parents' blessing."

"Oh, okay. Well, it's still fantastic news! I'm sure they will say 'yes.' Who wouldn't want you for a daughter?" Kelechi beamed at Mary and got her excited again.

She was getting married! And to the man she loved the most in the whole wide world! Mary beamed and giggled. "Thank you! We're expectant of God's blessings."

"Yeah, Mary. I want to be one of your bridesmaids, oh!" Aisha added and gave her a hug. "I'm so happy for you!"

The two other staff also congratulated her on her engagement before they all resumed their duties. Emails were sent, and one was to a blog with a tip about a secret engagement between Ifeanyi Chukwueke and Mary Uwanna, the pregnant corper from the Bolaji Scandal.

On Tuesday morning, the secret engagement wasn't so secret anymore. One of Chief Chukwueke's friends called him to confirm the story about Ifeanyi and Mary that his daughter had read on a blog. Chief Chukwueke denied the story, that it was a media hype, and thanked him for the tip off.

He paced his room, angry at Ifeanyi for going behind his back to announce his engagement to Mary. He had thought that with time, Ifeanyi would get over her, and he would be able to put in a good word for Ijeoma. He had discussed with Mr Njokwu, and their families stood to form a strong alliance if the two were to marry. Now, Ifeanyi had gone and messed things up.

Mrs Chukwueke came into the room and knew immediately that something was wrong with her husband. "What is the matter, dear?"

"I just got off the phone with Wale. Apparently, there is a story about Ifeanyi and Mary in one blog! I don't understand what is wrong with that boy!"

"He's in love," Mrs Chukwueke said, petting her husband.

"He's stupid, that's what he is! Now, he has forced my hand."

"Calm down, calm down, darling. It is well," Mrs Chukwueke rubbed her husband's back and got him to sit down on the sofa with her.

"Have you prayed about it?" Chief Chukwueke asked his wife.

"Prayed about what, dear?" Mrs Chukwueke replied.

"The marriage, *nau*...? We said we would pray about it and get back to him."

"You were serious? I thought you were just giving him time to sweat a little. We like her, *nau*... I just thought they were rushing it, that's all," Mrs Chukwueke replied.

"Eh heh...? I don't know, oh. I think he should marry Ijeoma. They have a baby together. Plus, there are great opportunities for collaboration between our families. Marriage is about more than love, and the way Ifeanyi is going, it's like he is ready to throw his life away for this girl."

"Hmmm..." Mrs Chukwueke muttered, thinking how he sounded just like she had done last year, before she got to know Mary. "He's not going to agree to marry Ijeoma, oh. We should probably just give them time and see how it works out. We'll go for a long engagement. *Abi*?"

"No. I've made up my mind. He needs to get serious, and Mary is clouding his judgement. It's better he marries Ijeoma," Chief Chukwueke said, conclusively. "I'll speak to him when I get back from work tonight."

"Ijeoma! Come, quick! You're going to *love* me!" Mrs Njokwu was dancing in her room. Mr Njokwu had just gotten off the phone with Chief Chukwueke. The engagement between Ifeanyi and Ijeoma was confirmed.

"Yes, Mum. What's going on?" Ijeoma came in, smiling at her happy mother, wondering what she was dancing about.

"Guess who is getting *marr-ried*?" Mrs Njokwu wrapped her arms around her daughter and did a little shimmy.

"Who?" Ijeoma asked, trying not to rush to any conclusions.

"You and Ifeanyi! In four months! Don't you just love me?" Mrs Njokwu beamed.

"NO!" Ijeoma pushed her mother away. "I don't want to marry him, and he doesn't want to marry *me*! Why won't you just let things be, Mum?"

"Young girl, are you going to talk to your mother like that?" Mr Njokwu rebuked his daughter.

"She won't stop meddling in my life, Daddy. I don't want to marry Ifeanyi. I don't want to be his pity bride!"

"You are nobody's pity bride. You are getting what you deserve! Ifeanyi is a good man. He will take care of you."

"You don't understand. You don't even know him! This is just business to you. Well, I don't want any of it," Ijeoma replied, boldly.

Wham! She got a slap across her face for her boldness.

"Phillip!" Mrs Njokwu protested.

"Stop talking like a stupid child! Do you know the trouble your mother and I went through for you to make this arrangement? You're going to marry Ifeanyi, and that is the end of it," he said, resolutely.

Ijeoma stared at her father, dumbstruck. He had never raised his hands on her before. The tears rushed down her cheeks, and she ran out of their room.

When she got to her room, she sobbed bitterly. She didn't know what was worse - marrying a man who didn't love her or marrying a man she didn't love!

Chuka called Ijeoma on Tuesday night. He had called her the night before, and they had arranged to get together on Wednesday at lunchtime. He worked in Lekki and planned on taking a break to see her in the afternoon when her parents would be at work.

"Hey, darling... What's wrong?" She sounded awful, he thought.

"I don't want to talk about it. I'm fine."

"Come on... It's me. You can tell me. What's going on?" Chuka prodded.

"My parents are forcing me to marry Ifeanyi."

"But I thought he was engaged to Mary...?" Chuka was shocked and confused.

"Well, it seems his family are in on it too. I don't know what to do. I told them that I don't love him, but they don't care!"

"Why would they force you guys to marry when you don't love each other? That's barbaric!"

"I know! And I'm stuck, because of Emeka. I don't have anywhere else to go! I don't know what to do!"

"Ummm... Talk to Ifeanyi. If you both don't want it, I'm sure you can stand against the marriage together. Don't worry, Ijay, it's going to be okay."

"Okay, I will. I'll talk to him tomorrow. Thanks."

"No problem, dear. Can I still come over tomorrow?"

Ijeoma swallowed. She missed him too. "Yeah, sure."

Chuka released a sigh. "Okay. I'll see you tomorrow. Don't think too much about it. Everything will be fine. Sleep tight, my love."

"Good night, Chuka."

Chuka heard the line click off. He had sounded more optimistic than he felt. He worried if he wasn't getting himself mixed up in something his heart could not survive.

What if Ifeanyi changed his mind and decided he wanted to marry Ijeoma? Would she change her mind too? He was fairly confident in himself, but he wasn't so confident about going against Ifeanyi in a battle over a woman...and even worse, the mother of his child.

VOLUME
FOUR

19

"Verily, verily, I say unto you, except
a corn of wheat fall into the ground
and die, it abideth alone: but if it die,
it bringeth forth much fruit."

JOHN 12:24

Ifeanyi got home just after 11 pm. He was half expecting to
find himself locked out, for his rebellion, but was relieved
when he got into his home without a problem. He fell on his
bed as soon as he got in, physically and emotionally exhausted.
He wanted to sleep, but he remembered Mary's words to pray,
and his spirit urged him on to pray.

He'd thought a lot on the drive back, and he could see things
clearer now. He got on his knees and was quiet for a while, not
knowing where to begin. He had to search his heart because he
wanted to speak sincerely about all he was thinking and feeling.

"I'm sorry, Lord," he began. "Please forgive me. I know it is all about You, but I've made it all about me and my love for Mary. The truth is that I think I still love Mary more than You. I know that makes me unworthy of You and unworthy of her. I really want to know You more, to love You more. I need Your help, Lord.

"It is easy for me to love Mary. I can see her, touch her, and hear her voice. She also led me to You, and for that I will always be grateful to her and love her. But You are the One who died for me, and I know You love me more than she can ever love me. I know it is because of You that I am even alive today. I just need You to be more real to me.

"Father, I'm ready to do things Your way. I'm ready to forsake her, if that is Your will. I'm ready to be led. I've made a mess of my life, Lord, and right now, I don't even know what to do with it. I just know that I want You, and I need You to take control.

"I know that this is more than whether or not I ever marry. I know You died to give me so much more. I want all of it, Lord, even if marriage is not part of Your will for me. I surrender to You, Lord. I trust You to lead me in the way that is best and that will draw more people to come to know You too.

"Father, I don't know what Your will is for me and Ijeoma. My parents are forcing me to marry her, and I feel so much dread about it. But if You say I should, I am willing... If it is the price I must pay for my sin, I am willing. Please tell me what to do."

Love her.

"I do love her. Not like Mary, but I care for her..."

Love her like I loved and love you...

Ifeanyi swallowed hard. "You're right, Lord. I don't and haven't loved anyone like that. Please teach me to love like that. Please help me to overcome my selfishness."

You just have to let Me live through you, and you can do anything.

Ifeanyi was comforted by his brief prayer time. He had been able to discern God's voice, and he knew what he had to do now. He had to walk in love; surrendering all and letting God lead the way.

He was no longer afraid that it would be too much for him. He somehow knew that he could do whatever God called him to do, even if he was to marry Ijeoma. He could love her, with the love Christ loved him. He was surrendered.

In the morning, Ifeanyi got a call from Ijeoma. He picked up on the second ring.

"Hey, Ijay. Thanks for calling. How are you?"

"You know what's funny? A few days ago, I learnt of your pending marriage to Mary from Chuka. And then *yesterday*, I learned that I am now the supposed bride...? So, Ifeanyi, *you* tell me... What is going on?"

"Yeah... I'm sorry. I should have been the one to tell you about Mary. Look, we need to talk face to face. Are you free tonight?"

"As it so happens, I am," Ijeoma said, sarcastically.

"Good. I'll come to you. Say about 7 pm? I'm sorry about everything. Have a good day, okay?"

Ijeoma sighed. "Yeah, thanks. You too." She cut the call, thinking he was sounding a little sober. She wondered if he was going to beg her to refuse to marry him, so he could marry his *precious* Mary. She smiled as she imagined the look on his face when she told him that she couldn't stand to be married to him either!

Ifeanyi sighed and prayed for more grace. Ijeoma was clearly upset, and it was his fault. How was he going to make it up to her?

As he drove to his office, he thought of Mary. He wondered what she was doing now. He wanted to talk to her, to tell her of his breakthrough last night and thank her. Her prayer had really blessed him.

Before he entered his office to start his day, he called her. Her phone rang through both times he tried. Maybe she was busy. He would send her a message.

Taking a refreshing breath, he faced the day with joy, hope, and peace. God was in control.

❤ ❤ ❤

Mary saw the WhatsApp message from Ifeanyi when she got into her office. She was of two minds; read and delete or simply delete. She chose to read it first.

"Hi, Mary, I've been trying to call you, but I guess you are busy. I just wanted to say I now understand why we can't be together. I can't love you the way I want to, nor the way you need to be loved, while I am not wholly surrendered to Christ. You deserve that kind of love. I don't know what the future holds, but I know that I have to let you go and let God take control. Thank you for loving me. I will always bless God for you. May God bless and keep you and save His best for you. Bye. Ifeanyi."

Mary cried as she read his message, again and again. She wanted to reply, but she knew it would only prolong her sorrow. He had said goodbye, and she had said goodbye last night. She was happy to know that God had ministered to him too, and that he was now surrendering his will to Him. She decided to keep the message and not delete it. She would read whenever she was weak and remember that God is in control and working out His will in their lives.

Ijeoma was excited and nervous. It was 2 pm, and Chuka hadn't called her yet. They hadn't set a time, as he had only said he would come over during his lunch break, which she figured would be around 1 pm. She didn't want to call or send a text reminder, because she didn't want to come off over eager. But, where was he?

Just that minute, she heard his horn. She let out a deep breath. *He is here.* And her heart raced with excitement. She checked her reflection in the mirror. She looked good. She hadn't known how to dress, because she didn't know if he would be taking her out or where they would go, so she just wore a simple mini dress that she'd worn out to parties a few times. Not too flashy, not too under-dressed, she thought.

She went to open the door for him, and the look he gave her when he saw her made her heart leap.

"Wow! You look *hot*!" Chuka said.

She beamed at him. "Thanks. I didn't really know what to wear, 'cos I didn't know if we were going out."

"*Mehn*, I'd love to take you out looking like this, but I really can't stay too long. I only have one hour break, and I've already used up 15 minutes," Chuka said, before he kissed her. "I brought you lunch, though. Thought we could eat in."

Ijeoma smiled. "That works for me."

They stayed in the living area downstairs, by the bar. Chuka had bought some assorted African dishes from The Place, a restaurant in Lekki, so they had a feast. He also got her a box of doughnuts with different toppings. When they had finished their meal, they both reached for the same doughnut.

Chuka retrieved his hand. "You go on, dear. Ladies first!"

Ijeoma giggled. "Thanks. The caramel and peanut one is my favourite!"

"*Really*? Mine too! Most people prefer the chocolate," Chuka said.

"Naaah... I like chocolate, but I'm a nut lover."

"I'll remember that," Chuka said, with a knowing smile.

Their time was fast spent, and they had enjoyed themselves thoroughly. Ijeoma wished he could stay longer but was grateful that he had made time to visit and, mostly, that it wasn't just about sex. They hadn't even talked about it.

"What are you doing Friday night?" Chuka asked.

"I'll be home with Emeka."

"Oh, of course. I wanted you to come with me to a friend's party. You can't get anyone to watch him?"

Ijeoma shook her head. "I doubt it. I'm sure my mum wouldn't want to babysit while I go on a date with another man. Her heart is set on Ifeanyi."

"Hmmm... So, have you guys spoken yet?"

"No. He said he'll come over tonight."

"Okay... Let me know how it goes." Ijeoma and Chuka held hands as she escorted him to his car. "I had a lovely time with you, Ijay! I wish we could do this every day!" He kissed her one last time. "I'll call you."

"Okay. Thanks for coming over. I had fun!" Ijeoma watched him leave and smiled to herself as she re-entered her home. If only she could close the book on Ifeanyi once and for all, she and Chuka might have a future.

Ifeanyi arrived at Ijeoma's home at 7 pm, as he had promised. Ijeoma was taken by surprise when she saw that he had bought her flowers. She smiled as she took them from him.

"What have I done to deserve these?" she asked, with a raised brow.

"I believe I owe you an apology. That's just the beginning. Where's Emeka?"

"He's in his playpen upstairs."

Ifeanyi bounded the stairs to go to Ijeoma's room, where a little nursery area had been arranged for Emeka. He picked him up, and the boy chuckled excitedly.

"He's growing well," Ifeanyi said. "You're doing a great job with him."

Ijeoma leaned on the door and watched him. There was something different about him, and the way he was looking at her. "So, I hear apologies are in order..."

"Yeah... Have you eaten? I thought I could take you out, and we could talk over dinner."

"What about Emeka?"

"He can come with us. Is that okay?"

Ijeoma sighed. "Alright. Let me get changed. You guys can go downstairs and wait for me."

"Cool!" Ifeanyi said, as he carried his son out of the room and downstairs to play on the sofa.

Ijeoma returned, wearing the same mini dress she had worn in the afternoon. She didn't get the same reaction from Ifeanyi as she had gotten from Chuka. He smiled at her, but she could tell he didn't quite approve.

"Is this not appropriate?"

"Ummm... Not really. Do you have something more reserved? You kind of look like you're going clubbing."

Ijeoma rolled her eyes and went to try something else on. When she returned, she didn't ask his opinion.

"Better," he offered, with a smile. "You look like a lady."

Yeah, whatever, Ijeoma thought. She was wondering when they would get to the part when he would apologise. That, she could not wait to see.

At last, they got to the restaurant and were seated at their table. Emeka was in his car seat next to Ijeoma and was already starting to doze off. The waiter came by and presented them with their menus. Ijeoma was not interested in it. She was looking at Ifeanyi expectantly.

He cleared his throat. "I know it's much too late, and it probably doesn't mean anything to you, but I want you to know that I am sorry for the way I treated you in camp, and since then. I was selfish and didn't know how to care about anyone but myself. Please can you forgive me?"

Ijeoma just stared at him. Where was he going with this, she wondered?

"I want a do-over. I want to make things right between us. You're a great girl - lady - but I never really gave you a chance. I blamed you for getting pregnant and intruding on my life, but that was wrong. I see things clearer now."

"Why the sudden change, Ifeanyi? How do I know if this is real?"

"I don't know. But I hope, in time, I can prove to you that I have changed."

"So, what are you saying? You want to marry me now?"

"No. No, that's not what I am saying. I'm not ruling it out either," Ifeanyi sighed. This was harder than he thought. "If that is God's will for us..."

"Please don't bring God into this. I don't want you to marry me because God said so. Is that what you are doing?"

Ifeanyi looked at her, stunned. "Don't you believe in God?"

"I do," Ijeoma replied, soberly. "But people like to throw Him in when it's convenient. If I marry, I want it to be for love, not out of obligation."

"Me too," Ifeanyi replied, and Ijeoma fell silent as her eyes met with his.

"You still love Mary."

Ifeanyi swallowed. "Yes. But I don't believe there's only one person for us. Sometimes, the greatest love comes from the most unexpected places. I think we owe it to ourselves to try. I am willing to try."

Ijeoma thought about Chuka when Ifeanyi mentioned love from the most unexpected places. She looked away from Ifeanyi, feeling guilty.

Ifeanyi slid his hand across the table to hold hers. "We don't have to get married if you don't want to. I am not proposing marriage. I just want a chance to know you better...and to love you. What do you say?"

Ijeoma thought he looked so cute and sincere. She remembered their brief affair in camp. Even though he had deceived her, and the feelings were not mutual, she had been happy with him. She knew she could fall in love with him. But now Chuka was in the picture, and he made her feel wonderful. But she had to think of Emeka. If Ifeanyi was willing to love her from his heart, she could try too.

Ijeoma swallowed. "I am willing to try..."

20

"Verily, verily, I say unto you, except
a corn of wheat fall into the ground
and die, it abideth alone: but if it die,
it bringeth forth much fruit."

JOHN 12:24

Ifeanyi dropped Ijeoma at home and helped her carry Emeka up to her room. On his way out, he met her mother and bowed in greeting. "Good evening, ma."

"Good evening, Ifeanyi," Mrs Njokwu said, with a knowing smile. "How was your outing?"

"Fine, ma. How is Daddy?"

Mrs Njokwu's grin widened. *Daddy*, eh? "He's fine, my son. It's good to see you. You should come around more often."

Ifeanyi nodded and smiled at Ijeoma. "I will. Thank you, ma." He gave Ijeoma a goodbye hug. "Goodnight, Ijay."

"Goodnight," Ijeoma said, returning his smile. It had been a nice evening. Unexpected, but lovely. She'd forgotten what it was like to date Ifeanyi.

After he left, her mother squealed, and Ijeoma was embarrassed beyond measure. She was sure Ifeanyi would have heard her squeal, even if he had reached the end of their street by then!

"Mummy! Are you a child?!"

"I'm just so happy for you! But you have to admit, it is sweet, isn't it?" Mrs Njokwu asked, beaming at her child.

"Please don't get too excited, yeah? We're not talking marriage or anything, just being friendlier. Actually, I'm not even sure what we're doing, but please, don't get your hopes up."

"Hmmm... You can shush me all you want, but you can't stop me from dreaming...and planning. Just start dieting, because you'll be fitting into a size eight wedding gown in four months!" Mrs Njokwu chuckled.

Ijeoma rolled her eyes. She loved her mother dearly, but she was really one-track minded. "Goodnight, Mum," she said, and gave her mother a hug, before returning to her room.

Ijeoma got into her room just as her phone began to ring again. She ran to it, so that the call wouldn't wake Emeka. It was Chuka. He'd called twice already tonight. She considered cutting the call, because she knew what he was calling to ask about, and she wasn't sure she was ready to answer him. She quickly decided to answer it. She could always rush him off the phone.

"Hey... It's kinda late, Chuka. Emeka's sleeping," Ijeoma answered.

"Oh, sorry... I keep forgetting. I just wanted to know how it went with Ifeanyi tonight."

"It was okay. Can we talk tomorrow? I'm pretty tired now." She forced a yawn.

"Oh, okay. Goodnight, sweetheart. I'll call you tomorrow," Chuka said.

"Goodnight, Chuka."

Ijeoma hung up the line and sighed. What was she doing? She really liked Chuka, but she also liked Ifeanyi. And they had history. Ifeanyi was the safer bet, though. Her parents loved him. Emeka loved him. He was rich! Attractive. She wasn't keen on his new religious fanaticism, though. But she thought at least that meant he would be a faithful husband.

However, she connected with Chuka on so many levels. They had bonded easily, and he also showed genuine interest and love for Emeka. She had told Ifeanyi that she would try, but she really didn't understand his proposal. Were they dating? And were they exclusive? Couldn't she still continue her relationship with Chuka on the *hush hush* and see where that leads?

She was in turmoil over what to do. She wasn't the sort of Christian that carried such issues to God. He usually stayed out of her personal life, and she wanted to keep it that way. She was just going to play it by ear and watch Ifeanyi. If he really brings his 'A' game, then she'd kick Chuka to the curb, otherwise, she wasn't about to sabotage a good thing based on one of Ifeanyi's emotional or religious mood swings.

There! Now, she could sleep peacefully.

"Waaaaeeh!" Emeka cried, in time to remind her that new mothers never sleep peacefully!

It had been very embarrassing going to work after her third break up with Ifeanyi and, technically, second engagement cancellation! Especially with the gossip in the media about their 'secret' engagement. Mary had been receiving calls from old contacts, friends and family, who were calling to express their wishes, to enquire more into it, or to see if she would let them have a major part in her upcoming, high-profile wedding! It was like the nightmare wasn't ending.

At some point, she stopped answering calls because she got tired of giving the standard, "No, false alarm. I am not engaged," response and receiving the comeback, "Oh...okay. Soon, dear. Keep trusting God."

At the office, everyone knew by now that Ifeanyi was not a name to be mentioned ever again. They'd all been surprised to see her down cast when she had resumed work on Wednesday. And when she'd told them of the break-up, that there would be no more future with Ifeanyi, and she hoped they wouldn't ever bring his name up again, they got the message loud and clear.

Still, she got the occasional pity look from Aisha. And there were also the occasional slip ups by colleagues, who mentioned weddings they planned to attend in the month or had attended, and then everyone would remember Mary and look at her sadly or with shock, as if they had just stabbed her in the heart. And she would have to say, "It's okay. I'm fine," with a smile.

Mary withdrew and kept to herself more, as people kept on treating her as though she was glass or a fragile baby. Even Kelechi couldn't help but jump on the pity train. She would give her smiles, which carried the question, "How are you feeling today?" or "Oh, do you need a hug?" or "Poor thing. It is well." She knew that they were only trying to be nice, and she would have to give them time to work through her break-up with Ifeanyi too!

When others were not compelling her to think about her broken heart, she had enough trouble forgetting about it too. Her brothers were good about not bringing Ifeanyi up, although Daniel made the occasional slip and would receive a slap at the back of his head from either Samson or Samuel, who knew better. It was always met with a stern, "Leave your brother alone," from Mary.

Mary prayed more to get her mind off Ifeanyi and focused on God's will. But soon after praying, something else would remind her about him, and she would indulge in some 'poor me's for a while. She used poetry to express her feelings of loss, disappointment, confusion, and anger. Soon, she found the activity so relaxing and refreshing that she began to write more and expressed all her thoughts and anxieties through writing. It was quite therapeutic, as she was able to counsel herself, and the writings remained for her to reflect and learn from.

She kept the writings private, as she was careful what she shared on her blog, "Speak Now For Freedom." Her blog was not so popular yet, but Ifeanyi's family was well known, and so was her relationship with him, seeing as they were once publicly engaged. People were constantly looking for gossip to share about them, and she didn't want to give them anything to write about.

Mary also took advantage of her new church and busied herself with volunteering and serving in as many capacities as she could. They didn't know her well, and she was happy to have a safe place, where she was only known as Mary, and not Ifeanyi Chukwueke's ex.

It had been a month since his break-up with Mary. Ifeanyi still thought of her often. He'd called her a few times since, but she never picked his calls nor returned his messages. He figured that was her way of moving on, but it hurt that she could so easily forsake him. There was even a day he had been tempted to pay her a visit, but he had resisted the temptation and prayed instead.

He sighed as he realised that his resolve to forsake her had weakened. He had come to know the song "One day at a time, sweet Jesus" well. It was his silent mantra.

He realised that part of the problem was that he had no mentor nor confidant to help him through this time, to inspire and encourage him in his Faith. Mary had been his confidant, and she had been the one inspiring and encouraging him in the Faith too. His family were all Christian, in the sense that they believed in God and went to church, but he couldn't talk about spiritual things with them.

Whenever he wanted to discuss something he was reading in the Bible with one of them, their eyes would cloud over, or they would quickly change the topic to something in the news or some other random event. And even when they were interested in talking about their Faith or other spiritual things, they tended to disagree on their understanding of many things. So, their discussions would quickly turn to debates, and he would end up confused or frustrated.

Even the issue with pre-marital sex, for example. They all thought he was being fanatical about it. Well, Chidinma also claimed to believe in abstinence until marriage, but her belief was strictly regarding sex. She thought other things were okay, and Ifeanyi knew from experience that they weren't.

He felt like his faith was being put out, and he needed real fellowship with like-minded believers, who would help him stay on track and keep his eyes on God's will. He'd begun to attend mid-week fellowship at his church. The first time he attended, he was really rejuvenated, as what they talked about resonated with much of the challenges he had been having with his family. He had been so buzzed that he had collected the number of the pastor who led the mid-week service, with hopes that he could call him and discuss spiritual things on occasion.

He'd been intentional about making new friends at church, hoping to find more people he could connect with on a deep spiritual level. However, it seemed most of the men were keener on gaining business contacts than making new friends. They were always excited when they realised that he was a Chukwueke. They often asked if his father's group of companies would be interested in their business or idea. He had only made one friend since he started attending these services three weeks ago.

While the men were mostly interested in business, he was surprised to find that a lot of the women seemed only interested in finding a husband. There were a few that bore holes at the back of his head, during every meeting, with their stares. He had even been approached by a couple of young women after service on two separate occasions.

They came off friendly, but their mannerisms told him that they were interested in something more. He knew because that used to be his forte. He intentionally refused to ask for their numbers. However, that didn't stop one girl, who had apprehended him after his third week.

"Hey, Ifeanyi..." She had fluttered her lashes and given him a sweet smile.

"Hi... Ummm..." Ifeanyi had tried to recall her name.

"Kemi. We met last week. How are you doing?" Kemi had asked.

"I'm good. You?" Ifeanyi had replied, keeping his charm in check.

"Good. I liked your contribution today."

"Ummm... Thanks."

"Can I get your number?"

"Ummm... Okay." Ifeanyi had pulled out his business card and offered Kemi a smile.

"Aight... I'll talk to you later," Kemi had said before turning around and walking sensually away. Her tight blue jeans showed off her fantastic figure. Ifeanyi had closed his eyes and prayed for grace.

Ifeanyi thought of Ijeoma. He sighed. He wasn't sure if he was making any progress there either. They were as different as night and day. They connected on few things, and mainly Emeka. She talked a lot about the past and NYSC days. She never wanted to talk about anything spiritual, and he always wondered what sort of Christian she was.

But God had said to love her. He wondered if that meant he would eventually fall in love with her. He couldn't see it happening.

He made more effort to call her often, and they did more things together than before. He'd taken her to the movies a couple of times, and they went out to dinner once. He also visited her at home every Sunday because he knew her parents would be around and they would appreciate it. He also didn't want to be alone with her in her home after the last time she had tricked him.

He pressed his eyes shut and sighed deeply. He prayed in his spirit. *God, what am I doing wrong? Do I have this Christianity thing all wrong? I'm doing my best to be loving to Ijeoma, but apart from that, I really don't know what else You want me to do. It's three* months 'til the wedding, and our parents are still moving ahead with plans. Is marrying Ijeoma really Your will for me?

Wait. Trust Me.

Okay, Lord. Thank You.

21

"Verily, verily, I say unto you, except a corn of wheat fall into the ground and die, it abideth alone: but if it die, it bringeth forth much fruit."

JOHN 12:24

"I think we're going to need a bigger size," Ijeoma said, after they had struggled to fasten the size 8 wedding gown at the back.

Mrs Njokwu frowned. "Is it me or are your breasts bigger?"

Ijeoma looked up from admiring the ivory gown to her mother. "I don't know about bigger, but they are definitely firmer!" Ijeoma smiled to herself, admiring her reflection in the mirror. Her boobs looked delightful in the dress. If only they had been able to zip it up.

"When last did you get your period, honey?" Mrs Njokwu continued.

Ijeoma thought for a while. It had been like six weeks or so. "I don't know exactly, but it's definitely due. Believe me, I haven't *missed* it at all!" she giggled, stepping out of the dress and handing it to the Sales Assistant.

"Excuse us," Mrs Njokwu said to the Sales Assistant, to get some privacy. "Ijeoma, have you and Ifeanyi slept together?"

"No. He doesn't even touch me. Why do you ask?"

"Well, if I didn't know better, I'd think you were pregnant. I guess it's just delayed because of stress," Mrs Njokwu sighed.

Ijeoma finally caught on. She hadn't even considered that she could be. They had been using protection. "Ummm..." she muttered, not wanting to give anything away. "Maybe the fertility pills you gave me are affecting my cycle."

"Hmmm... Maybe that's it. Excuse us! Yes, we'll try the size 10," Mrs Njokwu called to the Sales Assistant.

"You're what?" Chuka gasped. "Are you *sure*? But how?"

Ijeoma wiped her nose with her sleeve. She had confirmed her mother's suspicions with a home pregnancy test, and she had driven over to see Chuka at his home in Yaba. Having another baby was the last thing she wanted or needed right then. And for another man?! What would people think?

"Yes, I'm sure! What do you mean, *how*? We've had sex a few times."

"Yes, I know. I was just surprised, 'cos we've been careful. And I know you're on the pill, so...it's like double protection." Chuka rubbed her back lovingly.

"What pill? I'm not on the pill."

"You're not? Sorry, I assumed you were because I found some small white pills in the drawer where you kept your condoms. I just thought they were contraceptives too," Chuka said.

"You went through my drawer?!" Ijeoma was alarmed. "Did you take any of the condoms?"

"Yeah... I took a few. I mean, you had so many. Was that wrong?"

Ijeoma plumped on the bed. *Damn it!* "What were you even doing, going through my drawer?"

"Sorry, I didn't mean to snoop. It's just that after the first time, I had used mine. I only had one on me, and I thought you wouldn't mind if we used yours. What's the problem? Aren't they *normal* condoms?"

Ijeoma rubbed her temples and pulled herself together. She couldn't give too much away. "Yes, they are. Sorry for making a fuss. I just like my privacy, you know?"

Actually, Chuka didn't, because Ijeoma had always been free with him. Her carefree and open personality was what had endeared her to him. She didn't appear to be the secretive nor private type. He couldn't understand why she had made a big deal about the condoms. "What are those pills for?" he asked, with suspicion.

Ijeoma looked up at him. She couldn't understand his expression. "What pills?"

"The white pills in your drawer, Ijay. Are you still taking them?"

"No, I'm not still taking them." Ijeoma was afraid of the direction of their discussion. "Look, I have to go." She stood up and picked up her handbag.

Chuka held her hand to prevent her from leaving. "What are the pills for, Ijay?"

Ijeoma swallowed. "They are fertility pills. But I stopped taking them ages ago."

Chuka dropped his hand and stared at Ijeoma as though he was trying to figure out who she was. "Why were you taking fertility pills?"

Ijeoma held her breath as she returned Chuka's look. They both knew why, but she was afraid to confess it. "Please, just forget about the pills, Chuka."

"How or why should I forget about the fact that you were taking fertility pills, and now you are SURPRISED that you are pregnant?! Tell me. Where the condoms spiked?"

"What? How can you ask me that?"

"Ijay, I'm losing patience and respect for you right now. You better tell me the truth, or I swear, I'll walk," Chuka fumed.

Ijeoma dropped to her knees. "Please, please. I'm sorry. I didn't mean to. It was my mum. She wanted me to seduce Ifeanyi so I could get pregnant for him again. Please, I was just under so much pressure."

Chuka took a deep breath. "So, you're telling me that I fell into the trap you and your mother had set for Ifeanyi? And now, *I'm* going to be a father, because of YOUR own scheming?"

Ijeoma just sobbed.

Chuka walked to the door and flung it open. "Get out!"

"No! Please, please, please, Chuka. Please. I love you..."

"LIAR!" He barked at her, as the tears gathered in his eyes. "Get out!"

"Please, Chuka. You can't throw me out. I am carrying your child."

"You listen to me. That child is not mine! Take it to Ifeanyi. See if he will take responsibility." Ijeoma scurried out of his room, ashamed and heartbroken. "And so you know, I never want to see you again." With that said, Chuka slammed the door shut in Ijeoma's face.

Ijeoma ran to her car and balled her eyes out.

"See what you've done?! See what you've done?!" Ijeoma exclaimed, after barging into her mother's room.

"What? What's wrong with you? How dare you–"

"Shut up, Mother! Just shut up! I should *never* have listened to you!" Ijeoma shouted hysterically.

Mr Njokwu stood up from where he was seated to investigate. Had Ijeoma gone mad? How could she talk to her mother like that?

"I'm pregnant!" Ijeoma declared, observing her father from a distance. "Your *stupid* plan backfired, Mother. The baby is not Ifeanyi's!"

"What plan?" Mr Njokwu turned his attention to his wife. He had been about ready to knock some sense into Ijeoma.

Mrs Njokwu looked between her husband and her child.

"Tell him, Mother! Tell him how you ruined my life with your juju and incessant plotting!" Ijeoma cried.

"*Juju*?" Mr Njokwu was even more confused now. "Ngozi, what is she talking about?"

"Philip, I don't know what has gotten into her. Ijeoma, if you're pregnant for another man other than Ifeanyi, you've only got yourself to blame!"

"*WHAT*?" Ijeoma exclaimed.

"And who is this unfortunate man? How did you manage to sneak about having sex with Emeka in tow?" Mrs Njokwu continued.

"Please, can someone tell me what the hell is going on here?" Mr Njokwu shouted, looking between his wife and his child. "And Ijeoma, I know we raised you better than to be talking to your mother as if she's your mate! Before you say another word, I want you to apologise to your mother!"

Ijeoma just stood fuming, looking at her mother. She couldn't bring herself to say sorry. What kind of mother would do what she had done? "I hate you! I hate you for this!" she said at last, before she ran out of their room.

"Come back here!" Mr Njokwu shouted to no avail. "Ngozi, what was Ijeoma talking about? Why is she talking to you this way?"

Mrs Njokwu swallowed. How was she going to explain this to her husband? "She's pregnant. I don't know what's gotten into her, but she thinks I am to blame."

"And why would she think that?"

"Because I gave her fertility drugs. You know, so that if she and Ifeanyi were to make love, she would be able to have another baby quickly."

"And why would she want to have another baby quickly? You couldn't wait until they got married? And what is this talk of juju?" Mr Njokwu studied his wife. She wasn't telling the whole truth.

"It's nothing, darling. It's just that Ifeanyi wasn't proposing, and he was still philandering with that Mary girl. We thought that if Ijeoma got pregnant again, he would finally settle down and marry her."

"So, you decided on *witchcraft*?" Mr Njokwu looked at his wife, shocked. "You were pregnant when we married... Was it by *juju* too?"

"No, Philip! Of course not!"

"Why don't I believe you? I always wondered why I haven't been able to father another child... Is Ijeoma even *mine*?!"

"Jesus! Philip?! How can you ask me that?" Mrs Njokwu couldn't believe how the conversation had turned so quickly.

"I don't know. I guess when I hear juju, I tend not to trust people anymore. And things are beginning to make sense."

Mrs Njokwu went to her husband and wrapped her arms around him. "Philip, I love you. I made a mistake, but Ijeoma is yours. I didn't do any juju on you."

"I want a paternity test," he said coldly and took her hands from around his neck. "And I want it done today!"

Oh God, oh God, oh God! Mrs Njokwu was shaking. What had she done?

Ijeoma didn't look up when her door opened. "Go away, Mother!"

"Ijay, baby, I'm sorry." Mrs Njokwu sat at the end of the bed.

"Please, just go away. You've done enough!"

"Please, forgive me. I only did what I did because I love you. I wanted what was best for you and Emeka," Mrs Njokwu pleaded.

"Then why didn't you just *pray*, Mum?! Why didn't you just *help* me? I could have gotten a job, met a nice guy...had a life! You had only *one* plan, Mum, and that was Ifeanyi! Even from the first time I told you we were dating in camp, all you ever cared about was Ifeanyi. In fact..." Ijeoma's eyes widened as realisation dawned on her. "NOOOO! You wouldn't have..."

Ijeoma turned to her mother, as the pieces fell into place. She shifted away from her in fear. *Who was this woman?*

Mrs Njokwu realised that she had been found out. Her shame was all over her face.

"*YOU!* You gave me the condoms I used with Ifeanyi in camp! You spiked them too!" Ijeoma accused. "*Mother*? You said you wanted me to be safe! What if I had gotten infected? What kind of mother *are* you?!"

"I don't know why you are angry and hating me all of a sudden," Mrs Njokwu said defensively. "Are you not months away from marrying Ifeanyi?"

"Mum, that's what YOU want! Not me! You never even bothered to ask me what I wanted. Emeka is *your* doing... And you made me feel bad? That will never happen again. Oh, you're *soooo* going to pay for this!" she said with pure disdain.

Mrs Njokwu looked at her child with terror. How did she get to be so vindictive? "I'm sorry," was all she could say. She stood up to leave, with all the dignity she could muster. "We need to go to the hospital."

"What for?" Ijeoma looked at her mother. All respect gone.

"Your first prenatal, of course, and to check that everything is fine with you. Like you said, you could be infected."

"No thanks to you," Ijeoma hissed.

Disgraced, Mrs Njokwu walked out of her daughter's room. She'd lost her daughter, and she was now afraid that she was about to lose her husband. Even though he had not been her first choice, she had grown to love him dearly.

Her first choice had been a man named Mr Gregory Edochie. His father owned an oil rig. She'd slept with both of them about the same time. When she found out she was pregnant, she had gone first to Greg, but he'd asked her to abort the baby, that he didn't love her. Philip, however, was excited that he could be a father and pledged his love and commitment.

She prayed that the paternity test would come back positive, otherwise, her life was over! Philip would surely throw her out of their home. And if he threw Ijeoma out too, she would never forgive herself.

♥ ♥ ♥

Ifeanyi was at home watching TV with his sister. His phone rang, and he lazily picked it up.

"Uh, slow down, Ijay. What's going on? WHAT? How? You mean *you* and *Chuka*? Oh, wow. Calm down, calm down."

"Oh, Ifeanyi, I don't know what to do, and I don't have anyone else to turn to. Please, I need you. Emeka needs you!" Ijeoma cried into the phone.

"Don't worry. I'm coming. Everything will be okay. Just stay calm and don't do anything rash, until I get there." He hung up the call.

"What's going on?" Chidinma asked, curiously.

"There seems to be some commotion at Ijeoma's house. I have to go and see," he said, getting up and going to his room to get dressed more appropriately.

"That family is so strange. I can't believe you're actually planning on marrying into that!" Chidinma said.

Ifeanyi smiled. "I don't think there's going to be a wedding after all!"

22

"Verily, verily, I say unto you, except a corn of wheat fall into the ground and die, it abideth alone: but if it die, it bringeth forth much fruit."

JOHN 12:24

When Ifeanyi got to Ijeoma's house, the sun was just going down. He was surprised to see Ijeoma, Emeka, and Mrs Njokwu outside their home crying. As he approached them, the door opened, and Mr Njokwu flung out a few more bags belonging to his wife on their driveway. Ifeanyi quickly ran to the man before he closed the door.

"Sir... Sir! Please, what is going on?" he asked as he took in the scene.

Mr Njokwu didn't answer him but shut the door. Ifeanyi turned to Mrs Njokwu, "Mummy, what happened?" But she was too hysterical to answer him. She just wailed with her hands on her head.

Ijeoma was rocking a crying Emeka and sobbing quietly. "Ijay, what happened?" Ifeanyi asked.

"My father is throwing us out of the house! Apparently, it was something my mother did years ago. I can't even understand how he will throw me and his grandson out for what his wife did to him," Ijeoma responded, bitterly.

Ifeanyi didn't know what to make of her response. Mr Njokwu appeared again and threw out another couple of bags. "Ahmed! Come and carry this rubbish out! And lock the gate!" He eyed Ifeanyi. "Eh, what do you want?"

"Sir, please. I just want to understand what is going on. Please, can I come in?" Ifeanyi asked, bowing his knee.

"You have not asked the witch? Let her tell you."

"Sir, please. She's too distraught to answer me. I just thought we could talk, man to man. Please." Ifeanyi prostrated.

Mr Njokwu sighed deeply but decided to open the door for Ifeanyi to enter. Ahmed arrived just as Ifeanyi was going inside. "Carry these things and throw them out of my compound!" Mr Njokwu said, before he shut and locked the door behind them.

Ifeanyi followed Mr Njokwu to the bar in their living room, where the older man brought down two glasses and a bottle of vodka. Ifeanyi raised his hand to turn down the drink, but the look Mr Njokwu gave him made him rescind. "I'll just have a little, sir. Not much of a drinker."

"You'll drink some more when you realise what you just escaped!" Mr Njokwu joked, his eyes filled with bitterness.

Ifeanyi tried on a smile while he got some coke to mix with his vodka. He took a sip, swallowed, then proceeded with his question. "What happened, sir?"

"Ijeoma is not mine," Mr Njokwu said and took a swig of his undiluted drink.

Ifeanyi almost choked on the mixture he had just taken and then almost spat it out before he composed himself. His eyes widened. "How do you know that?"

"I requested a paternity test. It turns out my wife has been lying to me for 24 years!"

"I'm so sorry, sir," Ifeanyi said genuinely. "But maybe she didn't know. Maybe she really believed you were the father..."

Mr Njokwu raised an eyebrow at Ifeanyi. "Do you really believe that?"

Ifeanyi swallowed. For some reason, he didn't. He cleared his throat. "But, sir, Ijeoma is still your daughter. You're the only father she knows. You raised her up. Don't you love her? And Emeka, he's your grandson too..."

Mr Njokwu gritted his teeth. "I've done my duty! 24 years of caring for another man's child, believing that she is mine. No... I owe them nothing."

"But you must love her... You can't have raised her up all these years and not have one trace of love for her. She didn't know she was not your daughter. She loves you as the only father she has ever known and will ever know! Do you really want to throw away your relationship with her and your grandchild because of what her mother did? Sir, that's not fair."

Mr Njokwu frowned and reached for the bottle of vodka to top up his drink, but Ifeanyi placed a gentle hand on his, causing their eyes to meet. "Do you have other children, sir?" he dared to ask. Mr Njokwu's dark eyes revealed the truth, though he didn't answer. "Do you want more children, sir?" Mr Njokwu clenched his jaw. "Even if you had more children, Ijeoma is irreplaceable. She was a gift, even if she wasn't yours by blood. You are a father! Show her a father's love."

Mr Njokwu relaxed. "Do you know that Ijeoma is pregnant again?"

Ifeanyi nodded. "I do, sir."

"Did she by any chance tell you the baby isn't yours?"

"Well, she didn't have to, sir," Ifeanyi replied.

Mr Njokwu raised an eyebrow. "So, do you still plan on marrying her? Will you look after her child and love him or her like you love Emeka?"

Ifeanyi swallowed. "Well, marriage wasn't our plan. But I will look after Ijeoma and her children because I love her, and we are family."

"Because of Emeka?"

"Yes, we have a lifelong bond now."

"Hmmm... So, it doesn't bother you that she plotted with my wife to trap you with another baby?" Mr Njokwu asked, looking intently at Ifeanyi. The widening of his eyes revealed that he didn't know that part. "So, she didn't tell you that part." Mr Njokwu slid Ifeanyi's hand from his and poured himself another drink while he watched Ifeanyi's expression change. "It hurts, doesn't it?"

Ifeanyi remained quiet as he processed the new information and tried to think of something more he could say in Ijeoma's favour.

"You think you know someone, but you only know what they reveal. I thought I knew my wife... I thought I knew Ijeoma. But they were two strangers in my house. And Ijeoma is a replica of her mother! Down to her deceitful ways. I'd rather be childless!" He took another swig.

Ifeanyi shook his head. "No, Ijeoma is not like her mother at all. She has a good heart. I think she takes after you more than you realise!"

Mr Njokwu grunted and took another swig.

"Daddy, please... Don't cast Ijeoma away. Forgive, or you'll be the one to suffer. Find it in your heart to forgive your wife too."

"I think it's time for you to go," Mr Njokwu said, conclusively. "If you love them so much, take them into your house!"

"I can't take what is yours, sir. You need them. Yes, they messed up. That's what people do. But we forgive, and we try again. Now the truth is out, you can love even *deeper*. You can *choose* to love..."

"It's enough! It's only *Christians* that will make the injured party look like the guilty one! Have you saved any speech for them? Get out of my house!" Mr Njokwu hissed.

"Sir, please don't act out of blind rage! You will regret it. And your drink is clouding your judgement–"

Whaamm! Ifeanyi received a hard slap across his face for his daring. He was stunned, and so was Mr Njokwu. But he still raised another threatening hand at Ifeanyi. To his surprise, Ifeanyi didn't resist but rather closed his eyes and turned his other cheek to him. The second slap didn't come.

"I'm sorry. I don't know what got into me," Mr Njokwu said, soberly.

Ifeanyi swallowed and rubbed his bruised cheek. "It's okay. I forgive you."

"How can you be so forgiving? You would forgive two women who connived to ruin your life? Why don't you just walk away?" Mr Njokwu looked at Ifeanyi, perplexed.

"Because I know who I was and how much mercy God has shown me. We all need forgiveness. And those who have been forgiven much, love much. That's what Jesus said," Ifeanyi replied. "How much has God forgiven you?"

To his surprise, Mr Njokwu started to cry. "You're the son I always wanted!" he sobbed.

"I am still your son! As long as Ijeoma is your daughter, you can count me as a son, Dad. See how much God has blessed you?"

Mr Njokwu pulled Ifeanyi into his arms and hugged him. "Thank you! Thank you, son!"

Emeka was sleeping when Ifeanyi and Mr Njokwu finally opened the door. Ijeoma stood up quickly from where she was sitting by the doorway and turned to look at both of them, wishing for good news. Mr Njokwu went to her, wrapped her in his embrace, and cried.

Mrs Njokwu looked at Ifeanyi and then at her husband and child, unsure what was going on and what the verdict on her was. Ifeanyi gave her a reassuring smile, and hope resurfaced in her heart. Mr Njokwu turned to his wife. Despite her deception, he still loved her. And he knew that was why it had hurt him so much.

He remembered Ifeanyi's words, *"Now the truth is out, you can love even deeper."* He opened his arms to invite his wife into their embrace, and she ran to him and cried.

"I'm so sorry, Philip. I'm so sorry," she said.

"I love you. I love you both," was all Mr Njokwu could say through the lump in his throat. And this felt so much better than the rage that had begun to consume him. Forgiveness felt better.

Mary walked to the bus stop, to wait for a bus to Ajegunle, after attending mid-week service at her church. As she walked, she pondered on the message that had been shared. They had read the story of Jonah, and different people had shared various lessons. One girl had shared a lesson that really stuck with Mary.

She had talked about how we can know that we are walking out of God's will by the chaos in our lives. That when we are disobedient to God's revealed will, we can only meet turbulence on the path we choose, as He will frustrate us to guide us back on track. But if we are walking in God's will, He will certainly give us peace on every side.

As she pondered on the lesson and what others had shared, Mary considered her life. Since she met Ifeanyi, there had been one turbulence after the other hindering them from being together. She wondered if deciding to date him in the first place was an act of disobedience, and God had been trying to get her back on track by frustrating their plans to be together. But she was still unsure what His will was for her. Had He already shown her His will, and she had run from it, Mary wondered?

She realised that she had been waiting for the bus for a while, and it was unusually late in coming tonight. She didn't feel good asking people for lifts, since she knew her home was a bit out of the way for most people. She also liked the space to think through her thoughts after the service, and usually, when she accepted offers for lifts, she ended up having to engage in small talk with the kind driver, so she wasn't really able to think.

Just then, she heard a horn. A man had stopped and wound down his window. "Hey, can I give you a lift?"

Mary stepped back. She didn't like to take lifts from strangers, though she knew there were many well-meaning people who were just trying to be charitable, who offered lifts to strangers. However, she tended to turn down such offers, especially at night.

"Mary, it's me, David," the man stuck his head out and smiled. "Come on, let me take you home."

Mary was shocked to see that it was David who was offering her a lift. She considered the coincidence because she had just been thinking about whether or not God had revealed His will to her and she had rejected it. She remembered how David had told her that God had told him that she was his wife. Mary swallowed hard. *God, are You saying something to me?* Just then, it started to drizzle.

Mary approached David's car. "Thank you. But I'll be fine. My bus will be here any minute, and I don't want to inconvenience you."

"Mary, get in already. It's raining!" David said, smiling at her as if he could read her mind.

Mary ran to the passenger side and got into the car. "Thank you," she said, returning his smile. After what she had done to him, she never thought she would see him again, let alone that he would be so forgiving and kind towards her.

"You're one tough cookie, you know?" David said, and giggled, before driving away.

23

"Verily, verily, I say unto you, except a corn of wheat fall into the ground and die, it abideth alone: but if it die, it bringeth forth much fruit."

JOHN 12:24

Mary hugged David and wished him "good night" before letting herself out of his car. She smiled to herself as she shut the door. They had had a surprisingly pleasant ride and caught up on each other's lives.

Mary was happy to know that David was in a new relationship. He recently started dating a lady from his church, who was also called Mary. They had been friends in their childhood but had lost touch when she travelled to America to complete her studies. He had always fancied her, so when he noticed her in church about a week after Mary dumped him, he was excited.

They started talking again, and he finally got the nerve to ask her out about a fortnight ago. They are blissfully happy!

He was no longer resentful over their break-up and felt that Mary had freed him to fall in love with his true love. He had been happy to find Mary waiting at the bus-stop, and it was good closure for him; to forgive and to let her know that he was happy and had found *his* Mary!

Mary didn't have to tell him that things didn't work out between her and Ifeanyi. He already knew, but he didn't rub it in. He simply told her that he had come to know that "timing is everything," and she should continue to trust in God for her 'soul mate.'

Mary turned and waved goodbye as David drove away. She sighed deeply. So, he was not 'the *One*' either... She was relieved and also hopeful. She had no more ties in the past and was excited about what the future might have in store for her.

Chuka was on his bed, browsing on his phone and scrolling endlessly through Facebook. He didn't know what he was looking for, since he had unfriended Ijeoma and even blocked her from contacting him on any of his social media platforms. He knew he missed her, but he couldn't forgive her betrayal.

There was a knock on the door. He wasn't expecting anyone, and he didn't want to be disturbed, so he just ignored it. It came again. He got up and went to see who it was. He was stunned to find Ifeanyi at his doorway. He had only ever visited him at home once, but he didn't have to guess what this visit was about.

"Hi, Chuka," Ifeanyi greeted. "Won't you let me in?"

"What do you want?" he asked coldly, not giving way for Ifeanyi to enter.

"I came to say I'm sorry. I really am, Chuka. I was not a good friend to you. I was totally selfish, and I was wrong to have dated Ijeoma, knowing that you had feelings for her. Please forgive me."

Chuka sighed deeply and moved out of the way so Ifeanyi could come in. "Is that all you came to say?" He remained by the door and crossed his arms protectively over his chest.

"I know Ijeoma's pregnant with your baby."

"That baby is not mine," Chuka replied, coldly.

"If you want to disown the baby, that's fine. But you can't deny that the child is *your* seed. And Ijeoma loves you. You could be happy with her if you would just forgive..."

"Forgive what exactly? That she used me to get over you? That she had intended to carry *your* baby and is now stuck with mine? That because of her cunning, I am now a father, before I am ready?"

"Do you love her?" Ifeanyi asked simply.

"No."

Ifeanyi stared down at Chuka, who returned a glare. "Okay, well. I guess it doesn't matter then. I'm sorry I bothered you."

Ifeanyi approached the door, and Chuka stopped him. "What if I do? What difference does it make?"

Ifeanyi sighed. "It means you can forgive. And you can have what you've always wanted... Ijeoma, and a child of your own. You can choose to be a victim, or you can realise that YOU won! The woman you love loves you too, and you're going to have a family, but the only thing standing in your way is your ability to forgive. The moment you do, everything changes. So, what will it be?"

Chuka sighed and went to sit on the bed. "You make it sound so simple..."

"It really is that simple. This won't be the last fight you will have with Ijeoma! But it can be the first. You can enjoy a loving relationship, once you realise that no one is perfect. Don't stand in the way of your own happiness."

"But how can I ever trust her again? She tricked me."

"No, she didn't. She meant to trick me. I am the one who ought to be angry with her."

"Yeah... But now you're off the hook," Chuka grunted spitefully.

"How can you say that? I'm still Emeka's father. I love Ijeoma." Chuka frowned. "Not like you, but I *do* love her. And if you want to pass up on this opportunity, this blessing to have her as *your* family, that's *your* loss. She'll always be my family."

"Wow, you've really changed! What about Mary?" Chuka asked, soberly.

Ifeanyi closed his eyes for a moment and sighed. "I don't know. We broke up, and I don't think we're ever getting back together. I can't think of her right now. This is not about us. Right now, I'm more concerned about Ijeoma, and I just want to know if you're going to be a man and stand by her, or if I'll be doing that on my own..."

"Did she tell you that she loves me...?" Chuka asked, nervously.

"She didn't have to tell me. And I know you know it too."

"Oh God! This was not my plan at all. I am not ready to be a father, not even ready to be a husband. But she needs me to be," Chuka said, rubbing his hand over his head. "This is too much."

"No one is saying you have to marry each other... At least, not now. Of course, if you both love each other, it's better you than me..."

"You can't possibly marry her now... *Would you?*" Ifeanyi just stared at Chuka.

"Oh, God! I've got to make an honest woman out of her, haven't I?"

Ifeanyi grinned and nodded. "Yup. I think it's time to grow up, Chuka. Things don't always go as we planned. Sometimes, they work out better."

"You're right. You're so right. Come here, man!" Chuka stood up and received Ifeanyi in his embrace. "I'm going to be a father! We're going to be family!"

Ifeanyi laughed. "We're already family!" And the friends embraced again.

When they pulled apart, Chuka looked at Ifeanyi, squarely. "Thank you. I really appreciate this. And I'm sorry for what I said about Mary being a whore and getting pregnant for someone else. I didn't mean it. I was just angry."

Ifeanyi swallowed and gave a slight smile. "Thank you for your apology. All's forgiven."

Ijeoma was sitting in Ifeanyi's car. He had asked her to wait while he went in and talked to Chuka. Her stomach was tied up in knots as she waited to see if Ifeanyi would work the same magic he had worked on her father. She kept remembering Chuka's angry words and was afraid that he would reject her again.

It seemed like forever before she saw Ifeanyi walk alone out of Chuka's home. Her heart sank. Chuka didn't want her.

Then she saw him come out of the door moments later. Her heart leaped for joy. She composed herself and got out of the car.

Chuka smiled when he saw Ijeoma. His heart was filled with warmth at the sight of her. She looked even more beautiful since he last saw her.

"Baby, I'm sorry..." she started to say, but he pulled her into his arms and silenced her with a kiss. Ijeoma kissed him back passionately, pressing her body against his.

Ifeanyi went into his car to sit and wait for the lovers to separate. He distracted himself with his mobile phone, as he checked his notifications on social media. After five minutes, and they were still kissing, he started his engine and honked. Chuka waved for him to leave, his lips still meshed with Ijeoma's.

Ifeanyi shook his head and giggled before driving away.

When Ifeanyi got home, he was filled with joy and began to praise and worship God in his room. He finally understood why God had wanted him to wait and what He had meant by *love* Ijeoma. He really could not have been used to intervene in her life if he didn't love her genuinely and deeply.

Over the last couple of days, he'd felt God's love and grace in his life more and more, and he understood more the power and wisdom of the cross. He had a deeper appreciation of the Gospel message and the new life he had been called to. He rejoiced, not so much in his freedom from no longer having to marry Ijeoma, but in the mysterious, wonderful ways God had worked all things out for the good of all.

As he thanked and worshipped God, Mary was the last thing on his mind. He had no desire to bring her name to Him again... to bless their love. He had learnt to trust God and had experienced how amazing it was to walk in God's will and he just wanted to be led and used by Him. He truly believed that whatever God had in mind for him would far surpass his own imagination and expectations, and he glorified God in that knowledge.

After his time of praise and worship, Ifeanyi settled down to study the Scriptures and pray. He was disturbed by a knock on the door. The person opened before he could respond. He turned around to see that it was his father.

"I hope I am not disturbing you," Chief Chukwueke said, with a short smile, as he stood at the door.

Ifeanyi sat up straight on his bed. "No, it's okay, Dad. What is it?"

His father looked around his room. It had been a long time since he had been in there. He settled down on the three-seater sofa across from Ifeanyi's bed and smiled at him. "How are you doing?"

"I'm fine, Dad," Ifeanyi said, with a closed smile. He was wondering what the purpose of this unexpected visit was.

Chief Chukwueke cleared his throat. "Mr Njokwu told me what you did for him and his family yesterday. He was very impressed by your actions actually."

Ifeanyi maintained his smile, not knowing what to say.

"I was wrong about you. You've really proven yourself, and I want you to know that I'm proud of you."

Ifeanyi met his father's gaze and opened his smile. "Thanks, Dad. I appreciate that."

"I think I was wrong about Mary too... I shouldn't have forbidden you from seeing her. I just..." he sighed and leaned forward in his seat. "I was just worried that you were not thinking straight, and..."

"It's okay, Dad. I understand."

"Are you guys still in touch?" Chief Chukwueke asked. Ifeanyi shook his head.

"Wow... So, you mean you *obeyed* me?" Chief Chukwueke said, a smile curving his lips. He was more than a little surprised.

"Well, not quite. I wanted to stay in touch, but she cut me off," Ifeanyi replied honestly.

"Oh. But you still love her, don't you?" Chief Chukwueke asked.

"It doesn't matter anymore, Dad. It's in the past now."

"No... I think it matters. She really brought out the best in you. When you find someone like that, you hang on to them," Chief Chukwueke said, holding Ifeanyi's gaze. "Get in touch with her, and let's iron this thing out."

Ifeanyi was starting to get emotional. "Daddy, please. It's okay. I appreciate what you're trying to do, but what has been done has been done. It's good to know you're no longer against us, but what is more important to me is what God says. I need to follow His leading on this. I hope you understand."

Chief Chukwueke stood up from his seat. "Alright. You do what you feel is right." He sighed. "I just want you to be happy. I love you, son."

Ifeanyi stood up and hugged his father. "I love you too, Dad. Thank you."

Father and son separated, and Chief Chukwueke left Ifeanyi's room. Ifeanyi let out a deep sigh after he was gone. The truth was that his father's removal of his objection had made him excited about Mary again, such that he was afraid that he would revert to making her the centre of his world. He was still learning to distinguish God's voice, and after the mess his emotions had caused earlier, he wanted to be careful about acting on them again.

He wondered if he would ever be able to hear God say 'yes' for Mary, now that he was so on guard against self-deception, due to his own strong feelings. He prayed again his prayer of surrender, asking God to change his heart and desires according to His will. He asked that, if God wanted him to reconcile with Mary, that He would reveal His will undeniably and unambiguously, otherwise, she would remain forsaken. He prayed also that God would minister to her and reveal His will to her too.

Ifeanyi continued with his reading of the second chapter of Paul's second letter to Timothy. At verse 22, the words jumped at him, and he felt he had just heard God clearly concerning the direction and focus his life ought to take. He read it again and again. It read:

"Flee also youthful lusts: but follow righteousness, faith, charity, peace, with them that call on the Lord out of a pure heart."

24

"Verily, verily, I say unto you, except a corn of wheat fall into the ground and die, it abideth alone: but if it die, it bringeth forth much fruit."

JOHN 12:24

T he months passed. Slowly at first, but soon, the season of Christmas was upon the Lagosians. The shops had their sale items on display, and the malls were decorated in red and green. The churches didn't delay in joining the hype and putting up their Christmas trees, even in November.

Mary had finally settled into her new church and had made new friends too. She was among a team of four Sunday School teachers and was taking the lead to organise the Christmas drama that the Young Teens, ages 13 to 16, would be presenting. The story of Joseph and Mary, and Jesus in the Manger, was about to get a Nigerian make-over. Mary smiled to herself as she looked over the script she was working on.

The twins had completed their secondary schooling and passed their WAEC and JAMB exams with flying colours. They were now doing one year of A'Level, with plans to study Computer and Electrical Engineering at the University of Lagos. Mary was saving towards their tuition, even though they had been promised a scholarship from a charity organisation if the boys would make 'A' in both A'Level Maths and Physics. Unless they got distracted, that would be an easy feat for them.

Daniel was now in Junior Secondary Level Two and was very studious. Now that he was in a public school, there were lots of children in his class, and his teachers didn't allow much time for questions. He did a lot of extra reading to ensure that he understood. Fortunately, his brilliant brothers were kind to help him in the subjects which they excelled at.

Mary continued to work on her blog, "Speak Now For Freedom," even though things had slowed down since the initial buzz around 'the Bolaji Scandal,' as it was still called in media circles. There were still many women and young girls who approached her for advice and guidance, and a few had even benefited from Browne Law Firm's intervention. Even though she helped a lot of women, she hardly got any feedback to know if things had improved in their lives, but she always remembered to bring their cases to God for Him to intervene and work all things out to His glory.

She was happy when she got an invitation by email to attend a Marriage Renewal ceremony for one of the women who had come to her for counselling. She'd only met 29-year-old Tejumola once, and at the time, it seemed like a hopeless case because she wasn't ready to receive Jesus. Mary had attended the ceremony, which was held at their home, just last week. It was a small beautiful ceremony, and she was so happy to hear their testimony, which they shared during the reception.

Mary still thought of Ifeanyi from time to time, and each time he came to mind, she would simply say a prayer for him. It was her way of loving him, by entrusting him to God's love and care, rather than selfishly pining for his affections. Lately, he had been coming to mind more often, and so she had been praying for him a lot.

The other day, she had a dream, which she didn't quite understand. In the dream, she was at the market and had lost her ring. It was the second diamond engagement ring Ifeanyi had purchased for her. She was in tears because she was sure she would never find it. If she had dropped it in a market stall, anyone who saw it would surely keep it. She looked around for it, crying.

A market woman asked her what the problem was, and she told her about her ring and how important it was to her. The lady told her not to worry. She rounded everyone to search for the ring, and Mary was surprised as everyone stopped what they were doing to look for her ring. A small boy was the one who found it and brought it to her. She was so joyful and tearful, seeing how they had all come together to restore her ring to her. She thanked them all profusely.

The market woman said, *"Wear it, so that you don't lose it again!"* And that was when she woke up. She prayed for a meaning, but she received no understanding. She had the ring in her drawer, and she had never worn it out of her home since they broke up. After that dream, she checked for the ring, and found it exactly where she had left it. She put it away and decided to put the dream up to anxiety. Again, she prayed for Ifeanyi.

Ifeanyi and Chuka were best friends again. This time, they were also Brothers in Christ. After his reconciliation with both Ijeoma and Ifeanyi, Chuka was so moved by Ifeanyi's transformation that he invited himself to Ifeanyi's church. Ijeoma started to attend the church with them about a month later. They both gave their lives to Christ in September.

Ifeanyi was overjoyed for them. He remembered when he had given his life to Jesus more than a year before. He had grown so much since then. He remembered Mary and wondered how she was doing. He prayed for her and hoped she was happy.

In October, Chuka proposed to Ijeoma, and she said "yes" without hesitation. They set their wedding date for Valentine's Day, the following year, a month after their baby would have been born. The Njokwus and Uzokas realised that they were already family friends, with at least four marriages across their tribes in the last three generations.

Baby Emeka turned one year old in the first week of December, and they held a small house party for him at Ijeoma's home last weekend. He was growing fast and had already started walking short distances by the time he celebrated his first birthday. He also loved to say 'Daddy.' It was his first word, and he used it whenever he saw Ifeanyi.

Ifeanyi continued to attend the mid-week services at his church regularly and was now actively serving in the church, as part of the Evangelism Team. He made and kept many friends, as he became well known at the church. Kemi was among his friends. She had hoped for something more, but he had told her honestly that he wasn't ready to pursue a serious relationship with anyone. She was now dating another guy from church and liked to pick Ifeanyi's brain about how men think!

Chief and Mrs Chukwueke observed all the changes in their son and were inspired about taking the Faith they professed more seriously. They took the Discipleship Course together and were strengthened in their Faith and devotion to one another. They maintained an alliance with the Njokwus, which was profitable for both families. Mr and Mrs Njokwu had given their lives to Christ in May and joined the Chukwuekes in taking the discipleship programme, which ran at their church.

Chidinma was in a serious relationship. Ifeanyi knew it was serious, because she actually wanted to talk about it with him. Most of the time, she would keep her affairs to herself. But she had been dating this guy for six months now, and Ifeanyi finally learnt what his name was; Emmanuel Atiyota. At 30, Chidinma was anxious about getting married, and Ifeanyi tried to tell her she shouldn't be.

Nomnso would be coming home next week for Christmas, and Ifeanyi was looking forward to having him around. They mostly connected on Facebook, which Nomnso was very active on. He posted photos almost every day. He was enjoying his life in the States, but he always talked about how he missed 'Naija.'

Christmas time was always a good time to be home in Nigeria. The weather was perfectly hot and breezy too, so it was always a chance for those who hated the cold to return to a warm and more pleasant climate. It was also the time for lots of parties and weddings. Ifeanyi had been invited to three weddings already. That's almost one wedding a week in December.

He wasn't too keen on all the fanfare around this time. He felt that the true meaning of Christmas was hidden in all the commercialism, even though he had always liked the colourful Christmas decorations. He thought he had seen it all, until someone walked into his office wearing a 'Christmas' t-shirt. It wasn't the usual Christmas t-shirt with a rain-deer, or Santa, or even a nativity scene. This particular t-shirt just had a Bible verse on it in big green print.

"Matthew one twenty," Ifeanyi read the verse aloud.

"Do not be afraid to take Mary as your wife, for the One conceived in her is from the Holy Spirit," the man recited off-hand.

"*Huh*?" Ifeanyi creased his brows and looked strangely at the man.

"That's what the verse says. Well, the second half. You're the first person to ever ask me about this shirt! Most people just ignore it," he continued.

"Hmmm... Interesting. Why that verse?" Ifeanyi asked, intrigued.

"Oh, I've got others... I actually design t-shirts to spark people's curiosity about the Bible. This is from my collection of "Random Bible Verses." It's one of my favourite ones to wear around Christmas time," the man said.

"Oh, okay. Do you work here? I've never seen you before." Ifeanyi sat up straight and looked at the stranger squarely.

"No. Do you know Jesus?"

Ifeanyi smiled. "Yes, I do."

"Will you buy my t-shirt? Then you can wear it, and maybe you can spark up a conversation with the next person who asks you..."

Hmmm... Ifeanyi thought. *What a strange way to preach the Gospel.* "Okay. How much?"

He paid for the t-shirt and watched the strange man walk away. He noticed that he didn't bother to solicit anyone else to buy his t-shirts. He looked at the red t-shirt and shook his head before putting it aside to continue his work.

Later that afternoon, his pen began to bleed and wasn't working properly. He shook it gently, and it fell apart, causing the ink to splash on his white office shirt. It was a horrible mess. He went out to wash his hands, and people kept staring at his shirt. On his way back to his office, someone said, "Don't you have a t-shirt you can change into? Your shirt is distracting."

So, he changed into the t-shirt that he had just purchased, even though it was bright red. The green writing was all that was on it. His boss came in and asked why he was wearing that, and he explained what happened with his pen.

"Okay. I need you to run down to Mega Plaza and get me these things. My P.A had to go for a medical appointment. Pregnant women, eh?"

"Okay, sir." Ifeanyi frowned at the list of things. *He could have sent the security guard to get these*, he thought.

Fortunately, Mega Plaza was just down the street from his office in Victoria Island, so he didn't have to drive. As he walked down the street, he got a lot more strange looks than he had gotten with his ink blotted shirt. When he had picked up the items and was at the cashier, the lady in front of him said, "Don't be afraid to take Mary as your wife..."

Ifeanyi looked up confused, then smiled. "Oh, the t-shirt. You know your Bible verses." The lady simply smiled.

By the time he got back to his office, five more people had said the exact same thing to him, and he wondered if the sales-man was being completely honest that people normally ignore him! He presented the things he had gotten to his boss, who collected them and smiled at him.

"Don't be afraid to take Mary for your wife..." his boss said, looking at Ifeanyi pointedly, as if he was speaking to him and not reciting a verse. Ifeanyi was dumbfounded. *What was going on?!*

"You *too*?" he asked his boss. "But the verse isn't that popular."

"Oh... I looked it up," he admitted. "When I first saw it, I didn't know what it said, so I looked it up. Are you okay?"

Ifeanyi rubbed his head and excused himself. His heart was racing. When he got to his office, he shut the door and prayed. "God, is this YOU trying to tell me something?"

You asked Me to be clear.

Ifeanyi laughed when he received that word in his spirit. He punched the air and shouted, "Praise God!" He began to sing praises to God and worship Him, speaking in tongues as the Spirit gave him utterance.

He couldn't focus on his work after that revelation. He was too excited, and thinking of all the ways he could propose to Mary. It had to be perfect. He would need some help. He decided to call Chuka.

"Hey, bro... What's up?" Chuka asked, cheerfully.

"Do you know if Mary still works at Browne Law Firm? I need a favour," Ifeanyi started.

"At last!" Chuka shouted with glee, when Ifeanyi had told him of his intentions. "Praise God! Man, we've been waiting for you to get on board. I'm so happy for you."

Ifeanyi chuckled. It was time. And this time, no one and *nothing* would stand in the way of their love...

25

"Verily, verily, I say unto you, except a corn of wheat fall into the ground and die, it abideth alone: but if it die, it bringeth forth much fruit."

JOHN 12:24

Mary knocked on Kelechi's door and waited for her to say, "Come in," before she opened it to enter. Kelechi was engrossed in something on her desk but smiled radiantly at Mary when she saw her.

"Excuse me, ma," Mary began, nervously. "I noticed the bonus you gave me for this year. It's a lot, ma. I was wondering if it was a mistake."

Kelechi's smile widened. *Trust Mary to ask.* She shook her head. "No. I think you earned it."

Mary breathed out a sigh of relief. She smiled. "Thank you. I'm so grateful."

"No problem at all. By the way, what are you doing this weekend?" Kelechi asked.

Mary thought for a moment. They had drama rehearsals for the Christmas play. "I have rehearsals at church. Why?"

"I wanted to invite you to my brother's engagement party. Wouldn't you like to come?"

"You mean Chuka is getting married?" Mary asked, excitedly. *That means Ifeanyi will be there.* "I don't think I can make it, but I'm happy for him."

"Are you worried about seeing Ifeanyi again?" Kelechi asked.

Mary looked down nervously and nodded. "Besides, I don't have anything to wear."

"Can't you get a nice dress with your bonus?" Kelechi asked and winked. "Come on, it will be fun! It's Christmas, and you need a family celebration. So, will you come?"

"Oh, I don't know... Let me pray about it," Mary said at last. "Thanks for inviting me. I appreciate it."

"Okay. But let me know by tomorrow, okay? It's a closed affair, and I need to let the caterers know how many we're expecting."

"Okay, ma. Thank you," Mary said and then left Kelechi's office.

She was already excited at the thought of seeing Ifeanyi again, but she remembered her dream about their affair, and she wondered if she wouldn't revert to her old longing for him after seeing him again. She prayed for God's guidance, and she received a peaceful word. *Go. Don't be afraid.* It was discernible from all the chaos in her head, and she knew she could trust it.

Mary bought a nice dress from Ikeja City Mall. It was the first time that she had bought anything so lovely for herself. She tried to get something as close to her budget as possible, so she could still save some of her bonus. She had settled for a lavender, knee-length, cocktail dress, and she looked really pretty with her hair packed up and her face made up.

Kelechi had arranged to pick her up, even though she had insisted that she could find her way. "You're not coming to the party by public transport! I'll come and get you," she had insisted.

Mary waited nervously, wondering if she had heard God right about going. She prayed for strength and grace to deal with seeing Ifeanyi again, and wisdom to know when it was time to leave. But her stomach was already filling up with butterflies at the thought of him.

She had thought she was over him... What if he was over her? What if he had a girlfriend? She was beginning to hyperventilate. She hadn't thought of that possibility before.

Go. Don't be afraid.

Mary calmed down, and then her phone rang. Kelechi was in her neighbourhood but wanted directions. Mary left her building to stand by the street so Kelechi wouldn't miss her when she passed.

"What a lovely dress," Kelechi said when Mary had entered the car.

"Thank you," Mary smiled.

Kelechi asked after her brothers, and she said they were fine.

"You'll be meeting my husband for the first time today. He will be so happy to meet you," Kelechi said, as she tried to keep small talk going to get Mary to relax. She could tell the girl was nervous. Mary returned her smile and sighed deeply. *It is just a party...it's not a date*, she told herself.

They arrived at the venue of the event centre where the party was being held. Mary was surprised that it was such a big affair. There were lots of expensive cars parked outside, which meant that a lot of prestigious people had been invited. She didn't know Chuka's family were so privileged. She suddenly felt under-dressed.

Mary looked at Kelechi and smiled. "This is a big thing!" Kelechi chuckled in response.

Kelechi walked her through the entrance, and she was stunned to see that the place was empty. Well, it was richly decorated, but no one was there. She turned to Kelechi, who had suddenly disappeared too. Then a familiar instrumental started to play through the speakers.

She walked into the hall, thinking that she should turn around and go look for Kelechi when she saw him. *Ifeanyi*. Her heart leaped. What was going on?

Ifeanyi began to sing the beautiful love song by Michael Masser, "Nothing's Gonna Change My Love For You." He walked slowly towards her, his eyes fixated on her. Mary was riveted where she stood, taking in every word and note he sang. He had such a beautiful voice.

Ifeanyi reached Mary and held out his hand to her. She took it, with tears in her eyes as he sang the chorus. He could not have chosen a better song to convey his love. Mary's knees were weak as she listened to him.

It was too much. She wasn't prepared for this. Ifeanyi got down on one knee as the instrumental continued to play in the background.

"Mary, you are the love of my life. I have never loved anyone the way I love you, and I know that I will love you forever. I want you... I *need* you in my life. I need to make you happy. I *want* to make you as happy as you make me. For the third time, I am a humble man before you, desperate for you to be my wife..."

Mary was crying now, and Ifeanyi pulled out a handkerchief for her. "My heart can't take any more of this, Ifeanyi. I love you, but everything else seems to be against us. Your parents forbade you from seeing me; how can I know that they won't still oppose us?"

Just then, Chief and Mrs Chukwueke walked into the hall, and the lovers turned to them. "Because we love you too, Mary. We want you to be in our family. We see the difference in Ifeanyi's life since he met you, and we would be foolish to keep you from him," Chief Chukwueke said, as his wife wiped tears from her eyes.

Mary turned to Ifeanyi again. "What about Ijeoma?" she asked, looking into his eyes.

A heavily pregnant Ijeoma and Chuka entered the hall together, holding hands and smiling at Mary. Mary was shocked to see that Ijeoma was the bride she had come to celebrate. She looked from Ifeanyi to Chuka and to Ijeoma, beginning to understand, but being slow to believe.

Ifeanyi stood up and began to sing the last verse. He wiped away tears that trickled down her cheeks. Mary couldn't take her eyes off him as he continued to sing. Was she dreaming again? Was this really happening?

A choir suddenly started singing the chorus on the stage, and she gasped. Ifeanyi drew her into his arms, and they danced. The room began to fill with all the guests that had been invited to the engagement party.

Ifeanyi whispered softly into Mary's ear, "Nothing's standing in the way of our love, Mary. They've all come to celebrate us...if you say you will marry me."

Mary closed her eyes, looked into her heart, and felt the peace she had always longed for. She now remembered her dream about Ifeanyi's ring, and it suddenly made sense. Just as everyone in the market had come together to restore her ring, they had all come together to restore her engagement to Ifeanyi. She knew the truth, and that God was with them.

There was really nothing hindering them...except her fear. Her fear of failure... Her fear that when she finally got all she ever wanted, it wouldn't be enough. Her fear that it could still all fall apart, when she needed it to work.

Perfect love casts out all fear...

Mary stopped dancing and looked at her beloved. "Ifeanyi, I love you with all my heart. I don't want to live without you either. Thank you for making me feel like the most important person in the world. I am yours...and yours only."

Ifeanyi pulled her in his arms, and hugged her tightly, not ashamed of the tears that ran down his cheeks. All their family and friends that had been invited to witness the occasion applauded, and many roared and cheered the couple on. A new, more bubbly song played on the speakers, and Ijeoma and Chuka ran up to the couple to hug and congratulate them.

Mary hugged Ijeoma and smiled at her. "I thought this was yours and Chuka's engagement party..."

"It was meant to be. Ifeanyi suggested we do a joint celebration. And after ruining your special day, it was the least I could do," Ijeoma smiled. "Forgive me?"

"There's nothing to forgive," Mary beamed, and they hugged again.

"And who knew Ifeanyi could sing?" Ijeoma asked, as she chuckled.

"I know, right?" Mary giggled.

Ifeanyi had a bashful grin on his face. He kissed Mary's forehead. All the things he could and would do for love...

Three months later, Mary and Ifeanyi stood in front of a Minister to exchange their vows. Mary was a glorious bride, dressed in a white, satin gown adorned in diamonds and pearls, with a lace veil. She smiled, delighting in every moment, knowing that it was no longer a dream - it was real. All she had suffered in her life paled in comparison to her joy, on this special day, as she stood before her groom, peaceful and content.

The church was packed with invited and uninvited guests, who wanted to witness this special occasion. Considering the high profile of the Chukwuekes, and Mary's scandalous past, there was a representative from every media house at their wedding ceremony to capture the day in pictures and juicy details about who came, who wore what, and more...

The moment came for the minister to say, "If anyone knows any reason why these two should not be lawfully joined together, let them speak now or forever hold their peace."

The whole assembly was quiet, until...

"I object!" A woman in the congregation stood up brazenly. Everyone turned to look at her. "We belong together, Ifeanyi! It's supposed to be you and me, forever!"

The sound of whispers filled the air, as people began to speculate on who she could be, and her relationship with Ifeanyi. Ifeanyi was mortified to see who it was. Keisha Akindele, his ex-girlfriend.

He swallowed hard and looked at Mary, who was surprisingly calm. He prayed a silent prayer, as he raised his eyes to Heaven. *Father, do something! This can't be happening...*

"SECURITY!" Chief Chukwueke shouted, and the security guards quickly arrived at the scene to escort the shameless woman out of the church.

After she left, the whispers continued, until Chief Chukwueke said, "Sorry for the outburst. My son is hard to get over." To which everyone, including Mary, chuckled. This she knew too well.

"If we may proceed," the minister said, soberly. "Is there anyone else, who knows of any reason why these two cannot be lawfully wed? Speak now, or forever hold your peace!"

The room was filled with silence. Mary and Ifeanyi looked around and saw their friends and family smiling back at them. They looked at each other, and their smiles widened.

"By the powers vested in me, I now pronounce you, Man and Wife! What God has joined together, let not man separate!"

And the whole congregation shouted a mighty "AMEN!"

Ifeanyi took the veil from his wife's face and drew her into his arms for their first and most blessed kiss as man and wife. And it was definitely worth the wait!

"Verily, verily, I say unto you, except a corn of wheat fall into the ground and die, it abideth alone: but if it die, it bringeth forth much fruit. He that loveth his life shall lose it; and he that hateth his life in this world shall keep it unto life eternal..."

JOHN 12:24-25

THE END OF BOOK ONE.

"By this shall all men know that ye are my disciples, if ye have love one to another."

JOHN 13:35

MATURING IN LOVE

BOOK TWO

VOLUME
FIVE

26

"Be sober, be vigilant; because your adversary the devil, as a roaring lion, walketh about, seeking whom he may devour."

1 PETER 5:8

On the night of their wedding, when they were finally alone, Mary and Ifeanyi looked at each other with longing. This was the moment they had been waiting for, had dreamt of often, and sometimes even daydreamed about. Ifeanyi wanted it to be perfect for Mary. He wanted her to remember every touch and kiss and caress. But he could see she was tired and a little tipsy.

Mary smiled at Ifeanyi nervously. Her heart raced in anticipation of their first time. She wanted so badly to please him and hoped he wouldn't be disappointed with her lack of experience.

Sure, she was familiar with the act of sexual intercourse. She had learnt a few things from her time with the late and infamous Pastor. But it had never been about her nor her enjoyment. It had been about him; his perversion and dominion. She had never given herself to him in the way of love nor received him in that way.

Mary sat on the bed and kicked off her shoes. How she had spent the whole day in those heels was beyond her. Ifeanyi sat next to her and took her hand in his. He slid his fingers playfully through hers, arousing sensations in her body. With his other hand, he touched her face gently, lifting her chin up and kissing her, ever so gently, on her full, pink, glossy lips.

He let his hands run along her back, as he looked for the zip to release her from the obstructive white dress. He found it, and the hook, and unhooked the fitted dress. Mary enjoyed the cool breeze from the hotel's air conditioner on her body when the dress had given way. She enjoyed the sensations his touch stimulated as his hands caressed her breasts through the lace fabric of the lingerie she had worn underneath.

Ifeanyi stopped to take off his tuxedo jacket, neck piece, and belt, so he could be more comfortable. They continued to kiss with increasing passion. Mary shut her eyes dreamily as Ifeanyi kissed her neck and shoulders and trailed his tongue down south.

"Hmmm…" she sighed, lost between the dream and reality.

The light from the Sunday sun rushed into the hotel suite and awakened the lovebirds from their slumber. Mary stirred first. At first, she was confused about where she was. It was the first time she had woken up in a room other than hers. When her eyes took in her environment, and she remembered where she was and why, she looked down and saw that she was still in her wedding dress.

A long, strong, fair hand held her body close. He wore a wedding band that matched the one on her slender fourth finger.

Mary smiled at the sight. Looking further down, she saw that her husband was still dressed in his trousers and socks, as one of his legs lay on top of her full bridal skirt. She felt his breathing change as he stirred from sleep.

Mary turned around in his embrace, and his sleepy smile made her heart skip. She loved to look at him this way. She could look at him forever. He was so peaceful, handsome, and happy.

"Good morning, Wifey," Ifeanyi said with a grin.

"Good morning, Hubby," Mary smiled.

She took in the sight of him with unguarded eyes. He had broad shoulders and a firm muscular chest, with some scatterings of hair, that gathered at the point where his trousers hugged his hips. Mary instinctively touched his chest and swallowed as she felt his instant response to her touch.

"You slept off on me last night…" Ifeanyi said, without accusation, as a smile played on his lips.

Mary blushed with embarrassment. "Sorry, I was so tired."

"Not to worry. I've got you for the rest of my life. I'm ready when you are…"

He gently stroked her face and kissed her nose. She lifted her head and pressed her lips against his. She was ready now.

Despite her anxieties last night, Mary made love to Ifeanyi with wild abandon. It was the most natural thing to do, to become one with him physically, as she was already, spiritually and emotionally. Ifeanyi was gentle and firm all at once, taking the time to awaken all her senses, so that when he finally took possession of her body, she was but a bundle of nerves in his arms. Mary had never felt the feelings that coursed through her body that morning, and she couldn't hold back her cries of delight as she climaxed in his arms.

Later that afternoon, after they had had some brunch and enjoyed a second round of love making, Ifeanyi and Mary got ready for their trip to the airport to travel for their honeymoon.

They were scheduled on a Mediterranean cruise the following day, leaving from Egypt. Mary hadn't ever been outside of the country, and Ifeanyi thought this was the best way to begin to show her the world. He hoped that one year, they would travel to every country, exploring the world together.

Now that they could freely kiss and touch, they didn't hesitate to, and their preparations were much delayed by the brief, but frequent, intervals they stole to make out. Mary's body had been awakened to Ifeanyi's touch, and now, only a look from him kindled a fire within her. She longed for him, even when he was near. And it was always his pleasure to bring her to satisfaction.

Mary and Ifeanyi returned from their cruise a month later to begin their new life as husband and wife. Mary's brothers had moved into the Chukwueke mansion while their former abode was rented out. When they returned from their honeymoon, Chief and Mrs Chinedu Chukwueke presented the lovebirds with their wedding gift; a five-bedroom, fully furnished and equipped house in the new, thriving residential complex at Victoria Garden City, Lekki. Mary and Ifeanyi were overjoyed and expressed their gratitude profusely.

For the next three months of their marriage, Mary's brothers remained living with the chief and his wife so that the newly-weds could enjoy their privacy. When the boys eventually moved in with them, Mary discovered that she was pregnant! Soon, all the rooms in their home would be filled up. Mary was relieved to know that she could get pregnant again, as she'd had some fears about conceiving after her miscarriage. She was also delighted and ecstatic to be carrying Ifeanyi's baby.

Samson and Samuel excelled in their A' Levels as expected, but they no longer qualified for the scholarships, since their fortunes had changed with their sister's marriage. They began their new courses in Computer and Electrical Engineering at the University of Lagos and lived on campus. In September,

Daniel was enrolled in a private school in Lekki, to complete his junior secondary education. He adjusted easily and took advantage of the library and other resources to improve his learning.

Ifeanyi got a job offer from Solomon Investment Bank, which was much more promising than his current employment in accounting. It had long been his desire to run and own a bank, and this was a move in the right direction. Plus, the pay was encouraging. Especially with a baby on the way. He took the job and applied himself to it diligently, hoping to climb quickly up the career ladder.

Mary continued with her work at Browne Law Firm and also invested more time in her blog. Both vocations brought her so much joy, as they represented her ministry in obedience to God. Through her writings, she shared her faith in God and helped many to know Him more. And through her advocacy, she was actually able to see lives transformed and people delivered from life-long bondage. Her friendship with her boss, Kelechi, also grew, and she received a promotion for her diligence at work.

Life was good all-around for the couple. Mary enjoyed married life very much. Ifeanyi was an amazing lover. Very romantic and passionate. He loved Mary with complete devotion, as she did him. And her passion for him rivalled her passion for God. She was in awe of his love.

Ifeanyi scaled new heights in the attention and love he showered on Mary during her pregnancy. He was so happy that she was carrying his baby and always looked at her with adoration. He would often return from work and plant kisses on her stomach, then he would proceed to give her a foot massage while talking about his day. Sometimes, he even came home to cook and ran her a hot bath most nights.

They were blessed with twin boys in April, the following year. The Chukwuekes were overjoyed. However, the twins were a handful, and motherhood was a shock to Mary's system. It destabilised the fantasy world she had been living in over the past year. She didn't cope with the change well, even though Ifeanyi was very understanding and helpful.

As she had been caring for her brothers for a good part of her life, she had been looking forward to enjoying her husband, without any mothering obligations for a while. She thought she would have been happy with only one child. At least for the first few years.

The arrival of the boys also took a toll on their sex life for a while. For the first year, Mary was tired and stressed a lot of the time. She was also afraid of getting pregnant again, in case she had another set of twins. She was always careful to make sure Ifeanyi used a condom, even though she was also on the pill. Ifeanyi wasn't too pleased about that because he eagerly wanted more children and even hoped for twin girls.

They tried to talk about their feelings, and Mary told him how she missed the time when it was just them. Ifeanyi was surprised because he had thought that having a big family was what they both wanted. He couldn't understand why that would make her unhappy when it was a fulfilment of a dream to him. He thought that she had changed and told her as much. So, Mary tried even more to bury her feelings and rise to the occasion of her new role as a mother.

In October, when the twins were six months old, Chidinma got married to Emmanuel Atiyota. He had proposed over Christmas after they had been dating for over eighteen months. Chidinma was a beautiful bride, and being the first child and only daughter of her parents, they had thrown her a grand celebration.

Mary was reminded of how grand her wedding day had been. It was truly the best day of her life. She had felt like Esther, chosen as the most beautiful woman in the kingdom to marry the prince. And indeed, life with Ifeanyi had been everything she had imagined and more...

Though she had known that their lives would never be the same once they started having children, she wasn't prepared for how her kids would take all the focus of her life. She was suddenly thrust into being a full-time mother, and her dreams of a blissful, easy life with Ifeanyi and pursuing her passion for human rights' activism were put aside. Mary felt anxious and inadequate a lot, and she constantly worried about her parenting abilities. She often wondered about those women who seemed to be able to do it and have it all!

Mary couldn't understand her feelings, so she did a little research online, asking why she felt the way she did and reading about other women's perspectives from forums on motherhood. She learnt that her feelings were quite common. She had the symptoms of those who suffered from Postpartum Depression. Though she wished she could snap out of it, and prayed many times for God to restore love and joy in her heart for her children, she still felt cheated. She felt like her idea of marriage was a camouflage, like she was living someone else's dream.

Not long after the twins' first birthday, Mary found out that she was pregnant again. She wasn't as happy as she had been during her first expectancy. She was just relieved that she was not pregnant with twins again.

Ifeanyi felt that it would be best for Mary to quit her employment with Browne Law Firm, in order to focus on the children, while she could work on her blog from home. He thought Mary needed to spend more time at home with the boys so that they could bond and that she would be happier without the distraction and stress of nine to five work. But she was passionate about her work. It gave her purpose and joy, which she seemed to lack in motherhood. Mary honoured Ifeanyi's wishes and quit her job with Browne Law Firm because she wanted to please him.

However, while she was pregnant this time around, she noticed a change in Ifeanyi. He tried to be as doting as he had been when she was first pregnant with the twins, but Mary could tell that it wasn't coming naturally anymore. At times, she thought he looked at her strangely, as though he was disappointed...as though he was uncertain who she was.

Mary did not know that Ifeanyi was fighting his own demons and going through a trial of his own. He wished he could talk to her about it, but he feared it would only make her worry and not help the situation at all. So, he bore his burden in silence.

27

"Be sober, be vigilant; because your adversary the devil, as a roaring lion, walketh about, seeking whom he may devour."

1 PETER 5:8

M ary and Ifeanyi were a beautiful couple who were gen-uinely happy in their marriage and the envy of every-one who knew them. No one would have foreseen the storm that lay ahead for them. It was a storm that would rock them and test the depths of their love for each other and their faith in God.

It all began on this warm Friday night in September. Mary and Ifeanyi were preparing to attend the 30th Anniversary celebra-tion for his bank, Solomon Investment Bank. They were having a cocktail party and launching their new headquarters in Lekki

Phase 1. Ifeanyi was already dressed and waiting, while Mary couldn't decide on a dress to wear. Her pregnancy bump was causing an issue with fitting into any of her lovely gowns.

Ifeanyi came into the room and leaned against the door. She knew she was keeping him, but he was a patient man. He smiled at her and nodded at the green dress she had just taken off. "Wear that one," he said.

"It's too short," Mary said. It would have been perfect, except her five-month-old bump made it ride up higher than knee length.

"Let me see," he said and sat on the bed while Mary put it on again. "Gorgeous!" He grinned and pulled her into his arms for a kiss. "Now for the shoes..."

"That's easy. I'm wearing my flats," she giggled.

"Not with this gorgeous dress. Don't you have some cute low heels? They'll make your legs pop!"

"Who wants to see my fat pregnancy legs?" Mary laughed as she looked about for her golden sandals. They had small heels and were not too uncomfortable.

"I do. And they are not fat. They are beautiful, just like every part of you!"

"Awww... You're the sweetest," she said and went back for more kisses. The golden sandals worked, and she easily matched them with a gold and diamond jewellery set that Ifeanyi had gotten for her on her birthday, two months ago.

The twins, Chukwudi and Uchechukwu, came rushing towards them when they saw that they were leaving. Ifeanyi scooped them up in his arms and kissed them, while Mary gave their nanny instructions for their dinner and bedtime routine. The boys started crying when they realised they wouldn't be going with them. Mary hugged and kissed them both and tried not to let their cries get to her. Sandra was experienced with them, having been with the family for over a year now. Mary knew she could handle them, and soon they would forget about them.

The air was fresh as they stepped out into their driveway. Victoria Garden City was in the heart of Lekki, the peninsula surrounded by the Atlantic Ocean, the Lagos Lagoon, and the Lekki Lagoon. The drive to Lekki Phase 1 was short and breezy, as they were going against traffic.

Mary marvelled at the new marble building when they got in sight of it. There were cars parked everywhere, as the parking lot was already filled up. However, one of the security guards had already spotted Ifeanyi's car and pulled a traffic cone from a reserved spot for them to park. Mary was relieved to not have to walk far in her short golden heels.

The building was even more glorious inside, with a grand spacious hall. Waiters with trays of various small chops, delicacies, and cocktails, floated through the crowd, serving all the guests, who were dressed in their finest. Mary looked around for somewhere to sit, but the only seating was the orange sofa that lined the sides of the hall. She decided she'd wait a while before she sought out a seat.

"This is my wife, Mary," Ifeanyi introduced her to a colleague. She smiled and took his hand to shake it. Mary held on to Ifeanyi's hand as he made his way through the hall to greet his co-workers and bosses. A few of them knew her already and didn't hesitate to hug her and ask about the baby and the twins.

Ifeanyi and Mary separated briefly while his boss took him to introduce him to some other people. Mary had his colleague, Dare Olayinka, to keep her company. She was a newly-wed who kept gushing about Mary's life and how she couldn't wait to get pregnant.

"Whoa! Who is *that*?" Dare gushed, drawing attention to the tall, attractive woman who had just walked into the hall. It seemed all eyes were on her, even though the man who hung on her arm was also quite attractive. Mary didn't pay much attention to her until she saw how she greeted Ifeanyi.

Ifeanyi was making his way back to her, and they had locked eyes. Suddenly, the tall woman stood between them and called his name. "Ifeanyi, is that you?"

Ifeanyi broke eye contact with Mary to look at the woman standing in front of him. He was visibly surprised to see his old crush from high school. He gave her a once over before saying, "*Amaka*? Wow!" They hugged warmly. "You look good! How long has it been?" he asked, rubbing his hand through his head. She was stunning. Even more so than he had remembered.

"I don't know... Like *forever*! You look good too," Amaka said in a distinct Californian accent. She looked Ifeanyi up and down, enjoying the stunned expression on his face. She introduced her companion. "Meet my fiancé, Jamie Solomon."

At last, Ifeanyi remembered his manners and went to his wife, such that Amaka and Jamie turned around. "Nice to meet you, Jamie. This is my w..wife, Mary," he replied with a stutter. "Amaka's an old friend from secondary school," he said by way of explanation.

"Hi," Mary stretched out her hand to Amaka, their eyes meeting.

Mary thought Amaka had the strangest eyes. They seemed to dance with mischief. She withdrew her hand and shook Jamie's. Ifeanyi had his arm around her, and Mary could feel his heart pounding in his chest. Who was Amaka to him, she wondered?

"Jamie So-lo-mon? Is your father the MD of this bank?" Ifeanyi asked, nervously.

Jamie appraised Ifeanyi and gave a slight smile. "Yes, that's him. And you are?"

"I am currently the General Manager at the Victoria Island branch," Ifeanyi responded.

"Hmmm... I thought that was Victor Uneke?" Jamie replied.

"Victor's going to be running this branch. I am his replacement."

"Oh, congratulations to you," Jamie said, not sounding all that impressed. He tugged at Amaka, who was still staring shamelessly at Ifeanyi, caring little that his pregnant wife was by his side. A mischievous smile played on her lips. "Darling, you're ready?"

"We really should catch up, Ifeanyi! It's been too long," Amaka said as she leaned in to kiss him on his cheek. "It was nice to meet you, Marie."

"Mary," Mary corrected her, but Amaka had already turned on her high heels and sauntered away. She turned to look at her husband, not sure what had just happened. "Who *was* that?"

Ifeanyi's dazed look finally went away, and he looked at his wife while taking a sip of his cocktail. "She's an old friend."

"You said that. But, did you guys *ever...?*" Mary couldn't stop herself from asking. Amaka had given off a very bad vibe, and she wanted to be sure how dangerous she was.

Ifeanyi giggled, nervously. "No. Never." He sighed deeply. *Oh, I wish! Oh, God, please forgive that thought.* Ifeanyi swallowed hard.

Mary wasn't sure if she believed him, but she had to. Ifeanyi was a changed man. He had no reason to lie to her, she thought. "Okay. Well, I don't like her."

"What? *Why?* You're Christian. How can you not like someone you don't even know?" Ifeanyi asked.

"Being Christian doesn't mean we like everybody. I think she's trouble. I hope you will be careful with her."

Ifeanyi drew Mary into his arms and kissed her forehead. "Darling, you have nothing to worry about. I doubt I'll ever see her again after today, anyway."

Good. Mary smiled and rested in his arms briefly. Soon, she was tired of standing and was ready to find that sofa to rest on. Ifeanyi escorted her to the sofa and got her some small chops, then he made his way back into the crowd and mingled with his co-workers and clients. Mary sat, observing everything and everyone. She smiled and chit-chatted with a few people who recognised her, but it wasn't long before she was looking at her watch and thinking of her bed.

She looked around for Ifeanyi but couldn't find him anywhere. She instinctively looked around for Amaka and couldn't spot her either. She found Jamie talking with his father.

"Hi, Jamie, have you seen Ifeanyi?"

Just then, Ifeanyi reappeared. He was with a man, and they were engrossed in a conversation. She went to them. "I'm ready to go, babe."

"Okay, darl, hold on," Ifeanyi said, while continuing his discussion, which appeared to be a disagreement. Eventually, they cleared up the confusion, and the man walked away. Ifeanyi sighed. "Okay, dear. Let's go."

As they were leaving, Mary saw Amaka. She almost smiled, but for the look Amaka gave her. It was a cold icy look, dripping with contempt. Ifeanyi didn't appear to notice her as he left the building with his wife, holding hands.

When they got home, the boys were already asleep. Ifeanyi kissed Mary with vigour. She giggled.

"Aren't you tired?" she asked, getting a little excited herself.

"I want you..." he whispered in her ear as he tugged at her dress. "You're beautiful...and sexy..." He started his sweet-talking, which always got her eager to please.

They kissed passionately, and Ifeanyi caressed Mary's body intensely. That night, he made love to her with the passion of their first night together. All her fears about Amaka were cast away, as he reminded her that she was the one he had chosen. The one he loved.

The months passed by and Mary never gave Amaka another thought. Ifeanyi returned home every night, and they made love often. Occasionally, he had to work late, but it was nothing unexpected or out of the ordinary. He had new responsibilities at work and was very diligent in his business. Mary kept herself busy with her responsibilities at church, her blog, keeping the home, and nurturing their children.

The twins hung out with their elder brother, Emeka, most weekends. Ijeoma and Chuka brought him and his baby brother, Ekene, once a fortnight for a visit, and they returned the favour every other weekend. Ijeoma and Chuka had found a place to settle at Gbagada and were also expecting their second child together. Ijeoma's baby was expected two months after Mary's, in March. Mary thought it was weird how the woman, who had sought to tear her home apart, had suddenly become one of her best friends.

That Christmas, Ifeanyi took Mary for a week's getaway at a resort on the outskirts of Lagos while the twins stayed with their grandparents. It was like a second honeymoon for them. Mary enjoyed lazy days by the pool, long professional massages, and having Ifeanyi all to herself. The break was just what she needed to get back to her old self.

Mary travelled to the States just after the New Year and was delivered of Chioma Abigail Chukwueke in early February. She was a week past her due date, and Ifeanyi made it in time to be with them during the delivery. Abigail was the prettiest thing, and Mary loved the way Ifeanyi looked at his daughter when he carried her in his arms. It had been a long and stressful labour, and she fell asleep soon after delivery.

Mary returned home a month later with Abigail to a house full of friends and family. Ifeanyi had organised a surprise welcome home party for her and a baby shower for Abigail. He was truly the sweetest, most thoughtful man, Mary thought.

Everyone who was dear to her was there. Even Daniel, who had been enrolled in a private boarding school for his senior secondary education, had been able to take leave to attend the small family gathering. When the twins were born, they had thought it would be best for him to go to boarding school so that he could focus on his studies. Mary had missed him a lot, even though he came home during the holidays.

Chidinma came and sat with Mary when everyone was saying their goodbyes. "Are you okay?" she asked.

Mary sighed and smiled. "I am. Don't I look okay?"

"You seem a little distant, that's all. Abigail is a real cutie. Congrats again."

"Thanks," Mary offered her a big smile.

Ifeanyi joined them and sat on the arm of the sofa beside his wife.

"Are you guys going for the Solomon wedding next month?" Chidinma asked.

"What Solomon wedding?" Mary asked, looking between Ifeanyi and Chidinma.

"Oh, you should know about it, Ifeanyi. Isn't that your boss? Well, he's dad's friend, and it's going to be a big shindig," Chidinma said.

"Yeah, we just got the IV this week," Ifeanyi said, then coughed. "We'll probably make an appearance."

"Oh, okay. Well, I gotta go! I hope you had fun today, Mary," Chidinma added as she hugged Mary goodbye.

"Yes, I did! And don't think I don't know you had a hand in the planning! Thanks so much, sis."

Chidinma chuckled.

Ifeanyi and Mary escorted Chidinma and her husband, Emmanuel, out to the gate before walking back into their home together. There was a strange silence that hung in the air, and Mary couldn't help but wonder if it had to do with the Solomon wedding coming up.

28

"Be sober, be vigilant; because your adversary the devil, as a roaring lion, walketh about, seeking whom he may devour."

1 PETER 5:8

O ver the next few days, Mary noticed a change in Ifeanyi. He seemed to be bothered by something and appeared a little anxious. They hadn't made love since Mary returned. She thought maybe he was giving her space to recover, but it'd been more than six weeks since she delivered, and she wanted to be intimate with him again.

One day, she came up behind him for a cuddle while he was dressing, and he jumped, startled by her touch.

"Hey, darling... Is everything okay?" Mary asked.

"Fine, fine..." He gave a small strained smile. "I just have a lot on my mind, that's all. How are you?"

Before Mary could answer him, a call came through on his phone, and he quickly answered it. He said he had to rush and might be back late. That morning, he didn't take his breakfast, as he hurried to leave home for the office.

In the afternoon, Mary decided to surprise him with a visit at work. She prepared a meal of fried rice, dodo, and chicken and packed some for his lunch. It was not something she did often, but she just felt a certain urge to visit and encourage him that day. The boys were at crèche, and she took Abigail to visit her grandmother.

Mary knocked once and popped her head into his office. She was surprised to see that he had company. She instantly remembered the woman's face, and her name came back to her - Amaka. Mary looked at her and then at her husband, who looked not all that happy to see her.

Amaka stood up from her seat and strode over to Mary. Her tight dress revealed too much cleavage and long legs. Mary tried not to stare. "Hi, Marie. Congrats on your baby girl..."

"Abigail," Mary completed her sentence, looking at her squarely. "Thank you."

"I just came to extend my wishes to Ifeanyi," Amaka explained. Mary was surprised that she was so visibly nervous, as though she knew she had been caught in a wrong.

"We didn't see you at the party," Mary replied, hoping her implication that she had not been invited was clear.

"Oh, I couldn't make it," Amaka said. Apparently, it wasn't clear enough. She picked up her handbag. "Well, I'll leave you two lovebirds alone. Ifeanyi, let's talk later."

Amaka breezed past Mary and shut the door behind herself, leaving Mary to wonder what was going on between her and her husband. Her expensive perfume lingered in the air. Ifeanyi stood up at last and went to Mary.

"Hey, babe, this is a nice surprise..." He kissed her cheek.

Mary swallowed hard. "Is it? You don't seem too pleased to see me."

"I was just surprised, that's all. And with Amaka around, I didn't know what you might be thinking. I know you don't like her."

"What should I be thinking?" Mary asked, boldly looking into his eyes...looking for the man she had married.

To her amazement, he smiled and met her gaze. "Nothing! She just happened to be visiting when you decided to pay me a visit too." He took the food basket she had prepared from her hand and kissed her. "Thanks for lunch!"

Mary watched him walk back to his desk while she struggled to process everything she had seen and tried to align it with the explanation she had received. It didn't look nor feel innocent at all. They looked guilty. But she wasn't sure how guilty.

There was that awkward silence again. Ifeanyi made up for it with his, "Hmmm... Hmmm... This is delicious, babe," commentary on his food. Mary just sat there, on his sofa, feeling like someone was lying to her but unsure how she was going to get the truth.

"I thought you said you'd never see her again," she finally blurted out. "Are you guys friends now?"

Ifeanyi took a drink from his glass of water before answering her. "I think maybe we should have this conversation later."

"What's wrong with *now*, Ifeanyi?"

"Well, I can see you're already getting worked up, and that's not going to help us. I appreciate the food and your visit, but I really need to get back to work," he replied, coolly.

"Sorry? What is more important? Is it really that complicated that you can't answer me now? Who is she to you?"

"Nobody. She's nobody. Can you believe that? Do you trust me?" He asked, looking her in the eye.

Mary sighed deeply. The truth was she didn't know what to believe. All she knew was that Ifeanyi loved her, and he would do anything for her. She had to appeal to that love, in case, somehow, he had forgotten what was at stake.

"Ifeanyi, I love you. I don't know what is going on right now... I don't know if I should be worried or not, but I am going to trust you because I know you love me. But if we are going to work, honey, you have to be honest with me! You need to tell me what's going on. Whatever you have done, you know that I love you, and how ever hard it might be, I will *forgive* you, but you have to tell me the truth."

Ifeanyi sighed, stood up, and walked over to her. "Like I said, let's talk about this later. Okay, babe? I love you."

"Okay," Mary conceded. She hugged him and let him kiss her.

He escorted her out of his office to her car and held her in his arms for a long while. "Drive home safe, love."

Mary smiled, entered her car, and drove off. As she was driving, she started praying. She prayed for her marriage, for her husband, and for herself. She prayed that God would minister to both of them and lead them in unity and love.

Mary continued praying when she got home because her spirit wasn't relieved. Something was wrong, and she needed strength from God to handle it. The last thing she wanted was to lose her marriage with a careless move.

Ifeanyi didn't work late, as they had both anticipated. Mary was pleased and surprised to see him home even earlier than usual. She smiled, hugged, and kissed him at the door. But his kiss was lacking.

"We need to talk," he said. "Where are the kids?"

"They're in their playroom. What's wrong?"

"I think we should take them over to my parents' tonight."

"Why? What's the matter?" Mary asked, getting a little worried.

"I just want us to be alone tonight," he replied.

"Okay," she nodded and went to pack the children's bags for their nightcap at her in-laws'. Mary was shaking because she knew it had to be serious if Ifeanyi felt they needed to send the kids away for the night. She kept praying for grace, love, and wisdom through it all.

It was a little late when they returned home, and neither of them had had any dinner. Mary went to the kitchen to see what she could whip up quickly, then she felt his hand on her shoulder. "Leave that for now. Let's talk."

"I thought you might be hungry," she said nervously. The truth was that she was a little afraid to hear this truth she had asked for. She wasn't sure she was as mentally prepared as she'd thought.

"No, I'm not. Please...just sit down." Ifeanyi sat on the arm chair and directed Mary to sit on the sofa perpendicular to it. He looked her in the eyes, and she could see that he was shaking too. "Something happened... While you were away."

Mary took a big gulp of saliva, her eyes fixed on her husband.

"I... I... Slept with Amaka," he finally said, then covered his mouth as though he hadn't meant to say that. She blinked twice and breathed in deeply. "I swear, I didn't plan for it to happen. It didn't mean anything - she doesn't mean anything to me. It was the biggest mistake of my life...and I love you so much!"

Mary just sat there looking at him while he broke down in front of her. Her head was spinning in confusion as different emotions flooded through her. She didn't know how to feel. Angry that he had cheated on her? Offended that he had lied to her? Relieved that he had told her?

And what was to happen now? Now that she knew he cheated on her, what was she to do with that? And what was Amaka doing in his office...?

"What was she doing in your office today?" Of all the things she could have said, she was surprised that that was what she asked.

"She wants us to have an affair. But I told her it was a mistake, and it will never happen again."

"So, you only slept with her once?"

He sobbed and shook his head. "Please, Mary. Please forgive me. It will never happen again."

Mary closed her eyes as she felt the beginnings of rage in her soul. The thought of her husband, her *Ifeanyi*, with another woman was the thing of nightmares! "How many times did you cheat on me with her?" It took all the strength she had to look him in the eyes.

"Just twice. And it was like the same time..."

JUST twice? Mary was fuming. "Ifeanyi, you had SEX with another woman *twice*, and you want me to believe you never meant for it to happen?" She raised her voice. "I warned you about her! I told you she was trouble, and you LET it happen!"

He just sat there with his head in his hands.

Mary stood up angrily and towered over him. "Was it *good*? Tell me, Ifeanyi, was it WORTH IT?!"

He looked at her, blatant fear in his eyes.

"Answer me, Ifeanyi!"

"No, it wasn't."

"It wasn't good? But you did it twice?"

"It wasn't worth it, baby. I am so sorry..."

"But it was good, wasn't it?" Mary didn't know what had gotten into her, but she didn't seem to be able to stop herself. "Was she *better* than me?"

"Jesus! Mary, please, I'm sorry. Don't do this. You said I should be honest with you. I'm just..."

She sniffled and wiped the tears from her eyes and nose. She stared at him blankly. "You haven't answered me."

"No, she wasn't. It was just...different. Please sit down."

"Nice dodge!" *Calm down and listen.* She knew she should heed the Spirit, but she wasn't ready to be appeased. She wanted to be angry. She wanted to be mad! She deserved to have her own fall, she thought. She also wanted a turn to wallow in the mud for a while. "So, tell me...how this SUDDENLY came about, that you were in bed with another woman. Did she come to *our* home, or did you *go* to her?"

"Oh, God, Mary. I've told you the truth, and I'm sorry. I promise, it will–"

"Your promise means NOTHING! It means SHIT right now," Mary spat the words at him. "Do you remember when you *promised* to love me...and be *faithful* to me? What the hell happened with that?"

"Please calm down."

"Don't you dare tell me to calm down! Ifeanyi, you had an affair! What do you expect from me? To stand up and say, "Okay, what do you want for dinner, *honey?*"? God! You sit there crying, talking about how you never meant for it to happen, and you can't even answer me. I don't want your *tears*... I want answers! How do you expect me to ever trust you again?"

Ifeanyi got down on his knees before her and begged. "Please, Mary. Please forgive me. I will do anything and everything I can to regain your trust. Please, it was a moment of weakness, and I will always regret it. I love you so much, and it kills me to think how much I hurt you and sabotaged all that we have. I pro... It will never happen again. *Never.* Please, you have to believe me."

Mary sat down, still angry and hurt. She remembered how people say, "*once a cheater, always a cheater,*" and she began to cry. She had married a cheater! What did she expect? And could she ever trust him never to cheat on her again?

Yes, he was a changed man when she had married him. He had given his life to Christ and was walking in love and obedience. So, how did they get here? Where was God in all of this?

"Ifeanyi," she said soberly. "What about God? Did He never cross your mind when you were in bed with another woman? Didn't He minister to you at all?"

Ifeanyi just cried.

"If God can't stop you from cheating on me, what chance do *I* have?" she asked as she sniffled and wiped away her tears. Curiously, she asked, "When last did you talk to God?"

Ifeanyi looked up at her. "Today. After you came to see me. I prayed."

"So, what did God say?"

"He told me to confess," Ifeanyi said.

"Okay. So, tell me. I want to know *how* you could do this. When did this start? Tell me everything."

29

"Be sober, be vigilant; because your adversary the devil, as a roaring lion, walketh about, seeking whom he may devour."

1 PETER 5:8

Ifeanyi looked at Mary, shocked and unsure whether she really wanted to know all the juicy details of his betrayal.

"I just need you to make me understand how you can *love* me and *cheat* on me...and with someone who meant *nothing* to you," she said, afraid but desperate to know.

Ifeanyi comported himself and began, with a sigh. "Well, like I said, we were friends back in school. She was the new girl when we met. Her father travelled a lot because of the army, so she moved schools often. She was only with us for two terms. She was my first crush."

He took in a deep breath and continued. "It took me a while to come clean about my feelings for her. For the first term, I really just watched her from afar and fronted like I didn't care. I asked her out in the second term, and she turned me down. She later explained after the third time I asked that she didn't want to get into a relationship that she knew wouldn't last. We stayed friends, and when I learnt she was leaving - the notice was really quite short - we kissed. Well, made out."

Ifeanyi looked at Mary, and she sighed deeply. "I guess I have carried her in my heart all these years, and I always wondered what would have happened if we had been together. We never met, and I never heard anything about her. When I saw her at my bank's anniversary party, all the feelings came rushing back, and I was really surprised because I *love* you, and I am happy... and I never wanted to hurt you."

Mary swallowed hard. "Go on..."

"The night of the party, something happened." Her eyes opened wider as she realised that he had kept another secret from her all that time. "I went to the bathroom to comport my-self, and she followed me. I didn't even know. I saw her through the mirrors and was shocked. She just ran into my arms and kissed me. I kissed her back, but only for like a few seconds before I realised what we were doing. I was just so surprised to see her and to be feeling that way for someone else besides you."

Mary's eyes narrowed as she watched him. "Was that all you did?"

Ifeanyi nodded. "I had to push her away. She was trying to get physical, and I had to forcefully get her off me. I told her that I am married, and that I love you and can never cheat on you. I ended up fleeing the bathroom and going out for some fresh air."

"Why didn't you tell me this before?" she asked.

"I thought that was the end of it. I honestly never planned to meet or speak with her again. But some days later, she added me on Facebook..." Ifeanyi swallowed. "I accepted her invitation against my better judgement. She began to send me messages, and we would chat. I went through her pictures. She's a model, so she had a lot, and she even sent me some private personal shots. I told her to stop sending me the pictures, but we still sent messages often."

"What sort of messages? Can I see them?"

"I deleted them."

Mary sighed. "So, you knew what you were doing. You were entertaining an affair - Facebook stalking your ex! Please, don't let me stop you. Continue..."

Ifeanyi swallowed. "Before we travelled for Christmas, I told her we couldn't continue our chats and friendship because it wasn't fair to you nor her fiancé. I unfriended her and deleted everything. I hoped that was the end. But one day, in the New Year, just before you travelled, she showed up at my office. She said she wanted to invite me for her engagement party, and since I had blocked her on Facebook, she had to come and see me in person."

"You knew that was bull, right? Please tell me you knew her game."

"I suspected that it was. But I gave her the benefit of the doubt. She didn't try anything funny that day. She was actually angry with me for blocking her on Facebook and said that I didn't need to do that, and she had gotten the message when I said no more private chats. I ended up apologising."

"Did you *re-add* her?"

Ifeanyi shook his head. "Well, I went to the venue for the engagement party, but she told me that the date had been shifted to the upper week. She said if I had re-added her on Facebook, I would have known."

"So, she doesn't have your number...?"

"Yeah, that's what I said too. She confessed that she had wanted to see me. She said she had pre-wedding jitters and wanted to talk to someone she knew was happily married, to calm her nerves."

Mary laughed scornfully. "This is unbelievable..."

"We had lunch at the venue. It was a hotel. We talked about her relationship. She asked about mine. I talked about you, and she said you must be really special to have won my heart. I relaxed, and we talked about our pasts.

"We reconnected, and I encouraged her to pray about her decision to marry because she was clearly double-minded about the man, especially if she was trying to have an affair with me. She said I was the only one who could do that to her...and that she loved him. She just always wondered what life would have been like if we had dated back in school. I thought it was weird that she said that because it was sort of how I felt."

"So, if she had come into the picture while we were broken up before, you might have gotten back with her?" Mary asked, a little dumbfounded.

"It's possible. But that's not what happened. And I don't wish that my life was different. You are my destiny, Mary, and I will always choose you. You have to realise that I love you *sooo* much. I don't understand my attraction to Amaka, but I know that she is not you, and she would never have been enough for me."

"But *I* wasn't enough for you either. You *cheated* on me!"

Ifeanyi took in a deep breath. "I was vulnerable, and I was foolish. I gave in to temptation. I guess because she was the only girl I ever wanted that I had never had..."

"Oh my God! Is that what *this* is? Some male chauvinistic sexual *ego*? Should I be worried about the next girl who takes your fancy, seeing as you must bed *every* woman you fancy?!"

Ifeanyi looked at her, shocked. "I didn't mean it like that. I have self-control... Amaka was just..."

"*Special? Irresistible?* What honey?" Mary was getting mad again.

Ifeanyi sighed. "Do you want me to finish telling the story?"

She sighed. "Continue..."

"So, I attended the engagement party the following week. I got to meet the guy again, and he is quite nice, I suppose. He wanted us to do a double date, but I told him you had travelled to deliver our daughter. After meeting him again and seeing how happy Amaka was with him, I sort of let my guard down. She was getting married, and she was happy, and I thought there was no more risk."

His eyes met and held Mary's gaze. Mary knew this was the bit she was going to hate the most. She swallowed hard. "She called me a few days later, crying that they had had a fight, and she wasn't sure if there was going to be a wedding after all. She said she had no one else to talk to and begged me to come and see her. I did." Ifeanyi paused. He couldn't look her in the eye anymore. "I went to her place, and I listened to her and tried to reassure her. And she kissed me. And...you know what happened next."

Mary broke down with uncontrollable sobs. She folded her legs, wrapped her arms around them, and rocked...and cried. "Where was God?"

"I didn't listen. I wanted to give in."

She looked at him and wailed as he spoke the truth. *He wanted it.* And he didn't care about her or God. Ifeanyi reached for her, and she pushed him away. "NOOO!" she screamed out in pain. "You *promised* me! How could you be so *careless* about us?"

Ifeanyi knelt down before her. "Mary, I am sorry I wasn't the man you needed me to be. I'm sorry I put myself in that situation. I'm so sorry I hurt you."

"I was in the States, moments away from having *your child*, and you were here having *sex* with another woman! I suffered 13 hours of *strenuous* labour, and I could have *died*... And you were here *not* thinking of me! What about your children? Did you spare them a thought at all?"

"Please, Mary. I'm sorry. It was spontaneous."

"What about the second time, *huh*? Was that spontaneous too?"

Ifeanyi swallowed and looked down at his hands. "That was in the morning..."

"You SLEPT with her? You mean to tell me, you spent the night with *that woman*?!" Mary yelled and cried. She looked at her husband, and her heart broke. He didn't love her. He couldn't have done this if he did...

Ifeanyi looked up, pained. "I swear, it will never happen again."

"WHY?! Why Ifeanyi? Because you want to be a *nice* guy? You think that's what I want to hear? Don't tell me any more lies or give me false hope. If you want to have an affair, I'm not going to stop you. Not like I could, anyway."

He reached for her. "Mary, calm down. I'm saying I never want to hurt you again."

She shrugged him away. "Did you want to hurt me before? You said you never planned on it; you just went with your feelings... When your feelings stir you up again, you'll be singing that stupid, sad tune! Your kind of *love* is USELESS!"

"Please, Mary..." He began to cry again. "You said you would forgive me if I told you the truth."

"Yeah... Well, we all say things we don't mean." His eyes widened with undisguised fear. "Tell you what... I won't bank on your *faithfulness*, and you shouldn't bank on my *forgiveness*!"

"No, Mary, you don't mean that..." Ifeanyi cried. "I made a mistake. I know it was the worst possible mistake, but it was a mistake, and I need you to forgive me and give me another chance to make things right."

"I *needed* you to be faithful! Your *children* needed you to be faithful! You should have thought about that!" Mary stood up with finality. She had had enough. There was nothing more to be said.

Was her marriage over? She didn't know. She didn't want to care, because he hadn't cared... And if he hadn't cared, then maybe she had nothing to care about. He had treated her like nothing. He threw away what they had, as if it wasn't precious, for NOTHING!

Mary heard him call for her, but she didn't stop. She feared she might say something she would regret. She slammed their bedroom door shut, climbed into bed, and cried herself to sleep.

In the morning, there was a knock on the door. Mary didn't stir. Ifeanyi opened the door and walked in with a tray. He had made her breakfast.

On any other day, Mary might have given him props. A for effort, and A+ for presentation. But not today.

"Darling, have something to eat," he said, sitting on the bed with the tray.

She sat up, and he put it over her legs. She looked at him as he made her tea. The one thing she had always believed and would have banked on, she could no longer rest on. And that was his love for her.

She no longer believed he loved her. Maybe he had married her because he had to work so hard to get her into bed, she thought. But love...? Love didn't feel like this.

Ifeanyi smiled, after making the tea, happy that she seemed calmer and hopeful that she would forgive him. Mary lifted the mug and threw it at him. He screamed and jumped off the bed as the hot liquid scalded his face. She poured the rest of the food on the floor and turned her back to him.

If he thinks that is all it would take, he has another thing coming!

30

"Be sober, be vigilant; because your adversary the devil, as a roaring lion, walketh about, seeking whom he may devour."

1 PETER 5:8

Ifeanyi was stunned by Mary's display of anger. He quickly grabbed the napkin and dabbed his face, and the parts of his body where the tea had poured. Fortunately for him, it was a small mug, and most of it had missed their target.

He watched as she scattered the remains of the tray on the floor, leaving a mess of eggs, baked beans, and sausages for him to clean up. He was saddened by her response but was not angry. It only showed him how deeply he had hurt her. He knew then that he had a long wait to go to reconciliation.

He quietly returned to clean up the mess after using a cool towel on the parts of his body that still burned from where the hot tea had splashed on him. Afterwards, he had his shower and prepared for work. He ate the remains of the breakfast he had made, as he was famished after skipping dinner yesterday.

He went to see Mary before leaving for the office. She still had her back turned to him, but he could tell she was awake. He sat on the bed and sighed deeply.

"Mary, I know nothing I do will ever make what happened okay. Nothing will ever change what has already happened, even though I wish I could go back in time and make a different decision. In fact, there are so many things I wish never happened now, but what's done is done. And I am deeply sorry for that.

"I am so sorry for doing this to you. I hope that will be enough, and I hope that you will see that I can never let this happen again. Please give me another chance. Please give *us* another chance. I love you so much, and I am going to do all I can to make sure you believe in me again."

Mary didn't stir, and when he looked at her face, her eyes were closed. He swallowed, then leaned in and kissed her cheek. "I'll be home early tonight. I love you."

He got up and went to the door. After one final look back, he opened it and left the room and his home for work.

Ifeanyi had expected to find Mary up and about when he returned from work. He hadn't expected her to cook, so he had brought home some Chinese for them to eat, if by any chance she had found it in her heart to forgive him. He also brought flowers and her favourite chocolates, with a card saying: "*I'm sorry. Love, your husband.*" Inside the card read: "*Please forgive me. I will always love you.*" And he had signed it: "*Forever yours, Ifeanyi.*"

He was surprised to find that nothing had changed in the house since he left. The whole house was dark. He was worried that she might have left, so he hastened to their bedroom. She was sleeping. He sighed out of relief, even though he was concerned.

He kicked off his shoes, took off his suit, tie, and belt, and pulled off his trousers. He left her sleeping and went to the living room downstairs. He decided to call his mother to let her know that they couldn't pick up the children tonight as planned.

"What's the matter, Ife?" Mrs Chukwueke asked.

"It's nothing, Mum. Mary and I just need some time alone," he said.

"Are you sure? Did anything happen?"

"Mummy, please. Just help us with the kids. I'll come by tomorrow, and we can talk."

"Okay, dear. In case you want to know, the children are fine. Can I speak with Mary?"

"No, she's sleeping. We'll talk to you later. Goodnight, Mum."

He held his head in his hand and sighed deeply. What if Mary didn't forgive him? His heart ached, and he lost his appetite. *Lord, please help us!*

An hour later, Ifeanyi woke up to find that he had dozed off on the sofa. He had hardly slept last night, as he had tossed and turned, feeling cold and lonely in the spare room. The house was even darker, as he hadn't put on any light, and it was now 7:30 pm.

He got up and switched on the light in the living room. He considered putting on the television, but he felt an instant resistance in his spirit. *Pray.* So, he did.

After ten minutes, he didn't know what to say again. He felt he was beginning to sound repetitive in his prayers. He had been praying constantly since God had told him to confess. He had prayed for forgiveness from God and Mary, deliverance from further temptation, restoration of his marriage, and wisdom to live righteously. He had bound the enemy and annulled his work in their lives. And he had prayed his usual prayer points for his wife, children, and family.

"Lord, what do you want me to do? What can I do to make this right? Please, how do I get through to her? Please show me what to do?" he pleaded.

He waited in expectation for another five minutes, before his stomach growled. He was hungry. He made a move to rise and get his dinner. *Fast.*

Ifeanyi had never been good at fasting. He had been prone to resist it or do it minimally. But this time, he knew it was what he needed to do. The smell of the Chinese take-out had filled the room, and he was very tempted to begin his fast the next day. But he heeded the Spirit, resisted his flesh, and packed the food into the fridge. He would observe a fast, and only have a simple breakfast each day until Mary forgave him.

Ifeanyi went up to his bedroom to check on Mary. He carried the flowers, card, and chocolates with him, hoping he would find her awake. She was still sleeping. Wasn't she going to eat, he wondered? She should at least drink something. He decided he would go down and get her some water and some juice. He wasn't going to chance bringing her a hot beverage again.

He returned to find that she had risen from the bed and gone to the bathroom. He smiled, encouraged, and sat on the bed to wait for her. When she exited the bathroom, he gave her a small smile, but he might as well have been invisible. She looked right through him, passed him, and climbed into bed again, resuming the same position. He sighed.

He put on a lamp to illuminate the room. She pulled the covers over her head. He swallowed.

"I got you some Chinese...and chocolates... Why don't you get up and eat something?"

She ignored him.

"At least have something to drink. Baby, you need to take care of yourself. Please get up and have something."

She ignored him.

"Okay. Well, I'm going to leave them here. In case you change your mind. The Chinese is in the fridge downstairs."

Defeated, Ifeanyi returned to the spare room, where he made himself comfortable for the second night. The pain in his heart was even stronger. But he knew it was nothing compared to the pain in Mary's heart. How he wished he could cure her pain. But his proclamations were not nearly enough.

Ifeanyi checked on Mary in the morning. Apart from the lamp being switched off, nothing had changed in the room. She hadn't drunk the water nor the juice, and his card and chocolates laid unopened, where he had placed them.

He went downstairs and had a time of devotion and prayer. Afterwards, he broke his fast with a bowl of cereal. He brought some milk and cereal up for Mary, hoping that he could encourage her to eat something today. When he returned, she was awake and facing him, though she still lay in bed. He smiled at her.

"Good morning, love," he said.

She didn't say anything. He sat down and stroked some hair out of her face. "Will you have something to eat this morning?"

She swallowed but said nothing.

He was encouraged that she appeared to be listening to him, and he continued talking. "I'm going to my parent's place this morning. I need to check on the kids. Do you think we can bring them back today?"

A tear ran down Mary's cheek, and Ifeanyi instinctively reached to wipe it. Mary turned away from him.

"Baby, please. I'm sorry. We can get through this. Please forgive me, Mary. Please, I don't know what I would do without you."

Mary's shoulders heaved, revealing that she was crying. Ifeanyi got down on his knees and kissed her shoulder. "I'm never going to hurt you like that again. I promise."

Mary's sobs soon died down in intensity. Ifeanyi had tears in his own eyes from watching his wife in pain. Three days of misery for one lousy night of fornication. It *sooo* wasn't worth it. Not at all. How had he been so stupid?!

"I can stay home with you today...if you want me to. We can just lie in bed together. What do you say?"

"Please leave me alone, Ifeanyi. Do what you have to do, but leave me alone."

Ifeanyi swallowed. Mary shifted away from his reach, further into the bed. He got up and wiped the tears from his eyes. He carried the breakfast tray back down with him and cried in the kitchen.

Ifeanyi carried some more clothes and provisions for the children when he visited his mother that morning. When she saw his face, she knew immediately that something was seriously wrong. Ifeanyi said he was not ready to talk about it and pleaded with her to continue to watch his kids, as Mary was not feeling fine. He simply asked for her prayers for them.

Ifeanyi returned home to find things the same way as the day before. He continued in prayer, fasting, and making appeals to Mary. He even climbed on the bed with her, hoping that would bridge the communication gap between them. She had begged him to leave her alone, and he had had no choice but to honour her wishes.

The next morning, nothing had changed. Ifeanyi was running out of ideas, but he persisted in making breakfast for Mary and talking to her, hoping that at last he would succeed. She stopped responding to him altogether, and most times, he couldn't tell if she was awake or not. He was shut out.

By Sunday, Day Five, Ifeanyi had to admit that he needed counsel and external intervention. He swallowed his pride and called his mother. He was deeply ashamed when he finally confessed his fault to her. Even though he had done it to many women before, he had truly believed he could and would never cheat on Mary. The words, "I cheated!" burned his mouth as he said them.

♥ ♥ ♥

Mrs Chukwueke told her son to give it some time and to per-
sist in prayer and showing his wife his love and concern. She
told him not to be discouraged, that they should be happy that
at least she hadn't packed out, and she wasn't exchanging words
with him. "Mary has a strong character, and she will come out of
this. She will forgive you. Just give her time and trust God," she
said.

Ifeanyi also confessed his sin to his pastor that Sunday and
asked for prayers to be said for his home. He admitted that he
had been a habitual cheater in the past, and he was worried
about whether or not he could be trusted to keep his promise
never to cheat on Mary again. Like Mary had said, he never set
out to cheat on her, yet he did. And who could say he would
never do it again, even though he were to make a thousand
promises? Her words still echoed in his ears: "*Your kind of love
is USELESS!*"

He had actually almost given in to Amaka's pleas for an affair.
If Mary had not visited him that day at the office, their story
might have been quite different altogether. He wondered how
all this fit in with the teaching that he was now a new creature
in Christ, and the old had passed away, when he had been taken
again in an old vice. Could he really change? *For good?*

His pastor had shown him that his fall was not uncommon.
He reminded him of Paul's writings, in the seventh chapter of
the book of Romans, when he lamented about doing things
he hated because his flesh was still ruled by the law of sin and
death. The pastor told him that when believers lose their de-
pendence on God, it is easy for them to fall into sin, because
they are relying on their own strength (which is foolishness,
because the flesh is weak and sinful by nature) and are given
to pride and self-righteousness. But if any would walk by the
Spirit, they wouldn't fall into sin because their gaze would be
on God and not themselves.

He shared some scriptures with Ifeanyi to encourage him to
persevere. One of them was found in Proverbs 24:16 – "*For a*

just man falleth seven times, and riseth up again: but the wicked shall fall into mischief..." Ifeanyi was no longer counted among the wicked, but the just, and he would surely rise from his fall.

Ifeanyi was much relieved after his counselling session. He used the scriptures to counter the devil's ministrations, which had been causing him to despair. One thing was clear; when his gaze was on God, he had hope and strength, as he was reminded that he could do all things through Christ who strengthened him, as written in Philippians 4:13. However, when his gaze was on himself and his situation, he easily despaired of hope and courage.

So, Ifeanyi rather meditated on God and His goodness and power, His love and wisdom, choosing to trust in His grace against the odds.

31

"Be sober, be vigilant; because your adversary the devil, as a roaring lion, walketh about, seeking whom he may devour."

1 PETER 5:8

The news of her husband's betrayal broke Mary's heart and spirit. She could hardly believe that he could cheat on her. She had been so sure of his love and had revelled in it for almost three years of marriage. They were just a few days shy of their anniversary when he'd told her the horrible thing he had done.

She felt like she had been hit by a freight train that she hadn't seen coming. She wondered if she would be able to survive it, especially as she didn't want to survive it. As far as she was concerned, living with the pain of his betrayal was more torturous than succumbing to death.

The days that followed his confession were indeed the most miserable of her life. Mary fell into a great depression, with the fall of her esteemed Prince Charming. She couldn't fathom how it could have happened. After all that they had been through - that *she* had been through - how could he do this to her? She had not driven him to cheat; she had respected him, honoured him, and denied him nothing. It hurt so badly because it seemed so unnecessary, unprovoked, and callous.

His fall, in her eyes, was a judgement on his love. She didn't see it as a moment of weakness as he believed, because there had been many moments and many chances for him to tell her the truth and to do the right thing. And Mary thought the fact that he could betray her and lay in the arms of another woman all night, conscious of the evil he had done, only to do it again the following morning, was simply unforgivable. He was heartless!

She believed he was lying that Amaka meant nothing to him. She thought he was also lying that it just happened without his plan nor intention. She felt he was still lying to her. Perhaps it was because he was still lying to himself. Maybe it was only a matter of time before he realised his true feelings, that he didn't actually love her at all.

Mary couldn't bear to be deceived any longer. She was resigned to embrace the truth she knew, even if he never confessed it, believing that the truth would set her free. Free from pretence, free from hope...

Without any work obligations, Mary chose to spend her days in bed, sleeping and dreaming and falling into a greater depression than she had ever known. She no longer cared about anything. She felt he was all that was hers and all that was good in her life, and now he was not. Their marriage was a joke. And she thought if she got out of bed, she would just be playing a character in a play she no longer believed in.

She was tired of playing. She was tired of the misery that had been her life and longed for it to end. She lay in bed, longing for death, convinced that life had nothing more to offer her.

Because now, there would be no more kisses... No more "I love you"s...

Mary lamented her loss for days. *Oh God! Why did he betray me? How could he throw our love away? How could You let this happen, Lord? O God, why?* She cried, endlessly. *Oh, Ifeanyi, how could you break my heart? How could you fail me when I needed you?*

Her dreams were the same every time she closed her eyes. She dreamt she was walking in a field, lost and alone. It was a beautiful field that seemed to be endless, but she was looking for home. There was no home for her. She would see her parents in the distance and would run to them, and they would receive her in their arms, and she would cry tears of joy. She was home. But they wouldn't let her follow them. They kept saying to go back.

"Please, let me go with you. I've had enough. Please, I don't want any more."

"Go back and work it out. Go back. Your children need you. Your husband needs you."

"He doesn't love me, Mum. He lied to me... I don't want any more. The children will be fine without me. Please, I'm tired. I want to go home..."

Then she would wake up, and cry for her children. Because she couldn't be a mother to them. She felt she was too selfish. Life had been unkind to her, and she wished she had never brought them into this cruel world. But she had done it for Ifeanyi. And he didn't love her. Maybe he would love them. She cried.

Several days went by this way. Her wishing for death didn't make it happen. Every time she opened her eyes and realised that she was still alive, and that Ifeanyi had betrayed her, she was disappointed. Every time she remembered their children, she was pained.

And where was God? Whether He was hiding from her or she was hiding from Him, she didn't know. She only knew He couldn't help her now. He couldn't make her husband love her, and that was all she had ever wanted. She was disappointed in Him and hadn't prayed since Ifeanyi confessed to her.

Perhaps it was because she knew His way was forgiveness, and that was something she didn't want to do. She didn't want to forgive and pretend that her husband still loved her and had only made a 'mistake,' only for her heart to be shattered again. She wanted to remember the pain. She wanted to remember the truth.

She wanted him to know that he couldn't have his cake and eat it too! If he wanted to cheat, she knew she could never stop him. The only power she had was her decision to forgive or not, and she wasn't giving it away.

"Is she still in bed?" Mary heard someone say. She closed her eyes.

"Yes, Mum. And she's not eating," Ifeanyi said.

She heard the kids crying. She pressed her eyes shut. Mrs Chukwueke shook her, and she pretended to be asleep. *Please leave me alone*, she cried.

"Mary, wake up! Mary... Haaa! You can't just give up! Please wake up, let's talk. What Ifeanyi did was terrible, but God is still God. If you will not get up for Ifeanyi, at least get up for your children."

Mary stirred, enough for her mother-in-law to know she was awake and listening, but she didn't turn to her. She owed no-body anything. What could they do to her now? She supposed they could throw her out. Maybe death would come faster.

"Come and have something to eat. I brought peppersoup," Mrs Chukwueke said as she arose from the bed. Mary didn't move. Food would only keep her alive, and she had no interest in that.

The next thing she knew, the nanny brought the children into bed with her, and their cries prevented her from falling back to sleep. Mary got up to use the bathroom. She saw her reflection in the mirror. She looked terrible. She cried.

There was a knock on the door. "Are you alright in there?" Mrs Chukwueke asked.

Mary washed her face and came out of the bathroom. She wondered where Ifeanyi was. She didn't want to see him. He was sitting at the dining table.

She froze when she saw him. She wanted to run back to bed. She couldn't deal with him now. Mrs Chukwueke signalled for him to leave and, thankfully, he did.

Mary made it to the dining table. She poured herself a glass of water and took a few sips.

"Eat something," Mrs Chukwueke said. Mary shook her head. "Mary, you need to eat. If you think you are punishing him by starving yourself, you are not. If you die, he will still marry again."

For some reason, that hurt. She had thought she didn't care anymore. Evidently, she still cared about Ifeanyi's love life. How horrible it is to love someone who doesn't love you, she thought.

She picked up a bread roll and bit into it. She pulled her face in a grimace because it tasted awful. She remembered then that she hadn't brushed her teeth in a few days.

Her mother-in-law smiled as she watched her eat the bread roll. Mary just looked at her, expressionless. Did she know anything about this sort of pain, she wondered? She didn't need or want a pep talk, Mary thought. She didn't want anyone to give her hope that things would get better. The one thing she needed and wanted could not be done, and that was for the clock to rewind itself, and her husband to have never gone to that wicked woman's home!

To Mary's surprise, Mrs Chukwueke didn't try to counsel her. Rather she told her about the children and how they had been doing at her house. They had been there since the day they had dropped them off, over a week ago.

Mrs Chukwueke recounted something funny that the twins had done, and a small smile crept on Mary's face. She straightened her expression. Mary realised what she was doing. Her mother-in-law wanted her to appreciate life so that she would want to live again.

Mary finished the bread roll. "Thank you. I'm tired," she said, standing up to return to bed.

"Sit down!" Mrs Chukwueke spoke sternly. Mary did as she was told. "Mary, you have to snap out of this. This isn't you. Don't let the devil win."

"Isn't it too late for that?" she asked sullenly, thinking about the devil that had slept with her husband.

"No. You're still very much alive. And you have people who love you and need you. Ifeanyi still loves you, even if you can't believe that right now. Please forgive him."

"And then what?" Mary asked.

"Then *live*... Enjoy the beautiful life you have, with your children and devoted husband." Mary laughed at that description of her cheating husband. "Believe me, I know my son. He will never do this again. This has really shaken him up. And you know I've had to talk to him seriously too."

Mary sighed. *Here comes the pep talk*, she thought. She knew everything her mother-in-law would say before she said it. She had done her fair share of counselling. But life still had no more appeal to her. Death was now her desire.

"Look, if you won't forgive him for him, forgive him for you," Mrs Chukwueke continued. "Don't you deserve a second chance? Don't you deserve happiness? Don't you want to see your children grow up? This unforgiveness in your heart is a faulty gun. It shoots backwards, and you're the only one who will suffer. If you continue like this, Ifeanyi will move on, your children will have a new mother, and because they are so young, they won't even remember you!"

Despite herself, Mary cried. Her mother-in-law was right, but she wasn't ready to let go. She knew it would kill her, but in a sick, twisted way, she just wanted to be gone. Caring was too much work. She was tired of caring.

"And have you thought about the afterlife? Do you think you will not be judged?" Mrs Chukwueke said, looking at Mary with pain in her eyes. "Yes, he sinned. But you are sinning too. Do you know that Jesus has forgiven him? But He said that if you don't forgive, you will not be forgiven. If you die in unforgiveness, Mary, you're in danger of hellfire! Please, don't let the devil win!"

Mary gasped and covered her mouth with her hand in shame, as she looked at her mother-in-law. So, God had shown up, she thought. She could hear Him through her words, and as usual, His truth softened her heart. She cried.

Mrs Chukwueke went over to her and comforted her, and she wept more. Her world had been shattered, but there was still hope, because God was still God! Even if she didn't have the strength, her willingness was all that was needed for His grace to abound. Her faith was returning to her, and she was sorry for what she had almost done to herself and her children. "God help me!" she cried.

"He will, darling. He will. Just take it one step at a time, one day at a time. We all love you so much. Life tries to knock us down, but we must never stop fighting.

"Remember, Jesus fought for you the day He died on that cross. He could have said it was too hard. He could have said you were not worth it, but He faced His fears, carried that cross, and stayed there until it killed Him!

"He did it as an example to us...so we can fight for one another. It is a horrible battle, but we must keep fighting. Fight for Ifeanyi. He fell because the devil was trying to destroy your home. His job is to steal, kill, and destroy. Don't help him! Fight! *Okay*? You and Ifeanyi can win this - *together*!"

Mary nodded. She really needed that pep talk after all. She cried again. This time, she cried for her husband. She cried for his fall. She should have seen that the devil was the enemy, not her husband, and fought the devil. But she was blinded and didn't see that she was being deceived by the devil to complete his work of destruction in their lives. It was time to forgive. And though it was still hard, though she felt like she was giving away the only power she had left, it was what she needed to do to save her family.

"Thank you, Mummy. God bless you," Mary said and hugged her mother-in-law.

"God loves you, dear! And you have to believe that Ifeanyi does too. Give him a chance to show you again, okay?" Mary nodded and sniffed.

"Ifeanyi!" Mrs Chukwueke called out.

Ifeanyi came in from the visitor's waiting area, where he had been waiting. Mary took one look at him, and she knew he was sorry. He looked at her, unsure, and then went to her.

He got on his knees. "Mary, I know what I did was horrible. The last thing I wanted was to lose you. You're such an amazing person. You're a wonderful mother to our children. You've been my strength, my inspiration... Watching you give up on us, on life...nearly killed me. I never want to see you like that again.

"I didn't realise how great an evil I did to you until I saw you lose hope. Baby, please, don't change because of what I did. Forgive me, and I...I *promise* you, I will never make you cry like that again. I love you with all my heart."

Mary embraced him. Her redeemed husband. She forgave him. And she began to heal.

32

"Be sober, be vigilant; because your adversary the devil, as a roaring lion, walketh about, seeking whom he may devour."

1 PETER 5:8

Ifeanyi nuzzled Mary's neck affectionately, and she knew that he desired to kiss her again. Even though she had forgiven him, she was not ready for that level of intimacy. She was still in sorrow, still hurting, as the memory of his betrayal was still fresh in her mind. When she closed her eyes, she easily imagined him with another woman, more specifically, Amaka, and the pain was still real.

She knew it would take some time for her to kiss him without thinking of another woman's lips on his. Or feel his touch and not be jealous that he had touched another woman that way.

She still desired him... He was indeed a very desirable man. And being such a wonderful lover too, it was quite understandable how the thought of him with another woman would drive her mad.

She breathed in deeply as he kissed her neck and then her chin. She hugged him to stop him from kissing her lips. It was too much too soon. She hoped he would understand that it would take some time for her to be sexually intimate with him again. It would take trust, and that had nothing to do with forgiveness.

It was as though he had thrown hot oil on her face. She had been able to forgive the assault, but she still had the scars and may still live with the injury for a long time to come. She would have to learn to love the new disfigured face and appreciate the ways the pain and suffering were rebuilding her character and self-image. She might even need some physiotherapy to heal fully. And she would also have to learn to trust him again, to allow him to get close enough to hurt her, believing that he wouldn't abuse such privilege ever again.

"Ifeanyi, take it slow with her," Mrs Chukwueke said, as though reading Mary's thoughts. "Sit down. I want to talk to you both."

Ifeanyi pulled a seat next to his wife and held her hand. He wiped tears from his face.

"I hope you've realised what an awful thing you have done to Mary and to your home, Ifeanyi. Thank God she forgave you. Thank God she is Christian! Don't ever take her Faith or forgiveness for granted, do you hear me?" Ifeanyi nodded. "I want you to remember what we discussed, about you being the Guardian of your home. Do you remember?"

Ifeanyi nodded.

"I want to say it again for emphasis so that Mary understands too. God has appointed you as the head of this family, and it stands or falls with you. He has given you the authority to rebuke and the power to resist every attack of the enemy in your home. You are the gatekeeper, the protector, and the defender of this home, and you must be diligent to ensure that those God has entrusted to your care are safe and secure within it!"

Mary looked at Ifeanyi, whose eyes were fixed on his mother. She continued. "Do you know why they call it 'The Fall of Man'?" Ifeanyi and Mary looked at each other, unsure what she meant, and shook their heads. "Because the fall was attributed to Adam. He was the leader and spiritual head of the first family. If he had not taken of that fruit, it is my firm belief that God would not have cast them out of the Garden! Even though Eve fell, Adam was able to deliver her and bind the devil. But he was likewise deceived. If he had been attentive to his role as a guardian, he wouldn't have let Eve get near that tree to begin with. Do you understand what I am saying here?" They both nodded.

"This is not to say that the woman is without blame or responsibility, but there is a reason the scriptures say *"smite the Shepherd and the sheep will scatter."* That is in Zechariah, chapter thirteen, verse seven, I think... Yes, it is verse seven. It is about Jesus, but it connects. Because the Apostle Paul also tells us in Ephesians Five that the Christian husband represents Christ in the home, as the leader and head of the home. The woman who sins will be judged for her sins, but her husband, as the Guardian, will not go without giving account as well! That is the responsibility that comes with the power and authority, however great or small, bestowed on *all* leaders!"

Ifeanyi swallowed hard at that revelation. "So, Ifeanyi, you must be very vigilant! Don't use your position as leader to rule your home like the kings of this world. You must rule like Christ, whom you represent. Like a *servant*. You do not have the privilege of doing as you please, because you will give account for yourself, your wife, AND your children! So, this foolish thing that you have done, it must never repeat itself."

"I've learned my lesson, and I'm truly sorry," Ifeanyi said, releasing a deep sigh and looking at Mary apologetically. She gave him a small smile.

"So, for you, Mary," Mrs Chukwueke said, and Mary met her gaze. "I have always been impressed by your faith and strength of character. I know that you are a lady who knows the Lord intimately, so I was quite surprised to see your reaction to this testing of your marriage. I know what Ifeanyi did was extremely bad, and many would have fallen in your situation, but you are not like them. If the Lord is truly your hope and anchor, you can't lose faith because of what *any* man does! It appears that you have put all your hope in your husband when your hope should only be in God! *Trust* your husband, but lay your expectations with God."

Mary breathed in deeply. Her mother-in-law continued. "Ifeanyi *cannot* be your everything. God *is* your everything! I even suspect that was why this trial was sent, so that you will get your connection with God right again. You know God is a very jealous God, and if you have exalted your husband to such a position that your life starts and ends with him, you will certainly not be directed by God and will be in grave danger. I know you love Ifeanyi very much, and your marriage is a wonderful gift, but you must use this gift to the glory of God, even as you delight in each other."

Ifeanyi squeezed Mary's hand. His mother continued. "Let's not kid ourselves. He will offend you again, and you will offend him too. But if you are both walking in love, you will not use someone else's offence as a cause to fall into sin. You really can't afford to be selfish when their *salvation* is at stake. Rather, you will plead the grace and mercy of Christ so that as you hold on to your Anchor, you might even be able to deliver your fallen spouse. That is why the scripture also says, "...*for if they fall, the one will lift up his fellow: but woe to him that is alone when he falls; for he doesn't have another to help him up,*" and "...*if one prevails against him, two shall withstand him; and a threefold cord is not easily broken.*" That is Ecclesiastes Four, verses ten and twelve. Those are two of my favourite scriptures." Mrs Chukwueke smiled at them.

Mary smiled because they were among her favourites too. Her mother-in-law was serious again as she continued. "Mary, Ifeanyi is the head, but without you, he is nothing but a man without a home to lead! You must support him in his role as the head; you are to *help* him.

"I know that it will take some time, and it may be hard, but I hope you won't deny him sexually. You need to come together again so that you won't give the devil another foothold in your marriage. Ifeanyi has a lot of responsibility on his head, as the Guardian, and you will need to do your part to make sure that he is STRONG and not weak and vulnerable. It's good that you have forgiven him. Please find your way back to trust and intimacy. It is not in the length of time you allow but in the *quality* of your faith - and in *whom* you place it. Do you understand?"

Mary nodded and looked at Ifeanyi. He leaned in and kissed her cheek. She sighed. So, this was marriage, she thought. They had had their first trial, first fight, first reconciliation. Mrs Chukwueke had said a lot of things, and Mary hoped that she would remember them all. She had truly blessed them with God's wisdom and truth. "Thank you, Mum," she said.

"Thank you, Mum," Ifeanyi said.

"I am just glad that we could resolve this quickly and keep it within the family. You guys both need to work on your relationship with God. Your marriage is only as strong as your connection to the One who *binds* you. Have you been praying together every day?"

Ifeanyi shook his head. "We haven't been consistent, because of work..."

"And see where that has gotten you. First things first! Get your priorities right, and you won't be wasting time on all these grievances and resolutions. Keep God first in your home, *you hear*? Change your habits and start walking in the love and faith you profess to have. If you do this, you will enjoy a long and happy marriage."

"We will be more diligent and faithful going forward. And I will be vigilant," Ifeanyi said, soberly.

"Let me pray for you, before I go," Mrs Chukwueke said. They joined their hands and bowed their heads in reverence to God. "Father God, I just want to thank You for what You have taught Ifeanyi and Mary through this ordeal. Thank You for faithfully bringing them through and giving them the grace to win this victory over the devil. I pray that their love and faith will be stronger for it, and this testing will ultimately bring more glory to Your name.

"Please continue to minister to them and help them to walk in love and humility towards each other, forgiving all wrongs and forsaking all others. Please heal hearts that have been broken and restore trust in this marriage. I pray that Your blessing and favour will continue to flow in and through their lives so that others will be blessed by their amazing witness of Your love, in Jesus' mighty name. Amen."

"Amen," Ifeanyi and Mary chorused. They all stood up and embraced each other.

"I wish I could have kept the kids longer, but I have my own husband to attend to," Mrs Chukwueke said, with a wink. Mary and Ifeanyi smiled. "By the way, congratulations on your wedding anniversary! I'm sure you both forgot it is today."

Ifeanyi pulled Mary in for a side hug and kissed the top of her head. "I didn't." She looked up at him and smiled. He stole a quick kiss.

Mary hadn't kept track of time and wasn't sure which day it was. She was glad they hadn't missed the opportunity to celebrate their third anniversary and was happy that there would be many more ahead to celebrate after all. The day was even more significant now because it was also the day they reconciled from their first battle.

"Thank you, Mum. I don't know how we could have handled this without you. God bless you so much. I love you," Ifeanyi said.

"Yes, Mum. Thank you for the push and the counsel," Mary added.

"It is well with you both. God is in control. Never forget that, no matter what happens. Bye..." Mrs Chukwueke said as she walked to her car.

The driver opened the door for her, and she entered the back seat. Mary and Ifeanyi stood outside and watched them drive away, waving their goodbyes. Ifeanyi held his wife in his arms after his mother had driven out of sight. He breathed in her scent, and she remembered that she hadn't showered in several days. He didn't seem to care.

"Thank you for forgiving me, Mary. I'm sorry..." he began.

"Ifeanyi..." He stopped and looked down at her. "You never have to say sorry to me again about this. I know you are sorry, and I have forgiven you. Let's move past this, okay?" Ifeanyi held her tighter and breathed out a huge sigh of relief. More tears escaped his eyes. He was so very blessed.

Mary never imagined that they could be reconciled so quickly. God had truly shown up for them and delivered her from a fearful end. She trembled at the thought of where she would have been if she had succeeded in dying from a broken heart - because she wouldn't forgive her husband.

When they got back into the house, Ifeanyi prepared Mary's bath while she got re-acquainted with their children. She hadn't realised how much she had missed them and how much joy they brought to her. As she played with her children, the pain and sorrow she had been holding on to melted away. Ifeanyi came back to find her laughing with the twins, something she hadn't done in a long time. He smiled tenderly at her, and she returned his smile.

That night, Mary made love to her husband again, though she had thought she wouldn't be able to do so for at least a couple of months. She did because she was free. And the truth that set her free was the knowledge that God loved her *soooo* much, enough to restore her home from the clutches of the enemy and her to Himself.

VOLUME
SIX

33

"Let thy fountain be blessed: and rejoice with the wife of thy youth. Let her be as the loving hind and pleasant roe; let her breasts satisfy thee at all times; and be thou ravished always with her love."

PROVERBS 5:18-19

Ifeanyi lay in bed watching his wife, who had fallen asleep in his arms. She looked so beautiful as she slept and snored quietly. He thought of how lucky he was that he hadn't lost her after his sexual indiscretion.

For a moment there, he had been very afraid that she would never forgive him, that she would want to leave him. He hadn't expected that his actions would drive her to the point of losing hope and even seeking death. If not for his mother's intervention, he wondered what would have become of them because he chose to succumb to temptation.

He breathed in deeply, remembering their lovemaking that evening. He had been surprised when she came to him to kiss him on the lips. He had been prepared to wait. He thought maybe it might take a few weeks before she would trust him again, enough to let him get so close.

Her gentle touch on his cheek reminded him of the first time she had told him she loved him. Her sweet kiss reminded him of the love he very nearly threw away. He had watched as she had undressed before him, daring to be vulnerable again. She was courageous. And how he loved her.

But their love making tonight was bittersweet. Every time he touched her, his hands reminded him of his betrayal. Her body was different. Her scent was different. She moved differently and touched him differently. He looked in her eyes, which were filled with love and desire while his were pained with guilt from his transgression.

With each touch, he remembered the foreign body he had caressed and the other woman he had pleased, and he was haunted by his own infidelity. He was emotional as he took possession of her body again and felt her tremble in his arms. His wife had no clue about the torment he was going through, reliving his betrayal, while loving her. The visual of him in bed with Amaka came to mind, and he had sworn under his breath. He had bit down on his lower lip and looked at his wife who lay beneath his body.

Thankfully, Mary hadn't heard him, being in the throes of passion. Her cries of delight came soon after, and Ifeanyi had kissed her passionately on the lips, knowing how that thrilled her more. Even her sound was different. "I love you," she had cried, passionately clinging to him as he also released his tension and came with sweet relief.

When he said "I love you," his voice had croaked from his anguish. How could he have done what he did to a woman so wonderful...?

He released her from his arms and placed her head gently on the pillow. He crept out of bed and went to his study. He closed the door and went on his knees to pray.

"Father, thank You so much for what happened today between Mary and me. Thank You for delivering my marriage from the grip of the enemy and delivering my wife from her depressive mindset. Thank You for giving her the grace to not only forgive me, but to be intimate with me again, so soon after. Thank You for how You used my mother to help us to get to this point.

"I am so sorry for disobeying your command and for dishonouring my marriage and cheating on my wife. I'm sorry that I have not been diligent or consistent with my responsibilities as the leader in this home. I'm sorry for the opportunity I gave the devil to ravish my home. Thank you for the victory we won today. It was only by Your grace.

"Lord, I still need Your help to overcome temptation and not to fall into sin again. I need Your wisdom to guide me in all my dealings with Amaka. I pray, Lord, that she will relent from coming after me and finally get the message that I love my wife, and I will never step out on my marriage again.

"Lord, even with the wedding coming up, please I need Your counsel on how to proceed. I really don't want to have anything to do with her anymore, and I don't think I can or should go to her wedding. Lord, what do I do? Should I quit my job?"

Silence.

"Oh, Lord, please, I really need to hear from You. Please guide my heart, and show me what Your will is. I promise to obey."

Ifeanyi sighed deeply and continued after a moment's pause to listen to what the Spirit was saying to him. "Lord, I thank You for Your forgiveness, but I am still plagued with guilt. I want to be able to make love to my wife without constantly remembering my infidelity. I pray Your deliverance from every bondage of the enemy in my life. Please renew a right spirit within me and cleanse my mind of its corruption. I thank You because I know You have answered and will yet answer my prayer, in Jesus' name. Amen."

After that short prayer, his spirit was not yet relieved, so he continued in waiting, listening, and praying in tongues as the Holy Spirit led him to.

Mary opened her eyes to find herself alone in bed. For a moment, she wondered if she had dreamt it, or if truly she had reconciled with her husband and had made love to him that night. Her naked, sensitised body told her that it hadn't been a dream.

She thanked God for their reconciliation and began to pray. When she heard her two-month-old baby crying, she smiled, realising that life goes on, and she was happy to have her life, family, and marriage back. She looked at the clock, which said it was 11:13 pm. She wasn't sleepy at all. She'd indulged in sleep over the past ten days, and now, she was tired of sleeping.

She slipped on a robe and went to her baby to find out what she needed. Her diaper was soiled and she was hungry. Mary prepared Abigail's bottle and changed her diaper. She carried her baby, sat on the arm chair in her nursery, and fed her. Mary hummed softly as she fed her daughter.

Ifeanyi popped his head in the nursery, just as Abigail finished her bottle. He smiled at Mary, and she returned his smile. "Do you want me to take over?" he asked.

"No, I'm done. She's falling asleep," Mary said. "Where were you?"

"I was in my study. I'm going to have my bath."

"Okay, dear."

After putting Abigail down and checking on her twin boys, Mary settled in the private lounge she shared with her husband to watch a show on TV. She'd thought of checking her blog, which she hadn't checked over the last ten days when she had lain in bed depressed after hearing the news of her husband's betrayal. But she wasn't mentally ready to read about other people's problems yet. She needed something light and entertaining. There was nothing on, so she put on one of her favourite girly movies that she had watched many times before, which was guaranteed to make her smile and chuckle.

Ifeanyi saw what she was watching when he got out of the bathroom and smiled. He dressed in his pyjamas and joined her on the sofa. Mary snuggled in his arms and rested her head on his chest. His strong heartbeat was soothing to her.

Ifeanyi kissed the top of her head. "Happy Anniversary, baby."

Mary looked up at him and smiled. "Happy Anniversary," she muttered.

His lips came down to hers, and they shared a light kiss. "I love you, Mary. You know that, right?"

She swallowed. "I know. And I love you..."

He kissed her again, more passionately this time.

They soon forgot about the movie, as they made love on the sofa. This time, Ifeanyi wasn't plagued with guilt. His heart was full to overflowing with the love he felt for his wife and his appreciation at the grace he had received. He had been given a second chance, and he wasn't going to mess it up again.

It was 1:30 am in the morning, and Mary had been up for the last ten minutes, watching her husband sleeping while lying in his arms. She swallowed hard at the realisation of her vulnerability, having so easily and quickly forgiven him after such a major betrayal of trust and disrespect of her and their marriage. The last thing she wanted to do was send the message that she would take anything because she loved him, but she knew that there was nothing he could do that she could never forgive. And that scared her.

She was even amazed to realise how much more deeply she loved him now than before. She never thought it was possible that she could love him more. But somehow, she did.

Their lovemaking tonight reminded her of her desperate desire for him, and the thought of never being so intimate with him again was a pain she didn't want to inflict on herself. She had it bad for him. *Bad.*

She sighed as she remembered her mother-in-law's counsel to them yesterday, especially what she had said to her. "*Ifeanyi cannot be your everything. God is your everything!*" *Yes, but God doesn't make love like Ifeanyi*, she thought.

This time around, she had to be careful to keep her faith, hope, and expectations with God, and not with Ifeanyi. She had to learn to trust him again, and honestly, she wasn't there yet. But even with trust regained, there was still every possibility that he would fall again. They both needed to be spiritually stronger, to resist the enemy and fight for their marriage.

She got down from bed and went to her private place to pray. This was a private closet and spa room within their home that Ifeanyi had installed for her. She could access it directly from their bedroom or bathroom. When she was in there, she hardly heard a sound from the outside world. She had her own inbuilt stereo system that played different relaxing acoustic tunes or nature sounds, which were great for helping her to relax. Sometimes, she played her Christian worship songs to get her in the mood for praise and worship.

Today, she just listened to the calming sound of nature, as she got into the spirit of worship. She sang one of her favourite songs, "Jesus, Lover Of My Soul (It's All About You)" written by Paul Oakley. She let the truth in the words wash over her and get things into the right perspective.

She had to lift Jesus higher; high above her marriage, high above Ifeanyi, high above her children - high above any problem that may yet arise in her life. With Him rightly placed in her life, she could survive anything, endure all things, and do all things. She could truly do *all* to the glory of God and give unconditional, unselfish love to her husband and children, loving them as Christ loved and loves her.

She began to pray. "Thank You, Lord, for reminding me of what is most important. For a while, I lost sight of You and Your purpose in my marriage. Thank You for forgiving me for this idolatry, and Lord, please keep me from falling into it again. Let my eyes be stayed on You and You alone. I place all my hopes and dreams at Your feet, Lord, and receive from You the joy of Life Eternal; the joy of knowing You...

"Thank You for saving my marriage, despite myself...despite my husband's adultery. I know that You are in control and that this testing will bear the right fruit in our lives. I pray that You will make Ifeanyi stronger and give him a deeper love for You and appreciation of our marriage. May he always hold it in honour and protect and cherish it as he should. Help me to trust him, to be patient and understanding with his flaws, to show him the love You have shown me; a love that defies human wisdom and conquers all things.

"Please prepare us for the trials and temptations ahead. You said You would never give us more than we can bear, and Lord, You have been faithful! Please keep us in Your grace and lead us in the path of peace. I pray, Lord, for more of Your wisdom to handle the issues of life and to continue to walk in Your love, even loving my enemies.

"I lift up this woman to You, Lord. Father, You know her and Your plans for her. I pray that Your purpose in her life will be fulfilled. Deliver her from the grip of her enemy, the devil, and set her free to worship You. I pray for the grace to love her, if ever I should meet her again, that maybe she may see You in me and repent of her evil thoughts and plans towards my family. Lord, have mercy on her.

"Thank You for Your love which empowers me to do all things. Thank You for restoring me to Yourself. Thank You for what You are doing that we may not see or know or understand. Take all the glory, Lord. I love You."

You are My child, and I love you.

Mary was relieved in her spirit. She was strengthened by God and knew that whatever lay in store for them, the glory of God would shine through.

34

"Let thy fountain be blessed: and re-joice with the wife of thy youth. Let her be as the loving hind and pleas-ant roe; let her breasts satisfy thee at all times; and be thou ravished always with her love."

PROVERBS 5:18-19

"Good morning, gorgeous..."

Mary turned from her slumber to a familiar sight. Ifeanyi had made her breakfast again, but he had a big smile on his face this morning. Today, he also dared to bring tea. Mary smiled and lifted herself up slightly to receive his kiss.

"Good morning, dear," she replied and sat up against a couple of pillows.

"How are you feeling this morning?" Ifeanyi asked while he prepared their tea.

"Good..."

"I hope you have a big appetite..." Ifeanyi had prepared a big spread for them. Mary's tummy growled at the sight and smell of it, and they giggled.

"I'm kind of tired of the bed. Do you mind if we eat out on the balcony? I'd love the breeze and sunshine."

"It sounds perfect to me."

Ifeanyi carried one of the trays to the balcony and placed it on the small round table. He went back for the second, which Mary was already attempting to carry. "Please, let me," he said, retrieving it from her. She smiled.

"I need to check on the kids," Mary said.

"I already checked on them. They are fine. The boys have already had their baths and are playing, while Sandra is attending to Abi."

"Wow, what time is it?" Mary asked, looking for her phone to confirm the time. It was 9 am on a Saturday morning. "I didn't think I could still sleep so much."

"I guess it is the quality of sleep. Your mind must have been at peace last night," Ifeanyi offered an explanation.

Mary sighed. "I guess. Thanks for making breakfast."

"It was my pleasure. Let's pray." Ifeanyi took Mary's hand in his and prayed over the food and over their family and home, thanking God for their love and His many blessings.

"Amen!" Mary said when he was done and grabbed a sausage to quieten her growling tummy.

They enjoyed their meal quietly, and Mary appreciated the view from the balcony and the gentle breeze that caressed her exposed skin. It was a beautiful day. She tried to think of the things she needed to do, but her mind was uncooperative. She still needed to take things easy before she got back into her routine.

"So, I was thinking... Since we missed celebrating our anniversary, maybe we could make up for it by doing something special today?" Ifeanyi said.

"What do you have in mind?"

"Well, I had a reservation at Sky Lounge for us yesterday. Maybe we could go tonight? And we could spend the day together. Maybe go for a boat ride on the Lagoon, watch a movie...? What do you think?"

"Ummm... It sounds good. But aren't Ijay and Chuka supposed to come with Emeka and Ekene today? It's their week to bring them."

"I already called them. Ijay's due any day now, so they want to stay at home."

Mary nodded. "I guess I'm all yours, then."

Uche started crying loudly. *I spoke too soon*, Mary thought. She wondered what could be the matter. But it was only the usual commotion with little children. Chukwudi had pushed his younger brother down, as they fought over a toy.

Ifeanyi giggled. "Maybe we should do something we can all enjoy this afternoon. And then I'll have you all to myself for dinner?"

Mary smiled, shyly. "Sounds like a plan..."

Mary and Ifeanyi had a time of devotion after their meal, then Mary went to attend to the children, and Ifeanyi went to his study to do a little work. After some time with the twins on their play mat, where they had practised their knowledge of the alphabet and numbers, Mary decided to check her blog activity. Abigail was in her swing, enjoying some musical tunes, and Sandra took over minding the boys as they put big puzzle pieces together.

Mary saw that she had been missed. There were lots of comments on her last posting that were still pending approval, and some people expressed their concern in their comments. She also had a few emails to respond to. A couple were marked urgent.

After a couple of hours, Mary had responded to every email sent and comment made, and she even published a poem on forgiveness. She read it over and smiled in wonder of the gift that is forgiveness.

The Lord gave me a gift,
And He said that in order to keep it,
I must give it away...
As often as I am offended;
As often as I am hurt,
I must give it away...

For in that moment,
They need it so much more...
They need it to restore
They need it to heal...
Just as it was given for my healing,
I, too, must give it away...

I used to wonder about this gift...
How could I keep it
By giving it away?
But I have come to realise that
It has no value with me,
Until it is passed on to another...

And though I give it away,
It is mine still...
And my portion is all the more precious.
Yet, though it is hard to give away,
And it can feel like you are losing,
You gain your gift and your friend...

The gift of forgiveness
Is one I didn't deserve and never earned.

Every time I give it away,
I am reminded of how desperately I need it still...
And I affirm the Lord's love and wisdom
In entrusting me with this most blessed gift...

Mary explained her absence briefly with the expression, "God called me to fellowship," which was certainly true. Sometimes, it takes a trial for people to stop and hear what God is trying to communicate to them. She sighed deeply. She hoped she would become more attune with the Lord's Spirit so that she wouldn't need a trial to hear Him loud and clear. She remembered the Lord's words as written in John 15:4; "*Abide in Me, and I in you. As the branch cannot bear fruit of itself, except it abide in the vine; no more can ye, except ye abide in Me.*"

At 1 pm, Ifeanyi came up behind Mary and bent down to kiss her cheeks while rubbing his hands on her arms. "How's it going?"

She sighed. "It's good. Caught up on blogging. How about you?"

"Good too. What do you want to do for lunch?"

"I'm actually still full from breakfast. Plus, I want to save room for our dinner."

"True... But I thought you'd like to get out of the house," Ifeanyi said. "We can take the kids to the park, or Fun Factory, and just hang out."

Mary looked at the boys, who were clearly tired. They had just had their lunch. "I think they are about ready for a nap."

"Even better. They can stay home, and we can go out. Fancy a walk or a drive?"

"Ummm... A drive," Mary said with a grin.

Ifeanyi drove them down to the beach, and they took a walk along the shore, holding hands and enjoying the sand, the water, and the cool breeze. They talked easily, and enjoyed brief moments of quiet, as they appreciated just being together.

Ifeanyi kept thinking he should apologise again, but he remembered that Mary had said not to. He sighed and looked at her. She looked peaceful and happy. He wanted her to remain that way. His guilt was his problem, and he would have to work through it, like any other emotion.

"Hey, Mary? I thought that was you." The couple's path was blocked by a man, who seemed to have come out of nowhere. Ifeanyi thought he looked familiar. "I see you've put on some baby weight. It looks good on you."

Mary wasn't pleased with his reference to her appearance, which seemed more like an off-handed insult. "Hi, David," she said, receiving him in an embrace. "Meet my husband, Ifeanyi."

"The notorious!" David said, trying to be funny. "At last, we meet."

Mary wasn't sure what he meant by "*the notorious.*" Was that a reference to Ifeanyi's previous lifestyle or his popularity? It instantly reminded her of the conversation she had had with David, on their first date, when he had said men like Ifeanyi never changed. Would he be pleased to know that he had been right about Ifeanyi cheating on her after all? She swallowed.

Ifeanyi took an instant dislike to David. He took his hand and shook it, with a short smile. He held on to Mary tighter. David didn't miss it.

"So, how are you? It's been ages!" David didn't appear to want to leave.

"Good," Mary nodded and tried on a smile. She was afraid to look David in the eye. She feared he might see that he had been right about Ifeanyi breaking her heart. "We're celebrating our anniversary, actually." She smiled up at her husband.

"Wow, congratulations! How many years?"

"Three amazing years," Ifeanyi said, smiling down at Mary. He kissed her cheek.

"Wow, that's a long time," David said as sincerely as he could. "I must say I had you all wrong. Didn't think you could do it. You know, with your reputation and all. But with God, all things are possible, eh? I'm happy for you." David looked between Ifeanyi and Mary, whose expressions had suddenly dulled.

Ifeanyi gritted his teeth, knowing exactly what David was trying to do. He was trying to stir up trouble. And it was so unfortunate that he happened to have been right about him. He hoped Mary wouldn't give David the satisfaction of knowing that he had been right. David was just the sort of worm to take advantage of an emotionally vulnerable woman, Ifeanyi thought.

"Thanks," Mary said, aware of the tension between the two men. "What about you and your Mary? Did you guys get married?"

"No, actually. It didn't work out."

"Oh, sorry to hear that," Mary said sincerely. There was an awkward silence.

"Well, it was nice seeing you again, Mary. Nice to meet you, Ifeanyi."

"And you," Ifeanyi replied, curtly, knowing that David had succeeded in disturbing Mary's peace and happiness. But he knew he had no one else to blame but himself.

After David left, Ifeanyi pulled Mary in for an embrace. "I'm sorry," he couldn't help but say. And he meant it.

Mary hugged him back, and a couple of tears found their way out of her eyes. She prayed again for her husband. That he would be stronger and live up to his new potential in Christ.

Fortunately, that little cloudy patch in the afternoon didn't disrupt the whole day. Mary was introspective for a while as they drove home, but she soon came out of it and smiled sincerely at Ifeanyi. When they returned home, they made out and cuddled on the sofa in their private quarters.

The door of their lounge pushed open, and the twins ran in, followed by their nanny, who was carrying the baby.

"Sorry, madam," Sandra said, trying to get a hold of the boys, who had run and climbed on their parents' bed to escape her reach.

Mary stood up and tidied herself. She reached for Abigail and took her in her arms. "It's okay. Let them play with us."

Mary shut and locked the door. She turned to the sofa, where Ifeanyi was. However, he was already on the bed with the boys, having a pillow fight. She smiled. He looked helpless as the two boys jumped on him simultaneously. Ifeanyi chuckled loudly.

The boys went for their baths while Mary attended to Abigail. Ifeanyi was catching up on some sleep. When the boys were done and having their dinner, Mary handed Abigail back to Sandra to look after before preparing for her dinner date with Ifeanyi.

When she got out of the shower, he was awake and almost dressed. He gave her a look that sent shivers up and down her spine. Her look told him he would have to wait until after dinner to satisfy his sexual appetite. His grin told her that the anticipation was the best part!

They enjoyed their meal and good conversation at the Sky Lounge, Eko Hotel and Suites in Victoria Island. They were seated by the tall windows and had a lovely view of the city of Lagos and the Atlantic Ocean. The interior decor, pleasant fragrances, and acoustic tunes were the perfect combination for a romantic ambiance.

When they had finished their main course, and the waiter had returned to clear their table, Ifeanyi took Mary's hand in his. He gently stroked it as he looked at her finger, which held his engagement ring and wedding band. He caressed them.

"I could never have asked for a more precious gift..." he began, with emotion. "Mary, I adore you. I bless the day I laid eyes on you. It was the day I woke up and knew I could be so much more. I wanted to be a man worthy of you, but I know now that I can never be. And that is why your love means so much. Thank you for loving me, Mary."

Ifeanyi ran his fingers through hers and locked their hands together. "Thank you for being so loveable," Mary said, her lips curved up.

"Me? Loveable?" Ifeanyi raised an eyebrow.

"So *very* loveable…" Mary took his other hand, and they locked them too. "You give good love, Ifeanyi. You fill me up to overflowing, and loving you is the least I can do. And while I know you could have your pick of any woman, it is my honour to be your wife."

Ifeanyi's heart was full with joy at her words. "You mean it? You don't have regrets…?"

"No. Never. I would marry you again. I know I am the luckiest woman in the world. And when you realise your potential in Christ, you will know it too."

Ifeanyi pulled Mary into his arms and kissed her passionately. He wished, that very moment, that they were in the privacy of their own home so he could show her, in every way, just how deeply he loved her.

35

"Let thy fountain be blessed: and rejoice with the wife of thy youth. Let her be as the loving hind and pleasant roe; let her breasts satisfy thee at all times; and be thou ravished always with her love."

PROVERBS 5:18-19

Jamie Solomon was a man of mixed blood, who enjoyed the benefits of the multiple races to which he belonged. He stood tall at six feet three inches, fair in complexion, with a head of soft black curls. He had movie star looks, which he gained from his beautiful mixed-race mother, who was half Nigerian and half Indian. His father was a Caucasian American, who also sported good looks and broad shoulders.

Jamie was born in the United States of America, where he also spent his early years. He moved with his family to Nigeria 25 years ago, when his father bought and took over the small investment bank that was later renamed Solomon Investment Bank. He returned to California to do a degree in Accounting at the University of California. It was while he was in Los Angeles, living as a bachelor and working at an accounting firm, that he had met the beautiful Amaka Nkechi, the younger sister of his friend, Adania.

Amaka was a glamour model at the time, five feet eleven inches tall, who was not shy of adding more inches, with her passion for stiletto heels. She modelled mostly lingerie and swimwear, but sometimes, she featured in rap music videos. She had an amazing physique, typical of women in these videos. Jamie had been stunned to see her and made it his mission to make her his woman.

Three years later, they were about to walk down the aisle as man and wife. Jamie smiled at his reflection in the mirror as he admired his black tuxedo. This was his day, and he looked good.

Jamie had two younger brothers, Jimmy and Jason. They were known as 'The Solomon Brothers,' not for their wisdom however. They were actually quite fond of mischief and had a bit of a reputation back in the States, where they ran with a gang. Jason was still in the States completing his studies, while Jimmy had returned to Nigeria two years ago and married his long-time girlfriend, Fatima.

John Solomon Jnr, Jamie's father, set up a company for his sons, The Solomon Brothers' Realty, which Jamie now ran as the CEO, and Jimmy worked as the COO. Jason was going to be taking over his father's bank but was still a director to The Solomon Brothers' Realty. He had returned last week in preparation to celebrate his eldest brother's nuptials.

Though he loved Amaka, Jamie didn't trust her. She was too beautiful to be trusted. Men gawked at her everywhere they went, and it was hard not to be suspicious of her. He had found out that she'd cheated on him once. The poor fool didn't live long enough to do it again! The brothers were very good about handling such matters.

He remembered the day Amaka had met her old friend Ifeanyi at his father's bank's 30th anniversary party. He had sensed a certain chemistry between them, and his concerns had been raised when Ifeanyi's wife had come to ask him about their whereabouts. Amaka hadn't divulged anything that night, but he'd followed his hunch and decided to look into Ifeanyi's background.

It turned out the now devoted husband was once a woman charmer! All reports showed that he had changed his ways since he met his wife and even became a devout Christian too. But Jamie knew better. Men of Ifeanyi's calibre never change; they just adapt.

When Ifeanyi came for his engagement party back in January, he had used that opportunity to suss him out and see if there was anything going on between him and Amaka. He had Jimmy on the watch too, and Jimmy had reported back that there had been some longing stares passed from Amaka to Ifeanyi and the other way around too. But that was nothing much to go on. Jamie knew many men looked at Amaka with longing.

It wasn't until one of his friends at the engagement party had mentioned that he'd seen Amaka having lunch with Ifeanyi at the hotel just a week before that he knew he was on to something. He had decided to ask her about it, and at first, she had pretended as if she didn't know what he was talking about. That made him angrier. When she finally confessed that she had had a late lunch with Ifeanyi, he had thrown a fit and they'd had a heated argument.

She had said it was just old friends catching up, and nothing ever happened or would ever happen between them because he was happily married, and she would never cheat on him because she was in love with him. He said he didn't believe her, and they'd kept on arguing until she had let it slip about the kiss they had shared in the bathroom during the bank's anniversary party. Jamie had lost it and slapped her hard before storming out.

He didn't know what to believe about how far things had gone between them, but he still loved her and wanted to marry her, so he forgave her that indiscretion. They got back together about a week after that. He'd kept a closer eye on her and had learnt of at least three recent occasions that she had visited Ifeanyi at his office. One of these days he would have to pay him a visit himself to find out why Amaka couldn't stay away from him and let him know what grave danger he was in messing with his woman.

"Bro, it's time," Jimmy said, with a huge smile. They had had a mad time at the bachelor's party last night. Jimmy had organised it and ensured that Jamie had the time of his life. And Jamie never needed persuasion. Jimmy wondered if he had kept the stripper's number. She was a fox! "Ready to be a one-woman man?"

"There's no such thing," Jamie said, with a straight face and a final appraisal of his reflection. He hugged his brothers and let out a big sigh. It was time to make an honest woman out of Amaka.

Amaka sat with her legs crossed, looking longingly at Ifeanyi, wondering when he was going to quit this "good guy" act and stop playing hard to get. She knew his reputation. She had done her homework. His wife couldn't be so fantastic that she had spoiled him for all women. No, she wasn't going to take "no" for an answer!

"Look, Amaka. What happened between us was a mistake. It can never happen again," Ifeanyi said. He looked serious, but she didn't believe him.

"You've said that before, remember? You said you could never cheat on your wife, but then you *did*. You want me, just admit it, and all our lives will be better. Marie doesn't have to know..."

He stood up and went to the door. He opened it. "Please leave."

Amaka stood up. This game was getting long. She went to him and touched his face. "Don't you remember how good it felt to give in?" she whispered in his ears. She dared to kiss his lips, and he shut and locked the door.

They continued to kiss as they made their way to his office desk. The contents went tumbling on the floor, as he brushed them away and carried her and placed her on it. *At last,* she thought, frantically removing his shirt. "Say my name, baby. Say my name..."

"Amaka! Amaka! Chiamaka!"

Amaka snapped out of her daydream and looked at her mother. "Huh?"

"Where were you?" Mrs Nkechi asked, staring weirdly at her daughter.

Amaka sighed deeply. These daydreams were becoming an occupational hazard. She couldn't get Ifeanyi out of her head. She offered her mother a smile. "I was just...dreaming..."

"I can imagine... But you guys have already done the deed, *nau...* You can't be worried about your wedding night," Mrs Nkechi said.

"Hmmm..." Amaka muttered. That was truly the last thing on her mind. Jamie wasn't bad in bed, though. She had been quite content with him...until Ifeanyi. Compared to Ifeanyi, Amaka realised what a selfish lover Jamie was. She was now bored of him sexually and craved more of Ifeanyi.

If only he would get over his stupid conscience and just accept her offer to have an affair. Didn't he realise how lucky he was? How many men would want to be in his shoes? She didn't give herself to just anyone! And besides, it was just sex, not like she wanted a relationship or anything. *That* she would leave for his poor, pitiful wife!

"Okay, well... This is the day we've all been waiting for! I'm so happy for you, darling. You look beautiful," Mrs Nkechi gushed at her daughter, who was the most beautiful bride Lagos had seen in a while.

As if she needed to be told... Amaka smiled at her mother. She had chosen the dress specifically for how it accentuated all her curves and revealed just enough cleavage, but not too much to look slutty. She looked dynamite. She could just imagine Ifeanyi's face when he sees her today! They'd probably be having sex in a closet somewhere, before the reception was over. She smiled to herself as she played that small daydream in her head.

Her elder sister, Adania, entered the changing room. "Good, you're ready. Everyone's waiting. Let's go."

Ifeanyi was in two minds about going to the Solomon wedding. He hadn't received a word from God about it, and his father had counselled him to still go. He said that if he didn't go, it would raise questions and possibly suspicions. All he had to do was show up at the reception, enjoy the meal, take some photos, and say his goodbye to his boss. Ideally, if Mary could stomach it, she should accompany him. The fewer questions, the better.

Ifeanyi swallowed. Mary, surprisingly, had taken it coolly when he had relayed his father's counsel and requested for her to accompany him for support. "If you need me to come with you, then I will be there with you," she had said.

He sighed. As he watched her get ready, he thought how unfair it was that she should have to attend the wedding of the woman who had slept with her husband. Could she really handle it? What if she broke down during the reception? What if Amaka said something really stupid to her? What if Amaka tried something…?

He would have felt more confident about going if he didn't know how relentless Amaka was. She hadn't stopped sending him messages and visiting him at the office. Anyone observing would believe they were having an affair, even though they were not! He had told her repeatedly to stop coming to see him and stop sending him messages, and he'd even threatened that he would notify the security to bar her from entering his building.

"You wouldn't dare! Don't you know who I am? I'm about to become the newest *Mrs Solomon*. You will need an explanation for why you want me barred." She had smiled mischievously. She was pure evil! What had he done?

The last time she had come to his office, just a few days ago, he had decided that he would have to quit his job! He didn't need it anyway. He could work for his father, or better yet, start something on his own. He intended to present his notice after the wedding, and hopefully, he wouldn't still be there when Amaka returned from her honeymoon. He didn't need anyone's advice on that one. There seemed no other way around it.

Mary came to him and said, "I'm ready. How do I look?"

Like a million dollars, Ifeanyi thought. Mary was a sensational beauty, even after three kids. She was always so hard on herself, as if she didn't know how beautiful she was. She was taller than average, at five feet six inches, and had a slender frame. He stood a whole head above her at six feet two inches. She had curves in all the right places, and they were even more pronounced now that she had given birth. "You look amazing, Mary. You're still the most beautiful woman in the world to me."

Mary smiled shyly. She swallowed. *What else would he say?* She knew Amaka was very beautiful. Even as a woman, she couldn't deny it.

However, while Amaka had the loud, in your face type of beauty, Mary had a more classical look. They were different. And Mary had so much more going for her. She had the very desirable meek spirit of a woman who feared the Lord. And that was the fundamental reason Ifeanyi loved her so much.

He took hold of her hand and stroked it tenderly while looking intently into her eyes. "Baby, we don't have to go if you don't want to. I want you to decide. We can stay home and make love," Mary smiled, "or we can go, then come back and make love?"

Mary swallowed and stroked Ifeanyi's face. "It would feel so nice, leaving the wedding and knowing that I am the one taking you home..." she joked. Ifeanyi smiled. "Let's go. I'll be okay."

Ifeanyi kissed his wife passionately. She was truly the best thing that had ever happened to him.

36

"Let thy fountain be blessed: and rejoice with the wife of thy youth. Let her be as the loving hind and pleasant roe; let her breasts satisfy thee at all times; and be thou ravished always with her love."

PROVERBS 5:18-19

It was a beautiful, sunny Saturday in early April. The socialites, and everyone who was anybody in Lagos, were at the reception of the wedding ceremony between John Solomon Jnr's first son, Jamie, and Chiamaka, the second daughter to the late General Uzoma Nkechi. The security guards at the three entrances of the banquet hall did their best to follow protocol, but Nigerians always had their way of getting past protocol. Many were seated at the wedding who had never seen the invitation card!

Ifeanyi and Mary arrived at the hall in time to see the newest Bride and Groom of Lagos do their celebration dance. Ifeanyi went to greet his boss, who was happy to see him and asked if he would be joining their long banquet table. Ifeanyi humbly declined and showed him the table where his beautiful wife was sitting. She waved at them when they looked her way.

Ifeanyi returned with a bottle of champagne his boss had given him from his high table. He pulled up a seat and drew closer to his wife. "Thank you for coming with me," he whispered in her ear. She smiled at him.

The bridal party made their way to the centre of the hall, where an area had been prepared for the couple's first dance. It was difficult to see the bride and groom through the crowd surrounding them, but the video footage was showing on the big screens for all to see. The bride was certainly looking her best as she ground provocatively against her husband, to the envy of many of the men in the hall. Their friends cheered them on as they danced to several Nigerian wedding favourites.

Chuka and Ijeoma were not able to make it, as Ijeoma had just been delivered of her baby boy in late March. Mary was happy to see her former boss, Mrs Kelechi Nwachukwu, who had attended with her husband. She excused herself and went to greet them.

"Hey! Long time!" Kelechi grinned when she saw Mary. "How are you?"

"I'm fine! Good afternoon, sir," Mary greeted Mr Nwachukwu. He smiled at her pleasantly.

"How are the kids? I hear we are on number three," Kelechi said.

"Yeah," Mary giggled. "They are all doing fine. How are you? How's work?"

"We're good. Well, you know we are missing you... You should stop by the office once in a while. No one said you can't visit, right?" she said.

"Yeah, I will. I've missed you too."

"Where's Ifeanyi?" Kelechi asked, looking behind Mary to see if she could spot him.

Mary looked around. He wasn't at their table. She swallowed, remembering to trust and not fear. "He's here somewhere... He's probably greeting his colleagues."

"Okay. Well, greet him for me. It was nice catching up, Mary."

"Yeah; I'll drop by for a visit soon. Bye." Mary returned to her seat to wait for Ifeanyi. Thankfully, Amaka was seated with her husband on their special love-seat, so Ifeanyi could not have been doing anything sneaky with her.

"Hey, Mary, where's Ifeanyi?"

Mary turned to see her sister-in-law and her husband. She stood up and hugged them.

"I don't know, but he should be here soon," she replied.

Chidinma and Emmanuel sat down at the table. Mary noticed the special care Emmanuel used in settling his wife in her seat. "Didn't you guys come together?" Chidinma asked.

"Yes, we did. He went..."

"To rustle up some grub," Ifeanyi said as he returned. He had brought waiters to their table. He leaned in and kissed his wife softly on her lips. He hugged his brother-in-law and kissed his sister's cheek. "Are we expecting?" he asked, looking at his sister, whose expression broke into a big smile.

"How did you know?" she beamed.

"I've come to recognise the glow of a pregnant woman. Call it a gift," he grinned. "Congrats to you both."

"Congratulations!" Mary said, cheerfully.

"Thanks," Emmanuel and Chidinma said together. Emmanuel kissed his wife on the cheek. "It's been a long wait. We couldn't be happier. But please, we're not telling anyone else for now. Don't want to jinx it."

"How many weeks?"

"Four," Chidinma said. "They said twelve weeks is the ideal time for telling family and friends. Then, it's more likely to result in labour."

"I wouldn't be so negative, Chidinma. There is power in faith. Believe God will see you through. I am happy for you," Mary said.

"Thank you," Chidinma smiled, letting out a sigh of relief. "I'm starving!"

"I can just imagine," Mary said and giggled.

They all tucked into their meal. Ifeanyi looked at his wife and smiled. Looking at her, no one would ever know the torment she would be going through, being at that wedding. He leaned into her and kissed her affectionately on the cheek. "You're amazing, you know that?" he whispered.

She turned to him and kissed him back. "You owe me, BIG!" she whispered back.

"Don't worry, it will be my pleasure," Ifeanyi teased, and Mary giggled. "I love you."

"I love you too," Mary beamed.

"Do you guys want a room?" Chidinma asked, and Emmanuel laughed. The lovebirds cooled it and focused on their meal.

Amaka frowned at the offensive sight. Ifeanyi was playing happy families with his wife! How pathetic. No one would know what a cheater he was, the way he was carrying on.

She pitied his wife. She was so clueless. She probably didn't even know that her husband had spent a steamy night at her house. She wished she could tell her so she would wipe that "I'm the luckiest woman in the world" smile off her pretty little face!

Amaka plastered a smile on her face as another group of their friends came to snap a photograph with the newly-wed couple. She was seething inside. Ifeanyi hadn't even looked in her direction once! She needed an excuse to go over to their table.

"Kiss!" the photographer said to the happy couple. Amaka dutifully leaned into her husband and planted a big kiss on his lips for the photo. He converted it to a smooch, and those observing laughed while Amaka pretended to be embarrassed.

The compère was still introducing the many dignitaries that had come to grace the occasion with their presence. Soon, they would be cutting their wedding cake. Amaka tried to look around so that it wasn't obvious that a particular table was holding her attention, but she couldn't help looking at Ifeanyi's table once every minute. His wife seemed to be having the time of her life. She wondered what they were laughing about.

Damilola Ogunyemi, Mary's old friend from the NYSC camp, was also at the wedding and was seated at Mary's table. She had come with her new boyfriend, Sola Olatunji. The man was a joker and had them all in stitches with laughter. And a Nigerian wedding was never short of material to draw upon, not to talk of a Nigerian/American wedding! The atmosphere was charged with political tension, Sola had said, not realising just how close to the truth he actually was.

"Man, they should have called you to MC this wedding," Emmanuel said, between giggles, tears in his eyes from laughter.

"*You wan die? Or you wan make dem kill me?*" Sola said in broken English and giggled.

"But seriously, dude... Do you MC?" Emmanuel asked.

"Yeah, but mostly conferences and smaller parties," Sola replied, encouraged by the reaction he had gotten at the table.

"You're ready to go home?" Ifeanyi asked Mary. She was having a good time, but she knew what awaited her at home. She nodded.

"Alright guys, we're going to start heading," Ifeanyi said.

"So soon?" Chidinma frowned. "The party is just getting started."

"*Dem get their own party for house. Shey na true talk I dey yan*?" Emmanuel asked with a wink.

"You're in the Spirit," Ifeanyi said with a giggle.

Mary blushed and hugged Chidinma and Emmanuel. She went and hugged Damilola too. She was going to settle for a wave for Sola, but he stood up and requested a hug. She chuckled as she gave him a hug too.

Mary was surprised with how easy and drama-free the wedding had been. She was glad that they had attended and had been able to catch up with friends and family. She had gone to greet her mother and father-in-law at the high table when they had arrived. They had been pleased to see her and Ifeanyi. Mrs Chukwueke had winked at her, which she had found encouraging. Now, she had done her duty, she couldn't wait to go home so Ifeanyi could perform his...

"You're leaving so soon...?"

Mary was surprised to be standing face to face with the bride, who was blocking their path to the exit. She turned to look at her husband.

"We just came to say congratulations and show our support. But we have other plans for the day now," Ifeanyi replied, pulling his wife close for a kiss on the cheek.

"Well, the whole gang's here, and they want to meet you," Amaka said, waving at some friends who were approaching from behind the couple. "They didn't believe me when I told them you were now married with *three* kids - or is it FOUR?!"

Ifeanyi and Mary turned around and saw five beautiful ladies dressed in *aso ebi*. They all hugged Ifeanyi one by one, then proceeded to ignore Mary's presence. Ifeanyi was very uncomfortable about the whole thing, especially as he was sure he had had sexual relations with every one of those women! How they all happened to be present at this wedding couldn't have been a coincidence.

He released his grip from the last woman and said as politely as he could, "Lolade, Funmi, Amina, Omi, and Teni, meet my beautiful wife, Mary." They eventually acknowledged her presence with smiles. She smiled politely in return. "It was lovely meeting you all again, but we have to be going."

"Oh, why, Ifeanyi...?" they moaned in unison. "Stay for one dance at least! Mary won't mind..." Amina appealed to him, as they pulled him away from Mary.

Ifeanyi knew what they were trying to do, and he had been afraid that Amaka would try to embarrass Mary. He couldn't let that happen. He pulled himself free and ignored their protests. He took Mary's hand, and they walked determinedly away from the banquet.

When they got to his car, he apologised. "I'm so sorry for what happened back there..."

Mary smiled and said cheekily, "Less talk and more action!"

"You got it, ma'am!" Ifeanyi beamed. He got behind the wheel and started the car excitedly. He couldn't wait to get home!

After making love, Mary and Ifeanyi lay naked in each other's arms, reminiscing about the party.

"So, how is it that you remembered all their names?" Mary asked, her head on his chest as she looked up at the ceiling.

"I was a player, not a slut. When you juggle so many women, you have to learn to remember their names," he said.

"Hmmm... So, you remember *all* their names? How many?"

"Mary, this is not a good conversation," Ifeanyi objected.

"Come on... Tell! You know all of mine..."

"Yeah, well, that's because there was just me and that dead... bastard. I'm sorry, there was no better word!"

"So, if I hadn't come with you today, do you think you would still be dancing at the party with those girls?" Mary turned and looked at him.

"No, I honestly think I would have run home to you! That was a miserable life, Mary. Why do you think I came after you with all I had?! I was desperate for something and someone more, and I knew you were the real deal when I met you. I can't go back to that life..." Ifeanyi said sincerely.

"Awww, so sweet…" Mary smiled.

Ifeanyi nibbled her lips. "One of you, Mary, is better than a thousand of them! I feel richer than King Solomon."

Mary's heart was full with love at his declaration. "Thank God I found you then…"

"THANK GOD!" Ifeanyi exclaimed and pulled his wife under him again. He was ready for round two. She chuckled with glee when she saw the glint in his eye.

37

"Let thy fountain be blessed: and rejoice with the wife of thy youth. Let her be as the loving hind and pleasant roe; let her breasts satisfy thee at all times; and be thou ravished always with her love."

PROVERBS 5:18-19

Ifeanyi handed in his letter of resignation when he resumed work on Monday. Unfortunately, due to his high-level position, he wouldn't be able to leave the job for three months or until a replacement could be found and trained, whichever was sooner. He wasn't too pleased about that, but he trusted God to work everything out for his favour.

He was happier than he had ever been with Mary. Life was good. Somehow, they had gotten closer since they reconciled after his infidelity, and he was glad that he had listened to God and confessed. The lie had been eating him up inside.

Even though things seemed better now, he had no plans of slipping again, not that he would want to. But he wouldn't even put himself close to that situation again and risk losing the good thing he had with Mary. His fall had been shocking to him too because he had thought he was stronger than that. He still found Amaka attractive, and he knew he was still vulnerable, so he had to be brutal and cut all ties.

He had spoken to his dad about his decision to quit at Solomon Investment Bank, and his father had offered him a managerial position in one of his companies while he trained to take over. Everything was going to work out fine, he thought and sighed.

He picked up a picture of himself and Mary on his desk, which he had framed, and smiled. What had he done to deserve a woman like her? He decided to call her at home.

"Hey, darling... How are you?" he asked when she had picked up.

Mary smiled, pausing from her work briefly. "I'm fine, honey. How are you?"

"Missing you..." Ifeanyi said sweetly into the phone.

Mary grinned. He was such a sweetheart. "I miss you too. How's work?"

"It's okay. I handed in my resignation today. It's time for a change."

"Okay, good. As long as you're sure that's what you want. I know you loved the job," Mary replied.

"Yes... It's the best thing. How's blogging?" Ifeanyi asked.

"Good, good. Catching up on my mail and reading up on other bloggers' sites."

"Cool... Well, I just wanted to check in with you and hear your voice. I love you."

"I love you, too, babe. Have a great day at work! Abi, Uche, and Chuks send their love."

Ifeanyi made three kiss sounds on the phone. "And for you, muaaah!" He made a loud kissing sound. Mary giggled and blew one back before hanging up.

Ifeanyi sighed. *This love, oh...* He gave the picture one last look before placing it down gently and getting back to work.

The days and weeks that followed flew by in a haze as the passion between Mary and Ifeanyi burned ever hotter. They were the sort of couple that made singles wish they were married and the unhappily married wish they had waited for true love. Ifeanyi did all he could to make sure that Mary forgot that he ever betrayed her. No one would have suspected from observing the couple that they had ever suffered such a storm in their marriage.

Mary was positively glowing, when she walked into her former office to greet her former boss and colleagues. She was smart and caring enough not to come empty handed. She smelt of the delicious chocolate chip cookies she had baked just that morning to share with them.

Aisha was the first to spot her and literally screamed when she saw Mary. "Aaaahhh! Mrs *Ifeanyi* Chukwueke! At last, you've come to greet us," she said, dramatically.

Mary chuckled and received Aisha in a big, warm hug. "I'm so sorry. I brought cookies as a show of repentance."

"You're forgiven. Hmmm... Chocolate chip, my favourite!" Aisha beamed, carrying the whole box to her desk.

Her other co-workers turned from their seats to greet Mary. A couple stood up to hug her too and promptly joined Aisha in devouring the cookies. Mary noticed that one of them had gone, and there were two new faces in the office.

"Oh, this is Mary? We've heard so much about you... Aisha won't stop going on about you. She reads your blog every day!" one of the newbies said. "Hi, I'm Nwanda."

"Nice to meet you, Nwanda. I hope you like chocolate chip cookies," Mary said.

The other newbie was shy. Her name was Lucy. She looked like she was still in school. She was obviously a trainee.

Mary knocked on Kelechi's door. "Come in," came her response.

A bright smile broke on her face when Kelechi saw who her visitor was. Now that they were no longer boss and employee, Kelechi didn't hesitate to show her affection for Mary. They hugged warmly, and Mary realised what a disservice it had been for her not to have visited for so long. She missed the woman so.

"Hmmm... So, tell me; how's married life? Is it all you ever hoped it would be?"

Mary beamed. Her face said it all. But to fulfil all righteousness, she said, "That and more..."

Kelechi chuckled. "That's great. It's written all over your face. I told you it would all work out."

"Yes, you did. Thanks for always believing in me...in us. Sometimes I think you are my guardian angel!"

Kelechi blushed at that compliment, and her eyes watered. Why was it that any time Mary was in her office, someone had to be in tears? She wondered as she reached for her box of tissues.

Mary and Ifeanyi took the twins and Abigail to visit with Ijeoma and Chuka and to spend time with Emeka, Ifeanyi's son. They brought gifts for their new baby, Chika, who was the spitting image of Chuka. Emeka and Ekene were excited to see them as usual.

At almost four and half years old, Emeka was a big kid. He doted on his mother and was protective of his younger brother, Ekene, who was only three years old. Both boys were fascinated with Chika and were eager to carry out small errands for their mother, like bringing Baby's blanket and helping to shake his bottle. However, when Mary and Ifeanyi arrived with the twins, Chukwudi and Uche, they quickly abandoned their duties to play with their younger brothers, who were far more fascinating, because they could do a lot more things than cry!

"Congratulations!" Mary sang, presenting the gift bag she and Ifeanyi had packed for Chika. Ijeoma beamed at her. Motherhood looked good on Ijeoma, Mary thought.

"Thanks, guys," Ijeoma smiled, not able to arise from her seat, as Chika was latched to her breast, enjoying his lunch. Chuka arose to collect the gift bag and give Mary and Ifeanyi hugs and kisses.

"Thanks for coming over." Chuka sounded tired, as though he was the one that had just delivered the 9lb baby boy.

"Congratulations, man! Three boys!" Ifeanyi marvelled. "Are you going to try for a girl?"

"I think we're done. Am I right, babe?" Chuka turned to his wife, giving her a half-smile.

"Don't mind him, *joor*... He's just thinking about the money," Ijeoma hissed, fondly. "I think a girl will round us off nicely. I've always wanted a little girl, but maybe we'll try in a year or so."

"What about you guys?" Chuka asked, hoping to turn the attention from himself.

Ifeanyi looked at Mary. He still desired more kids. Her eyes told him she wasn't *totally* opposed to the idea. He smiled. "Maybe... We'll see how it goes. But only one more, I think. Right, Mary?" She simply nodded in agreement.

Mary placed Abigail down to sleep in her stroller and turned to Ijeoma. "So, how was the labour?"

"It was a breeze. I was barely in there for an hour. Apparently, it gets easier the more kids you have," Ijeoma said, with a grin.

"Hmmm..." Mary muttered. That hadn't been her experience. She also wondered how Ijeoma managed to look slimmer than she had done before her pregnancy. Mary was still conscious of the extra weight she had put on, but she was actively working it off. Her frequent bedroom sessions with Ifeanyi gave her some much-needed exercise as well. She smiled to herself remembering their session this morning.

Chuka asked the maid to bring drinks and small chops for his guests before signalling for Ifeanyi to follow him to the veranda while the women carried on their pregnancy, delivery, and maternity discussions. Ifeanyi gave Mary a wink as he followed Chuka through the glass sliding doors. Ijeoma didn't miss it.

"Hmmm... So, it's still hot, *eh*?" she joked, and Mary blushed.

Red hot, she thought but simply smiled.

When Ijeoma was still looking at her pointedly, Mary asked, "Isn't it supposed to be? I guess I don't really have anything to compare our relationship to. He's my first everything - and the last! As far as I'm concerned, he's the best in the world."

"Yeah, I guess you don't. Well, we're still hot too. It's just, Chuka worries a lot about money, you know? Besides that, we get on great. He's definitely the best *I've* ever had," Ijeoma smiled.

"Hey! Don't throw that!" Ijeoma suddenly shouted at Emeka, who had just picked up his big toy truck and was about to hurl it across the room. "You might hurt someone. You guys should play safe, okay? Glory!"

The nanny came moments later. "Please watch these boys... They are starting to play rough. And tell Mike that we are still waiting for the drinks and small chops."

Ijeoma turned to Mary again. "Mike's the cook. That's the only way I can function with three kids!" She laughed.

Mary gave her a small smile. She now understood why Chuka was anxious about money and sounded so tired. Especially if Ijeoma wasn't working either. She wondered how she would broach the subject with Ijeoma, and if it was even her place to. Maybe she would write a blogpost about it. She decided she would do just that, and her face brightened again.

"Hmmm... This is awesome," Ijeoma sighed, her head facing the tiled floor in the dimly lit room.

"Hmmm..." Mary muttered, inhaling deeply. The incense filled room was relaxing all her muscles. "I really needed this."

The masseuse finished her work on Mary's legs, completing the full body massage. "When you're ready, you can go to the steam room," she said, as she left the double room with her colleague.

Mary let out a deep breath as she turned on her back, thoroughly relaxed. Ijeoma had a good stretch.

"It was so nice of Ifeanyi to include me," Ijeoma said. "Please thank him for me."

"Don't worry, I will," Mary smiled, exhaling. "Now, I don't know what to do for his birthday..."

"Oh, that's right. Isn't it this weekend?" Ijeoma asked.

Mary nodded. "I've been racking my brain trying to think of something to do. And then he springs me with a surprise day at the spa!"

"Men don't need much. A nice gift, a meal, and sex!" Ijeoma giggled. "It's not like it's his big 4.0, is it? You can just take him out to dinner or something."

"Yeah, I got his gift already. Bought it while I was in America."

"There you go. Now, all you have to do is ship those kids off to their gran's and prepare a sensual treat for him when he gets home from work tomorrow!"

Not a bad idea, Mary thought. Ifeanyi was certainly easy to please.

The house was unusually quiet when Mary returned home from her spa day. She was shimmering glossy all over from the treatments she had received. She was surprised to see that the living room was lit only with candles when she opened the door to the main house. She instantly perceived the mouth-watering smell of food from the kitchen. A smile broke on her face. What was Ifeanyi up to?

Her hand flew to her mouth when she saw a buck naked Ifeanyi in her kitchen. He turned around to reveal his short apron, which covered his manhood, but made him look so deliciously scrumptious that Mary had no more appetite for the food. He smiled when he saw the look in her eyes. That was the effect he was going for.

"How was your day, honey?" he asked casually, as if he wasn't cooking naked in the kitchen.

Mary swallowed some saliva that had gathered in her mouth. "It was great... Thank you. And yours?" she asked, breathlessly.

"Pretty good," Ifeanyi said with a nod and a smile. "I took the day off."

"I can see that..." Mary's eyes scanned the kitchen. He had been very busy in there. So many lovely delicacies, she wondered if he had really made them all. "Baby, what are you up to? Where are the kids?"

"They're at my mum's," he said, licking his fingers. "You don't mind, do you? I wanted the house to ourselves for the next few days." Ifeanyi put down the cooking spoon and the napkin in his hand and walked slowly over to Mary, who seemed to be riveted where she stood.

"*Days*? What's the matter? Have you finally been given leave? Or...is there something you want to tell me?" Mary's voice trailed off with the last question. She thought of the unexpected spa day and wondered if Ifeanyi was buttering her for another fall. She swallowed hard as she looked at him for an explanation of his behaviour, her heart pounding in her chest.

Ifeanyi reached her and silenced all her fears with his kiss. That kiss with the adventurous tongue that always made her go weak at the knees. Mary gasped when his mouth left hers and his tongue trailed up and down her neck to finally settle on her shoulder, where he planted more sweet kisses. She quivered in anticipation of their lovemaking.

"It's my birthday this Saturday. And you're all I want," he spoke softly into her ear, heat in his breath. He sucked on her lips while his hands roamed freely all over her body, relieving her of her clothing. "Oh, yeah... And world peace," he added with a grin, his lips still pressed against hers. Mary couldn't help the giggle that escaped her lips.

He claimed her lips again in a most delicious kiss, with his hands on her buttocks and her back pressed against the wall. Without further ado, Ifeanyi swept Mary off her feet and proceeded to savour his birthday treat, freshly marinated and tenderised from the spa.

They never made it to the bedroom.

38

"Let thy fountain be blessed: and rejoice with the wife of thy youth. Let
her be as the loving hind and pleasant roe; let her breasts satisfy thee
at all times; and be thou ravished
always with her love."

PROVERBS 5:18-19

The lovers eventually got around to eating the delicious
spread Ifeanyi had cooked up. He was indeed a man of
many talents. With the house all to themselves, they sat
in their underwear on the rug in the living room, with a small
mat laid for the food, as though they were having a picnic. They
ceremoniously fed each other with their hands, enjoying the
opportunity to keep touching and teasing themselves.

Mary was unbelievably happy. She was so happy, she worried if it was sinful. Ifeanyi made her laugh, and she enjoyed teasing him too. She wished every day was like this, but she immediately realised that if every day was like that, then she wouldn't appreciate such occasions. She sighed and swallowed.

After their meal, she cleared up the mat and took everything to the kitchen. She would return to wash them later, she thought to herself as she returned to her husband, where he was still sitting on the rug. She sat in his embrace and enjoyed being close to him and not having a care in the world.

"I was thinking..." he said. Mary turned to look at him then relaxed in his embrace again. "If we had more kids, I don't think we'd have many more occasions like this."

"Hmmm..." Mary muttered. She liked where his mind was going.

"And I promised to take you around the world sometime..."

"Hm hmm."

"We've been fortunate - blessed - to have three children in as many years, haven't we?"

"Yes, dear. We've been very blessed," Mary said and nodded.

Ifeanyi sighed deeply. It had taken a while for him to get to this point, but he had to admit it. "I am content. I mean, if we had another child, I would be *happy*. But, I don't think we should try for another child. I am content with our family as we are."

Mary turned to him fully to look at his face. "Do you mean that?"

Ifeanyi nodded.

"So, it's not the sex that has turned your head...? You are thinking straight, right?" Mary joked, waving a finger in his face.

Ifeanyi giggled. "Well, it did sort of... But yeah, I'm thinking straight."

Mary couldn't help but continue the tease. "How many fingers am I holding up?"

Ifeanyi laughed and tickled her, and she giggled like a child. "I'm serious, baby. I'm content. And most of all, I want you to be happy. I know you want more from life than raising children, and I want you to enjoy all you do. And for that, we need balance.

Three is a good number. And honestly, I *love* this… I want more of this."

"Me too…" Mary said, sincerely. "I'm glad you finally came around."

"Well, with the way you put it on me…" Ifeanyi teased.

Mary laughed out loud.

The next day, Friday, Mary took over treating Ifeanyi. She made him breakfast in bed. Afterwards, they showered together, stealing pleasures while at it. After they had dressed, they settled down to study the Bible together and then prayed.

"So, what do you want to do today?" Mary asked when they had completed their time of devotion, and she had tidied up the kitchen. "Want to go to the mall?"

"I thought it was *my* birthday we are celebrating," Ifeanyi baulked, raising an eyebrow.

Mary giggled. "So, you mean you wouldn't like to treat yourself to something nice? I promise, I'll close my eyes and pay!"

"Hmmm… Tempting. But, I think I'd rather go to Get Arena, then we can catch a movie at the Palms after…"

"I'm up for it," Mary said, enthusiastically. "Don't think because it's your birthday I'll go easy on you. Be prepared to race!"

"It's ON!" Ifeanyi laughed.

Ifeanyi beat Mary each time around the tracks at Get Arena. She took it like a champ. They drove the short distance to the Palms Shopping Mall, where they had some lunch and enjoyed a late afternoon movie.

Ifeanyi noticed Mary was distracted on her phone during the movie. He wondered who could be demanding so much of her attention. She was usually good at switching off other things when they were having time together.

"Who you chatting with?" he finally asked, unable to contain his curiosity.

Mary looked up and smiled. "Sorry, I'll be done soon."

Ifeanyi raised an eyebrow. She hadn't answered him. "Is it someone I know?"

He wondered if Mary was chatting with David. Ever since they had bumped into each other at the beach, he had become a little anxious that David would try something with Mary. He knew he shouldn't think like that... And Mary wasn't that kind of a woman. Still, he was nervous.

Mary typed fast and put her phone away. "Done. And yes, you do. But it's confidential."

Confidential? Ifeanyi swallowed hard. Was David pouring out his heart to his wife? Why was he being so paranoid? He knew that Mary sometimes had confidential conversations with people because of her blog, but not usually people he knew...

Mary could tell that Ifeanyi was uncomfortable with her answer, but she really couldn't tell him more. She snuggled into his arms, and he relaxed. They enjoyed the rest of the movie, with occasional kisses and giggles shared.

After the movie, the lights came back on, and Ifeanyi noticed that Mary was missing an ear-ring. They looked for it around their seat but couldn't find it anywhere. They checked outside the cinema hall too. Still nothing.

"Maybe I dropped it at Get Arena," Mary said. "Can we check it on our way home?"

"Sure," Ifeanyi said. But he was sure she had it on when they arrived at the Palms.

"Suurprissse! Happy Birthday!"

The lounge at Get Arena was filled with Ifeanyi's friends. He turned to look at his wife, who smiled sheepishly at him. She put on her missing ear-ring, which she had hidden in her handbag.

"You?!" Ifeanyi laughed, pointing an accusing finger at Mary. She chuckled. "You really got me, there!"

"Happy Birthday, bro!" the greetings started coming in as his friends surrounded him.

Mary smiled to herself and greeted everyone, hugging the few that she knew well. She'd thought fast on her feet when Ifeanyi had said he wanted to go to Get Arena. When she saw the lounge, she knew it would be a perfect place to have a get together. She'd contacted Chuka, and he'd taken care of the rest. Being a Friday night, many of Ifeanyi's friends were happy to come out and join them.

Ifeanyi was pleasantly surprised by the party. It was a good crowd of mostly friends from church and the NYSC camp, with just a few of his old friends who he still talked to and occasionally met at events. It was also a good mix of men and women, and they mingled easily. However, those from camp kept to one side of the lounge, and those from church took up the other. Ifeanyi settled somewhere in the middle with Mary, Chuka, and Ijay.

Chuka, always the party starter, got everyone's attention and suggested some party and drinking games they could play. It was just what was needed to get the group more relaxed, and soon, instead of two main groups, they became one big group, laughing and joking, drinking and eating.

A few people arrived late when the party was in full swing. One of them was Kemi Ojo, Ifeanyi's friend from church. She came over to give him a hug. Mary thought the hug was longer than he had given others but tried not to think too much about it. She knew they were good friends, and she didn't want to start getting paranoid over every woman he knew. Kemi hugged Mary, Chuka, and Ijay too, and found somewhere in the middle to sit across from Ifeanyi. She had come with a friend, who obviously didn't know anyone.

Mary couldn't help noticing the way Kemi kept looking at Ifeanyi. Whatever his feelings for her, it was clear she wanted more than his friendship. Mary had noticed this before, but then, she'd trusted Ifeanyi. Now, she was nervous and uncomfortable. She looked at Ifeanyi to see if he could tell that Kemi was into him. His behaviour didn't suggest that he knew anything nor that he was interested in her. Still, Mary couldn't help but wonder.

Ifeanyi smiled at Mary. She seemed oddly quiet, he thought. Maybe she had had enough and was ready to go home. He was having a good time, but by 10 pm, he was ready to call it a night himself. He was no longer the late night or party all night type of guy. He wanted to be alone with Mary, in their home.

He noticed Kemi looking at him. She smiled her usual sweet smile. *Hmmm...* Was that why Mary was so quiet, he wondered? Did she think there was something between them?

He knew that Kemi still had a crush on him, but he had never looked at her in that way. Sure, she was attractive, and he had noticed, but he'd never been tempted. However, he knew what he had to do now. He couldn't take the risk, and Mary needed to know that she could trust him.

He'd stayed friends with Kemi because she had been dating someone else, and he thought that she'd moved on. However, she was single again and obviously desirous of attention, even from a married man. He sighed. It was a shame that even among supposedly Christian women he wasn't safe.

"Hey, Kemi, can I have a word?" Ifeanyi asked, suddenly. Everyone was quiet as they looked between them both. Kemi was stunned. Her heart was beating fast as she wondered what it might be about. "Please, carry on. It won't be a minute." Ifeanyi got up and tugged at Mary to follow him.

Kemi's heart dropped when she noticed that Mary had tagged along with Ifeanyi. They went out into the cool night. Mary wasn't sure what Ifeanyi was doing either, but she was glad he had asked her to come along. She would have been worried sick if he had gone out alone with Kemi.

"I was just wondering if you had something to tell me, Kemi. I couldn't help but notice that you've been paying me special attention of late. And no, it's not just tonight," Ifeanyi said, looking Kemi square in the eyes.

Kemi's mouth was dry. What was he talking about? She tried to think of something to say. She didn't know what to say. "I don't know what you're talking about..."

"Is it just me?" Ifeanyi looked at Mary. "Have you noticed anything, babe?"

Mary was taken aback by Ifeanyi's confrontation. She nodded. "Actually, I have. It does seem like there's something you want to tell my husband."

They both looked at Kemi. She swallowed hard. "Well, I guess... We used to talk a lot, and now we don't talk anymore," she offered.

"I thought you realised that once I got married, I couldn't be your confidant anymore. Mary's my best friend and my lover. I'm not looking for anyone to replace her in any area."

Mary looked at Kemi, who was clearly embarrassed. Even though she was trying to hide it, Mary saw that the woman was in love with her husband. She couldn't help but pity her. She wondered why Ifeanyi had decided to confront her like this.

"I'm not asking you to," Kemi said defensively.

"You don't have to say it with your mouth. Your eyes and your body do most of the talking. And it's not just me who noticed. My wife noticed too, and it makes US uncomfortable. I really don't think we can be friends anymore."

"Ifeanyi," Mary said, surprised. *That's a little drastic*, she thought. But deep down, she was relieved and happy that Ifeanyi was fighting the battle she didn't know how to fight.

Kemi was clearly upset. "Are you really saying I can't be your friend because you *suspect* that I have a crush on you?" Her tone was sardonic. "You really are full of yourself, Ifeanyi!"

"Look, I really don't care about your opinion of me. As long as you respect my wife and my marriage. You really have to be careful about the message you are communicating, especially when you profess to be Christian."

"That's rich! You're judging me, and I've done nothing. If you're worried about cheating on your wife, *own* that! Don't project unto me. But it's okay, though. I'll leave. Have a nice life!" Kemi stormed back into the lounge to get her purse and her friend.

Mary swallowed as she watched them walk away. Ifeanyi's hard expression hadn't changed. "Was that really necessary?"

Ifeanyi softened as he looked at Mary. He didn't know what to tell her. How could he tell her that he was so afraid of falling again that the thought made him sick? The thought of hurting her again or losing her actually made him physically sick!

Instead, he pulled her in his arms and kissed her until her knees went weak. And she knew he had to do that. A love like theirs had to be protected at all costs. Mary melted in his arms, savouring his kiss.

Mary and Ifeanyi got home at about 11 pm. After Kemi had stormed out, some other people, mostly their friends from church, had decided to go home too, and others went to a night-club for more fun. Ifeanyi had thanked Chuka for organising the surprise party and appreciated his friends who had attended before he decided to take his wife home.

Ifeanyi appreciated his wife for the outing in his own special way. They made love into his actual birthday. It was exactly the evening he had had in mind for them. Afterwards, they lay in each other's arms; satisfied, naked, vulnerable, and exhausted until the morning. And it was, indeed, a HAPPY Birthday!

VOLUME
SEVEN

39

"Wherefore let him that thinketh he standeth take heed lest he fall..."

1 CORINTHIANS 10:12

Seventeen years ago...

Amaka looked down at the folded white note that had just been passed to her by her neighbour and friend, Sade. Her heart flipped in her chest. She knew who it was from already. He had sent her two before, folded exactly the same way. She thought he was the sweetest thing, and his persistence was endearing. She swallowed as she picked up the paper and proceeded to open and read it under her desk.

> *"I don't know what it is about you, Amaka, but I can't stop thinking about you. Please meet me under the*

mango tree after class. I have something for you. x
Ifeanyi."

Amaka smiled. This one was different. The other two had read, *"Will you be my girlfriend?"* and *"Please go out with me.* ♡*Ifeanyi."* She had simply replied with a "no" both times. It was cruel, but she didn't have time for dating. She moved schools often, and she barely had time to study. She was always catching up, and her grades were poor. Having a boyfriend on top of that would be a definite failure, and her father wouldn't like that at all.

Besides, what if she fell in love and then had to leave him behind to follow her father on his next move? She had made the decision long ago that she didn't have time for boys. Even though Ifeanyi made her want to break the rule, she knew she would be the one hurting if they were to split up. She already liked him too much.

After class, Amaka was in two minds about meeting Ifeanyi. But he said he had something for her, and her curiosity got the better of her. She told Sade she would catch up with her later and followed the route behind the junior secondary building to the farmer's garden, where the mango tree was.

Ifeanyi was leaning on the tree waiting for her. He was too handsome. She took a deep breath and tried to remember her decision.

"Thanks for coming," Ifeanyi said, with a shy smile.

"You said you had something for me?" Amaka replied, emphasising her reason for coming.

Ifeanyi gave a nervous giggle. "Are you always so direct?"

"That's the only way to be," Amaka said. "So, where is it?"

"Can't we talk first?" Ifeanyi asked.

Amaka sighed. "Well, we don't have much time before the next class. What do you want to talk about?" She folded her arms across her full bosom. Even at fourteen years old, she was all filled out.

"Why won't you go out with me?" Ifeanyi decided to be direct too.

Amaka looked him in his eyes, and he was so sincere, her heart melted. She could make an exception... What if he was 'the one'? But the thought made her giggle. She didn't believe in fairy tales.

Ifeanyi was embarrassed by her giggle, misunderstanding her. He straightened his expression and pressed his lips together in a frown. She didn't have to be cruel.

"I'm sorry. It's really nothing personal. To be honest, I like you." Ifeanyi smiled again. There was hope. "It's just, my dad's in the Army, and we're constantly moving. This is my third school since I started junior secondary, and it is really destabilising." Ifeanyi nodded, showing that he understood. "I'm always catching up, relearning things, adjusting, and making new friends. I don't have time for a relationship, and mostly, I can't risk the heartbreak." She swallowed when she concluded her account.

"Thanks for being honest. I understand, and it's a shame. I really, *really* like you. But, I don't know if I could handle the heartbreak either if you were to suddenly go."

They were both quiet, as they looked at each other with longing. "I guess we can be friends at least... Maybe in the next life, or if we meet again when we're older, we could give love a try," Amaka said.

"Here's hoping you won't be taken! I know you will have a lot of suitors. But yeah, maybe..."

Amaka cut him off with a kiss on the lips. Ifeanyi smiled widely, his eyes dancing as he looked at her for an explanation. "You just looked so sweet, I couldn't resist."

"If we're going to be just friends, you can't be doing that," Ifeanyi joked, still gushing from the kiss and wishing she would do it again.

Amaka giggled. "So, we're friends."

Ifeanyi took off his school bag and opened it. He brought out the gift box he had bought for Amaka and handed it to her. She beamed with delight when she saw that it was jewellery.

Wow! She should have said "yes," she thought. They could have managed a long-distance relationship. People do it all the time.

She opened the box and pulled out a gold bracelet. Engraved inside were the words, "I love you." Amaka's eyes began to water.

"I know you're not my girlfriend, but I still want you to have it. I'm glad we can be friends," Ifeanyi said.

"Thank you. This is lovely. Beautiful! I'll cherish it. Forever..." Amaka said, giving Ifeanyi a hug.

The bell for the next class rang, and Ifeanyi escorted Amaka to her class before heading over to his.

♥ ♥ ♥

Present day...

Amaka looked down at the old, gold bracelet on her wrist. She had never taken it off. Even though she didn't believe in fairy tales, she had secretly hoped that one day, they would meet again, fall in love, and live happily ever after.

Even though she had had other toasters, flings, and relationships since, none of them quite compared to Ifeanyi, and the feelings she felt those few months when they were the best of friends. When she had learnt that she would be moving again, she had been half relieved and half disappointed. Relieved knowing that she had made the right decision, because a break up then would have been devastating. But disappointed because they still broke up...as friends. And she was very much emotionally involved and was going to miss him terribly.

She had waited until her last day to tell him because she didn't want it to be emotional. He had been angry that she hadn't said anything before and ignored her the whole day. But before the day was over, he found her and apologised for his reaction. And their last fifteen minutes together was spent making out in one of the abandoned classrooms. It was so intense. Amaka still remembered every move he made and how mind blowing his kisses were. It had made her wish she had agreed to a relationship.

Now, he was married and apparently happy with someone else. It should have been her! A tear ran down her cheek as she fingered the bracelet and remembered the Ifeanyi she had loved in school. Before he became the notorious player. Before he became a devout Christian. Before he became a devoted husband.

He was *her* Ifeanyi, and he loved her! He hadn't even gone out with anyone else while they were friends. It wasn't because there weren't other girls keen on him. Amaka knew it was his way of making their time together special, and she had loved him for that.

She looked at her wedding band and engagement ring and cried. She had only gone through with the wedding, because Ifeanyi had turned her down. If he had agreed to an affair, she was sure it would only be a matter of time before he realised that he had made a mistake getting married so early and decided to leave his wife for her. And she would never have gotten back together with Jamie.

She knew Ifeanyi still loved her. Their bond was unbreakable. The day he had come to see her at her home, he had said as much. He said they had 'a special bond.' That was what had prompted her to kiss him, and he had instantly responded.

That night he made love to her, she knew he loved her. She felt it. He was just afraid to be a bad guy. It was his religion that was holding him back. It wasn't because he loved his wife... It couldn't be. She was such a simple, dull, religious woman. What could he possibly see in her?

But what could she do about it now? She was now married too. If he said "no" before, there was even more reason to say "no" now. And there was still Jamie to consider. It's not like she didn't have feelings for him. It's just that the moment she saw Ifeanyi, she knew that what she had with Jamie would never be enough for her. It wasn't love.

Meeting Ifeanyi again made her realise that she had settled. And making love with him was what sealed the deal. She just couldn't go back to what she had been used to. Jamie no longer did it for her. Every day of her honeymoon, she had thought only of Ifeanyi.

No, she had to have him. It was worth risking everything to be with Ifeanyi again. If he still loved her, and she was sure he did, she would risk it all.

"Hey, what are you doing in there? Or have you finally decided to start cleaning?" Jamie chuckled at the image of his beautiful wife cleaning the toilet. That would be the day!

"I'm coming!" Amaka said cheerfully, trying to mask her emotional state.

She looked at herself in the mirror and knew what she had to do. Newly-weds were supposed to be over the moon, but this one was miserable. And to make matters worse, she just realised that she was pregnant. Her periods had been sporadic of late, so she couldn't rule out Ifeanyi, until she made a doctor's visit. She was excited at the possibility that it was his, even though it was a very slim chance.

Ifeanyi was engrossed in some paperwork, when he heard a knock on the door. He absent-mindedly said, "Come in," while never looking up from his work.

"Hm hmm..." the lady coughed so he would take notice of her.

Ifeanyi looked up and did a double take. He couldn't believe his eyes. What the hell was she wearing?

"Do you like it? I bought it especially for you," she said, seductively, throwing off the overcoat she had used to cover the sexy, one-piece lingerie she had worn to his office.

Ifeanyi swallowed hard. He could feel himself responding to her seduction already. What was she trying to do to him? Get him fired?!

"We can't do this... You need to leave..." he said, half-heartedly.

"*Or*..." she said, strutting towards the sofa and stretching out on it, in a sexy pose. "I could just lie here and wait for you... The sooner I get what we *both* want and leave, the sooner you can get back to concentrating on your work."

He closed his eyes and took in some deep breaths. This was crazy! "Amaka, please... I'm married! And so are you!"

"I don't mind if you don't. And who are we hurting anyway? They never need to know!" She sat upright on the sofa and spread her legs. Ifeanyi gulped. "Ifeanyi, I thought you were the *notorious player*... What happened to you? You've deceived many women before... And your wife is naive, if I may say so myself. Don't worry, I'll be discreet. You just come on over here."

"I'm not that guy anymore. I've changed! Please, just go."

"*Once* a cheat, *always* a cheater. You *know* that. You've already proved that theory is true. So, get over your guilt, and let's get *happy*!" Amaka said, with a wicked grin and a shake of her ample bosom. Ifeanyi was salivating. "Besides, if it's not me, you *will* do it again. At least, you know you're safe with me. I also have a reason to keep it quiet!" she said, putting a finger to her red, full lips.

Ifeanyi just sat there, staring at her. *Oh God!* The temptation was too much! Why did she have to be so damn sexy?!

She got up from her seat and strode over to him. He continued to stare, as if in a trance. She got close to him, so that his face was right before her big, bouncy breasts, held up by only a few red lace strings. How could a woman with such large breasts manage to keep them standing so firm, he wondered?

Without thinking, he took an exposed nipple in his mouth. *Oh God, this feels so good*, he gasped. "God, please forgive me," he muttered under his breath, then proceeded to have his way with her.

He hastily undid his tie, then his buckle, while kicking off his shoes. She assisted him with his shirt buttons. He carried her over to the sofa, eagerly, and pulled down his pants. She pulled him down on top of her.

There was another knock on the door, and it opened almost immediately. *Damn!* He had forgotten about securing the door!

Ifeanyi turned to look at Mary. The horrified expression on her face immediately transformed to one of disappointment and heartbreak as tears flooded her eyes. That look would haunt him forever. She hurriedly shut the door and ran.

"Mary, wait! No! Please, I can explain!" Ifeanyi shouted after her, quickly pulling up his trousers and running out of his office, a dishevelled mess.

Mary stopped and turned around. His face was riddled with the red print of another woman's lipstick. "No more explanations, Ifeanyi. It's *over*! I want a *divorce*!"

Ifeanyi woke up with a start. His heart was pounding in his chest as he turned to look at his wife, who lay sleeping peacefully beside him. The tears ran down his cheeks, and he swallowed hard.

He had had that dream before. And he was afraid now because he thought it might be more than a dream. Could it be a premonition? *God, please no!*

How could he still be having such dreams, after the amazing long weekend he had just spent with Mary? He got out of bed to pray. He prayed fervently in his spirit until the sun rose that morning.

40

"Wherefore let him that thinketh he standeth take heed lest he fall..."

1 CORINTHIANS 10:12

Something was wrong with Amaka. Jamie knew it, but he couldn't place it. She wasn't her usual lively and sensual self. She was often lost in her thoughts and had been this way even during their honeymoon.

Rather than ask her what the matter was, he studied her. Sometimes she smiled to herself, and other times, she looked on the verge of tears. She couldn't hold his gaze these days, and when they made love, it was like she wasn't even there. Had she lost interest in him? Was there someone else?

Ifeanyi. He'd almost forgotten about him. Could he be the reason she was so distracted? What were all those visits to his office really about anyway? It was time he found out. He couldn't stand to be in the dark any longer.

Jamie grunted and carelessly knocked the table when he arose from his seat, showing his irritation at his wife's mood swings. Amaka raised her head slightly, jolted from her thoughts. *What's eating him*, she wondered? She sighed. Now, she'd lost where she was in her daydream.

While she couldn't recollect it, she easily remembered a particularly memorable day in January. The memory always made her smile.

♥ ♥ ♥

It was a week before her engagement party...

Amaka was wearing a short, blue and white spotted cocktail dress. It didn't hug her figure, yet it accentuated her curves, which couldn't be hidden, even if she wore an oversized maternity gown. The dress clung in the right places and was loose in others, and she used a thin white belt to showcase her slim waist line and hourglass figure.

She wore her big designer shades and sat on a high stool at the bar. She wanted to recreate a Pretty Woman moment. When he arrived, she would turn from her stool, and he would do a double take, surprised that it was her sitting there. She had just done her weavon and knew he wouldn't recognise her by her hair style. The long brown and blonde wavy weave complimented her light skin tone and framed her face beautifully. She sipped her alcoholic cocktail as she waited for him.

"Can I get a Chapman?" she heard him say.

Ifeanyi stood right next to her, but he hadn't recognised her yet. She smiled to herself, waiting for the moment when he would. Butterflies lurched in her stomach in anticipation.

"Is there a party here? I was told there's an engagement party happening tonight," Ifeanyi asked the bartender.

"Maybe it's later. I don't know about any party, sir," the bartender replied and pushed his drink across to him.

Ifeanyi paid and brought the glass to his lips for a drink. He noticed the blonde-haired woman sitting beside him. She was pretty and had a hot body. Ifeanyi turned his back to her and pulled out his phone. He dialled Amaka's number. The lady's phone rang, but it still didn't register.

Amaka stood up, her phone still ringing. She tapped his shoulder. "Are you here for the party?"

He turned around to look at the person who had tapped him. He did a double take and then chuckled. "Hey, I didn't recognise you," he admitted. "Why were you just sitting there?"

Amaka shrugged. "You're late," she said instead.

"But no one's here! Where's the party?"

"It's next week."

"*Next* week?!" Ifeanyi raised his brows. "But you told me it was today. What game are you playing at, Amaka?"

"I'm sorry, we had to shift it yesterday. Jamie had to travel. We posted the update on Facebook..."

"You couldn't call and tell me?" Ifeanyi looked at her. Her beauty was distracting.

"I'm sorry. I thought you would have seen it. I didn't realise you hadn't added me back until today..."

"*Okay*. So, why didn't you call me this morning, or even this afternoon?"

"You can imagine it was a little upsetting for me that you'd still not added me back. I was actually going to let you come and find out for yourself. But by the afternoon, I figured I could meet you and tell you in person," she smiled mischievously. "I guess I also thought it would be nice to chat, without the noise of the party. I've missed you."

"Well, I would still have appreciated the call. You don't know what I had to put off to come here today."

"Why don't you just lighten up, Ifeanyi? It's no big deal. You're here now. Let's talk."

Ifeanyi rushed his Chapman and put down his glass with a thud. He was done. "I don't think we have anything to talk about. I just came to wish you well."

"Really? Well, I do. I think I've got the pre-wedding jitters. It might help me to talk to someone like you..."

"Someone like *me*?"

"Yeah... A happily married man. A rehabilitated *player*. What's your secret? Didn't you have cold feet at one point? I mean, settling for *one* woman for the rest of your life; it must have been daunting."

Hmmm... Ifeanyi eyed Amaka. He sighed. He actually had nothing else to do, and he was a bit lonely, with Mary not around and all. He figured a drink and a chat wouldn't hurt. And he thought he might find the chat interesting too. Maybe he could seize the opportunity to talk about Jesus. He smiled. Amaka returned his smile.

They topped up their glasses at the bar and found a table by the window. Ifeanyi was no gentleman. He didn't want her to get any ideas. Amaka pulled out her own seat. Ifeanyi relaxed in his, feeling in control of himself and the situation.

"You look good," Amaka said. She admired him in his dark suit and jeans.

"Thanks." Ifeanyi held his tongue from returning the compliment. Truth was, he hadn't seen Amaka look better. She was covered up, yet, still very sexy. She certainly knew how to dress, he thought. "What's with the shades?"

Amaka grinned. "Part of my disguise. It was either shades or a hat."

Ifeanyi nodded, not fully understanding the need for the disguise. "So, you have cold feet?"

"Ummm... Kinda." Amaka sighed.

A waiter came by and placed menus on their table. Amaka took one and opened it. She hoped Ifeanyi would relax and eat something. Maybe she would order a platter for them to share. That could be sexy, she thought. Dipping their hands together into the same dip, or hands brushing as they both went for a chicken wing. She smiled to herself.

"Marriage scares me. Until Jamie, I never thought I would ever settle down. There were just too many options. Marriage means I have to choose, and it is a choice I will be stuck with forever. It's far too daunting..."

"Hmmm... I feel you. How long have you been with Jamie?"

"Three years plus. By far my longest relationship. In fact, I don't think I've ever had a relationship. I just dated guys until I got bored or they became too clingy." She giggled.

Ifeanyi nodded and smiled. They were not too different. "But you know, you won't be beautiful forever... At some point, you just have to make a decision to love somebody and give them a chance to love you - the *real* you. And you won't know your real self until you settle down and stop playing games."

"I guess," Amaka sighed. She met Ifeanyi's gaze. She liked that he seemed more relaxed. "I'm going to order something. Do you want to eat anything?"

Ifeanyi shook his head. But he was lying. He had expected to eat at the party and hadn't eaten lunch.

"So, is that what you did? Just *chose* someone?" Amaka asked, looking intently into his eyes.

"Ummm...no. My case was different. I think it was a case of cupid's arrow. I just saw her, and I knew..."

"*Really?*"

"Well, it wasn't instant recognition... I didn't admit it to myself for a while. But I was drawn to her for a long time, and I thought it was the usual sexual attraction. But after our first date, I knew she was different. She was like a breath of fresh air, and I was gagging for more." Ifeanyi smiled to himself. He hadn't talked about this to anyone before.

"Hmmm... She must be pretty terrific," Amaka muttered, envy hidden behind a brilliant smile. *What did he see in her? Maybe she put a spell on him...*

Ifeanyi sighed. "She is. I didn't have cold feet with her. In fact, I was sick from not being able to have her. So many things kept getting in the way, and for a while, I thought she would never be mine. When I finally got the confirmation from God to proceed, it was the most joyous, liberating feeling."

Yes, definitely a spell! Some kind of religious enchantment, per-haps. "Hmmm..." Amaka didn't know what to say.

The waiter returned, and she placed her order. Ifeanyi changed his mind and picked up the menu. He quickly placed an order for fried rice and plantain with roasted chicken. Amaka eyed him mockingly, and he giggled.

"I'm starving!" he finally admitted. She smiled. He was finally being himself.

"I'm happy for you," Amaka lied.

Ifeanyi composed himself. He knew she wasn't being truth-ful. "So, why are you marrying Jamie? Do you even love him?"

"Of course, I do. We've been together for three years."

"It doesn't mean. You're not faithful to him."

"I have been. Until you..." *And that other guy*, she thought. But he didn't have to know about that. Their eyes met, and her de-sire for him was plain to see. Ifeanyi breathed in deeply. "Only you can do this to me, Ifeanyi. You know, I have always won-dered about you. I hoped we would meet one day, actually, and pick up where we left off. I was so surprised to finally find you and you were already taken." She leaned into him, flirtatiously.

"Yeah... That's a shock to a lot of people. And I always thought you would be the one married with children," Ifeanyi replied. "It's funny how things work out."

"Funny how..." Amaka sipped her drink, not finding it all that funny. She sighed. "So, you've been happily married for how long?"

"Three years in March."

Amaka nodded. "People say the first two years are the hard-est. Is that true?"

Ifeanyi shook his head. "Not for us... Well, things changed when we had the twins. It wasn't as hot as the first year, but we were still very happy."

"Yeah, I don't know if I want children. Marriage is a big enough commitment," Amaka giggled.

Ifeanyi smiled, somewhat relieved by her revelation. He sat up and folded his arms on the table, looking at her pointedly.

"Then I guess you and I wouldn't have worked out. I've always wanted kids."

Amaka mirrored his move and replied, without a moment's contemplation, "I would have had yours..." She swallowed, looking at him with longing. *Kiss me*, her eyes begged.

Ifeanyi looked at her, and he had a strange feeling in his stomach. He recognised it as a feeling of animal desire. It was highly unsettling. He didn't like it. He leaned back in his seat, creating distance between them again. She was getting to him. He looked away and swallowed.

There was a brief silence, as neither of them knew what to say after that. Ifeanyi thought he should make his excuse and leave, but he had already placed his order, and he was still hungry. Amaka hoped he wouldn't shut down again. She was enjoying their intimate discussion.

"Amaka," he said, at last. "I think you need to pray about your decision to marry Jamie. Marriage is a big commitment, and you seem very undecided. I know you are not a Christian, and you probably think you can always get divorced, but, trust me, you'll never be the same after. Marriage is God's design, and it's not something you should play with. I really wish you would meet someone you could love with your whole heart. Someone with whom marriage or having children wouldn't be the scariest thing but the most fulfilling thing you can do with and *for* them."

Amaka swallowed. "Thank you. I'll think about it."

"*Pray* about it," Ifeanyi emphasised.

"Don't I need to have a relationship with God for that?"

"That wouldn't be a bad idea either," Ifeanyi winked. Amaka giggled.

She sat back in her seat and breathed out a sigh. She looked at her handsome friend. He was so sincere. She wondered if he would ever give in to her. Until then, she would enjoy the chase and the tease.

Ifeanyi poured himself a glass of water, and Amaka sipped her cocktail. They enjoyed the quiet and the ambience until their meal orders arrived. When they resumed talking, they talked mostly about the past; their lives growing up, their adventures and misadventures, in the States and in England.

They had much in common, and Ifeanyi enjoyed their rapport. He wondered again about what life might have been like if they had dated back in school. Could he have fallen head over heels for her, the way he was with Mary? Was it possible to love two women equally?

He had never thought it was possible to love one with the intensity that he loved Mary. He wondered if he was in for another surprise. He looked at Amaka and openly appreciated her beauty and her personality. His guard was down.

She caught his look of admiration, and he averted his eyes. She smiled to herself. He was not untouchable after all... There was still a chance. She just had to be patient and wait for the right time. She knew it wouldn't be much longer until he gave in to his desire. They always do...

❤ ❤ ❤

Present day...

Jamie returned to the dining area, where Amaka was still seated, reminiscing. She'd hardly touched her food. Had she even noticed that he had left, he wondered.

Amaka looked up at Jamie. He was dressed as though he was going out. "Where are you off to?"

"Looking for my wife. Have you seen her?" he said, dryly.

A small smile crept on Amaka's face. She stood up and went to him. "I'm sorry. I haven't been myself. Just have some things on my mind..."

"What do you have to be worried about? What do you want that you do not have? You act like you don't want to be married. Half the time you're not here," he said, clearly hurt.

"Forgive me," Amaka swallowed. She'd never known Jamie to show so much emotion.

She kissed him. He kissed her back; a kiss that showed that he ached for her deeply. Why wasn't this enough? Amaka wondered as Jamie began to undress her. She closed her eyes and thought of Ifeanyi and his kisses. And she made love to Jamie as though he was Ifeanyi.

41

"Wherefore let him that thinketh he standeth take heed lest he fall..."

1 CORINTHIANS 10:12

It had been a month since he had submitted his notice, and Ifeanyi was still at Solomon Investment Bank. A replacement had been found, but he was still in his first week of training. After he had completed his first month, and Ifeanyi had handed over everything to his care, then he would be free to leave.

Mr Solomon had called him into his office to enquire about his decision to leave. He had simply said he wanted to learn his father's business. Mr Solomon had nodded and wished him well, expressing his sadness at his departure.

There was a familiar knock on the door. Ifeanyi had come to know that knock and dread it. He never needed to say "Come in" anymore. She usually just lets herself in moments after knocking.

"Hey, gorgeous. I'm back," Amaka announced gleefully, walking towards his desk to give him a hug. "You missed me?"

Ifeanyi's heart raced in a slight panic. After the three recurrent dreams, *more like nightmares*, he'd had about her since her wedding, he wasn't going to take any chances. He wouldn't even give her an inch, because he knew she would surely take a mile!

He stood up from his seat and crossed his arms protectively over his chest. "Get out now! I swear, I'll call your father-in-law right now if you don't leave. You're *married* for goodness sake!"

"It didn't stop you," Amaka immediately shot back.

Ifeanyi swallowed hard at that retort. "Look, I don't care who knows the truth anymore, because the most important person to me knows, and she has forgiven me. But I think you wouldn't like your husband or your in-laws to know your dirty little secret..."

"You know, I almost don't care," Amaka said, surprising herself with that revelation. What was the worst that could happen? She would be happy to get an annulment, anyway. She moved closer to Ifeanyi and swallowed. Looking in his eyes, she said, "This isn't just about the sex, Ifeanyi. I know I made it seem like it was, but I missed you while I was away. I *really* missed *you...us.* You can't say you didn't miss me at all..."

"I can, actually, because I didn't. Like I've told you about a thousand times, I love Mary. I am *in love* with my wife."

"Men don't cheat on women they love," Amaka replied with a hard stare.

"And that is *why* I am *never* making that *stupid* mistake again..."

"*Mistake?* You call what we did "a mistake"? That night was *poetry*, Ifeanyi. You made *love* to me. I am experienced enough to know the difference!"

Ifeanyi ran his hand through his head in exasperation. He shouldn't be engaging her in discussion over this. She was just trying to get under his skin. *Lord, please help me get through to this woman!*

"If I was gentle and passionate, it is only because that is the kind of lover I am. The only woman I make love to is my wife... and it is *because* she's the *only* one I love. I don't know what my feelings for you were, but I know it wasn't and isn't love. I'm sorry because it should *never* have happened, but it was *just sex*."

"You *slept* in my *arms*, Ifeanyi..." Amaka said, refusing to give up the fight. Why was he denying the truth? "Look, Ifeanyi, I know it's a hard truth, but you *love* me. I love you too. I should have never let you go, but I am ready to fight for us now. We love each other...we deserve to be together!"

"Okay. You're *clearly* deluded. I'm going to go ahead and make that phone call!" Ifeanyi picked up his telecom. It was time to put a stop to this!

"Ifeanyi, before you do that, you should know that I am pregnant!" Amaka said and watched as Ifeanyi crashed to his seat at the news.

On the night in question...

It was a little after 9 pm when Ifeanyi got the call from Amaka. He had just gotten off the phone with Mary, who was sounding stressed because she was three days past her due date. The doctor said that if she was still uncomfortable, they would induce labour when she was a week past due. Ifeanyi promised he would make it over to see her on the weekend and stay with her until she delivered. That made her happy.

He stared at the phone as it rang, being of two minds about whether or not to pick it up. He finally did, just because he was tired of the indecision, and also, he knew he wanted to talk to her. He was also curious about why she would be calling now.

The last time they had spoken was two days ago. He had been the one to call then, and it had been a little awkward. He had said he just wanted to say thanks for inviting him to the engagement party the previous weekend and wanted to know how she was doing.

The truth was that he had been thinking about her a lot since then. He had wanted to call earlier and finally did so - just because he was tired of the indecision, and he thought he was making a big deal out of calling. They were just friends, after all, he had told himself. She was happy he had called but said she couldn't talk because Jamie was around. That was when he realised the true nature of his call, and he awkwardly said, "No problem. Good night."

She'd texted him moments after to say it was sweet of him to call. But he knew it wasn't sweet. It was lust. He was at temptation's door, and he couldn't trust himself. He had prayed then for God to strengthen him and help him do right by Mary.

So, picking up her call today was a big deal. He had been reminded in his spirit about his prayer to God, so God had answered his prayer by granting him that warning. Yet, he had picked the call. Just because he *really* wanted to.

Her voice on the other end had been desperate. She was crying. Apparently, Jamie had been suspicious, and she'd slipped up and told him about their kiss at the party, and he had gotten mad and broken up with her. He hadn't returned since he stormed out two nights ago. On the night of Ifeanyi's call. Normally, if they were just fighting, he would have returned to her by now.

"Please, can you come over? I just feel so bad right now," she sobbed.

"Sure," he said the word without giving it much thought. *What about Mary?* His conscience pricked. *Nothing's going to happen,* he silenced it.

The drive to her place in Ajah, Lekki was long enough for the Spirit to minister to Ifeanyi. As he drove, his hands shook because he knew he was going against godly counsel. He was even afraid he might get into an accident, you know, as a sign from above that he was in error, just as Jonah had been swallowed by the fish. But unremarkably and thankfully, the road was free.

The Lord ministered to him as he recalled scriptures. *"Lust not after her beauty in thine heart; neither let her take thee with her eyelids. For by means of a whorish woman a man is brought to a piece of bread: and the adulteress will hunt for the precious life. Can a man take fire in his bosom, and his clothes not be burned? Can one go upon hot coals, and his feet not be burned?"* (Proverbs 6:25-28).

He drove on. He got to her house. Her directions had been on point. He parked outside. Last chance to go home.

Again, he was reminded by the Spirit. *"Flee fornication. Every sin that a man doeth is without the body; but he that committeth fornication sinneth against his own body. What? Know ye not that your body is the temple of the Holy Ghost which is in you, which ye have of God, and ye are not your own? For ye are bought with a price: therefore glorify God in your body, and in your spirit, which are God's"* (1 Corinthians 6:18-20).

Ifeanyi cried because he knew he was weak. He knew the truth. Tonight wasn't about comforting Amaka. It was about quenching the fire she had ignited in him from the moment he had seen her at the anniversary party. The fire she had fanned with her Facebook friendship and seductive display pictures. A fire *he* had fanned by devouring *all* her pictures as though they were porn.

He hadn't looked at them in months, but he still remembered the pictures vividly. One in particular, where her eyes seemed to be drawing him in, and her skin shone like gold. She was like a sex goddess, and he had been spell bound.

He remembered her cleavage from the night of her engagement party. That black lace dress she had worn was pure wickedness. There was hardly anything left to the imagination. He had hardly been able to keep his eyes off her. He swallowed and decided he would go home. He couldn't trust himself to behave.

His phone rang. He stared at it as it rang. It was Amaka. "I love Mary," he said in determination as he started the car.

And then she opened the door. She was in her nightgown, and she beckoned him to enter. He switched off the car. *Shit!* There would be no more ministration that night.

Ifeanyi pulled himself together and got out of the car. He took a deep breath. *Nothing has to happen. You have self- control,* he ministered to himself.

"Can I get you coffee?" Amaka asked, when they had hugged briefly at the door. She could sense his tension.

"Tea, please," Ifeanyi said, choosing to look around at her home to keep himself from staring at her. He sat on the three-seater sofa, in her small living room but then thought he might be safer on the armchair. She returned and took her seat at the armchair, and he let out a sigh of relief. Or was it disappointment? "You have a nice place, here."

"Thanks," she smiled. "I'm really glad you came. I didn't want to call you at first. I know you're happily married, but I thought... we go way back, and there was really no one else I felt I could talk to."

"I understand," Ifeanyi said, swallowing a gulp of saliva. He sipped his tea. "I think we share a special bond. You know, I'm not supposed to be here... But I felt bad because it was my fault... I shouldn't have called you that night. I guess I..." he was rambling.

Before he had finished his sentence, she was by his side. She looked in his eyes, and he knew she was going to kiss him. "You don't have to say it, I know why you came. It was the same reason you called." And then she kissed him. That was all it took.

Ifeanyi kissed her back with all the passion he had been holding on to, in a reserved place just for her. Somehow, they found their way to her bedroom, amid a flurry of clothes flying, limps flaring frantically, and hot kisses. "Oh God... I shouldn't do this," Ifeanyi mumbled, his lips against hers, as she fiddled with his buckle. "But I've been aching for you for so long..."

Amaka bent down, pulled down his jeans, and pushed him on top of the bed, his legs hanging off it. His boxers came off next, and the next thing he felt was her soft, wet mouth on him. He was conquered.

He woke up at 1 am to find her cuddled in his arms. *Shit! Shit! Shit!* He had done it.

He let her go gently and went in search of his clothing. He managed to gather them all. *Damn it!* Where did he keep his car keys? He was sure he had left them on the coffee table.

He couldn't find them, and he didn't want to wake her up, so he went back to sleep, next to her on the bed. Thank goodness Mary wasn't at home, he thought. He didn't want to have to lie to her about where he had been.

He woke up to the sound of the shower. It was 5:30 am. He had to be going, so he could get to work. He pulled on his clothes.

"Have you seen my keys?" he called to Amaka.

"What?" Amaka shouted from the shower.

"My keys! I am looking for my keys," Ifeanyi replied.

"I can't hear you. I am coming out soon."

Oh no! God no! He didn't want to see her come out of the shower. He just wanted to get the hell out of there and forget this ever happened.

She came out glistening, with the towel wrapped on her head. Her full, video vixen figure was in clear view. His mouth dropped open. He saw more than he had seen last night, and his manhood stood upright, as if in respect. *DOWN!* Ifeanyi commanded to no avail. The smile she gave him told him she knew just what he was thinking.

She pushed him back onto the bed. "Let me help you with that," she said, seductively.

She straddled him while releasing his hardened member from the confines of his jeans. All Ifeanyi could say was, "My keys!" before he went, "Oooohhh..."

He was overcome again. And this time, they did not use protection.

The keys, which had actually been in his jeans, had fallen out during their session last night, and had been thrown under the bed by the crafty temptress.

42

"Wherefore let him that thinketh he standeth take heed lest he fall..."

1 CORINTHIANS 10:12

Pregnant?

The word rang in his ears. Ifeanyi dropped the receiver and crashed in his seat, as though he had been hit by a bulldozer. He hadn't even imagined this possibility. He sat horrified, his mind racing, thinking about how he was going to break this shocker to Mary. She would be devastated. *Oh, God!* What had he done?

He looked at Amaka, who stood, watching him. He couldn't read her expression. He swallowed hard. "Are you sure?"

She simply nodded her head.

"How far along are you?" This would tell him if he was safe or not. Hopefully. He took in deep breaths while still holding Amaka's gaze.

"I'll tell you, on one condition," Amaka said, bargaining.

"What?" Ifeanyi creased his brows.

"I want an honest answer. If you knew it was your baby, would you want me to keep it?"

Wow! That was a big question. He knew the Christian thing to say. Of course, she should keep it. Abortion was wrong on so many levels. But this baby could potentially destroy his life and put his other children in jeopardy.

He decided to throw it back at her. "It depends... How far along are you?" If she was up to three months pregnant, there was really no going back, anyway. And that was about the length of time since their affair.

Amaka narrowed her eyes. "Are you dodging the question? I want you to tell me what to do...before *everybody* knows," she said.

Ifeanyi thought of Mary. He had put her through enough. Even if she forgave him, things would never be the same, because Amaka would always be in their lives, just as Ijeoma was now. But to abort a baby...? Ifeanyi knew Mary would never forgive him if she found out that he had aborted the baby. No matter what, she would keep it.

"Keep it," he practically whispered.

Amaka smiled. "I didn't hear you...?"

"So, why are you smiling?" Ifeanyi snapped.

"I just wanted you to say it again. Now I know you love me." She beamed and fluttered her lashes at him.

Ifeanyi stared at her as if she was mad. He stood up angrily. "Keeping it has *nothing* to do with you! Let me be clear; what happened between us was a *mistake*! The *biggest* of my life. Now, if the baby is mine, we will *deal* with it, but if not, I would ask you to kindly *leave my life!*"

Amaka swallowed hard, feeling the heat of his angry glare. "Is that really how you feel about me, Ifeanyi? After *everything*?"

"After *what*? We had sex! Get over it! All I want to know from you now is how far along you are, so I can know if I *could* be the father of your child." Ifeanyi gritted his teeth to cool his rising temper. Why was she stalling for goodness sake?!

"I thought we had a connection, Ifeanyi. You said we had a special bond. How can you make love to me and discard me the next minute as if I am nothing?" she sobbed.

"Can you even *hear* yourself? What about the man you just *married*? You don't seem to have any problem discarding him! What about my *wife*, who I make *mad* love to *every chance I get*? You want me to discard her...for the likes of *you*? Not in a *million years*!" Ifeanyi said, fuming.

About a minute passed in silence as they stared at each other. Ifeanyi was still waiting for her confirmation on her expectancy. Amaka was emotional. She had really believed he loved her. She hadn't imagined this outcome.

Ifeanyi eventually snapped. "You know what? Just get out! I don't care anymore. If the baby is mine, we'll find out soon enough. I know my marriage will survive it, because I married a *good* woman." He eyed her with disgust, every trace of attraction gone, then added, "I really wish I could say the same for you. You can take your leave now!"

Amaka was humbled and ashamed. "Okay. I'm sorry. It's just..."

But Ifeanyi wasn't listening to her anymore. He had sat back in his seat and was fiddling around with some papers on his desk. He had to get back to work. Hopefully, she would get the message and leave.

Amaka stepped closer to him, and he retreated in haste as though she was toxic waste. He rolled backwards in his seat and almost toppled over. Amaka was pained by his dramatic reaction.

She sighed deeply before saying, "I'm eight weeks pregnant. The baby isn't yours." Ifeanyi didn't look up at her. "I guess this is goodbye..."

Amaka fiddled with her wrist and dropped something on his desk on her way out. Ifeanyi didn't look up until he heard his door click shut. It was the sound of freedom. He let out a huge sigh of relief.

He looked for what she had dropped on his desk. It was the bracelet he had given her seventeen years ago when he was only fifteen. He picked it up and looked at it before throwing it into the bin. It was over. Thank God!

Jamie had had Ifeanyi's office bugged, believing that their conversations would reveal the truth behind why Amaka kept frequenting his office. He had asked her about it, but she'd lied and said he was giving her 'financial advice' about starting her new business. A business that she still had no business plan for!

He listened to the recording, getting madder by the minute. He had finally found out the truth. If only he had followed his suspicions sooner, he would not have married that cheating woman! Oh, who was he kidding? He would have married her anyway, just to know he had her.

But it pained him so much to learn that she had not only cheated on him with Ifeanyi, but she actually thought she was in love with him and was going back for more. What was it about this Ifeanyi anyway? What would make her disgrace herself, and disgrace him, for another *married* man?! And so soon after their honeymoon... Even while knowingly carrying *his* baby, for goodness sake! Oh, it was painful!

Amaka's voice played in the recording, as Jamie listened to it for the fourth time, "*This isn't just about the sex, Ifeanyi. I know I made it seem like it was, but I missed you while I was away. I really missed you...us. You can't say you didn't miss me at all...*"

Despite himself, he cried. It hurt that she had said she didn't care if he found out, as though she didn't even love him at all. And it hurt more than a little to learn of her pregnancy that way. She had obviously gone to confirm the dates, to rule out Ifeanyi, before divulging anything to him. Oh, women were so crafty!

He sat with murderous thoughts as he contemplated his next move. By the time he was through with that wretched bitch he called a wife, she would wish she was never born! It didn't bode well for Ifeanyi either, even though he had rejected her appeal, and apparently, she had thrown herself at him to get him to cheat on his wife. He had still done it; and no one slept with his woman and got away with it!

Jamie unlocked his phone and pressed '4' on his speed dial. "Hey, Jimmy. We've got DIY tonight. Come loaded!"

Jimmy hung up his phone and took a deep breath. It had been over a year since Jamie called him for a DIY. The last time, his wife had just delivered his second child, and she had been very angry with him that he had gone with Jamie.

"You have a family to think about, Jimmy! Why are you still rolling with that *boy*?" Fatima had shouted.

"Don't call him that! He is my brother. My *older* brother."

"Jimmy, as long as he refuses to grow up, he is a BOY! Please, promise me you will stop this..." she had pleaded.

"You don't understand. Jamie doesn't take "no" for an answer..." Jimmy had said, but his wife's look had told him she wouldn't take "no" for an answer either. "Okay, babe. I'll find a way..."

"Please... I need to feel safe, and you need to think of our children." Fatima had touched his arm affectionately. "I know you love your brother, but you're not helping him this way. I love you, and I know you love me too, so I need you to promise me... No more *funny* business."

Jimmy had nodded and kissed his wife on her forehead before he kissed his one-month-old baby girl, cradled in her arms. "Okay, I promise. I love you."

Jimmy sighed. He wondered what it was about this time. He suspected it had to do with Jamie's suspicions about Amaka and that Ifeanyi guy. If that was the case, then there really wasn't much to be worried about. He would go with Jamie but let him know that this would be the very last time.

Jimmy decided to send his wife a short message on WhatsApp instead of calling her. It read: *"Hey, babe. It's going to be a late night tonight. Don't wait up."*

♥ ♥ ♥

"Where have you been?" Jamie's voice was hoarse as he studied his wife, who had just returned home at 7:30 pm.

He had known she was not the type to cook or clean. That had never been an issue in their relationship. But he expected her to be home waiting for him when he returned from work, at least. What sort of husband waits at home for his wife, who doesn't even have a job? He thought, fuming!

"I went shopping... Why?" Amaka replied, dropping her handbag and the things she had purchased at Ikeja City Mall.

Shopping always boosted her morale and pride when she was down. It was the one thing no one could take from her. And today, she really needed some retail therapy.

"Where were you this afternoon?" Jamie asked.

"I just told you, I went shopping. What's the matter, babe?" Amaka went to him to give him a hug and a kiss, and he flinched. She stepped back, surprised at his reaction.

"I'm going to give you just one more chance to tell me the truth," Jamie met her eyes, but Amaka still didn't realise what danger she stood in.

"I don't know what 'truth' you are looking for, Jamie." He slammed his fist on the table, and she jumped. Sweat gathered on her temples, as Amaka was gripped with fear. She tried to still her trembling hand. What did he know? "Ummm... I also stopped over at Victoria Island for some business..." she swallowed hard, watching him rise from his seat and walk towards her.

"So, you're not screwing around on me...?" Jamie asked, in a low tone.

"No, never..." she cowered.

"LIAR!" Amaka gagged as she fought for breath. Jamie had his hands across her neck, squeezing it in his rage. When he saw how she was struggling to breathe, he released her. She gasped for air and moved away from him. "You are such a lying *whore!*"

Jamie played the recording from Amaka's visit to Ifeanyi's office today, and she finally knew all that he knew. "Baby, please, I..."

Jamie didn't want to listen. He slapped her hard across her face. He started removing his belt. He had given her a chance to be honest, and she had lied to him.

"Please, baby, please..." Amaka cried and begged, watching in terror as he removed his belt and folded it through his hand. "Please, forgive me..."

She received her first lash. She screamed in pain and began to run blindly away. The next one came. She fell to the floor and shielded herself from more lashes with her hands and legs.

"Did you think you would screw around on me and get away with it?" Jamie shouted at her, hitting her a third time with his belt. The buckle tore at her skin. Amaka wailed from the pain.

After a few more lashes, and when the belt stopped producing the desired impact, he began to kick her until he too broke down as he realised he had gone too far. "If you ever, *ever*, cross me again, I swear, it will be your *last!*" he threatened before he left her crouched on the floor and stormed out of their home in Banana Island, Ikoyi.

43

"Wherefore let him that thinketh he standeth take heed lest he fall…"

1 CORINTHIANS 10:12

Chukwudi and Uchechukwu were officially toddlers, having turned two years old in April. Mary and Ifeanyi had decided to skip throwing a birthday party for a family outing instead. They had taken lovely photos of the twins and Abigail and all the family, and some of them were now framed and displayed proudly in their home.

Mary managed to keep a good home, with a part-time cleaner and a full-time nanny. She was happy to do all the cooking because she loved to cook, and their fridge and freezer were always well stocked. But the job was beginning to be too much for just one nanny.

The twins were very mischievous, and Abigail also needed much attention. Mary was having a hard time working on her blog from home because of the constant distractions from the children. Even with the nanny around, they were constantly shouting, "Mummy! Mummy!"

She'd decided to let the boys stay in crèche later, as they had that provision for working mothers. This enabled her to work until 5 pm before going for them. Abigail was easy to handle at only three months old, and when Mary was engrossed, the nanny was able to attend to her, and the home was peaceful and quiet.

However, Mary soon realised that some things are really too good to be true. Today, after only a month with the late pick-ups, one of the carers at the crèche complained about the boys' behaviour. They said they couldn't handle them anymore for the rate they charged, and she would have to do early pick-ups or find a crèche that can give them the attention they needed! Mary was dumbfounded.

"But madam," the lady said, "how are you handling them at home?"

Mary didn't even know how to begin to answer that. Was the problem with the boys, or with her, or with the crèche? She didn't know. But one thing she knew, something had to change!

She could afford to get a second nanny. She knew other mothers with twins and triplets who had one nanny per child, but she always thought she would be able to manage with only one so that she could still be very much involved. She didn't want to completely delegate her mothering to nannies.

When she got home, she called her mother-in-law for advice.

"Hello, my dear, how are you and Ifeanyi?" Mrs Chukwueke asked when she had picked up the phone.

"We're happy. Everybody's fine, thank God. How about you and Daddy?"

"We bless God. Things are good. How about the kids? I hope the boys are not giving you too much trouble?"

"Oh, I was even calling you about them. They are fine, but they've been acting up a lot more lately. I just got a complaint from the crèche. I'm a bit stuck on what to do. How do you get them to behave when they are at yours?"

"Ummm… The truth is what works for me may not work for you. I am not their mother. At my house, they are quite different creatures, and they have my full attention when they visit," Mrs Chukwueke said. "Are you able to give them your full attention for lengthy periods of the day?"

"Ummm… Honestly, no. They are mostly with the nanny, and our times together are usually short, partly because I find them quite clingy and demanding," Mary said.

"They are clingy and demanding because your time with them is precious little. Give them more time, and they will settle. I can imagine it is harder now that you have Abigail, but you have to make the effort. They act out because they want your attention. You can't teach or enforce discipline when you are not attentive."

"Hmmm… You've given me a lot to think about, Mum. But I think it is a lot easier said than done. I do try to make time for them, it's just…"

"You have to be serious and determined about this, Mary. It is going to take time and commitment to break the bad cycle you have with them. But once you do, you will reap the benefits of a peaceful home. Children are not that complicated. The question is if you really want to be present or not."

Mary swallowed. "Thanks for the advice, Mum. I know what I need to work on now, and I'll make more effort."

"And if you need any help or break, don't be afraid to ask, or bring them over. They are my babies too."

Mary giggled. "Okay, Mummy! Thanks so much. I will remember to."

"No problem, dear. You also need to make sure you look after that husband of yours. He's your first baby."

Mary giggled again. "I hear you, Mum. But to be honest, he's the one looking after me these days."

Mrs Chukwueke smiled. "That one is even better."

When Mary got off the phone with her mother-in-law, she heard Ifeanyi's car horn and smiled excitedly. He was home unusually early today. She hoped it was for good reason.

♥ ♥ ♥

Amaka was still crying on the floor, twenty minutes after Jamie had stormed out. She had suffered a few cuts from where the belt buckle had snagged her skin, and she had bruises from the hard impact of the leather belt Jamie had used. She remembered her conversation with Ifeanyi today, and she easily sympathised with Jamie. She had said some unforgivable things... And now, she was truly at his mercy because Ifeanyi had rejected her.

Amaka had refused to believe that Jamie was an abuser. He was mostly an affectionate man. She had rarely seen his temper in their three-year relationship, but when she did, the times she had been unfaithful, it was always heated. She thought it was a reflection of his passionate love for her. A love that was sometimes suffocating...

From the first day she had met Jamie, Amaka knew he was trouble. But she was madly attracted to him. She didn't play hard to get for long, and once he had her, he had her! But she quickly saw that he was possessive, jealous, and controlling, and so she had tried to break it off early.

However, Jamie never heard "no" and never released his grip on her. He would shower her with gifts and flowers and apologise in the most romantic ways. And he was so feared among men who knew him that no one dared come after her, who he had branded 'his woman.' And if any ignorantly or foolishly did, they were easily scared off or chased away.

Even still, he cheated often, and she'd gotten mad the few times she had caught him. He always coldly told her, "*Men are wired differently from women,*" and demanded that she forgive him (without a promise that he would be faithful)! She soon accepted that her fate with him was sealed and gave up the struggle. She had adjusted and decided to have an affair of her own.

His name was Kubi Sulaiman. A sweet, simple guy with nothing to offer her but illicit sex. She felt she could trust him to be discreet, but after their first time together, Kubi had avoided her. It was also then that she'd tasted the first display of Jamie's rage. It wasn't long after that she had gotten wind of Kubi's demise. An unfortunate car accident caused by brake failure. However, she always suspected that there was more to the 'accident' than met the eye.

When she had met Ifeanyi at his bank's anniversary party last year, she had thrown caution to the wind and decided that she would get him, no matter what. Darn the consequences... After all, you only live once, she'd figured. And if anyone was a match for Jamie, Ifeanyi was. Unlike Kubi, he had a lot going for him. But she hadn't expected that he would make her work so hard for it.

The more she had worked to get him into bed, the more desperate she had become. And once she had him, she was unwilling to release her hold on him. It was an issue of pride; she couldn't stand to lose. It was also an issue of lust; he was phenomenal in bed. And somewhere in there, she had believed there was love.

They *did* have a special connection. She'd been reminded of that during their late lunch at the hotel before her engagement party. They had talked like best friends, and he had opened up his heart to her. She knew then it would only be a matter of time. And she had been sure he would do it again, but her desperation had made her careless. She swallowed.

Now they had been found out, and she had gotten the beating of her life...from a man who cheated on her on a regular basis. Life was so unfair! How did she, a woman as beautiful, bright and well to do as her, end up being someone else's property?!

Amaka arose from the floor and attended to her injuries. Her maid retired promptly at 7 pm every day, so she was home alone and expected that she would be until the morning. That was usually what happened whenever Jamie was mad at her.

She wondered where he would go tonight. He would probably go and blow off his steam on a night out with Jimmy. Then she wondered if he would try to go after Ifeanyi. Knowing him, he probably would, she thought. But she didn't want to care about Ifeanyi right now.

Amaka prepared a hot, relieving bath and took a bottle of wine with her, to enhance the treatment. After her bath, she served herself some food, which the maid had prepared and ate sparingly, as she grieved a loss she couldn't identify. Was it the dream of what could have been between her and Ifeanyi or the marriage she had jeopardised in pursuit of that dream? Or was it the realisation that she wasn't free nor happy, and perhaps, would never be, when she had once thought she was both?

Or maybe it was a combination of all these losses. She just wanted to be loved and to love passionately in return. She cried.

Even though she didn't want to, the thought kept gnawing at her to warn Ifeanyi about the fact that Jamie now knew of their affair. After all, he had a family, and if Jamie was as volatile as she knew him to be, anything could happen. She couldn't live with that on her conscience. And even though she now knew he didn't feel the same way about her, she still cared for him.

She sighed deeply and unlocked her phone. After a few attempts at calling, with no answer, Amaka decided to send a text message and then went to bed. She didn't think of the child in her womb. Nor did she think to pray. She had never been that kind of woman.

After Amaka had left his office, Ifeanyi had not been able to get back to work immediately. He was actually quite emotional, because things could have been worse. He could have returned home to his wife today to inform her that the woman he had cheated on her with was now, potentially, carrying his baby!

But thank God that wasn't the case! Thank God it was finally over. He was sure he would never see her face again. And the relief was overwhelming. He was so thankful for how God had graciously seen him through the mess he had made - again! He had spent some time in prayer and praise before he was able to return to work, but even then, he had been just too excited to focus.

Ifeanyi decided to return home early to spend the evening with his family. Mary was happy to have him home early and asked if everything was okay. He told her about the visit from Amaka, and that he knew she would never bother them again. She had her own family now, being pregnant for Jamie. Mary was relieved and thanked God.

They had a lovely family time, and the boys enjoyed having Daddy home. Mary observed that their behaviour was better that night. She wondered how much Ifeanyi's presence at home affected them. It seemed it was also a factor in the challenging behaviour they were presenting. Clearly, there was much merit in her mother-in-law's counsel about being 'present' and attentive.

By 9 pm, the kids were all in their cribs, and the nanny had retired to the boys' quarters for the night.

Ifeanyi and Mary were settling in for the night, and Mary went down to the kitchen to make them a hot beverage. She came back to their private lounge with hot chocolate for herself, tea for Ifeanyi, and crackers to share. She sipped her drink with her legs on his laps while she read blog posts from her WordPress reader. Ifeanyi had the TV on and was watching an action movie.

At 9:30 pm, Ifeanyi's phone began to buzz again. Three missed calls from Amaka. She must be really desperate, he thought. He never knew she was so crazy.

Ifeanyi hadn't told Mary about Amaka's frequent visits until today because he didn't want her to get worried. However, he had been sure that it was all finally resolved. He believed today would be the last time. But now that she was still calling him, he was beginning to wonder if the nightmare would ever end.

The doorbell rang, and Mary and Ifeanyi looked at each other. Neither of them was expecting company, and it was an unusual hour for visitors. Their neighbours also knew better than to disturb them at such a late hour.

Mary swung her legs from his so that he could stand up to get the door. She instinctively muted the television. She wondered if Amaka would be so bold and shameless as to come to her home.

Ifeanyi was surprised to see Jamie Solomon through the peephole. He opened the door ajar with the safety catch on, and saw that Jamie was not alone. His phone beeped, and he looked down to check the screen. The message from Amaka read:

"Ifeanyi, I've been trying to call you. Be careful! He knows!"

Before he could push the door back shut, Jamie forcibly kicked it open, breaking the latch. Ifeanyi recognised the bigger man as Jamie's brother. But before he could think to say or do anything, he received a blow that knocked him to the ground.

44

"Wherefore let him that thinketh he standeth take heed lest he fall..."

1 CORINTHIANS 10:12

In an instant, Ifeanyi remembered everything that had happened since that sinful night.

Amaka had been merciless in the morning when she rode on him. He had wanted to resist her. He really did. But somewhere along the ride, he lost his mind and applied himself 100% to the adulterous act. It was too late to pretend like it wasn't what he wanted. She was well pleased at the turn of events.

"Oh, you've gotta be kidding me," Amaka gasped, rolling off him, yet hanging on to him. It was even better than last night, she thought. "You know I'm never letting you go, right?" she giggled.

Despite himself, Ifeanyi smiled. He was used to that reaction from women. He had missed it. It was a pride booster. Though Mary was always appreciative of his bedroom talents, it was something else coming from an experienced woman.

He took a moment to get his breath back before sitting up in bed. He had to get out of there. He was starting to feel and think like his old self again. He had to think of Mary. She could never find out about this... Oh, he would take this to his grave!

Amaka sat up and began to touch and kiss him again. He pulled her away. "I need to find my keys."

"Where do you have to go so early?" she pouted.

"Work."

"I thought you were the boss. Doesn't that mean you get to show up when you're good and ready?" she continued to kiss his shoulder. She wanted more.

Ifeanyi stood up from the bed and began to put on his clothes. "Please help me find my keys."

"Only if you promise to come back," Amaka said, looking into his eyes.

Ifeanyi looked into her eyes. What was a lie when he had already done the unforgivable? "I promise."

She smiled, stood up, and wrapped her arms around his neck. She pulled him in for a snog. He gave in to her kiss.

When Amaka was satisfied that he meant to keep his promise and return, she turned to start looking for the keys on the bed. She tipped her head under the bed and found them right where she had thrown them. She retrieved the keys and handed them to him.

A muscle ticked on his temple as he took them from her. "Thank you," he said, stiffly. He did a final check that he had everything and then turned for the door.

She quickly slipped on a dressing gown and followed his hasty movements towards the front door. She caught his hand as he opened it. "Call me," she said, with pleading eyes.

Ifeanyi nodded and slipped away.

Ifeanyi had no intention of ever calling Amaka again. And he refused to pick her calls too. He didn't want to keep a woman on the side. He hadn't wanted to cheat on Mary to begin with. But Amaka had come upon him like an irresistible rash he had to itch.

Now, it felt like a sore he had opened. And he knew that if he kept picking at it, it would only get worse and worse and leave a terrible scar. The moment she had said, *"I'm never letting you go,"* he had begun to feel dread.

And then when he realised that she had intentionally hid his keys, he was convinced that she was not a woman to be played with. If she didn't get the message that it was just a one-off and came after him, Mary might find out what happened between them. Unless he intended to lose Mary, which he could not bear to imagine, he had to keep Amaka as far away as possible.

He hoped that by ignoring her calls and messages, she would get the idea. However, he was wrong. She paid him a visit about two weeks later after he had returned from his short visit to the US to be with Mary during her delivery.

He had been racked with guilt the whole time he was there, but he employed his skills from his years of juggling women and managed to conceal it from her. Being with Mary again also re-minded him of why he had turned his life around and married her. He made a commitment to himself that he would never fall again...and she must never find out about his betrayal.

Ifeanyi was not at all happy to see Amaka when she opened the door to his office and smiled sheepishly.

"What are you doing here, Amaka?"

"You promised to call," she said, resting her back against the door.

"I'm sorry. I lied."

Amaka sighed and walked slowly towards his desk. "She must be really something special..." She fingered and studied the framed picture of Ifeanyi and his wife on his desk.

"She is." Ifeanyi straightened the picture.

"When is she coming back?"

"Soon. If you don't mind, I have to get back to work."

Amaka took a seat on one of the visitor chairs in front of him. "I don't do this, you know... In case you think I make a habit of throwing myself at men. It's usually the other way around."

Ifeanyi nodded slowly.

"I know you're a changed man now... Believe me, that makes me happy. Even though it really hurt that you didn't call or pick my calls. But I think we have a rare opportunity here, to explore this chemistry between us...before Marie comes back," Amaka said, seeking out his leg under the desk.

"Mary. Her name is Mary. And I'm sorry, I'm going to have to take a pass on that." Ifeanyi withdrew his legs and sat up straight when he felt her bare foot riding up along his calf.

Amaka leaned in slowly, letting the spaghetti strap of her mini dress slip off her shoulder and exposing more of her already exposed breasts. "Do you really find me that easy to resist?"

Ifeanyi stared at her for a moment, then giggled nervously. "Please, can you go now? I need to get back to work."

Amaka slid her hand on the desk, on top of his. "You're not fooling me, Ifeanyi. I know you want me... I'm not going to wait for you forever."

He pulled his hand away. "How are wedding plans?" he asked instead.

Amaka raised an eyebrow. "Moving along. Though you've sort of put a spanner in the works..."

"*Me*? How?" A small smile crept on his face, despite his efforts to appear serious.

"By being so *phenomenal in bed*... I just want to check out my theory, to make sure it wasn't a fluke, you know?"

Hmmm... Ifeanyi thought. She was relentless. He sighed. "I thought you said you loved him?"

"What's love got to do with it? It's sex! He does it too..." Amaka stood up from her seat and walked around Ifeanyi's executive desk to his seat. "So, what do you say?" She leaned on his desk, holding his gaze.

"To *just* sex?"

Ifeanyi could feel his resolve dissolving. He dropped his gaze to her exposed thighs and licked his lips, which had suddenly gone dry. He trailed a hand along her inner thigh, enjoying the feel of them. He glanced at the picture of him and Mary on his desk, and closed his eyes, sighing deeply. If he gave in now, he knew he wouldn't stop. Mary deserved better than that. He swallowed hard. *God help me!*

"To *phenomenal* sex..." Amaka smiled, feeling triumphant as she leaped onto his desk. She played with his tie.

Ifeanyi stood up, carried her, and dumped her in front of his door. "NO!" he said resolutely. He straightened his tie and walked back to his seat.

Amaka pouted, then straightened her dress and straps. "This isn't over!"

And no, it wasn't over. With each visit and text, his resolve had weakened. He had also lost his connection with God. He couldn't pray like before because his heart wasn't contrite. He fully intended on keeping his secret from Mary, and well, God was in the business of confessions.

Rather than pray with his whole heart, he said short simple prayers. Usually asking for strength when tempted. And he was tempted a lot. He often fantasised about giving in again, and he listened to the devil's ministration, saying he was fighting the inevitable. Sadly, he was beginning to believe it.

The day Mary had visited him in his office to find Amaka there, he was facing another moment of weakness. He had been seriously considering Amaka's appeal for an affair. She had texted him the night before to say that Jamie was out of town until the weekend, and he was considering paying her another visit.

Amaka had been happy when she'd visited him that afternoon. It was her fourth visit in as many weeks. She knew she was wearing him down. He had actually replied her last text with, "*Okay.*"

She gave her signature rap on the door and opened it. This time, he gave her a shy but knowing smile. She had him. She beamed.

"I got your text," she said, strutting in. "What does 'Okay' mean?"

Ifeanyi smiled. "It means '*I hear you.*'"

"And what does *that* mean?" Amaka replied flirtatiously.

"It means you're relentless!" Ifeanyi giggled. "You really didn't need to come to my office today. I replied your text..."

"Hmmm... It sounds like you've been ignoring them, hoping I would pay you a visit...?"

Ifeanyi sighed. He didn't know what to think or say anymore. "Go home. I'll call you."

"You mean it?" She leaned across his desk, seductively, hoping for a kiss.

There was a knock on the door. Amaka immediately sat down on the visitor's chair, as they both turned their gaze to the door, and Mary popped her head in. Ifeanyi thought his heart had stopped beating for a second. He looked at her, unable to move, but hoping she wouldn't read anything into Amaka's visit.

Ifeanyi stood at the parking lot and watched Mary drive away, his heart pounding in his chest. Wow, that had been close, he thought. What the hell was he doing?

He rubbed his hand through his head as he walked back into his building. He was in trouble. He had completely lost sight of who he was and what he was about to throw away. He couldn't go through with his plans for tonight. He needed to pray.

Oh, but he was so ashamed. He had fallen so far. And right now, the only thing stopping him from going ahead with an affair was his love for Mary. It wasn't because of God, who he had shut out since that night. That was what was shameful; because now he needed Him.

As he got on his knees to pray, he was very aware that he was before God now because of his marriage, and not because of his salvation nor relationship. At the back of his mind, he had thought that he could always repent, *later*, when he'd had enough. But it could be too late for his marriage, even if he was forgiven by God. He had taken God's grace for granted.

He was silent for a long time, as he didn't know what to say nor how to say what needed to be said. He was still not ready to come clean to Mary. How could God help him to do the right thing, to resist temptation and be faithful to his wife, when he wasn't ready to do things His way?

Surrender. Stop resisting Me. You're not in control of this.

Ifeanyi cried as God ministered to him. He was pleasantly surprised to realise that God hadn't left him altogether.

"I'm so sorry..." he sobbed. "Lord, please take control of this! Please, don't leave me to myself. I'll mess it up!"

Confess. If you walk in the light, you will be restored in fellowship and cleansed from all your sin.

"God, it's going to kill her! What if she leaves me? Oh, God... I can't..."

You will not be free until you confess. The truth will set you free.

"Okay, I'll tell her. But please, help me. I can't lose her, Lord. I promise I won't do it again. Please help me! I'm so sorry..."

Let go, Ifeanyi. Not your will but Mine.

It was the hardest thing for him to do. To let go and not be in control. Letting go meant that he could lose his marriage by coming clean and doing God's will, but he would regain his fellowship with God. Before, he had thought that he could keep his marriage by deceit, while losing fellowship with God, not realising that he was losing fellowship and intimacy with his wife too. It was the lie of the enemy, to keep him in bondage to sin.

Ifeanyi sobbed as he let go of the idea of being in control. He had to accept that he was not the perfect husband he had hoped to be. And he was afraid of Mary's reaction when she saw the truth too. Would she ever trust him again? Would she love him still?

However hard, he knew letting go was the only way to win. To be in God's mercy was a good place to be, and Ifeanyi found strength and solace there. He was also at Mary's mercy now...

Ifeanyi was in turmoil that night when he confessed to Mary. He hadn't known what to expect, but he knew her to be gracious. However, as the days went by, he despaired of her forgiveness and feared for his marriage.

Ifeanyi did not call Amaka that night as promised. She waited up and resisted the urge to call or text him, even though she was furious at him for deceiving her again. She didn't pay him another visit until two weeks after. And this time, she was livid.

Ifeanyi stared at her as she vented, calling him all sorts of names. He was not at all moved by her outburst, especially after reconciling with his wife. "Since I have been so terrible to you, why do you keep showing your face around here? When will you get the message already? Jeez, you're like a dog with a bone! For God's sake, LET IT GO, otherwise I will have you *barred*! Don't make me call the security on you."

Amaka laughed wickedly. "You wouldn't *dare!*"

Oh, dear Lord! Who is this woman? She was dangerous. A woman obsessed, bent on getting her way. And Ifeanyi realised, in that moment, how true it was that he wasn't in control...

Present day...

Ifeanyi fell to the floor, at the feet and mercy of his adversary, Jamie Solomon. The man whose feelings he had not considered...until now. He had kept his secret from him, believing it was Amaka's place to tell - or not. But maybe tonight would have turned out differently if he had confessed and asked his forgiveness too.

He hoped it was not too late to beg for mercy...

VOLUME EIGHT

45

"But the God of all grace, who hath called us unto his eternal glory by Christ Jesus, after that ye have suffered a while, make you perfect, stablish, strengthen, settle you."

1 PETER 5:10

"**M**ary, hide!" Ifeanyi shouted as he used his right hand to rub the blood gushing from his nose. "Please leave my wife and kids out of this," he begged.

The two brothers entered the house and locked the door behind them. Jimmy crushed Ifeanyi's mobile phone under his feet and kicked it across the room. Jamie bent down and picked up Ifeanyi by his shirt. "Did you think you could screw my wife and get away with it?"

"I'm sorry! It was a mistake. Amaka said you guys broke up," Ifeanyi said in his defence.

"Did she now? I guess that gave you license... BIG MISTAKE!" Jamie spat at him before punching him in the face again.

Jimmy picked Ifeanyi from the floor and held him up while Jamie used him as a punching bag, breaking a couple of ribs in the process. Ifeanyi spat out blood. His instinct was to fight back, but he knew that would only make matters worse. Also, the odds of him prevailing against the two men were slim to none. They were both bigger than him, and Jimmy was also very muscular.

When Jamie had tired himself from punching Ifeanyi, Jimmy threw him to the ground, and they began to kick and step on him. "Hold on! Before he passes out!" Jamie said, restraining his brother. "I don't want him to miss the main action!" He laughed wickedly.

Ifeanyi was horrified, as he realised what they intended to do. "Please, I'm sorry," Ifeanyi mumbled. "Leave my—"

Jamie bent down and slapped him across the face. "*That* was for your *nerve*... To think you could stick your *little dick* in my wife! Now, you're going to have to watch us have fun with your pretty little wife too. I hear she's a bit of a freak." He laughed, and Jimmy giggled, watching Ifeanyi's horror. "Payback's a bitch!"

"God, please! NOOO!" Ifeanyi pleaded, hanging on to Jamie's leg, as they entered the main house. Jamie kicked his face and shook his leg free.

"Come out, come out, wherever you are!" Jamie sang, taunting Mary to come out of hiding.

Ifeanyi stumbled to his feet. He had to stop this. He had to do something! God strike him dead if those men were to lay their hands on his wife. He managed to get on his feet and picked up a weapon. A lamp stand.

"What do you think you're doing?" Jimmy asked, pointing a gun at him. Ifeanyi dropped the lamp stand and kept his hands up in surrender, now terrified. *How could this be happening?*

"Please, just go! I've learnt my lesson. Please, I'm begging you..."

"Tie him up!" Jamie ordered, and Jimmy found something to tie Ifeanyi up. He tied him to the stairway railing before following Jamie up the stairs.

Ifeanyi was sobbing, turning frantically to see where they were going. "Mary, hide! God help me. I'm so sorry for what I did. Please help us. Please don't let them harm Mary. God, please!" he cried and struggled with his restraint.

Mary had heard the first punch, and Ifeanyi's warning for her to hide. She first contemplated getting the kids, but she thought their cries wouldn't help, if she was to find somewhere to hide. She knew the perfect place to hide - her secret closet. She quickly sent a text message to her in-laws, which read, *"HELP! Armed robbers at our house!"*

She wasn't sure if they were armed robbers, but she knew well enough that such attackers tended to rape any women they found. When she got into her closet, she realised that they could be kidnappers, and she decided to go back for her kids. She was in the corridor, when she heard Ifeanyi apologise for sleeping with Amaka. That was when she knew what type of visit it was. She crept back to her hiding place, making sure that she opened the balcony door, so they would think she had climbed out of the balcony.

The closet had a secret entrance from the bathroom and their bedroom, which was covered by a full-length mirror that opened outward when a switch was pressed. It also acted as a safe for their valuables. No one would ever know there was a room behind the mirrors, so Mary could stay there all night unless they set the house on fire to smoke her out!

While there, she prayed. That was all she knew to do. The signal wasn't strong in the closet, so she couldn't make any calls, and she couldn't risk being found. It would take about 30 minutes for her in-laws to get to her house, depending on when they see the text message. She asked God to take control of the whole situation. To soften the hearts of their attackers and to give Ifeanyi wisdom to deal with them.

She also prayed for wisdom for herself and strength to handle anything that might befall her. She committed her children to God's care. That the enemy would neither see nor touch them. She prayed that their attackers would be blinded and confused and even turn their hatred on each other. She kept praying, trying not to panic nor cry, but calling on God's presence to fall upon them in their hour of trouble.

Then she heard someone in her bedroom. They went out onto the balcony and then the bathroom. "She's not here!" the person said. She could still hear the person hovering in the room. For a while she panicked that he would find the switch to the secret room, but then she heard his footsteps retreating. She let out a sigh of relief.

"I can't find her anywhere," Jimmy said.

"She couldn't have run out! What about the kids?" Jamie asked.

"Ummm... Bro, let's leave them out of this," Jimmy said. Having two kids of his own, he knew bringing them into this would be going too far. In fact, he thought they had done enough and hoped Jamie would blow off his steam already.

"But we've got to find her," Jamie said. Then an idea popped in his head. He took the gun from Jimmy and shot at Ifeanyi's right foot. Ifeanyi screamed and wailed. "Mary... Come out now, or the next one will be in his head!"

"Mary, DON'T!" Ifeanyi shouted through his pain and got hit with the gun.

"Shall we go for two," Jamie asked Jimmy, thoroughly enjoying himself and pointing the gun at Ifeanyi's left foot.

"Look, bro. I think we've gone far enough."

"Hey! Don't do this man! Imagine if it was YOUR woman! This bastard screwed my *wife*."

"But his wife had nothing to do with it. Let's just go. Besides, what if she's called for help?" Jimmy asked.

Jamie turned to Ifeanyi. "It looks like your wife doesn't give a shit about you!" he said, fuming. He was tempted to shoot the other foot just for the hell of it. That would teach him!

"Please, I'm sorry for what I did," Ifeanyi said, crying. "I will never have anything to do with Amaka again. Please leave my wife out of this. She's the kindest person you'll ever meet. She doesn't deserve this. In fact, I'd prefer if you just killed me!"

"Ifeanyi..."

Everyone turned to see Mary at the top of the stairs.

"NOOO! Mary, no. Hide!" Ifeanyi shouted, frantically struggling to get free. "Go back!"

Jamie and Jimmy smiled. "She's an angel, after all," Jimmy said. They both climbed the stairs to her as she stood frozen at the top of it.

Ifeanyi struggled frantically with his restraint and was making headway. Jamie turned back to him and fastened his restraints again. "You go first. I'll stay here and watch him squirm," Jamie said, pointing the gun at Ifeanyi so that he would be still.

"Shoot me! Just kill me already!" Ifeanyi resisted, refusing to be still.

"Nah, this is so much more fun," Jamie laughed.

Jimmy had reached Mary, and she stepped back from him. Jimmy caught hold of her hand, hating what he was about to do. She struggled free.

"Look, I came out of hiding willingly, didn't I?" she shouted. "I don't want you to rape me. If it is sex you want, then let us do it like grown-ups, okay? Ifeanyi didn't rape Amaka, she gave herself to him freely. I only ask for the same courtesy."

Jimmy looked at Jamie, who was smiling like he had won the jackpot. "That's cool, babe. Go do you, Jimmy."

"Mary, please, no..." Ifeanyi cried.

"It's okay, babe. I still love you. I just need these men out of my house before they terrify my children," Mary said.

"Noooo... God, no!" Ifeanyi wailed as he watched Mary walk away with Jimmy.

Jamie smiled and licked his lips. "Hmmm... She sounds like a pro! I bet she's wild in bed."

Ifeanyi just sobbed. His worst nightmare was about to happen, and there was nothing he could do to stop it. Where was God?

Mary led Jimmy to a spare bedroom upstairs, as she didn't want to defile her marital bed. She didn't know what she was doing, but she reasoned giving herself freely was far better than being raped. She prayed for strength to follow through.

Jimmy followed her and watched her, intrigued. He had never met a woman so brave. He wondered if she had some other trick in mind, or if she was really going to give herself to him. She was beautiful, and he would definitely enjoy it. But he wasn't feeling right about it. She was a good person and didn't deserve this.

She sat on the bed, nervously. "What's your name?" she asked.

"James. But you can call me Jimmy," he replied.

"I'm Mary," she said and swallowed.

"So... Can we get on with it, already?"

"Yes, but I want to be comfortable. Can you give me a minute to pray?" Mary asked.

"If that will make you feel better," Jimmy smiled. What a strange request, he thought. Was she stalling for time? "But don't make it a long one."

Mary got down on her knees while Jimmy settled into the bed to wait for her. "Lord, I just want to say thank You for Your grace upon my life. Thank You for the strength You gave me to forgive my husband's betrayal, by sleeping with another woman behind my back. I thank You that what was supposed to break us only made us stronger. I know Lord that even this act of evil against us tonight will make us stronger. I trust You because You are ALWAYS in control, even when it looks like You are not.

"You are the Lord who knows and sees the hearts of all men, and Lord, you know what is in Jimmy's heart. I thank You for his kindness, in agreeing not to rape me tonight, and even giving me this time to pray. I know that he loves his brother and feels his brother's pain and heartbreak, and if this is the only way for them to get resolution, then I pray that you will give me the strength to carry through on our agreement, even though it is against Your command.

"Please forgive us for what we are about to do tonight. I know that this is contrary to Your Spirit, but so is death, and You suffered Your Son, Jesus, to die on the cross for me, and for Jimmy, and for Jamie. Lord, tonight, I am going to carry my cross, and I pray that Your grace shall be sufficient for me. I also pray that Your grace will be upon Ifeanyi too. Please minister to him now so that he knows that You are here with me; that You are in this place of suffering, and we will yet praise You...because You are good!

"Thank You, Lord. I am strengthened, and I give You all the glory. I love You."

Mary stood up and looked at Jimmy. "I'm ready. Please be gentle."

Jamie was enjoying watching Ifeanyi roll and weep in torment, at the image of his wife with another man. Whether by force or by choice, it was the most horrible thing he could imagine. Ifeanyi knew she was doing it for him, but he couldn't fathom how or why she would go freely. And here he was, powerless to fight for her, to defend her honour. He was a failure!

Jamie looked up, wondering what was taking them long. It had been more than ten minutes. Or were they doing foreplay? He smiled, wondering if she would give him a blow job.

The unmistakable sound of Jimmy climaxing was heard through the hall, and Jamie chuckled while Ifeanyi could do nothing but cry. His wife was ruined. And it was all his fault.

46

"But the God of all grace, who hath called us unto his eternal glory by Christ Jesus, after that ye have suffered a while, make you perfect, stablish, strengthen, settle you."

1 PETER 5:10

Ifeanyi could barely look up when he heard footsteps on the stairway. He couldn't bear to see his wife, whom he had failed. His actions had brought this evil upon her, upon their home. Would she ever forgive him?

"How was it?" Jamie asked, hoping for juicy details. When he didn't see Mary, he figured she was still recovering from Jimmy's assault.

"As good as could be expected," Jimmy said with a smile. "Alright, let's go."

Jamie handed him the gun and began to bound the stairs. "No, it's my turn."

Jimmy held his hand. "She said she wanted the same courtesy as your wife. That's one man, and she's done it, so let's go."

Jamie pulled his hand away, grimacing. "What are you talking about? You think I came here to watch you fuck her? He screwed my wife, so this is payback!"

"No... You've had your payback. You beat the shit out of the guy and watched him squirm while I did his wife. What you are doing now is being a bloody bastard! She doesn't deserve this. So, come on..." Jimmy headed towards the door, hoping Jamie would get the drift.

"You fucking bastard. How can you screw me? You go... I'm getting mine!" Jamie continued up the stairs with more determination.

Jimmy fired the gun, and everybody jumped. "If you so much as touch her, I'll kill you."

Ifeanyi looked between the brothers, not sure what was going on, but thankful that Jimmy was at least preventing Jamie from violating his wife a second time.

"You wouldn't!" Jamie said, lingering at the top of the stairs. What the hell was the matter with Jimmy?

"Okay, maybe not," Jimmy replied. He untied Ifeanyi. "But her husband most certainly will. Jamie, it's over. You've had your revenge. Don't be cruel. Look, it's been almost 30 minutes already. We don't want to get caught out here."

Ifeanyi pulled himself up against the railing. His busted foot was still bleeding, and his whole body ached. But he was ready to spend his last strength fighting for his wife.

Jamie came down the stairs again, fuming. "The last guy who screwed my woman didn't live to talk about it. Consider yourself very lucky!" he said, glaring at Ifeanyi.

Ifeanyi spat blood in his face. Jamie cursed madly and began to kick him again until Jimmy successfully dragged him away. Jamie pulled himself free from Jimmy's grip angrily. "I can't believe you did that! You've grown soft on me, *mehn*. If you were not my brother, I swear…" he grumbled as they walked out of the house together.

"You'll get over it. Fair is fair, and they got what they deserved," Jimmy said.

"I should have gone first," Jamie muttered under his breath. He entered the car at the passenger side, and they drove away.

Mary came down the stairs after her attackers had gone and was shocked to see how badly injured her husband was. "Oh, baby…" she cried as she held him up in her arms. She supported him to rest on the sofa, then she called the nanny.

Ifeanyi couldn't look at his wife. He was too ashamed of himself. After what she had suffered, she was now the one taking care of him.

How could he have let this happen? How could he be so defenceless? What if they had been armed robbers? He had been so unprepared for the attack, and now, Mary would never be the same.

Mary returned with the security guard, who assisted Ifeanyi out to his car and supported him into the passenger seat. "How could you let those men into my compound?" Ifeanyi grumbled at the guard.

"They said they were Madam's brothers," the guard replied. "I'm sorry, sir."

Ifeanyi sighed. Ibrahim was a new guard and had never seen Samson and Samuel. It was his fault, though. He shouldn't have opened the door to them without doing his due diligence first. Even though he knew his 'what ifs' wouldn't change what had happened, it was all he could do as he derided himself for letting Mary down.

Mary asked the nanny to check on the children who, surprisingly, had not been disturbed by the events of the night. "Please stay with them until we come back. Abigail should be due for her feed now," she added before heading for the car.

Mary got a call from her mother-in-law saying they had been trying to reach them. She said she already sent their mobile police. Mary told them that the robbers had gone, and she was heading to the hospital with Ifeanyi. She said she'd call them when she got there.

Mary drove Ifeanyi to their family hospital in Lekki, and he was received by the Emergency Relief team. He was still bleeding when they got there. The medical staff prevented Mary from following them, asking her to wait for them to call her. Mary kissed Ifeanyi's forehead and said, "I love you," but he couldn't even look at her as he was rolled away on a stroller bed.

Adania Nkechi was asleep in her one-bedroom apartment, alone in her bed on this Thursday night. She lived a lonely life because the man she loved belonged to someone else. Though she had met him first, though they had been the best of friends, the moment he had set his eyes on her sister, she had been shoved aside and forgotten. It was her common experience; the curse of having a sister that was so beautiful. And it didn't help that Amaka knew it and flaunted it everywhere she went.

Adania tried to be a good sister to her. She tried not to be bitter and to always hold Amaka in positive regard. But it had never been harder than the day she married him, and she had to stand by as the doting sister.

Her doorbell rang. She checked her bedside clock and confirmed that it was 11:30 pm. Who could be ringing her bell at such an unholy hour? She looked out of the window and recognised his car.

She threw her robe on and walked briskly to the door. She confirmed that it was him through the peephole. She took in a deep breath and opened the door.

"Hi, Adania. Can I come in?" Jamie asked, soberly. He knew he could count on Adania for some comfort tonight. And it would be the best payback for Amaka.

Adania moved aside for him to enter and looked about for her sister. "What's the matter?"

"Amaka and I had a fight. She cheated on me, again," Jamie said. "I didn't know where else to go."

"Oh, I'm so sorry, dear. Come here. Everything will be okay," Adania said, receiving him in a hug.

"I hope I didn't disturb you," Jamie said, when they had separated.

"Of course not," Adania said. "Let me put the kettle on. I know you like your tea."

Adania was filling the kettle with water when she became aware of his presence behind her. "It should have been you, Adania. I'm so sorry I was blinded by Amaka's beauty and didn't appreciate yours. You know I always loved you."

Adania dropped the kettle on the counter. This couldn't be happening. Not now. Not this way. She didn't want to be "the other woman." For God's sake, he was her sister's husband! But she knew that if he touched her now, she couldn't and wouldn't resist him. She turned to him. "It's too late now..."

"Is it?" Jamie asked, stepping closer to her. He touched her face, and she closed her eyes, inhaling deeply. He had her. And he took her. Right there in her kitchen.

It was midnight, and Mary was still waiting for some feedback about her husband. She had called his parents when she got to the hospital but told them not to bother coming. There was no need for all of them to lose sleep. They said they would visit first thing in the morning. She also sent messages to Chidinma and Nomnso, telling them what happened and asking them to pray for their brother.

Another thirty minutes passed, and she was still waiting. She kept thinking about what had happened between her and Jimmy. She was surprised how calm she had been. She had appealed to him to dissuade his brother from trying to have his way with her. She knew Jamie would have been far from gentle and kind like Jimmy.

"Mrs Chukwueke," the on-call doctor called.

Mary arose to meet her. "Is my husband alright?" she asked.

"Yes, he's stable. You can come and see him now."

Mary followed the doctor into a private room, where Ifeanyi lay in bed, bandaged up, with his right foot suspended in the air. He looked like he had survived a very bad motor accident.

"Madam, we can see that there was gun violence involved. We've asked your husband for a statement, but he has refused to give any. We have a policy to involve the police with every case involving guns. We will need you to give a statement on what happened," the doctor said.

"Please, leave me to talk with my husband," Mary requested.

"Okay, ma'am," the doctor said before leaving with the nurse.

Mary sat and leaned over Ifeanyi and cried, seeing what his 'mistake' had brought upon them. She never wished for him to suffer this way, but somehow, she knew he would never forget the 'lesson.' She wondered how he had coped, imagining what Jimmy was doing with her upstairs while he was powerless to stop it.

She touched his face, and he turned away from her. "Hey, baby... Look at me. Are you angry with me?"

Ifeanyi had a lump in his throat. He choked through it as he replied. "I brought this on us. You're ruined now because of me..."

"I'm not ruined. Don't ever say that," Mary protested. "Did you think I wasn't *ruined* when you married me? Do you remember all I suffered before you came into my life? God has always been with me."

"But I couldn't protect you! I am your husband, and they would have raped you...and I couldn't protect you..." he broke down in sobs.

"I'm fine, Ifeanyi. Jimmy was kind," Mary said.

Ifeanyi turned to look at her. He wanted confirmation that she had slept with Jimmy. "But he still slept with you... Didn't he?"

Mary shook her head, and relief flooded Ifeanyi. "Thank GOD!" He pulled her into him with his strong left arm and hugged her, letting the tears run down his cheeks. "How did you manage to change his mind?"

"It wasn't me. It was God. I didn't even know what I was doing. I just thought...*follow Jesus*. You know, Jesus knew they wanted to kill him, but he didn't protest. He went willingly. And I was like, this is my death, my *cross*...and I must go willingly. I asked Jimmy to let me pray first, and God just took over."

"Wow..." Ifeanyi said, beholding his wife with new eyes. "When I finished praying, he was crying. He said that I was glowing like an angel. The glory of God was shining on my face, and he begged me to forgive him for what he had been about to do. I told him that I had already forgiven him, and he just wept. He asked me to pray for him to receive Jesus, and I did. It was so powerful, watching how my simple act of following Jesus opened the door for his salvation."

"But... But I heard him... Coming..." Ifeanyi said, remembering that haunting sound that had broken his spirit.

"He was putting on a show for Jamie. He said that his brother is hard-hearted, and if he knew Jimmy hadn't followed through, he would have insisted on violating me himself. I stayed back because I was still glowing. Well, that's what Jimmy said."

"God, thank You! You're my angel, Mary. I don't know how I would have gone on if Jimmy had slept with you. It was *sooo* unbelievably painful to imagine another man with you...and to know I was to blame."

"I guess, you got a taste of your own medicine, in a way... Even though nothing happened," Mary said with a small smile.

"I did! That was grace! I know you said I shouldn't apologise again, but I must. Mary, I was the worst sort of man to cheat on you; to even think that another woman could make me feel like you do. I gave into my basic instinct, and it could have been so much worse tonight...if you hadn't followed Jesus! You saved us, Mary. And I love you so much!"

Mary cried, listening to him. "All glory belongs to God. I'm glad you now know the pain I felt, even though I never wanted you to suffer. If only we would walk in the Spirit and not the flesh, we wouldn't have to learn the hard way."

Ifeanyi nodded. He pulled Mary in for a kiss, his mouth now devoid of blood. It was a long, sweet, relieving kiss as they connected in spirit, heart, mind, and body. "I would die for you..." Ifeanyi muttered when their lips parted briefly.

Mary swallowed and wiped away her tears. "I have died for you...and I will do it again. You don't know how in love I am with you. I'm so in love with you, Ifeanyi."

Her words stirred up passion in him, but his body was too weak to act on his desire. He just kissed her, with as much strength as he could muster. He was so unbelievably lucky to be loved by such an amazing woman.

47

"But the God of all grace, who hath called us unto his eternal glory by Christ Jesus, after that ye have suffered a while, make you perfect, stablish, strengthen, settle you."

1 PETER 5:10

As expected, Amaka woke up to find herself alone in her home. Her heart ached as she remembered what had transpired yesterday, between her and Ifeanyi, and the beating she'd received when she had gotten home. As she got out of bed, her whole body ached, and there was a numbing pain in her abdomen. That was when she remembered her baby. She would need to go to the hospital to verify that she hadn't lost it or suffered any internal bleeding.

She called the maid, who promptly attended to her. After a shower and cereal, she got ready to go to the hospital. She checked her phone. No calls or messages from her husband. She sighed. What had possessed her to marry such a man? He hadn't even cared that she was pregnant!

Amaka wondered if she could really take more abuse from Jamie. It was one thing to stay with a cheating husband, it was quite another to stay with a violent one. However, more than his occasional physical assault was the constant emotional abuse, which hurt the most. When he was happy, he treated her like a queen, and when he was not, he had a way of making her feel utterly worthless.

The trip to the hospital confirmed that she and the baby were fine, and she was advised to rest and take it easy. Amaka had been surprised to realise that she was happy that the child was unharmed. It was the last thing that gave her hope of love; someone to love who would love her in return.

Three days passed and Amaka was still home alone. Apart from their week's separation, this was the longest Jamie had gone without returning home after a fight. She called everyone she knew and could trust, and that was her sister, Adania, her mother, and Jamie's brother, Jimmy.

Jimmy said he last saw him the night he had found out about her infidelity. Adania said she hadn't seen him. Her mother said the same thing and told her to wait and be patient, that he would return home soon.

Adania hated to lie to her sister, but she had done worse already. She turned to the handsome man asleep in her bed and had no room in her heart for guilt. She was finally happy. She was finally 'the one.' After feeling like a nobody and playing second fiddle to her younger sister, she was finally the star of her own show.

The last three days had been amazing. At first, she hadn't believed it when he had returned to her the next day and asked for dinner. She had excitedly prepared his favourite dish, which they had eaten together at the table. They caught up on old times and made passionate love all night. He had come for more again the next day, and then the next.

Adania knew that this couldn't last forever and dreaded the moment when he would tell her that he was going back to his wife - her sister. Since that first day, they hadn't even mentioned her name at all. She braced herself for his return every day, but with each new day, her heart became more fragile and desperate, that if he had said those words, she was sure she would die of a broken heart.

It was on Day Five, that they had the dreaded discussion over dinner.

"I was wondering..." he started. "How would you feel about us living together?"

Adania swallowed. "I don't get it. You want to live here with me?"

Jamie shook his head. "I want you to come and live with me."

"But... But, Amaka's there..." Adania said, looking at him incredulously.

"Yes, I know. She's my wife. But I was wondering if you would be my wife too." Adania's jaw dropped as she stared at him in awe. "I know it's unusual...and may be strange because she's your sister. But I can't help who I love. I made a mistake marrying her. I see that now. But I don't want to go home without you."

Adania couldn't believe her ears. He wanted her to be his *second wife*? To her *sister*? What would her mother say? "Can't you just get an annulment or divorce? I don't like this arrangement at all."

An annulment didn't sound good to Jamie at all. He didn't want to divorce Amaka. He didn't want anyone else to have her. He just wanted to have what he wanted - the best of both worlds. A beautiful wife, for display, and an adoring, home-making wife. And he had also entertained fantasies of a threesome with the sisters. No, an annulment wasn't an option.

"No, an annulment is not an option. This is what I want. I can live without you, but I really don't want to. I would give you anything you want if you were my wife, Ada. Just think about it. Life's too short to be unhappy."

Adania took in all he said and couldn't believe that she was seriously considering sharing her sister's husband for the rest of her life. She loved him, but there had to be another way. There just had to be.

That night, Jamie returned home to his wife, leaving Adania to decide what she wanted to do. As usual, he made no attempt to explain his whereabouts to Amaka. As he was still understandably unhappy about her unfaithfulness, she had no leg to stand on regarding his undue absence. She welcomed him into their home, and their bed, and soon, all was history.

Ifeanyi was released from the hospital after a week's stay and was instructed to stay off his feet for at least a month. He had several broken bones, and he had to be careful not to rush the healing process. He had the best nurse on hand to look after him. His beautiful and devoted wife, Mary.

They gave their statement to the police but said that they didn't intend to press any charges. Rather, they chose to forgive and move on. Ifeanyi immediately installed additional security in their home and installed CCTV in their bedroom and in Mary's secret closet.

He wanted to be more prepared, should anyone seek to prey on them again. However, he was also well aware of the scripture that says, "...*unless the LORD guards the city, the watchman keeps awake in vain*" (Psalm 127:1). He knew he had given place to the devil, through his unfaithfulness, and if he was careless again, he could invite more trouble.

Ifeanyi never returned to Solomon Investment Bank. He took two months' sick leave, which completed his period of notice, and Mary assisted him in getting his office cleared out. After two months of recovery, an additional month taken for physiotherapy, Ifeanyi started work with his father's group of companies in the telecommunications industry. He took to the job well and actually enjoyed learning under his father.

Mary continued with her blog, and created a section for Marriage and Motherhood, where she shared lessons from her life about both callings. A lot of women, and even men, appreciated this new section of her blog, and she was surprised that there seemed no shortage of things to say about both topics.

With Ifeanyi's blessing and support, Mary published her first story, from a first-person perspective, on how she had learnt about, coped with, and forgiven her husband's infidelity. She titled it "He Cheated!" - an eye-grabbing title that was packed with emotion. The press quickly picked up the story, calling it a "brave and daring tell-all." It was just the promotion she needed to get the word out, and she got lots of visits on her blog because of it.

She hoped that the lessons from it would help other hurting women discover the freedom of forgiveness and also help men see how damaging infidelity is to their spouses, marriages, and homes. Infidelity was such a scourge in modern society that many women and men were resigned to its inevitability. But she knew the power of the cross. If only more people would choose to live it...

One day, someone commented anonymously on the story, wanting to know what she should do with a husband who habitually cheats on her, yet beats her up for cheating on him. Mary decided to let Ifeanyi respond to the enquirer. He wrote:

> *"I'm sorry about your situation, dear Anonymous. It is a horrible thing to be cheated on and a terrible thing to be abused in your home. From the sounds of things, neither you nor your husband are Christian, otherwise, you would not habitually cheat on each other. If you were Christian, and he cheated on you once, then I would say forgive him and give him another chance because anyone can fall once, especially if they were not on guard or had too much confidence in their own ability (1 Corinthians 10:12). Christian marriage is for life, and*

we have to be ready and willing to forgive all wrongs and give grace to each other, loving each other as Christ loved us (John 13:34).

"However, a Christian is someone who is submitted to God, and as such, cannot continue to sin (1 John 3:9). They won't continue to do wrong because of grace (Romans 6:1-2). And most certainly, they should be walking in love (Read 1 Corinthians 13). An abusive person cannot be a Christian, even if they go to or belong to or even lead a Church! Jesus said we shall distinguish the true and false believers by their fruits (Matt 7:16-18), and the world will know His disciples by their love towards one another (John 13:35).

"So, it is because of this that I suspect that neither you nor your husband is Christian. In which case, your marriage is not one of godly covenant, but of human contract, and is only as strong as **your own** will, your word or **mutual integrity**, and the legal framework that supports it. Legally, you can divorce, and in this case of physical abuse, I would recommend that you do divorce.

"Do you have children? It is important to take them into consideration too, especially in an abusive relationship. They can learn bad behaviour from watching you and your husband fight and hurt each other intentionally. Also, they are at risk of suffering physical, sexual, or mental abuse, or even neglect, as you are not able to give them the attention and care they need, because you also need help desperately. You shouldn't stay in an abusive relationship for the sake of your children because you will end up teaching them that that is what is normal and expected in life.

"Please get professional help. See a counsellor or a lawyer about getting a divorce and protecting yourself and any children from further abuse. If you believe in God at all, this is a time to pray and get His guidance too. He is gracious and will forgive you and give you the courage to start again, on a sure foundation of love. We *sincerely hope and pray that you will call on Him, in your hour of need. Mary and I wish you all the best!"*

❤ ❤ ❤

It had been three months since that awful night, when Jamie had found out about Amaka and Ifeanyi. Amaka had been wrong about him only beating her due to her unfaithfulness. Now that they were married, he didn't hesitate to show her that he owned her, and every and anything she did to offend or irritate him got her a slap, kick, or a punch. Maybe it was because he was still hurting over her infidelity, Amaka reasoned as she tried to be patient with him.

However, Amaka miscarried her child at the twelve-week mark, due to Jamie's constant battery. For once in her life, she had cried for someone other than herself. When she had told him that she had miscarried, he hadn't even batted an eyelid. He hadn't apologised or sought to comfort her. It was then that Amaka realised that she had married a monster.

She covered up her bruises and did well to keep the good public image of a happily married couple. She didn't even tell her mother about her husband's abusive behaviour. Whenever she complained to her about anything in her marriage, her mother had a way of making it her fault. She wasn't respectful enough. She wasn't submissive enough. Didn't she cheat on him? His ego was bruised.

"This is marriage, nobody's home is perfect," she would say.

Amaka couldn't tell her sister either. They had never been so close because she had always been jealous of her. Adania thought she had the easy life because everyone wanted a piece of her, or to be like her. She didn't know how lonely an existence it was to be the one everyone envied and to only be seen as a trophy wife or girlfriend. She didn't understand that her gift of beauty, which she had used to her advantage all her life, was also her curse! Nobody cared to look deeper, and the only man who had, and whom she had loved, now hated her and was happily married to Miss Perfect.

One sunny day in August, Amaka returned home from a day of retail therapy to find her sister, Adania, in her kitchen. She dropped her things on the dining table and went to her. "You didn't tell me you were coming, Ada. Is everything okay?"

Adania turned to her and revealed the slight rise of her stomach. Amaka screamed gleefully. "You are pregnant?! Who's the lucky guy? Come on, you have to tell me everything." She dragged her sister over to the dining table so they could sit and catch up.

Just then, Jamie walked into the living area in his boxer shorts, not caring to acknowledge Amaka's return from her day out.

"Jamie, put something on, abeg! Can't you see my sister is here?" Amaka said, feeling embarrassed for her sister.

"That's the thing, Amaka," Adania began. "Jamie is the lucky man..."

"What? I don't understand," Amaka said, looking between her husband and her sister.

Jamie was approaching them in the dining area. He put his arm around Adania and planted a wet kiss on her lips. "We're getting married," he said, with a big grin.

Amaka's fall to the marble floor, as she fainted, was far from graceful.

48

"But the God of all grace, who hath called us unto his eternal glory by Christ Jesus, after that ye have suffered a while, make you perfect, stablish, strengthen, settle you."

1 PETER 5:10

I t had been a long flight, and it was made even longer by the annoying Christian woman that had sat beside him, who couldn't stop going on and on about Jesus. Jason was glad to get off the plane and get out of the airport to breathe in the fresh air again. However, to his dismay, it wasn't all that fresh at the Murtala Muhammed International Airport, Lagos. It was always a buzz kill whenever he landed in Lagos and saw the many taxis and buses in disrepair, which ought to be off the roads, blowing white and black smoke into the air. He sighed.

His spirit was lifted when he saw his brother, Jimmy. The brothers hugged warmly, and Jimmy's driver took Jason's luggage and carried them to a Range Rover jeep. Jason gladly entered and sat beside his brother, smiling as he enjoyed the cool air conditioner, which was a huge relief from the heat and dusty air outside.

"How was your flight, man?" Jimmy asked when he had settled into the jeep and the driver was pulling out of his parking space.

"Mehn, don't ask. If I have to sit next to another one of those evangelists, I'll punch something," Jason giggled.

"Oh," Jimmy said, a little disappointed. He had hoped for a chance to talk to his brother about his new-found Faith. Perhaps he would save it until later. "That bad, eh?"

"Oh, this one was the *worst*! She even opened her Bible and everything. I guess she figured I had nowhere to run to. There should be a law against such evangelism on commercial aircrafts!" he groaned on. "Anyway, how are you? How've you been?"

Jimmy smiled, though his mood had been dampened by his brother's blatant hatred for religion. "I've been good... Going through some changes."

"Yeah, I noticed. You've been quiet in our WhatsApp group." Jason noticed a big black book on the seat beside Jimmy. He frowned when he saw what it was. "What are you doing with a Bible?!"

Jimmy looked down at it and smiled at the opening it had presented. "I'm reading it."

"You what? For real? What for?"

"Because I want to know God more," Jimmy said, looking at his brother sincerely. The driver watched the brothers through his rear-view mirror.

Jason laughed nervously. "Are you *kidding* me?! Since when?"

"It's been about three months now. I met this amazing woman..."

Jason's eyebrows shot up. "Huh? What about Fatima? You cheating on her with a *Christian*?"

"No...no... I'm not. I actually had an encounter with God when I was with this woman. I wasn't cheating, though...well, not really." Jimmy wondered why he was having such a hard time saying what actually happened.

"You're confusing me," Jason said.

"Don't worry, we can talk when we get home," Jimmy said, eyeing the driver, so Jason knew it was a private discussion.

"Ummm... Okay. So, you're a *Christian* now?"

"Yes, I believe in Jesus. And I hope we can talk about that sometime."

"Does Jamie know?"

Jimmy nodded. "Yes, but, I don't think he believes I'm serious."

"Hmmm... And how's Fatima taking this?"

"You can ask her yourself when you see her tonight."

Jason nodded and looked at his brother, then at the Bible. He looked out of his window. He didn't know what to say. Was Jimmy really serious? He believed in that 'pie-in-the-sky' *bullshit*? He had always looked up to Jimmy, but now, he didn't know what to make of him. And who was this woman he was talking about?

They drove on in silence for a long while before Jason remembered something funny that had happened to him on his journey from Los Angeles. Jimmy laughed, and the mood lightened a little bit. They carried on in silence.

Kemi approached Mary at the end of their women's meeting at church. She had been working up the courage for a few weeks now. "Can I have a word with you, please?"

Mary had noticed that Kemi had been looking at her during the meeting and was wondering what it was about. She'd thought to approach her, herself, but thought she might be picking at an old wound. They hadn't spoken since the day of Ifeanyi's party. It was strange that they were no longer friendly, and she had prayed for how to resolve that, since they were both Believers. She didn't hold any bitterness towards the woman and hoped that they could be reconciled.

Mary smiled warmly at her. "Sure."

They walked out of the room and the building together. Kemi didn't say anything until they were at Mary's car, and there was no one within earshot of them. Mary leaned on her car and looked at Kemi expectantly.

"I wanted to say that I'm sorry," Kemi said, at last.

Mary looked on at her, not fully understanding the purpose of the apology. "What are you sorry for?"

Kemi looked down, embarrassed, then up again. "Ifeanyi was right about me that night. I had to go home and pray about it because I couldn't see it then. I've been jealous of you for a long time, and it was wrong of me. I'm sorry."

"Thank you," Mary said. "I really appreciate your honesty and apology. But, why did you decide to say something now? All's been forgiven and forgotten."

"I read your story. And I understand you both better now."

"Oh," Mary muttered, not sure what more to say.

"I don't want to be a home-wrecker. It's just that I've been single for so long, and sometimes, I just want someone, *anyone*, to take notice of me. But it is so horribly selfish of me. I can't imagine it is easy for you, with so many women throwing themselves at your husband."

Mary gave a small smile. "No, it's not. I'm glad my story helped you to see my perspective. And I know it's hard being single, when you want to be married, but you have to value yourself enough to wait for your *own* man...and the *right* man, who will honour you with his love and faithfulness."

Kemi nodded. "I know that. I'm happy things worked out for you both. You were brave to forgive him. I don't know if I could have."

"It was hard, but I'm glad I did. We're happier than we have ever been, and we've learnt so much from what happened. It's also given me a way to reach out to others. But I pray you never have to experience such in your life, Kemi. Thanks again for your apology."

"Thank you for forgiving me. Please tell Ifeanyi that I'm sorry too."

The women hugged. "I will. Have a good night."

Kemi watched Mary drive away, feeling like a load had been lifted off her shoulders.

The three brothers were together again. Jamie showed up just in time for dinner at Jimmy's house. He greeted his brothers loudly, with manly hugs, and kissed his sister-in-law on her cheek. They all perceived that he had had a few to drink already.

"Hey, where's the beautiful wifey?" Jason asked.

"She couldn't make it," was all he said.

Jason and Jimmy exchanged looks and then decided to think nothing of it. Fatima laid food on the table. She had prepared a feast, as she knew the three brothers ate enough for six healthy, strong men.

"So, you said you had an encounter with God?" Jason asked, continuing their conversation from earlier today.

Jamie almost choked with laughter. His two brothers looked at him, perplexed. "Oh, you meant him?" he asked, indicating Jimmy.

"Uh huh…" Jimmy said, hoping Jamie wasn't so drunk that he would ruin his testimony with jests.

"Wait… Is this about that night or a different experience?" Jamie asked quietly, sober enough to know to keep their rendezvous discrete.

"That night. It was quite a special experience."

"So, what happened?" Jason asked. "Can we talk here?" He wondered if they were supposed to keep it hidden from Fatima.

"Yeah… Fatima knows."

"Fatima knows what?" she asked as she pulled up a seat.

"About my conversion story."

"Oh, that…" she swallowed. It still hurt thinking about what he had been doing at Mary's house. But she had seen and appreciated the changes in him.

"Okay... So, tell us," Jason said.

"I didn't come to hear this," Jamie objected. Everybody looked at him sternly, and he rolled his eyes. "Do tell," he said mockingly.

So, Jimmy recounted the story of how he had gone to Mary's house with Jamie, to carry out their mischief, and told of how Mary's face glowed after she had prayed. "It was the most unbelievable, amazing sight to watch her glow. I could feel the presence of God in the room, and I was afraid but also calm. I can never forget that experience in my life. When she prayed for me, I felt a touch on my head, like an anointing... My life hasn't been the same since."

"What's different?" Jason asked sincerely. The story seemed a bit far-fetched, but why would his brother pretend?

"Well, for starters, I pray now. Not just morning and night, but constantly. I am aware of God's presence, and He talks to me..."

"Like an audible voice?" Jason asked, sceptical.

"No... An inner voice."

"How do you know that's not just you thinking?" Jason looked at Jamie, who had a smirk on his face.

"I know the difference. Honestly, I'm not that wise. And often, He says things to me that contradict my common sense or desire, and He convinces me of His wisdom. I've started keeping a journal."

"Hmmm... Okay, what else?" Jason asked, not fully satisfied.

"I'm just a different person now. I have this desire to know more about Him. To do right. To do His will... I have been studying my Bible daily and joined a fellowship because I want to connect with other Believers."

Even as Jimmy was speaking, he realised that his former self would not have been convinced by such changes. He struggled to think of what might persuade them without having to boast about his good works. He wished God would reveal Himself again so they would see.

"So, you've become religious..." Jason interjected. "You're still the same guy, just religious now. You haven't cured cancer. You haven't raised the *dead*. Didn't Jesus say that such signs would follow those who believe?"

"Yes, as a collective body. We do not all have the same gifts, but the gifts are distributed within the Body of Christ so that the manifestation of the gifts are evidence that we are of the true Faith," Jimmy said, surprising himself. He hadn't known the answer to the question until he started speaking. It was as though God had helped him, and he too had gained a new understanding.

Jason just looked at him as if he had spoken jargon. Jimmy opened his Bible searching for the scripture that said, *"are all apostles? Are all prophets? Are all teachers? Are all workers of mira-cles? Have all the gifts of healing? Do all speak with tongues? Do all interpret?"* in 1 Corinthians 12:29-30. He was not well versed with the scriptures yet, so he couldn't locate it. He rather quoted it.

"So, what's *your* gift?" Jason challenged.

"I don't know yet, but I desire the greatest, which is love."

Jason looked at Jamie and chuckled. "Yeah, me too!" But his expression showed he was not amused.

Jamie scoffed, happy that Jason hadn't fallen for Jimmy's conversion story either. The first time Jimmy had told him, he hadn't known whether to be mad that he hadn't actually slept with Mary, as he had led him to believe, or sorry that he had lost his brother to religion. They had grown apart since that day, and he missed his brother. He had hoped that he would soon snap out of it.

Jimmy was saddened that they hadn't received his testimo-ny. Their hearts were hardened. He had been sure that if they would just hear what happened to him, they would also believe. Then the Lord reminded him of the scripture; *"If they hear not Moses and the prophets, neither will they be persuaded, though one rose from the dead"* (Luke 16:31). He had never understood it until that moment. True Believers were never won by the ev-idence of signs and wonders but by the preaching of the cross.

He knew his experience was not even as dramatic as a resur-rection, and he had no evidence to show them, like the dead per-son now alive. Even still, how many of those who had witnessed

Lazarus' resurrection had become Believers? He sighed. Only God could give them grace to believe, he realised.

And even though Fatima saw the changes in him and appreciated them, she still didn't accept his revelation of Jesus, though she believed in God. To her, Jesus was just a prophet, and Mohammed was the last prophet and considered greater. But Jimmy knew what he had seen and heard, and he knew that his relationship with God was real. He thanked God again for granting him the grace to see and decided that he would continue to pray for his family.

Jamie and Jason were happy to see him drop the discussion, even though Jason still wanted to know why Jimmy hadn't suddenly received the gift of healing with his salvation. However, he pondered on Jimmy's experience at Mary's house, trying to make sense of it.

Fatima also pondered on it. As someone who already believed in God, she wondered if she would have been convinced that Jesus was the Christ, the Son of the Living God, like Jimmy now believed, if she'd had that experience herself. She decided she would continue to watch Jimmy and see what becomes of his conversion.

"So, you'll never guess who approached me at church today..." Mary said. She was cuddling with Ifeanyi on the sofa after their dinner.

"Who? David?" he asked.

Mary frowned. She raised herself from her leaning position and looked into her husband's face. There was something about the way he had said David's name. He was jealous. "No, babe. David doesn't attend our church..."

"I wouldn't put it past him," Ifeanyi said. "So, who was it?"

"Before I tell you, what's your beef with David?"

Ifeanyi sighed. "I just...don't like him. And I don't trust him. He gave off a bad vibe the day we met."

"Do you trust me, though?"

Ifeanyi looked at his wife and was sorry. "I do. I'm sorry. For even implying anything... I know you would never cheat on me."

"Well, to be sincere, you don't *know* that." Ifeanyi raised an eyebrow. "But you have good reason to trust me. Anybody can fall, like you said. So, I don't expect you to look at me like some angel, but I do hope you will trust me."

Ifeanyi pulled Mary to himself. "I trust you. Completely. 100%. Do you trust me?"

Mary looked in her heart and spirit. She turned to him and smiled. "Yes, I do. Almost 100%." They laughed.

"Thank you. I want to earn it...and keep it," Ifeanyi said sincerely.

"I know you do. And I appreciate all you've done to show me that I can trust you again. In fact, that was where I was going. The person who approached me was Kemi."

Ifeanyi's expression darkened. "Really? What did she say? Did she upset you?"

Mary kissed him so he would relax. "No, she didn't. She just wanted to say sorry."

"Oh," Ifeanyi said, a little confused. "For what?"

"For trying to steal my husband..."

"So, she admitted it?"

"Yeah...and she was quite sincere. She said she read my story, and she understands us better now."

"Oh, really? Okay. That's good."

"Yeah... I think so too." Mary smiled and stroked Ifeanyi's arm tenderly. "I think she's hoping we will be friends again."

"Not a chance!" Ifeanyi said.

Mary looked at him, thinking the same thing, but wondering why she felt that way. "Why do you say that? She's apologised... And we've forgiven her...?"

"There's no need to give temptation breathing space. I know women. And I know me. We can be *friendly*, but not friends. It's safer that way," Ifeanyi said resolutely.

"But, isn't that like holding on to unforgiveness?" Mary still didn't completely understand.

"Trust me on this, babe. It's the best thing." Ifeanyi let out a deep sigh. "Not everyone can be your friend. You *choose* your friends, and they are the ones who will build you up. As a married couple, we have to be very careful of the friends we choose. We need to protect our union and surround ourselves with people who share our values, and who we trust. You didn't trust me immediately you forgave me, so we can't trust Kemi immediately either. Maybe when she gets married, we can be friends. But not now."

"I agree," Mary said, happy with his response. She settled back in his arms and smiled. "You're a wise man, Ifeanyi."

"Who learned the hard way..." He sighed. He kissed the top of her head. "It's you and me against the world, Mary. Just you and me."

"And Jesus..." Mary muttered.

"And Jesus."

49

"But the God of all grace, who hath called us unto his eternal glory by Christ Jesus, after that ye have suffered a while, make you perfect, stablish, strengthen, settle you."

1 PETER 5:10

Amaka woke up in the hospital, having suffered a mild concussion from her fall. She quickly shut her eyes when the bright light in the room aggravated her headache. She turned her head and tried opening her eyes again. A blurry face came into view.

"She's awake!" Adania cried to the medical staff and went to sit beside her sister. "Hey, dear... You okay?"

Amaka looked at her sister, trying to remember what had happened. The memory returned to her when she noticed her sister's slight bump. She shifted away in her bed.

Adania swallowed. "How are you, sis?"

"How could you?!" Amaka asked, tears stinging her eyes. "You're my sister! He is my husband! *How could you?*"

"We'll talk about it when you get home. Just take your rest, sis," Adania said, calmly.

"I'm not going anywhere with you! Where's Mummy?" Amaka asked.

"I've called her. She's on her way."

Amaka leaned back on the pillow, feeling a little dizzy still. A nurse came in to check her vision, reflexes, and other vital signs of recovery.

"You suffered quite a nasty fall there," the nurse said. "Do you remember what happened?"

"She slipped on some water," Adania lied.

Amaka shot daggers at her sister before turning to the nurse. "Will you please kindly ask her to leave?"

The nurse was surprised but did as she was told. Adania made her leave without another word, and the nurse continued with her assessment of Amaka's health. Amaka still had some mild symptoms, and the nurse recommended that she should stay in the hospital for the next 24 hours, until she was more stable.

When she was alone, Amaka cried bitterly. Her own *sister*?! *Pregnant* for her *husband*...and *engaged* to be married to her very own monster of a husband?! She felt both anger and pity for her dear sister. If she envied her so much, Adania was welcome to have her husband and her miserable life. She was done with it!

Amaka was stirred awake by her mother's touch. She cried when she saw her, and her mother hugged and kissed her.

"Adania told me what happened. How are you?" Mrs Nkechi asked.

"What did she tell you, Mum?" Amaka wondered if Adania had fed her mother lies.

"That you fainted when you found out. Please forgive your sister, Amaka."

"So, you knew? How long have you known about them?"

"Just a few days..." Amaka stared at her mother with disbelief. "She wanted my counsel and blessing. She was already pregnant. What could I say?"

Amaka began to shake her head. "You should have said '*no*,' Mum! Is this what you wanted for your daughters? For us to share a husband?"

"None of this would have happened, if you had been faithful to him. The deed is done now."

"Mum! I can't believe you're still blaming me for this!" Amaka was pained. Why wouldn't her mother see anything from her perspective?

"Amaka, not everything is about you. You have to think of that child. You just have to forgive and make the best of the situation."

"Mum, Jamie beats me! He is the reason I lost *my* child! I want to believe that if you knew that, you would never have given your blessing!"

"I know, my child. Please forgive him. You broke his heart!" Mrs Nkechi said.

"You *knew*? You mean, *all* this time you *knew*?" Amaka retracted her hand from her mother's. "And you thought that was what *I deserved*? I can't even believe you are my mother! Please, just go. You've never been on my side. I will not stay in this marriage another day! I'll die first!" Amaka turned her back on her mother, tears streaming down her cheeks.

"Amaka, listen to reason. Life is not a bed of roses. At least it was not a strange woman he brought home..." Mrs Nkechi continued.

Amaka just wept. She was truly alone. Even her own mother didn't love her. She shut her eyes and tried to shut her mother's words out. She soon fell back to sleep.

"What do you think you are doing?" Jamie asked, looking at his wife, who was busy folding clothes into a small suitcase.

Amaka didn't turn to him but continued with her activity. She hadn't expected him to, but still, she was pained that he hadn't bothered to visit her at the hospital. She was done with the marriage. And she was ready to fight for her freedom, that was if he still cared enough to prevent her from leaving.

"I asked you, what the hell do you think you are doing?" he asked again, his voice raised.

Amaka zipped the bag. She didn't have time to pack a lot. She just packed her essential things and planned to come back for the rest. She'd called an old friend, who was happy to accommodate her, until she could get her own place. Her former apartment had already been leased out. "I'm leaving you."

Jamie's smile sent a chill up her spine. "That easy, *eh*...? You don't want to talk about it?"

"There's nothing to talk about, Jamie. I wish you and Adania the best." Amaka carried her suitcase from the bed and approached the door. Jamie's tall, broad-shouldered frame blocked her exit. "Please get out of my way."

"Or else?"

"Get out of the way, Jamie!"

For some reason, Jamie found her boldness amusing. He smiled. "You're not going anywhere, darling." He picked up her left hand to make his point, only to find her ring finger devoid of his band. He frowned. "Where's your band?"

Amaka snatched her hand back. "I flushed it down the toilet. Right where our marriage went!" she spat the words at him. He slapped her. She pulled herself together instantly. Her defiant expression showed that she was ready for all he had. He slapped her again, harder. "With such tender affection, it is hard to imagine why I would want to *leave you*," she mocked.

Jamie pulled the suitcase from her angrily and threw it across the room. He pushed her back into the room and shut and locked the door behind him. "You started this, Amaka! *You* threw our marriage down the toilet!"

Amaka watched as he unbuckled his trousers, slightly afraid that he would beat her with his belt again. She looked for a weapon, but all she could lay her hands on was a wire hanger.

"Get away from me! I swear, if you touch me again, one of us will die tonight!" She waved it frantically.

Jamie pulled off his pants and threw it across the room, along with the belt. Amaka watched it and turned her gaze back to him, only to grimace and look away from the sight of his manhood pointing at her. She thought she was going to be sick.

She waved the hanger at his face. He grabbed her hand and twisted it, eliciting a scream from her. He peeled the hanger from her grip and threw it by his pants.

He pulled her into him. "I'm calling a truce. You hurt me, and I've hurt you back. We're even now." He leaned in to kiss her, but she resisted him vehemently, pushing him away with all her might.

"NO! NO! NO! We're no way even! Even is me having an affair with your *brother* and carrying *his baby*! Even is me kicking the shit out of you every freaking night, just for the hell of it! You killed our baby, Jamie! We will NEVER be even!"

Jamie wasn't listening to her. He was busy trying to get her undressed while she resisted him. He had her cornered and managed to get his hands past her underwear.

"Get away from me!" she screamed madly, pushing and punching him. "I'm not having sex with you!"

"Stop fighting me, for goodness sake!" Jamie said passionately, looking at Amaka square in the eye. "I said I'm sorry." *No, you didn't*, Amaka thought. And then as if reading her mind, he added: "I'm sorry, Amaka."

Amaka swallowed hard. He seemed sincere, but she knew him well enough to know he would say or do anything to keep his control. "If you're sorry, then don't do this. Don't force me to have sex with you. If you're sorry, let me decide what I want to do. Don't treat me like your property or a prisoner!"

Jamie released his grip and gave her some space. He breathed heavily as he watched her. She straightened her dress, and calmly went to pick up her suitcase again, then made for the door. He quickly grabbed her hand. "You're not leaving!"

"*Please*," she begged. "Just give me some space. A day or two to calm down..."

"NO! You're not leaving me *ever*!" He pulled her away from the door and pushed her onto the bed.

"Please, Jamie... Don't do this..." she pleaded, resisting him. He silenced her with his hand pressed against her mouth and forced her legs apart. Amaka gave up the fight and sobbed as Jamie raped her.

For a moment there, she had thought he was sincere.

It had been three days since she returned from the hospital. Three days since Jamie had forcefully had his way with her. Three horrible days that she'd abided with him in the place she once called her home and heard him having sex with her sister each night. He had even had the audacity to ask her to join them one night. She had slapped him in disgust.

Amaka fought back tears. Why had she stayed? Why had she given up the fight? Was it because she knew he wouldn't relent? Wherever she went, he was sure to find her and make her regret her existence. Was death really worse than this?

Those were Amaka's thoughts as she sat in church while others stood up singing praises to God. She had never been to the church before. *They* had never been to the church before. But today, she had insisted. If it was the last freedom he would grant her, she deserved the freedom of religion! He had decided to come along too.

So, there they sat, among the congregation on this fine Sunday morning in August. Amaka didn't know why she had a burden to come to this place. She had wanted to escape her home. To be relieved of Jamie's presence, but with him by her side, she might as well have stayed at home.

But she needed answers. Quite desperately. She needed to know what she had done so bad to deserve such a fate. Was she not worthy of love? Of respect? Of care and protection? If this was punishment for her sins, the price was far too much to pay.

She needed grace. She had heard that Jesus was gracious. That He saves... He saves sinners like her. She wondered if He could be just what she needed. Yet, she was sceptical. But she didn't know where else to go or who to turn to.

When the ministration started, Amaka paid attention as though she would be sitting an exam afterwards. The pastor started his sermon by saying that the Lord had put a burden on his heart for someone today. Amaka's ears itched. In her heart, she hoped she was the one. He asked the congregation to pray that this soul might be receptive to his word and that the message would not be as the seed that fell on the stony ground.

"*Come to Me all ye who are weary and heavy laden...*" he began, reading Matthew chapter 11, verses 29 to 30.

"Are you burdened today? Do you feel like giving up? Has everything you tried failed you? Has everyone deserted you? Jesus says 'come.' Come and learn from Me. Come and bear My yoke. It is not burdensome, and you will find rest for your soul.

"It doesn't matter what you've done. However bad you think you are, Jesus invites you to fellowship. He will not turn you away. He came for you. He gave up everything for you so that you will know how precious you are to Him. Come now..."

A woman arose from her seat and walked briskly to the front. Amaka watched as her heart ached. She also wanted to go. But maybe the word was for that woman. Then a man arose from his seat and walked to the altar too. Amaka swallowed. Was she worthy? What would Jamie say?

"I am still waiting for you to come," the pastor said, and Amaka immediately arose from her seat.

"Sit down!" Jamie hissed. She hesitated.

"Come, my child," the pastor beckoned. "Do not fear what men can do to you. Nothing can separate you from this love. Come boldly to the Throne of Grace and receive your freedom."

Jamie pulled her and forced her to sit again. The man behind him spoke up. "Who are you? The *devil*? How can you hinder a soul from going to God?"

Jamie turned to the man. "You mind your own damn business! She's my wife!"

The man ignored Jamie. "Sister, your liberty was bought at a great price. Do not allow yourself to be a slave to *any* man! Run to Jesus, and He will help you."

"That's it! Let's go!" Jamie said, tugging at Amaka as he got up to leave.

Amaka pulled herself free and practically ran to the front of the church. The people nearby who had observed the commotion clapped for her, and the whole congregation arose to applaud the woman who had run in desperation to the foot of the cross. Ashamed, Jamie sat back down again.

50

"But the God of all grace, who hath called us unto his eternal glory by Christ Jesus, after that ye have suffered a while, make you perfect, stablish, strengthen, settle you."

1 PETER 5:10

I t was a full house at Mr and Mrs Ifeanyi Chukwueke's home. Daniel, Samson, and Samuel, Mary's brothers, were all home for the summer break. Thankfully, the house was big enough to accommodate them all. However, for their trip to church that morning, they needed two cars. Mary decided she would let the twins fight over who would drive her car, while she rode with Ifeanyi and the kids, as usual.

The twins, Samson and Samuel, had one year left of their four-year engineering courses at the University of Lagos.

Daniel would be commencing his final level of senior secondary school, SS3, in September, and his grades were showing remarkable improvement. He had aspirations of becoming a pharmacist or biochemist. Ifeanyi and Mary had discussed sending him abroad to one of the top-ranking universities if he continued to perform well. That had inspired him to no end.

Even though they now stayed far away at Victoria Garden City, in Lekki, Mary and Ifeanyi still faithfully attended their fellowship at Grace and Truth Assembly (GTA), in Ikoyi. Today was supposed to be their Thanksgiving service, but the pastor had followed God's inspiration to do an altar call. The ministration was short and inspiring, and two people had already made their way to the front of the church to receive Jesus as their Lord and Saviour.

Unusually, there was some applause that quickly spread from one corner of the church to the whole congregation. Some people even stood up to clap as one woman made her way to the front in haste. Mary couldn't get a good look at the woman. She stood up and clapped along.

When everyone settled back in their seats, she thought she recognised the woman's distinct frame. But, no... It couldn't be. What would Amaka Nkechi be doing at their church?

"Is that...*Amaka*?" she turned to ask her husband, who had also turned to her to ask her the same thing. They exchanged nervous giggles.

The woman was very emotional. She was sobbing profusely. Mary wondered if she should go to her.

Go to her.

It was a simple, distinct voice, and Mary knew that God had called her to minister to Amaka. She got up, but Ifeanyi held her hand. "What are you doing?"

"I'm going to welcome her," Mary said.

Ifeanyi looked at her puzzled. Mary's heart was too soft for her own good. He shook his head. "I don't think it's a good idea, Mary."

Mary squeezed his hand. "Don't worry. It's the Lord's will," she said, looking into his eyes so he understood that she was acting on God's leading. He nodded and let her go.

Amaka stood before the altar, sobbing uncontrollable tears. She couldn't keep her cool. It was as though years of repressed emotion were gushing out of her. She was both excited and afraid.

She was excited because of the newness of this and the anticipation of getting to know God. And she was afraid because she still felt inadequate and was worried that she would embarrass Him or herself. But standing before this altar felt so right. She was ready to leave the past behind and be moulded into a whole new person.

Suddenly, she felt someone beside her. The person held her hand. It was a woman's hand. She turned to the woman and almost had a heart attack when she saw who it was. How could this woman be holding her hand? How could she be looking at her as though she didn't know the horrible things she had done?

And suddenly, the woman threw her arms around her and pulled her in for a hug. Who was this woman, Amaka wondered? Was she even human?

Amaka thought to resist, but she had no more fight in her. She just wanted to surrender to love. So, the two women hugged like long lost sisters, in the view of everyone in church. Including both their husbands. One man cried tears of joy and relief, while the other cried from shame and defeat.

"Welcome to the Family," Mary said, at last. "Don't be so surprised that I would hug you and receive you warmly. We are all in the same boat here. None of us deserved His grace, so we have no right to withhold it from others. I'm just so glad you accepted His call!"

Amaka cried and muttered, "Thank you!"

They separated, while still holding hands, as the pastor continued his ministration. Mary stayed with Amaka as she made her personal confession of faith in Jesus Christ and joined the Family of God. Amaka was invited to sit with the new guests at the front so that the ministers of the church could attend to her, get to know her, and support her in her decision to follow Jesus. Mary returned to sit with her husband, who had a whole new level of respect for her when he never imagined that he could love or respect her more!

At the end of the service, Amaka looked at the corner where she had been seated with Jamie and found that he was no longer there. She looked around for him, but it appeared that he had returned home without her. She was relieved about that, although she knew she still had to return home and get her things. She wondered what sort of reception she would receive when she returned. She didn't want to go alone.

Mary and Ifeanyi came down together to welcome her. Ifeanyi's gaze was guarded, but he smiled sincerely when he welcomed her to the Church. Amaka returned his smile.

"What about Jamie? Didn't he come with you?" Mary asked, looking around for him.

"He did, but he left already. I think we've split up..." Amaka said, soberly.

"Awww... *Really*? Do you want to talk about it?" Mary asked, even though she could feel Ifeanyi's resistance. He didn't want Mary to get involved in Amaka's affairs.

Amaka started crying again. Mary turned to Ifeanyi. "Baby, can you give us a moment, please?"

Ifeanyi didn't want to leave Mary alone with Amaka, but he trusted God. He kissed her lips softly. "Don't be long, we're waiting for you." He offered Amaka a closed smile before leaving the women to talk.

"Oh, wow! I never knew things were so bad between you two," Mary said, after Amaka had recounted her life since marriage. "I can see why you don't want to go back, and I think you definitely need someone to come with you...to talk to Jamie."

Amaka's eyes widened in shock. Was Mary suggesting she should return to that home, *that marriage*, after everything she had just revealed? She didn't want anyone to try to talk Jamie into changing. She couldn't trust him for a second.

Mary saw the fear in Amaka's eyes and quickly clarified her meaning. "So that he will let you go. It would take a mighty move of God to change a man like Jamie. You definitely need some space apart for your safety and sanity. And we can continue to pray for him." Mary smiled warmly at her.

"So, will you come with me? I know it's a lot to ask. Or maybe you can help me speak to one of the pastors," Amaka said.

"Oh, I think I would be the wrong person to go with you. Not even Ifeanyi." Mary swallowed. She suddenly got an idea. "What about Jimmy?"

Amaka shook her head. "No... He's Jamie's sidekick! He would probably hold me down while Jamie assaults me."

Mary smiled, and Amaka wondered what she could be smiling about. "Not anymore. Jimmy is saved now! Let's call him. I'm sure he would love to help."

Jimmy was just leaving service from his chosen fellowship, Salvation House, when he got Amaka's call. He wondered what could be the problem, as that was usually the only time she called. When she told him where she was and that she needed him, he said he would be there as soon as possible. The two churches were barely ten minutes apart.

By the time Jimmy got to GTA, almost everyone had gone. Even Mary's brothers had driven home because they couldn't handle the long wait any longer. They had taken the toddlers and their nanny, leaving Ifeanyi to attend to Abigail while he waited for his wife.

Jimmy was happy to see Ifeanyi. Ifeanyi had mixed feelings about seeing Jimmy again. It brought back bad memories of that awful night. But one thing that he was thankful for was that Jimmy had seen the light that night, and God had used him to shield his wife from an assault by Jamie, something he had been indisposed to do. They hugged briefly, and Ifeanyi followed Jimmy into the church to meet the women, who were still talking.

Jimmy hugged Mary warmly before he hugged his sister-in-law. "So, what's up, ladies? How can I help?"

Jimmy and Amaka arrived at her home to find her things thrown across the yard. Some were in bags, but most were littered around the compound and blowing in the wind. On a normal day, Amaka would have been furious, but today, she was happy! The sight was the vision of freedom. He had kicked her out!

She smiled, even though Jimmy was angry at his brother. While Jimmy pounded on the door, Amaka gathered her things, and maximised the bags he had thrown out, to arrange them properly. Some things were broken, stained, and irreparably damaged, like her perfumes, some jewellery, and expensive clothing. She knew that they wouldn't be complete either, but she was happy to take what she could and leave.

Jamie never opened the door to them. He later filed for a divorce on the grounds of Amaka's adultery. She happily signed for her freedom and never looked back.

Amaka forgave her mother, sister, and Jamie, but she was only able to maintain a relationship with her mother. Jamie kept the sisters apart, and Amaka would never know how married life was for Adania, even though there was never a wedding. She really wished her well and hoped she had found the love she had been longing for. Amaka continued to pray for their salvation.

When Jimmy asked Jamie why he'd finally decided to let Amaka go, his response was shocking.

"A stupid bitch, I can live with! But a Jesus *freak*? No fucking way!"

Hmmm... Jason had thought to himself. *Jamie doesn't sound rational.*

Jason had observed Jimmy for the three weeks he had stayed at his place during his visit to Lagos for the summer. There was definitely something different about him that he couldn't pinpoint. It wasn't just that he was religious. There was a deep spirituality about the new Jimmy that was honourable and admirable.

On his return trip to the US, Jason was surprised to meet the Christian woman who he had sat next to on their inbound flight at the airport. He was even more amazed to find that she was sitting next to him again. He thought it was more than a coincidence, so this time, he initiated a discussion with her. She was delighted and spoke freely with him. This time, he listened, and when she opened the scriptures to him, he was interested in what she read.

By the time they reached Los Angeles, Jason was converted. He never imagined then how his life would be turned upside down; the lengths he would go to nor the things he would suffer for the proclamation and defence of the Gospel. Nor did he know that the woman who sat beside him would one day become his wife, the mother of his children, and that they would travel the world together planting churches and transforming rural communities.

Mary and Ifeanyi made it home by 2:30 pm that fateful day, more than an hour later than they usually get home from church. Mary had cooked their brunch, jollof rice and chicken, before the service, so all they had to do was warm it up. Samson warmed up the food for everyone and fried plantains to eat with the meal. Daniel set the table, and Samuel was on dish-washing duty.

The big family sat around the table and held hands as Ifeanyi prayed over their meal. After saying the grace, Ifeanyi gave Mary's hand an extra squeeze before releasing it.

"I was so proud of you today," he said. Mary beamed.

"Why? What happened? And why was that woman crying?" Daniel asked.

Mary looked at Ifeanyi and giggled. "She was just so happy to meet Jesus and to be given a second chance."

"And I can tell you, it's the best feeling in the world to surrender your life to Christ," Ifeanyi added, giving Mary a wink.

Daniel smiled and nodded. "I know. I cried too. But mine wasn't that dramatic."

"And you two?" Mary looked between Samson and Samuel. "Have you given your lives to Jesus?"

"I think I still have time... When I get married, I will," Samson said, avoiding eye contact.

"Isn't that dumb? What if you die tomorrow?" Samuel asked.

"So, does that mean you're saved, Samuel?" Mary asked, an eye-brow raised.

"He's a secret disciple," Samson said, giggling.

"Is that so?" Ifeanyi asked. "There's nothing secret about discipleship. We are supposed to let our light shine and preach the Gospel with boldness. You should never be ashamed of Jesus! And Samson, tomorrow isn't promised to anyone. Besides, you can't marry wisely when you are living unwisely. You need Jesus, even before you marry. You will need His grace to appreciate and love a *phenomenal*, godly woman like my Mary."

At this, they all smiled while Ifeanyi leaned in and kissed his blushing wife. They enjoyed the rest of their meal with pleasant conversation. Chukwudi and Uche were not shy about making their voices heard either.

Mary's brothers returned to their studies in September, and Mary and Ifeanyi had their cosy home back. Samson still hadn't surrendered all to Jesus, but they believed God and prayed often for him to come to the knowledge of the Truth. They also prayed for more boldness for Samuel to minister with the empowerment of the Holy Spirit. Daniel had a spirit like his sister's. They both radiated Christ and His grace wherever they went.

Ifeanyi grew in grace and wisdom and remained faithful to Mary. He disproved the theory that said, "*once a cheat, always a cheater.*" Rather, he upheld the belief that he was in fact a new creature and could do all things through Christ, who strengthened him. And his wife's regained trust was a treasure he did not want to lose.

Their beautiful marriage was an inspiration to many people, especially those who knew of Ifeanyi's past. Mary's story, "He Cheated!", was a ray of hope to many, as it showed that infidelity was not a death sentence to a marriage but could be overcome with sincere faith and love. Mary's graciousness and faithfulness had turned the fiery trial from a consuming fire to a refining fire in their lives, purifying their hearts and binding them ever closer.

THE EPILOGUE

"For I know the thoughts that I think toward you, saith the LORD, thoughts of peace, and not of evil, to give you an expected end."

JEREMIAH 29:11

Every year, on the 21st of October, Mary and Ifeanyi commemorated the memory of Mary's parents with a special activity. This was their fourth year marking the date, since their wedding three and a half years ago. In their first year, they had simply paid a visit to their graves and laid flowers on their plots. They had shared a moment of silence and then prayed.

In their second year of marriage, when Mary was 26 years old, they marked ten years since her parents' passing with a small family gathering at their home. Ifeanyi's and Ijeoma's parents were also around to honour the dead, as well as several of Mary's relatives. Last year, Mary decided to plant a tree in their memory at Lufasi Nature Park, Lekki. They also made a sizable contribution to charity in their honour.

This year, as the date drew near, Mary wondered how she would honour them. It would be twelve years since their passing and she wanted to do something special.

As she looked about her home, she saw pictures of the family, including her in-laws, and it became obvious what was missing. There was no portrait of her parents. She decided that she would have one painted, using one or two old photos. That way, every time she looked at the painting, she would remember them, and not only during this special time of the year. Ifeanyi loved the idea.

So, Mary pulled out her old box of family memorabilia, which had pictures from her childhood and the last pictures her parents had ever taken. There really wasn't much. They were not rich and didn't take photos often. But the few they had, Mary kept well.

Ifeanyi came to sit on the floor with Mary, as she went through the pictures. He wrapped her in his arms and kissed her cheek. He picked up one of the pictures. "How come I've never seen these pictures before?"

"Because you never asked," Mary said cheekily.

She was stuck between two pictures. One of them made her father look really good, but her mother's eyes were shut. And in the other, her mum looked good, but her dad was somehow blurry.

Ifeanyi saw a picture that he found intriguing. There was something strangely familiar about the picture. Almost like he had seen it before. He studied it for a while, trying to recollect what it reminded him of.

"Oh, that's a very old one. I was only three in that picture," Mary said, taking it from him.

Ifeanyi pulled it back. "Why does it look so familiar?" He studied the picture some more. There was something in the background. It looked like his old toy truck. And the tree... "I think this is the tree in my parents' garden."

"What?" Mary looked at the picture again. She saw the resemblance between the tree in the picture and the one at Ifeanyi's parents' mansion.

"Oh, my God! I think I took that picture! This is *you*?"

"I think you must be mistaken, Ifeanyi. I'd never been to your house."

"You said you were only three in this picture, so you won't remember. Was your mum a cook?" Ifeanyi had the weirdest, biggest smile on his face. He was putting the pieces together.

"Well, yes... She was..."

Twenty-five years ago...

"Who's the little sweetheart?" Mrs Chukwueke gushed at the little girl in the pink dress. She shyly hid behind her mother's legs.

"I'm sorry, ma. I didn't have anyone to watch her today. The madam who normally helps me travelled for a burial," Elizabeth said apologetically.

"Oh, it's no problem. What's her name?" Mrs Chukwueke smiled as the girl finally found the courage to come out of hiding.

"Maryann. It's her birthday today!" Elizabeth said proudly.

"Awww... Happy Birthday, Maryann! How old are you?" Mrs Chukwueke asked, bending down to have a conversation with the girl.

Mary raised her hand and revealed three slim fingers. Ifeanyi came rushing into the room then, chasing after his two-year-old baby brother, Nomnso. He stopped when he saw the pretty little girl. He went to his mother and whispered something in her ear that made her laugh.

"It seems my son is quite smitten with you. Do you guys want to go out and play while your mum and I get some work done?"

Mary looked up at her mother shyly. Her mother had told her that she would have to behave herself and play quietly in a corner because she didn't want to be a bother to her employers. Elizabeth smiled and nodded. "It's okay if you want to play, Annie."

"Come on, Annie! Let's play!" Ifeanyi said, beckoning for her to follow him.

Mary took one last look at her mum before she followed the friendly boy outside to their play area. Nomnso chased after them, pushing his truck. Ifeanyi's older sister, Chidinma, soon joined them on the swings.

Elizabeth thanked Mrs Chukwueke for her kindness in letting Mary play with her children. She promised it wouldn't happen again, and it never did. After her shift, which concluded at 4 pm on Saturdays, she came out to find the children still playing outside. Ifeanyi appeared to be quite fond of her little Annie.

It was his idea to take photos, and he had taken them with his disposable camera. When he showed her the pictures the following week, after they were printed, she'd asked to keep the one with her and Mary, by the tree. Ifeanyi often asked her to bring little Annie to play again, but Elizabeth never did. And after she delivered her twins, she stopped working for the Chukwuekes.

Present day...

Ifeanyi stood up and went through his things. He was trying to remember where he had kept them. The pictures he had taken that day. For a strange reason, he had never wanted to throw them away. He eventually found them and brought them to Mary.

Mary couldn't believe her eyes. She remembered that day vaguely. But the pictures brought tears to her eyes. There were two with only her and Ifeanyi, and two of all the children, and another one with her, Ifeanyi, Nomnso and her mum. Chidinma must have taken that one.

Mary looked up at Ifeanyi, as though she was seeing him for the first time. He smiled softly at her. "You are my Annie! All these years, and I didn't know. Our love is written in the stars, Mary," he said with emotion, pulling her into his arms.

"I guess it is..." Mary swallowed, as Ifeanyi brought his face down to hers for a sweet, head-spinning kiss.

They eventually settled on a picture of Mary's parents, Mr Efe and Elizabeth Uwanna, to paint, and it now stood proudly on their wall, next to a painting of Ifeanyi's parents, and across the room from the best painting in the house. The one of the two lovebirds, seven-year-old Ifeanyi and three-year-old Maryann, whose love had transcended time and overcame all societal barriers. They were, indeed, meant to be.

Chidinma and Emmanuel Atiyota also marked their second wedding anniversary at the end of October and invited the whole family for a dinner at The Oriental Hotel in Victoria Island. Chidinma was in full bloom, at seven months pregnant. Emmanuel was an adoring husband, who took special care of his wife.

Nomnso had returned home in September, after completing his studies in the US. He would be part of the next batch of National Youth Service Corpers and hoped to be as lucky in love as his brother. He hadn't had much luck on the dating field back in the States. It was hard to meet a good Christian girl who upheld the values she professed to believe in.

The Atiyotas were outnumbered by the Chukwuekes at the dinner table. Emmanuel had just one sister, Sarah, who was thirteen years old, and his parents with him. Sarah sat next to Nomnso, so everyone was paired up. Mary and Ifeanyi were the last to arrive at the dinner but were still on time. Mary had slimmed down remarkably, and she received compliments on her outfit from the other women at the table.

"Happy Anniversary!" Mary said, hugging Chidinma, who couldn't get up. Emmanuel stood up to hug her and Ifeanyi, before they took their seats.

Chidinma had ordered a set buffet menu, so the food was already arranged for them to help themselves to. After Mr Atiyota, Emmanuel's father, said the grace, they all helped themselves to the mouth-watering spread. Emmanuel served his wife, and Mary served her husband. The elderly wives both served their husbands, who were busy talking business.

Ifeanyi shared an idea he had been working on for a while with his father that would combine banking and telecoms in a whole new way. Chief Chukwueke loved the idea and said they would discuss it further at the office. Mary smiled at her husband. He was finally going to realise his dream in banking, but to an even richer extent than he had originally envisioned.

Chidinma also talked about an idea she had been discussing with her mother to start an event management company. She was excellent at planning events and was passionate about it too. Everyone was excited about it. Event planning was now a big business in Nigeria, and it was about time Chidinma took her passion to the next level.

Ifeanyi looked at Mary as she ate and chatted happily. She had given up her passion for human rights advocacy with Browne Law Firm at his wish. He wondered if she was still okay with that or if she would like to pursue it again, now they had agreed on not having more children. Or maybe there was a new passion she wanted to pursue...

"You're alright?" he asked her.

She beamed at him. "I'm good. You want more food?"

"No. Thanks. I was just thinking maybe you would like to go back to work...?"

"Why?"

"I don't know... Are you happy just being a housewife?" he asked, almost whispering.

"I'm not just a housewife. But yeah, I'm happy. I'm doing what I love to do, and the time is not nearly enough even for that."

"You mean your blog?"

"Yeah... It's a ministry, you know?"

"Yes, it's got great potential!" Ifeanyi bopped his head up and down, as she smiled at his wife.

Mary laughed. "You don't even read my posts anymore."

"I do read your posts. Every Sunday, I make time to catch up." He gave her a cheeky grin.

"Oh, yeah? Thanks," Mary smiled. "Drop a comment now and then."

"Really? I thought it's a bit cheesy. Being your husband and all..."

"*Nah*... I love it. And then we can continue the banter offline." Mary winked at him, playfully.

Ifeanyi giggled. "No worries, babe. I will."

"Are you guys talking about Mary's blog?" Chidinma asked. They both nodded. "Yeah... I've been using it to prepare for motherhood. Good stuff!"

Mary beamed. The banter continued as they discussed current affairs and politics, amid other topics.

Mary looked about the room filled with the people she loved - her family - and her heart was glad. She thanked God that she hadn't given up hope in the dark seasons of her life, because the joy in the light was well worth her perseverance. And she just knew that the joy would last forever.

One night in November, after the kids were tucked in bed, Ifeanyi sat in bed watching his wife glow. She was radiant. He noticed her glow, usually when she was writing one of her inspiring stories. She never believed him when he told her she glowed.

"Hey... When are you coming to bed? I'm lonely up here," Ifeanyi said with a fake sulk.

"Won't be a minute, honey. Just need to finish this thought..." Mary said, typing fast on her keyboard.

The inspiration had been flowing easily lately, and she'd published almost twelve articles in the last week! Now that Abigail was nine months old and very mobile, and the twins, Chukwudi and Uche, were officially in their 'terrible twos,' she had lots of material to draw upon and many lessons to learn and share. People were beginning to ask her about when she would be publishing a book. It hadn't been in her plans or in her heart, so she simply answered them, "If it's God's will, soon."

Mary sighed as she hit 'publish' on her latest blogpost on marriage. She switched off her laptop and put it aside. "Done," she said, smiling at her patient husband. "I'm all yours now..."

Ifeanyi beamed at his wife. He received her into his arms and kissed her lips softly while running his hands through her body. This was the life. This was how he hoped to spend the rest of his days.

Mary straddled his laps as he lay with his back on the bed, looking up at her. She looked mad sexy dressed only in his t-shirt. He looked into her eyes and said with emotion, "Thank God I found you."

Mary smiled sweetly, playing with the few hairs on his bare chest. "Hmmm... You say that every night..." she replied flirtatiously.

"And I mean it every night..." He pulled her into him for the sweetest kiss, and Mary melted in his arms. If she was any happier, she was certain she would burst with joy!

And Mary and Ifeanyi lived happily ever after...

"And we know that all things work together for good to them that love God, to them who are the called according to his purpose."

ROMANS 8:28

THE END.

END NOTE

First of all, thank you for buying my book and reading it to the end. I sincerely hope you have been blessed by all you have read and pray that the seeds that have been sown in your heart, through this inspirational story, will germinate and bear lasting fruit in your life to the glory of God! I hope you are encouraged, inspired, challenged, and convicted to begin a walk with God or draw ever closer to Him.

There are so many lessons in this story, I can't list them all. I would encourage you to read it again so that you can draw more out of it. If you have been blessed, please be kind and share the blessing by telling your friends and family about the book *and* encouraging them to get their own copies to support the ministry. You can also support this ministry on **PATREON**.

Please, also take the time to write a review that will encourage others to take a chance and buy and read their own copy. You can post it on my website, as a comment when you visit **https://books.ufuomaee.org/the-church-girl** and/or at your favourite ebook store. Thank you so much!

If you are going through what Mary or Amaka went through, please seek help. Do not suffer in silence. You can also reach out to me by sending me an email at **me@ufuomaee.com**. I am not a counsellor or a therapist, but by God's grace, I give good Christian counsel. If you have any other questions or concerns, feel free to ask me, anonymously. I have a section on my blog to respond to questions by my readers, called "**Reader Questions**." You might find some of the counsel I have given there beneficial to your life and walk with God.

Finally, if you have decided to give your life to Jesus or re-dedicate your life to Him because of what you've read here, I would love to hear from you too! It was for this reason that I wrote the book, that all may come to the knowledge of the truth and submit to the Wisdom of God, Jesus Christ. And if you are yet to do so, I would implore you not to wait another day. As it written:

> "...now is the accepted time; behold, now is the day of salvation."
> (2 Corinthians 6:2)

I sincerely hope you will make the decision before it is too late. May God bless you and keep you by His grace. Amen.

Love,

Ufuomaee.

What will it take for you to give your life to jesus christ?

"Come unto Me, all ye that labour and are heavy laden, and I will give you rest. Take My yoke upon you, and learn of Me; for I am meek and lowly in heart: and ye shall find rest unto your souls. For My yoke is easy, and My burden is light."

MATTHEW 11:28-30

Jesus Christ is the Wisdom of God. Aren't you tired of doing life without Wisdom? Everything is better with Jesus. I can testify that He is truly the *only* Way, the *whole* Truth and the *abundant* Life! I wish you would answer the call of God to surrender your life and will to Him today.

ACKNOWLEDGE-MENTS

First of all, I just want to thank my Lord, Jesus Christ, for bestowing me with the *gift* of writing, the *love* of writing, and the constant *inspiration* to write. Without His Holy Spirit, I would not have been able to write this book at all. What started as a short story idea was soon transformed, with His help, into a life-changing series on my blog and, finally, what you have in your hands - a book that will remain a light to others for many years to come. To God be the glory!

I cannot but thank the man God has used from the beginning to establish me as the woman I am today, my amazing Daddy! His love and support for me throughout my life has been immeasurable and incomparable. Even when he didn't understand my passion, he gave me the wings to fly and was there when I needed to stand. I can never pay him back. I can only say, "Thank you, Daddy, for always believing in me."

I must also appreciate my mum and sisters, 'Rhe and Jite. I have been blessed with a supportive family, who have inspired and encouraged me through all my endeavours. They have been the wind beneath my wings! I thank God for you all.

I would also like to acknowledge my friend, Moses Ida-Michaels, one of the pastors I respect very much. He gladly read through my manuscript and helped me to think through my objectives and edit it accordingly so that the real message would be passed across. I really appreciate his input and the perspectives he brought.

Many thanks to Paul Ikonne, who worked with me on the cover redesign and layout for the new and improved edit. He was patient, thorough, and skilful in his delivery.

Finally, I want to thank my friends, fans, and faithful readers of my blog, **Grace and Truth**. Those who said, "*this story needs to be in a book!*", those who said, "*you will never know how this story changed me,*" and those who said, "*whatever book you're writing, I'm buying!*" I have been so encouraged by you all, and you helped me to see that this story needs a much wider audience and to believe in my gift. May God help you to discover and use yours to His glory too! Amen.

ABOUT THE AUTHOR

   Ufuomaee is a writer, blogger, and Christian fiction author. She tells stories to help young people make the right choice before marriage and deal with challenges that often arise during and after. She loves to use parables and poetry to teach about God's love. When she's not writing or working, Ufuomaee loves to watch action movies and romcoms on Netflix. She also loves reading romantic and inspiring books by other amazing authors, which she reviews at www.ufuomaee.blog.

CONNECT WITH ME

FIND MY BOOKS HERE

- www.amazon.com/author/ufuomaee
- www.goodreads.com/author/show/16833067.ufuomaee
- www.books.ufuomaee.org
- www.medium.com/@ufuomaee

FOLLOW ME

- @ufuomaeedotcom
- @UfuomaeeB
- @ufuomaee

VISIT/EMAIL ME

- www.ufuomaee.org
- blog.ufuomaee.org
- me@ufuomaee.com

OTHER TITLES BY
Ufuomaee

An Emotional Affair
Broken
A Small World - Season One
A Small World - Season Two
A Small World - Season Three
The House Girl
Perfect Love
Beauty and the Beast
The Atheist
The Naive Wife Trilogy

A
SMALL
WORLD
— PREVIEW

Are you wondering what happened to Amaka? Or Ijeoma and Chuka? Or Adania and Jamie? Or do you just wish the story could go on and on and you can draw more inspiration from Mary and Ifeanyi's love story? Well, **A Small World** is my way of doing that.

A Small World is a seasonal story series I will be continuing on my blog, by God's grace, which tells the stories of all my major characters from my first three stories series (An Emotional Affair, Broken, and The Church Girl), revealing how their lives are interconnected. It is a captivating, never-ending story that you mustn't miss if you are a fan of The Church Girl.

Why did I ever get married? Oh yeah, she was pregnant! Don't get me wrong, I love my wife, but she can be REALLY annoying sometimes. Okay, a lot of the time!

It was cute while we were dating, but now, not so much. She doesn't seem to understand the pressures I face and lives as though we have a goldmine in our backyard. I know she's used to having a lot. Being the only child of her rich parents, she's used to having whatever she wants. But I always thought she wanted me more...

Chuka sighed to himself. He had been thinking negatively about his marriage a lot lately. They were approaching their fourth anniversary, and Ijeoma had been dropping hints about what she wanted him to buy for her and do for her. The message was loud and clear, "You have to top last year!"

They hadn't really done much last year, because they were broke. They had spent all their money on hospital bills for their third son's birth, and Ijeoma couldn't resist getting all the cute baby things, even though they already had enough children's clothes and toys to open up a store!

He had decided to recreate their first date by ordering food from The Place and eating at home. She hadn't found that funny at all. She had called him cheap and sulked for days.

What's keeping Chuka? He's supposed to be home by now. Maybe he's got a new client. Hopefully, it's one big multinational company! The peanuts he's making in that bank can't keep us afloat much longer. I don't know why he's too proud to accept help! I can't believe I even agreed to move to Gbagada. My parents would have given us the difference to buy that four-bed house in Ikate... Men and their foolish pride!

Four years, and he still hasn't even taken me on a proper honeymoon. Jos! Jos, of all places... He better have something decent planned for Valentine's Day, oh. I should have known better than to use that date for our wedding too. I thought it would make it easy for him to remember. Now, he doesn't even make the effort, when I deserve DOUBLE celebration. For goodness sake, where is he?!

Ijeoma looked at her watch for the sixth time in five minutes. It was after ten. It was unlike Chuka to be returning home so late. Had something happened to him? With that horrible Third Mainland Bridge traffic, she always feared for his safety on the road. She never wanted to be caught on the bridge past 6 pm at night. She'd called him several times already, and now, his phone was switched off.

Ijeoma bit her lower lip anxiously. She hated to admit it, but she feared that he could be having an affair. She'd heard enough stories about bank marketers to be concerned. Of course, she knew she shouldn't be. He was Christian. But then, that hadn't stopped Ifeanyi, his best friend, from cheating on Mary. Even though Ifeanyi was probably the world's best husband now, she knew she couldn't put it past Chuka. He never could resist imitating Ifeanyi.

Since the day they first met, he had met Amaka about a dozen more times. Half the time in a professional capacity, and other times at church when he would make the effort to say hi. He had fallen under her spell and couldn't stop thinking of her. He knew of her past with Ifeanyi, and that was enough reason for him to be cautious with her. But he felt he could freely indulge in his fantasies, knowing that that was all they were and would ever be.

However, now he needed to fantasise about Amaka more and more, just to perform with Ijay in bed. He knew that if they didn't do something about their situation, it was going to end in a bad way. He didn't know how he would begin to broach the subject with Ijay. She was in constant denial over the fact that they had issues. And that was part of the problem.

As he packed up for the day, Chuka spotted a letter on his desk. It must have come in after he had left for marketing that day. He picked it up, opened it, and was completely stunned by what he read: "*We regret to notify you that you have been retrenched...*"

"What?!" Chuka exclaimed. He had bigger problems than he had even realised. How was he going to face Ijeoma tonight?

THE CHURCH GIRL

"Hey, no probs. See you on Sunday," Jimmy said, smiling to himself as he hung up the phone.

Fatima was looking at him curiously. "Who was that?"

"Amaka. She's coming to Salvation House this Sunday."

Fatima began shaking her head. "No, I don't like that... Why's she suddenly attaching herself to you?"

"It's church, Fatima. You can't stop people going to whatever church they like."

"And there are like a thousand and one churches..."

"Are you *serious*? You're *jealous*?"

Fatima swallowed. The thought of that woman anywhere near her husband was highly disturbing. She had never liked her... But then, she was Jamie's girlfriend, then fiancée, and, finally, wife. Now, she wasn't, and Fatima didn't trust her for one minute.

She had watched helplessly as Jimmy and Amaka grew closer. Talking on the phone, sending messages and Bible verses... She had prayed that some other guy would come and take the woman's attention, but she was still single, months later. Maybe she was gunning for her husband. She wouldn't put it past her... *the bitch*!

"Would you blame me?"

"She's my brother's *ex-wife*. She's like family..."

"Yes, your brother's EX-WIFE, so she's no longer family! And have you forgotten the lack of family values in *her* family? Isn't her sister the one who's pregnant for and living with your brother now? What if she wants revenge? Have you thought about that?"

Oh, I was so stupid! Why did I do it? Why?

He doesn't love me. He never loved me. I have never been so miserable in my life! For three months, he has not touched me! Oh God! And I know he's sleeping with other women. I knew that was the kind of man he was, yet, I was so desperate for a man, so desperate for him, that I didn't care that he was my sister's husband! And look at the hell I am in...

Jesus, forgive me! He won't even let me sleep in the master bedroom. He said, "it is for his wife!" Who the hell am I? He said he would marry me; he said he loved me. And here I am, wasting away for him... Oh, how I wish I had never gotten pregnant. How I wish I had never given in to him. Jesus, please, forgive me!

Adania cried, as she did most days. She pitied her miserable existence in Jamie's home. As soon as he had thrown her sister out of his house, she knew she was going to regret her decision.

She hadn't wanted to believe it before. She'd hoped that her sister would come around. She knew Amaka already knew that her husband was a philanderer. At least, the two of them could have satisfied his appetite.

But watching him that day broke her heart. He was a broken man. Amaka's rejection had broken him. It was Amaka he loved. And look what he had done to her. Adania had feared for herself and her child that day.

🌎 🌍 🌏

Ifeanyi entered through the gate, after finding a place to park on the street, and was directed to the backyard, where there was a barbecue and a pool party going. It was thriving with lots of young men and scantily dressed women and girls. As he searched for Chuka, someone called his name.

"Ifeanyi?" the lady drawled his name with contempt.

Ifeanyi sighed, afraid to discover who it was. His scandalous past wasn't letting go of him easy. He turned around and stood face to face with Keisha, his ex-girlfriend. He forced a smile.

"Hey, Keisha..." She slapped him. Hard.

He took it and hoped she would be appeased and walk away. She just stood there smiling wickedly at him. "Okay. Maybe I deserved that..."

She slapped him again, and his head spun.

"That's taking it too far, don't you think?"

She lifted her hand to slap him a third time, and he dodged it. He caught her hand and she winced. Then she smiled at him again, her eyes dancing mischievously. She's crazy, he thought, and let go of her hand.

"What are you doing here? *Backslidden*, are we?" she teased, rubbing her wrist.

"I'm looking for my friend..."

"*Right*... Gotcha," she said sarcastically. "What's *her* name?"

Ifeanyi ignored her presumptuous question. "Chuka. Have you seen him?"

"Oh, him... He was with my boyfriend earlier. Don't know where he is now..."

"Okay, thanks..." Ifeanyi turned to continue his search.

"I heard you cheated on your wife! Old habits die hard..." she shouted after him. Ifeanyi paused for a second, then continued walking away

🌍 🌍 🌍

Emmanuel is the best. We've been married for almost two and a half years now, and they have been the best years of my life. I'm so glad I decided to give him a chance and fell in love with him. You see, he's not the type I usually go for. I've always found myself attracted to the handsome, bad-boy types, like my brother used to be. Who knows, maybe it was observing Ifeanyi change, and appreciating how he honoured God, that made me find someone like Emmanuel so attractive?

Emmanuel is what you might call a church boy, to the core. He grew up churched, and he stayed churched due to his own passionate belief in God. But he wasn't boring, as I feared all church boys would be. He was just a man who loved God above all else, and I found security in that. I found that I could trust him easily and follow him. And every day, I just thank God for him...

Chidinma was happy, enjoying a peaceful, near perfect marriage. At Christmas, she had birthed her first child, a handsome baby boy, Jonathan. He was a cross between his mother and his father and was such a cute baby. He now lay in his crib, sleeping, as Chidinma and Emmanuel entertained friends and family.

Every Saturday since they returned home from the hospital, they had open house for friends to come, bestow gifts, and sight the precious little one. Today, Chidinma's old friend, Lola, had come, even though she too had just had a baby. In fact, they had delivered in the same hospital on Boxing Day, and they hadn't even noticed until they were checking out. Being from a privileged home, Chidinma had travelled abroad to continue with her secondary schooling, and so, they had lost touch after Junior Secondary Level Three (JSS3). It was nice to meet again after all these years.

"So, how's your husband? Bolu, right?"

While she ate, Amaka watched the couples and the singles mingle, as the place buzzed with people doing their last-minute shopping for Valentine's Day. She felt a little sad that she'd be missing out on it this year. She always loved Valentine's Day. Jamie loved to go overboard with gifts and romantic gestures. He was really quite the sweetheart, but she remembered that he usually bought gifts for his other female 'friends' too.

She hadn't thought much of it the first year they were together. But by the second, she knew they weren't just friends. She sighed. Why did he have to be a dog? They could have been happy if he would have just treated her right... She sighed.

Then she spotted a tall man with Jamie's frame. It seemed uncanny that she was just thinking about him, and he would show up. She kept watching his back, hoping he would turn, and she would be able to know whether or not it was him. The big man turned. It wasn't him. But she kept staring.

He was a fine-looking man. Not as dashing as Jamie, though. He was more rugged and a little bigger. He had some shopping too, but there was no woman with him. Was he a lonely shopper like her?

He caught her staring, and she looked away quickly, embarrassed. When she looked up, he also turned his gaze to her, and their eyes met. Amaka felt shivers down her spine. Few men had ever done that to her.

She swallowed and half-willed him to come over and talk to her. The other half of her was scared that he would. She hadn't yet found herself in a situation where she was tempted to fornicate, but this man was right up her alley. She could see herself backsliding for him. She shut her eyes and said a quick prayer.

When she opened them, he was standing before her. She gulped. He grinned.

"I was just wondering what a beautiful woman like you is doing here alone," he said with a genuine smile.

She didn't know what to say. She shyly responded, "Thanks..."

"I really never do this, but I just wanted to know your name..."

"Amaka," she replied.

"Hi! Nice to meet you, Amaka. I'm Bolu."

Keisha lay in bed thinking about her encounter with Ifeanyi today. She knew she should quit, but she just couldn't. She couldn't stand to see him happy. People like him didn't deserve to live happily ever after...

Keisha knew that it would be near impossible for him to fall for her advances again. He might never cheat on his wife with another woman, but all that was needed to accomplish her will was for Mary to find him in a very compromising position. And she could make up a sob story, talking about how they were in love and never intended for her to know...

Keisha giggled wickedly. She could just imagine the poor woman's face. That's if she didn't suffer a fainting spell or a heart attack. It had to be a really good set-up, and she would have just one chance to pull it off. For it to be really effective, she needed to start planting seeds of doubt so that when she told Mary her side of the story, she would readily believe.

Keisha smiled to herself and rolled on her side. She would begin work on her plan tomorrow. She couldn't wait...

Chuka woke up to a migraine. The sun was harsh as it poured into his room. He reached for his wife before he remembered that he wasn't at home. He had a vague recollection of what had happened yesterday.

He slowly got out of bed and sat on the edge of it, holding his throbbing head. He heard a tiny rap on the door and a gentle voice asking, "Can I come in?" Chuka grunted his reply, and Mary opened the door.

"Good, you're awake," she said with a smile. It turned into a frown when she saw his pained expression. "Are you okay?"

"Headache..." was all he could say.

Mary left, and moments later, returned with a glass of water and paracetamol.

"Do you have ibuprofen?" he asked.

"I think this might be a safer bet for you, considering..." Mary replied.

"That won't do anything for me," Chuka shook his head but took the medicine when Mary insisted.

"Come and have breakfast," Mary said with a smile. She turned at the door and said, "Happy Valentine's Day! Oh, and Happy Wedding Anniversary too!"

Jamie heard the car horn, and the gate open and close, and knew that Adania had left for church. He threw the sheets off himself and got out of bed. He had a good stretch and smiled at his reflection in the mirror.

He wrapped a small towel around his waist and went downstairs to eat his breakfast by himself. The house help came to inquire if he needed her this morning, or if she could leave for church as well. Being already fully dressed, her question was a bit presumptuous.

"Sit and have breakfast with me," Jamie said.

She hesitated and then smiled shyly and sat down. "Thank you, sir."

"Princess, is it?" Jamie asked after her name. He had heard Adania call her that several times before.

"Yes, sir," she said as she packed yam and egg onto her plate.

"Which church do you go to?" Jamie asked.

"The Redeemed down the road. Do you want to come to church today, sir?"

Jamie smiled at her question. "No... But thanks for the offer."

They ate quietly. Princess was a bit nervous and uncomfortable, realising that Jamie was naked, apart from his small towel. She had noticed him looking at her a few times, and she had been flattered. But she worried about Madam. Princess wondered if she was his wife or sister because she had never observed intimacy between them.

Jamie enjoyed the stewed sausages and licked his fingers loudly. Princess found the sounds very distracting. Jamie caught her looking at his lips as he smacked them, and he grinned. She averted her eyes, hurriedly finished her meal, and packed her plate into the kitchen. She returned to pack his and clear the table.

"Get me some more juice," he said, holding her hand as she tried to carry his glass away.

Princess let go of the glass, but his touch lingered on her hand. Her heart raced as she went into the kitchen to fetch his juice. She returned and didn't find him at the table. She called after him, "Sir?"

"Bring it upstairs!"

Made in the USA
Columbia, SC
18 January 2023